Only

Small Things

Are Good

or

The Open Letter

by

Micah Harris

Pagescape Press

2018

Only Small Things Are Good

Copyright © 2018 by Micah Harris

Published by Pagescape Press, 3101 Old Pecos Trail No. 629, Santa Fe, NM 87505

Publisher's Note: This novel is a work of fiction. Names, characters, places, and incidents are either products of the author's imagination or used fictitiously. All characters are fictional, and any similarity to people living or dead is purely coincidental.

Library of Congress Cataloging-in-Publication Data

Names: Harris, Micah
Title: Only Small Things Are Good or The Open Letter / Micah Harris
Identifiers: ISBN: 978-0-9993059-0-4 (paperback)
Subjects: 1. Pentagon—Fiction. 2. War and Military—Fiction. 3. Texas—Fiction. 4. Washington, DC—Fiction. 5. Political—Fiction.

Cover art by Lisa Shirk: www.lisashirk.com

Printed in the United States of America

Introduction

This deeply thoughtful and exquisitely written novel draws upon Micah Harris's time as a policy analyst—or "action officer"—in the Pentagon. Through the voice of his characters, Micah captures the nuances of defense policy development: navigating the bureaucracy, the inter-agency process, and working with the White House to shape policy.

This is not a tell-all tale, luckily for Micah's coworkers, directors, (and assistant secretary!) but, still, it builds a picture of the bureaucracy that can only be built by someone who has lived through the joy and frustration of making a difference. This is a novel that offers a lively portrait of the realistic and fantasy life of a Pentagon staff officer—using a startling sense of humor to color the thoughts of a *very* earnest narrator.

It was my pleasure to have Micah as an action officer in real life in my former office in the Pentagon policy shop. Like his character Joel, Micah made a lasting impression on the hearts and minds of OSD Policy.

This novel is a must-read for anyone who wants to understand life in the Pentagon.

Madelyn R. Creedon
Former Assistant Secretary of Defense
   for Global Strategic Affairs

He was determined—I learnt that very soon—to do good, not to any individual person but to a country, a continent, a world. – Graham Greene, The Quiet American

He was a skeptic. He was young, abstract, and therefore cruel. – Fyodor Dostoevsky, Crime and Punishment

Maybe justice will be on a larger scale in what is larger, and easier to find out about. So if you approve, why don't we start by finding out what sort of thing it is in cities? After that we can make a similar inquiry into the individual, trying to find the likeness of the larger version in the form the smaller takes. – Socrates in Plato's, The Republic

The Poem in Prose

The first time I knew a president to get inaugurated, I listened over a kerosene heater that roared in my father's shop like a jet engine. The next time, I stood patriotic by the cold Capitol while the president spoke, then I trundled off to ask for a job at the Heritage Foundation.

For the president after that, I rode my motorcycle through the African rain with grocery bags tied over my shoes. I coat-checked the bags, then lifted a flute of champagne from where it was offered on a tray. And I stood there watching my embassy's watch-a-peaceful-transition-of-power party. It made me proud then, to be honest.

But the last time our president swore in public, I holed up in my house with Sam-Bob and watched it on TV. Then I jogged the inauguration's secured perimeter. I ran for miles, dodging oily styrofoam that over-spilt the garbage bins and skidded among the people still enamored with politics.

I am lonely from the places I have been—from the people I have known. I missed a connection in Addis Ababa once and sat dumbly on the hotel roof with a beautiful woman. Whole sectors of the city fell dark, starved for power, then, after a long African minute, prickled back to view. Our turn came. The lights darkened, the a/c fell silent, and we drank quietly through the chirps and groans of a city ending its day.

"I believe population control is part of environmentalism," she said.

I killed rats one day as a boy. Clubbing them—rupturing them where they scuttled in upon themselves under the straw. Dozens of rats. Someone had asked for my help. But someone has denied my help now.

I see clearly at all times. Once I saw plainly, in a horse-headed nebula, that God made us. But, another night, as I lay unjustly in an African jail, I saw, stark in the silence, that there is no God. There never was. Only we had created him.

A man stood over me in the dark and pissed through the bars while generations lived their petty lives outside and died in the night. In the morning, their grandchildren unlocked the gates to laugh with me over our little mistake about who created who and in whose image.

I didn't pray after that, exhausted from no answer. I lived in Africa. I documented rape and repression for the State Department. And I saw no God.

That made me angry once—the loss of everything. Then I grew weary of anger and gave it up.

Every myth must die, of course. But why ours? Why so soon?

So, my friends, I ask you. Let us write our lonely memoirs. Let us read them to each other and shovel rubbish in on the gullies between us. Let us gather back the silt that was washed away and return it to its rightful place. Let us plant shrubs over our broken past. And these will become gardens where we clink our glasses with a slosh, and smile at a spot of foam absorbing into our soil—weary, joyful, and well aged in the twilight of our youth.

We will celebrate that thirty is the new seventy. Then we will find a myth that is still true. We will learn to be young again and our children will see that, despite it all, this world is a place worth keeping. And then, perhaps, we will look through their eyes and glimpse it too.

The Unwritten Rules

A bolt lies loose in the oil under your government, and the reason it broke and fell down there instead of holding things together like it should have done, is because this bolt is a bolt, and bolts are dead. Governments should be run by the living.

My name is Joel Alden. I became what I am in a mechanic's shop where the wrench slips and you skin the knuckles of God's hand that He gave you for the purpose of working. You curse not at all and the good people of the earth pay you a hard dollar for the trucks that were set right by your labor. I grew my handshake strong there, and my voice took such a tone that you cannot doubt but I have told you straight all that I have told.

Last year I started work in the Office of the Secretary of Defense (OSD) and, in that place, I found five facts, lined and balding in a row, each coming from the one before like a series of Russian dolls, and all of them judging the occupants of my desk:

1. Something is broken about my world
2. People expect me to fix it
3. I can't fix it, but …
4. I can possibly make it better by trying, and …
5. My job is to try.

My soul got stuffy real quick at that desk so I took to working in my head while I slept, or in the shower, or while I pedaled the elliptical.

How odd that a mechanic's son should pedal an elliptical.

They have north of twenty-thousand people working in the Pentagon, and somewhere near the top of it all is the Policy shop. (They actually call it a shop. Go figure.) It is supposed to work such that OSD Policy decides what the Department of Defense should do while everyone else gets on with doing it.

I work in OSD Policy's Special Operations and Counter Terrorism (CT) office where I advise a chain of civilians on CT issues. People think CT advisors sit around watching videos of bearded Islamists being blown up (along with their innocent wives, children, and neighbors), then we chink our shot-glasses, go bottoms-up, and cross another face off a wall chart that probably doubles as a dartboard.

Or people think of us huddled at a meeting table, engaged in a sober evaluation of the various theories for busting up terror networks and reintegrating the busted terrorists back into peace-loving societies. After this sober analysis, we will meet with the Secretary of Defense—the SecDef. Then the SecDef will whisper in the president's ear, with a nod of apology to the attendees of a disrupted meeting. The president will arch back in his chair, protecting the delicate microphone with his hand, his brow furrowing while he listens. Then he will nod and the SecDef will step away with a thanks-for-your-time glance to the disrupted room.

Huddled in the doorway, we remark to ourselves how these decisions have aged the president. "Is it just me or has he grown crow's feet by his eyes?" we say. "Is there one person in the whole world who can just chat with him as a friend?" Then someone trots out the old Truman quote: "If you want a friend in Washington, get a dog."

We will relay the president's decision to the military—casually calling him POTUS—and, in some remote mountain, the selected people are shattered in a micro-blast while, overhead, a Predator motors silently on its way. Others are arrested and secretly un-tortured; some are shuttled to GITMO where they will be held forever and eventually go on hunger strike, and still others hear an uncharacteristic message of peace from their bribed imams.

Do these things happen? Perhaps. But they never look like that. I saw the SecDef once in the Pentagon gym and I have only ever seen the president on TV.

Still, I'm lucky. Few people sit this close to the levers of power in their twenties. Or they sit here and never notice because the levers don't look like levers.

The first mistake people make when they think of power is they think of force, when they should be thinking of influence or persuasion.

People overthink power. That's because most don't have much of it and they assume you have to cheat to get it. But they're wrong. You can trust people in power. People don't understand that. But you should never trust someone who does better for himself in the power business (or the charity business, or whatever) than the other business he was in before.

So what is power? Most people won't answer that question. But it's not as complicated as you probably think if you grew up in America.

The core of power is credibility. The key to credibility is communication, and the first rule of communication is that you listen tremendously to learn who the other person is. The second rule is that you must know who *you* are. And the third rule comes after the first two: you must tell yourself generously to *that* person. If that sounds easy, it means you've never tried.

Our world contains thousands of things—millions probably—and, before you can tell so many things to so many people, you must listen with the enthusiasm of a squirrel and the patience of a horse, and then you must squeeze your message into the shape of a thousand different ears.

I learned this from Janet Lestersen before she left me, seven months ago, in the winter. Now the seasons have changed to a weepy, dripping summer, but I still try to follow her advice because she is the best person I know.

My father has also done all he will do for me in this life. That's because his story is closed. So I will follow Janet's second rule—I will tell you something about him and about me. I will speak of the past. Not of a time that was, but of a memory that is—the memory of a family yet unbroken and of a young stranger who lived there before he died to become me.

The Father-Son Conversation

Joel Alden is born into a world as the world should be, but something tilts under him, then it tilts again, and he must lean hard to keep his world right.

Ronnie Alden takes each son on a trip when he turns ten. He took Josiah. He took Jeremy. Only, maybe he will not take Joel, if Joel doesn't mind. The family already took a special trip a few months ago, didn't they?

Memories crowd Joel's head. He waves from the porch then, alone on the carpet, he repairs his red truck and the yellow one Josiah has abandoned. Then Jeremy goes and both boys return, glowing with stories of beaver cubs playing sentinel, slapping the alarm with their scaled tails, and of a bear pawing at their tent in the night until Father's flashlight set the tent aglow. Father called Jeremy dumb because he peed in a stream and poisoned the fish. So, when Father walked off to shower, Jeremy peed again and watched the fish, but they seemed okay.

"I want to go on a trip with you," Joel says.

"But, you don't even know where you want to go," Father replies.

"I want to climb Trinchera Mountain."

"But we already climbed most of it this summer."

"I want to climb it all."

"But it's too cold. We'd have to wait until the summer."

"Okay."

"If we wait for summer you'll be eleven for your ten-trip."

"Okay."

So Joel drives, with Father watching—Joel's chin tipped up to peer over his knuckles on the wheel, until they hit the first big road and then Father drives them over the parched plains, to eat lunch at La Loma in Clayton, because it is Christian-owned. Past Rabbit Ears and Capulin Mountain, to Cuchara, Trinchera, the Huajatolla, and the Bear Lakes—the Spoon, the Trench, the Earth Breasts, and the ponds of the beast—until Joel walks with his father in the high air, among marmots, pika, mountain goats, purple and yellow flowers that shiver cheerfully in the wind, and a vast herd of elk.

A skier with a death wish has woven tracks between the rocks on the mountain face. Climbing to the stony height, Joel stops.

"You okay?" Father asks.

"I'm just dizzy in my head."

"Take it easy and you'll be fine."

"Okay."

"It's a good thing we got that jeep to drive us for the first part or this climb would be more than a boy can do in a single day."

"Yes."

"And it's good only a jeep can drive that road or this mountain would be crawling with city slickers."

"Yes."

"Ready to make another go of it?"

"Yes."

Joel high-steps to a boulder and falters. Father catches his hand and they climb at a slower pace.

Standing on a ridge, Joel casts a stone and they watch it bounce over the rock face then slide across a field of snow and tumble thousands of feet below on the empty mountain. Father finds a heavier rock and heaves. It cracks into three and these pieces break again until a dozen rocklets tumble, clatter, and shrink to distant specks, crawling and bounding over the lowland grass.

"What would happen if we threw a really big rock over the edge?" Joel asks.

Father finds one too heavy to lift and tilts it off balance. It shatters fifty feet below, the pieces bounding and clattering after. They count twenty-three seconds in awe before this fragmented boulder has played out the laws of gravity and come to rest.

Then they climb on, looking for a stone to answer the one question in both their heads: how big can this go? Sitting in a crack near the peak, they push together with all four legs until, on the count of three, they unbalance a boulder the size of a freezer and set it rolling, thundering and echoing, with the bounding pieces airborne for seconds at a time before surfing like free turtles over ice, only to pass the snow and bounce, airborne again on their calamitous descent.

"We're almost to the peak," Father says. "Let's climb up and look for a way down on the other side."

"Okay."

Following the ridge past the peak and down the other side, Joel feels Father's grip on his shoulder and they stop, thirty feet from a bighorn sheep staring sublimely across the valley. It becomes alert and withdraws.

They stumble upon a crumpled fuselage and ponder the pilot's final hopes—did he have time to notice where he'd left the curiously absent tail of his plane? They cross a meadow and count the elk below—134 at Joel's count and 128 at Father's. Father says Joel double-counted and Joel says Father missed the babies. The elk gather, browse less-easily for being watched, and wander across the alpine grass.

"Isn't this amazing?" Father says. "It's good we thought of coming here for your ten-trip."

"Yes." Joel smiles.

"You know, it's important for us to spend time together and know what's going on with each other."

"Yes."

"That's why I decided to take each of you boys on a trip when you turned ten."

"Yes."

"And it's why your mom and I teach you at home." They walk with muffled footfalls through a field of tiny flowers. "When you were born, your mom and I knew we would answer to God for your safety and education." They pass the flowers and again crunch the sharp rocks underfoot. "Joel, I have something to tell you. That's why we are here, because I have something to tell you."

"You didn't want to bring me here?"

"You should ask me for vacations when I'm not tired."

"Like when?"

"Maybe on a Sunday afternoon, when I'm not working."

"Before your nap?"

"Joel, I have something to tell you."

Father looks at him but Joel looks away. Sensing that a thing reserved to be spoken, unwitnessed, on a mountain, is a brutal thing, he sits hard on a rock and listens, knowing that his father's brow has darkened while he determines whether Joel's behavior is sullen and therefore requires correction.

"You know Mr. Hendricks?" Father asks. "The one who lives catty-corner from your grandparents?"

Joel has seen Mr. Hendricks, in pleated khakis, watering his pretentious petunias. He waves and Joel waves back for decency's sake.

"Mr. Hendricks was my science teacher in high school and he's still a deacon at the Baptist church. He convinced them to make him principal of Sampson High School when your Uncle Bobby was there and I was in college." Joel glances at Father. "I need to tell you this, now that you're growing up," Father says. "After Mr. Hendricks became principal, some football players started taking your Uncle Bobby to the field across from school, where they did drugs and made Bobby do whatever things they wanted."

Joel listens.

"Mr. Hendricks found out that Coach Dickson was part of it and he told Coach Dickson to stop it. But that's all he did. They were having a good football season and the parents wanted to keep Coach Dickson."

Father stops and seats himself on a boulder that tumbled years ago and lodged itself a yard from where Joel now sits. His eyes look intense and his mustache sags while he thinks.

"The school knew what was happening, Joel. Your granddaddy knew what was happening, too—and he only told Bobby to take a stand. He told Bobby to get karate lessons so he could defend himself. But guess who taught karate?"

"Who?"

"Coach Dickson. Bobby wouldn't go to the lessons with Coach Dickson so Granddaddy said it was Bobby's fault for being bullied and maybe the experience would teach Bobby something about the need for self-discipline and for taking control of his life.

"Sometime about then Bobby had to start wearing diapers. He still wears them."

Father leans an elbow on his knee and looks into Joel's face until Joel looks away and selects a rock to scrape against his palm. "Our first responsibility is to protect weak people from being abused by strong people," Father says. "It's even more important than keeping the peace."

In his mind, Joel sees Uncle Bobby swishing the hose from one patch of grass to the next as he waters Granddaddy's lawn. Uncle Bobby doesn't talk, but he waters Granddaddy's lawn because he waters it best. And he sees Mr. Hendricks' flowers across the way.

"Your Uncle Bobby wasn't the only one that got bullied," Father says. "The Bruners had a boy Bobby's age, and the first time someone took advantage of the Bruner boy, Mr. Bruner asked his boy who'd done it. Then Mr. Bruner walked to the ringleader's house with a pipe wrench and he explained to the ringleader's dad that, if it ever happened again, Mr. Bruner would collapse his boy's skull with the very pipe wrench Mr. Bruner held there for him and his boy to look at. Then he asked whether they had any questions and they did not have questions. After that, the football players left the Bruner boy alone and they only picked on Bobby."

Before this story, Joel has seen terrifying flashes of Father's anger—the petty fury of a man whose life has not been all he hoped. But now, sitting on a stone in the scarce air, Joel sees a bitterness that always smolders and drives a man.

"Until high school, your Uncle Bobby was normal. He was shy and thin from rheumatic fever, but he studied hard and he was a loving kid. It was only because of those football players that he lost his ability to function. That's why he stays with your grandparents and mows people's yards for a job.

"And, you know what? The boys who bullied him still live in Sampson. One goes to the Methodist Church and another runs the insurance agency and sits on the school board."

Father squints and makes eye-wrinkles at the sun. Then he looks back at Joel. "So that's why we teach you kids at home. And it's why, when Mr. Hendricks and the school board decided to take me to court for it, I said these are my kids, not yours, and I will keep them safe. I told them that I would go to jail before I'd give him my kids."

"Did you go to jail?" Joel asks.

"No. The court threw the case out because a class-action lawsuit was about to settle it for the whole state of Texas. The home-schoolers won."

"I'm glad you didn't go to jail."

"Me, too."

Joel stares behind him at the field of flowers. Something white pops up from the grass. Then more white flecks bounce. Joel feels a tweak on his shoulder, then the ground is alive with bouncing ice that strikes clothes and caps but only stings when it hits your ears.

"Hail!" Father says. They run for protection among the nearest of the altitude-starved trees, but the storm spends itself suddenly and they stop in the abrupt sunshine, dizzy and laughing from hypoxia and hyperventilation.

A Bureaucratic Milieu

A: The Vivid Imagination of a Vague Problem

A year ago, last June, I stood behind a guy who wore Dockers in the checkout line at Safeway and we discovered a mutual acquaintance who was hiring at the Department of Defense. That's how I got myself on the inside of the Pentagon and it's why I can now report to you that your government is run by thirty-year-olds and that I am the only mechanic to be found among them.

It feels great to arrive. After hoping, learning, and putting in time at menial jobs, I set up shop in a cubicle and waited for people to ask my advice. And then the requests poured in like a trickle from a dike. My boss, Nick, asked me to answer a congressional query on DoD's public diplomacy efforts.[1] Before I finished the letter, someone asked me to review Ms. Holachek's statement to Congress on "Local reactions to private security contractors working in terrorist hotspots."[2] I tried to explain that this is a complicated issue, but no one listened. They asked me to make any necessary changes to the statement and wanted to know how soon I could have it done.

Those are just two examples from my second week at the Pentagon. Now I wish I had stuck my finger in the dike because, beneath all the questions and the quick-fire answers, I began to doubt

---

[1] Public diplomacy means convincing the man on the street that, despite the missiles and the bullets, the U.S. really means well. In theory, the U.S. does this as part of its holistic approach to countering terrorism. In reality, the U.S. is terrible at it.

[2] These are the strange, private armies the State Department hires to protect its diplomats. Their job is protection so they drive very fast with guns slung across their chests doing the exact opposite of public diplomacy.

that the people turning the bolts had stopped to see how the whole thing hangs together.

So, today, on my one-year anniversary at the Pentagon, I admitted something I have known for a long time: people like us shouldn't be running the world.

It's probably the last of my childhood illusions—that the world has grown-ups in charge. I'd thought I was just there to help them out. But now I've discovered that what the grown-ups really want is staff whose judgment they can trust.

Because I am a mechanic, I know that my job is to find what's wrong and, if I can, put it right. If I hear a noise, I look under the hood and see what's broken. Usually it's simple—a cracked exhaust pipe, for instance, must be replaced. But I am not done yet. When I've replaced the exhaust, I'll run the engine and see a vibration, then balance the flywheel to stop the shaking that cracked the exhaust. Do you think this makes me a good mechanic? No. A good mechanic would have balanced the flywheel before the exhaust cracked. If more people in government had dirt under their fingernails, they would understand this.

Soon after I started at the Pentagon, I learned that the U.S. passes ostensible terrorists to foreign governments for "de-radicalization"—something that sounded Soviet to my ear.[3] Sometimes we even pay for this service.

So what is de-radicalization? As in, what does it actually look like when it's happening?

In my second week on the job, I googled this question like any good researcher would do and found that some of the best investigative journalists were asking the same questions. But the journalists found themselves floating through a sort of intergalactic silence, where they ask a question and the question keeps echoing in space, but there is no answer.

---

[3] *We* would never call it a re-education camp, now, would we?

I have always had an over-active brain so, when I heard the journalists' echoes, I imagined in the missing pieces. It involved a sort of bearded, Islamic Stalin who unrolls a de-radicalization kit, consisting mostly of varied pincers. He cracks his knuckles while radicalism drains like sticky syrup from the face of a terrorist, professionally restrained on a stainless surface with circular, micro-scratches—the remnant of a previous session that was scrubbed away. The Stalin guy snaps his latex gloves over his hands, leaving the terrorist faint, lying there in the syrup and asking for a sip of water before they got into the main part of the de-radicalization procedure. It would help relieve the suffocation in the room, wouldn't it—the drink of water—and everyone could think the whole thing through before any mistakes were made?[4]

B: The Manipulative Conversation

This scene made me queasy so I called Harvey, who was identified as "your Detainee Affairs POC" (point of contact) on the contact sheet at my desk. Harvey would clear it all up for me and stop the question in my head from echoing in upon itself.

He told me that, once the U.S. returns a detainee to his nation-of-origin, we often lack insight into how that nation handles the rehabilitation. But, he said, we do seek assurances that the country will make a credible effort to de-radicalize[5] them before release.

---

[4] In my head, a theory presents itself in this hilariously sad way that maybe the world's major crimes were simply a result of personal dehydration. And, in the seconds after the theory reveals itself and stands steadily there in my gaze, it sucks this tremendous supporting evidence from the history books like an MRI efficiently collecting bits of jewelry from where they have been forgotten in some hapless body. I am now convinced that, to be safe, a man should always drink water before he does something rash.

[5] Maybe it's just this *word* that's setting off neurological storms in my brain. When Harvey said it, the bearded Stalin had morphed into a scientist

I played the dumb-new-guy card and asked him where I could find our policy for how the U.S. decides what types of de-radicalization programs are acceptable and which detainees to send. He told me that foreign de-radicalization programs are the most viable alternative to indefinite detention or releasing terrorists directly back into society. I told him I owed a brief to my DASD—my Deputy Assistant Secretary of Defense—on the issue and asked him to point me to the official policy on the matter.

Harvey told me *his* DASD could provide such a brief to my DASD. I told him I needed the policy in advance because *my* DASD always asks for a pre-brief to meet with another DASD.[6] Then he informed me that the de-radicalization policy predated the creation of the Detainee Affairs office so he wasn't the best suited to explain it.

That's when I started to think that

a. we don't have a policy on this,

b. my questions about it are unwelcome, and

c. if I wasn't hired to look into things like this, what the heck was I hired for?

Aren't we supposed to be debating these questions around a table in the evening with loosened ties and scotch?

My boss is Nick Anderson. He's a Director. His boss is the DASD—Bruce Horvath. The DASD's boss is the ASD—the

---

wearing a lab coat and I realized in a stroke of interpretive genius that the most revolting scenes in Stanley Kubrick's *A Clockwork Orange* are not the rapes, the beatings, and the murders. No. They're a prison chapel, aversion therapy, and the police beating a "rehabilitated" criminal.

[6] I was a bureaucrat before, at the State Department, and I know how to play the information-control game. I hate it, though. Because it's crap. It's the sort of thing people do when they don't know you yet and they haven't decided whether you're cool. It's also what they do when they know their "information" will crumble under scrutiny.

Assistant Secretary of Defense for Special Operations and Low Intensity Conflict, Ms. Holachek.

Nick is a man of goodwill, but he used to work for the CIA. They use other acronyms at CIA, so people can tell he's an outsider at DoD and he doesn't always get a lot of love.

He has an open-door policy so, after I had my go-around with Harvey, I walked in, skipped the pleasantries, and demanded to know who decides our de-radicalization policy. That, according to Nick, was a question for OSD's Detainee Affairs office.

"I already asked them," I said. "They said it's someone else's policy."

"Then your next step is to call NCTC."

I cursed not at all and looked up the National Counterterrorism Center on my contact sheet. This time I tried another tack. I told the voice on the other end I was the new OSD CT representative and that I hoped to meet and introduce myself sometime. He agreed and then I asked whether he could "shoot me the current de-radicalization policy" since I had come over from State Department and was trying to get smart on the issue. He asked me where I'd worked at State and I said "the Bureau of Democracy Human Rights and Labor."

"Ah, you were in DRL," he said, his words almost crawling out.[7] "You know, to be frank, the policy you're looking for probably originated with CIA." I asked and he gave me a number to call. "I'll give CIA a heads-up that you will be calling," he said.

I thanked the NCTC guy, took a breath, then pressed forward. CIA said they thought the de-radicalization policy came through the Director of National Intelligence, but DNI said such a ruling "would have been a White House decision." I was too junior to call the White House alone so Nick and I did it together on his

---

[7] In DC there are types of people and, as it happens, some of the counter-terror types don't like some of the human-rights types.

speakerphone. But no one there seemed to have any memory of the de-radicalization policy. "We would not normally get involved in the specifics of something like that unless there was an interagency disagreement," they said, suggesting I ask the State Department.

My usually-helpful counterpart at State said that, indeed such decisions are the purview of the State Department because, under the National Security Act of 1947, the State Department is tasked with the conduct of foreign relations, and transfers of prisoners to foreign countries is obviously part of foreign relations, but unfortunately, people "elsewhere in the government" had "taken over such decisions in the national security space" and now they only expect the State Department to help carry out those decisions.

Was this truly a virgin-born policy? The idea made me queasy again and I wondered if, by chance, my office was responsible. Probably not, of course: State Department is responsible for foreign relations, DNI is responsible for intelligence, and DoD and State both have special offices for detainee affairs. But I should at least find out. Then, if the decision was ours, we could make it an on-purpose decision rather than a by-accident one.

I pressed Nick on this and he looked annoyed, but he saw I was trying to do the right thing so he asked what I thought was wrong with the current policy. I said, to start with, it's not a policy, it's just what we're doing. He said, "What we do" is about as good a definition of policy as I'm likely to get.

I opened my mouth and briefly imagined Nick as some sort of wolverine, looking across his desk at me through wire glasses while restacking papers with his paw. Then he smiled. "Why don't you make some recommendations."

I said, "Thank you," more vehemently than I meant to, and, in a huff, sat with my entire throbbing soul in my cubicle. These detainees are real people, I raged. How can the government not have a thought-out, written-down policy for how to de-radicalize them or re-educate them, or whatever?

C: The Action Memo

I had to get my soul out of that cubicle. So I shuttled myself down the bright hospital halls of the Pentagon to the gym where I restored the pulsing thing to the place where it belonged in my chest. Then I ran it far above the 152 beats per minute recommended by elliptical manufacturers for thirty-year-olds who weigh 210 pounds. I ran it up to 165 and, in a torrent of indignation, wrote a memo in my head—a memo that would, over the next six months, be edited by over a dozen offices, become Ms. Holachek's official advice to the SecDef, and, eventually, turn my life into a scale-model of my disassembled country:

FROM: ASSISTANT SECRETARY OF DEFENSE FOR SPECIAL OPERATIONS AND LOW INTENSITY CONFLICT[8]

TO: SECRETARY OF DEFENSE

SUBJECT: Establishing a Policy for Detainee Reintegration

BLUF:[9] I recommend that you request a Principals Committee (PC)[10] meeting to review and establish U.S. policy for reintegrating[11] non-U.S. personnel detained in terror-related contingency operations.[12]

- In a number of cases, the U.S. returns detainees to their country of origin to be subjected[13] to a so-called "de-radicalization" regimen. (See demographics of current detainees at TAB A)

---

[8] I write it, of course, but a SecDef memo would never officially come *from* me. It comes from my ASD, Ms. Holachek.

[9] All SecDef memos must include the Bottom Line Up Front in the first line. They must also be written in bullet form and fit on a single page.

[10] The Principals Committee is a senior national security body that meets at the White House and includes the Secretaries of each of the national security departments and agencies. The National Security Advisor presides. If the president presides over it, this same body is called the National Security Council.

[11] This is my first step toward changing the vocabulary from the Stalinist "de-radicalization" to "reintegration."

[12] We don't call it war anymore.

[13] I estimate that I have invested twelve hours of my time defending the word "subjected" through successive versions of this memo. People thought it sounded biased and they were surprised when I doubled down to keep it.

- To date we have sent detainees to XX, XX, XX, and XX[14] for "de-radicalization."[15]
- This policy has not been considered at a senior level for some time:[16]
- The practice has expanded significantly in recent years
- Interagency standards have not been established for when such programs are appropriate
- The exact practices of the programs are opaque
- The data on these programs is inconsistent, incomplete, and inconclusive[17]
- Many of the "de-radicalization programs" advocate a non-violent, Islamic theology.
- U.S. support for theological education programs presents constitutional questions that merit review.[18]
- An in-depth briefing is available to you on request.[19]

---

[14] In the end I obtained the information to replace these xx's by drafting the memo and then getting Ms. Holachek to formally task the Joint Staff to fill in the blanks.

[15] I have placed the period inside of the quotation mark. I had to remind three or four of the Pentagon's self-appointed quality-control monitors that, whatever Britain does, this is standard American usage.

[16] I have masked the fact that, as best I can tell, it has *never* been formally considered at any level.

[17] I defended these adjectives from deletion by Navy, Joint Staff, and Detainee Affairs by repeatedly challenging them to provide consistent, complete, conclusive data.

[18] Office of General Counsel would not say whether the current programs had been legally "reviewed" *per se* but OGC also would not say that the programs have *not* been reviewed. Further, OGC would not state categorically that the programs *need* to be reviewed. But then, again (and OGC was very clear on this point), OGC was *not* saying the programs should *not* be reviewed. So "questions that merit review" is the language I negotiated with them.

[19] Of course, the SecDef knows he can request a briefing. I initially drafted this memo to recommend that the SecDef request a briefing but, during

RECOMMENDATION I: Request a Principals' Committee meeting to establish U.S. policy for returning non-U.S. detainees to reintegration programs in their countries-of-origin.

Agree__________   Disagree__________   Other__________

RECOMMENDATION II: Have OSD-Policy draft a position paper[20] to be proposed for review by an interagency policy committee (IPC)[21] in advance of the PC meeting.

---

review, I was bargained down to this mere hint. I almost lost this, too; it was touch-and-go for a while.

[20] This gives me more work to do and that's not great. It means that I will be constantly holding up my ideas for people to throw darts at them. But the power of suggestion is half the power; it lets me establish my own ideas as the default ideas, then others will have to make compelling arguments to overturn them. It establishes me as the person with ideas. It also makes me the compiler of other people's ideas and that's essential because, where there is a contradiction, as "the one with the pen," I can resolve the discrepancies in my favor.

[21] An IPC is a much lower-level version of the PC. IPCs usually meet at the White House and develop materials for the PC to review. By jumping from an IPC to a PC, I have avoided the intermediate level which is a Deputies Committee (DC), because a DC would typically be attended by the Undersecretary of Defense for Policy or the Undersecretary of Defense for Intelligence and I have discovered by careful snooping that neither of them is favorably-inclined to my recommendations. They are not opposed, really—this is simply not one of their pet issues so they dislike spending DoD's "political capital" on it. Both undersecretaries will approve this memo before the SecDef reads it but, in their massive piles of paperwork, they are unlikely to notice that we have proposed a process that bypasses them.

Nick and I thought up this little scheme and then solicited some well-placed help in sliding our paperwork through the system. As a curious note, Nick had not made up his mind about detainees but, because we became such good scheming buddies, he started thinking he agreed with me completely. (There are many methods of communication—many methods of persuasion. You must use the one that works for a given topic, for a

Agree_________   Disagree_________   Other_________

Attachment(s)

TAB A: Detainee Demographics

Prepared by: Joel Alden, OSD/Policy/SOLIC/CT

After extensive comments from her staff, the Acting Assistant Secretary over Detainee Affairs, a woman named Cynthia Donaldson, approved the memo with "no comment."

D: The Non-Paper

It took many months of persistence, depression, anger, asking other offices to review my memo, asking my boss to ask other offices to review my memo, and tons of late-night hand-holding from my friends after work. Then this much-revised memo got read and initialed by the United States Secretary of Defense, the sixth in order of succession to the president. And, beside the last bullet—the one that offered a briefing—the SecDef hand-wrote "Yes, please!"

I'm a quiet guy when I'm not trying to be funny but, when I saw this memo, I emitted a primal roar, startling my cubicle mate and giving all the other poor chumps in the office an excuse to emerge, eyebrows arched, from their boxes and re-acquaint themselves with their ignored souls. I ran through Nick's "open door" to where he sat talking into his desktop video screen. I held up the SecDef-blessed paper for his view and got a smile. He looked back to his screen and said, "I see that the SecDef approved Joel's de-radicalization memo."

I winced at "de-radicalization," stage-whispered "reintegration," then grinned despite myself.

---

given person, at a given time. This is the secret, if there ever was one, for success.)

24

It's funny what a SecDef signature can do for you. After months of being treated as an agitator and a pain in the rear, people couldn't wait to hear from me. The demand was overwhelming. It was 1 p.m. Tuesday, and the SecDef's staff wanted him to receive the requested briefing on Thursday morning while the issue was fresh and before he left Saturday for Southeast Asia.

Two days to prep for a briefing should be no problem, right? After all, I'd been working on this for nearly a year. Wrong! The SecDef's office reminded us that all meeting-prep materials are due in the SecDef's office twenty-four hours before the briefing. The Undersecretary's office reminded us that, "In accordance with standard procedure, all materials are due to the Undersecretary of Defense for Policy forty-eight hours in advance to give the Undersecretary time to review." We laughed because we were only notified by the SecDef's office forty-four hours in advance. But my "non-responsiveness" lodged me on the Undersecretary's shit-list of lousy staffers who don't meet deadlines and I could hardly draft anything because people were asking me every three minutes when I was going to be done, politely reminding me that the materials had been due four hours ago.

I also had a Director, a Deputy Assistant Secretary, and an Assistant Secretary who all expected to review and edit my materials before they went to the Undersecretary's office—and each of them had a deputy who passive-aggressively offered to help me out with the whole thing. All this when, just yesterday, I wasn't sure they cared! I was melting into sheer stress by 2 p.m. on Tuesday, when Ms. Holachek scheduled a meeting for 3:30 in her office to discuss our prep for the SecDef meeting.

It was a crappy situation—I hadn't really envisioned what a brief to the SecDef would look like. I'd vaguely assumed I would go to his office and ask him if he had any questions about what he'd read in my memo. Then I would talk with him about the legal and ethical problems of forcing terrorists into theology training—like sending juvenile delinquents to Mormon seminary or something. Not any other kind of Christianity, and not any other kind of faith—just Mormon. And why Mormon? Because Mormons offer a program that teaches people not to kill Americans, and that's the point, isn't it? We don't care if people believe in God, and we don't care which version of which god they believe in, so long as he/she/it can replace the Islamist killer theology with something harmless—and by harmless we mean something that isn't a killer theology. Beyond that, what do we care if it's Mormonism, Islam, Buddhism, or whatever?

"Really, Mr. Secretary," I'd say sympathetically, while redirecting the conversation from Mormonism back into a teachable channel, "I understand the sentiment, but there may be a better way to accomplish the same strategic objective[22] without using a particular brand of religious training." Having piqued the Secretary's interest with this line, I would transition flawlessly into a set of recommendations that could be proposed for interagency consideration.[23]

"Joel!"

"Yikes! What?" Nick stood behind me in my cubicle. "Sorry, Nick, I didn't see you there."

"Ms. Holachek said that, even if we don't have the full brief prepared, we should at least print off a draft of the interagency recommendations' paper for her to review at our 3:30 meeting."

"Um, sure. I'll read over it again and see if it needs any updates."

---

[22] I always try to say "strategic objective" if someone doesn't take my plain talk seriously enough.

[23] "Interagency consideration," means the White House national security staff will distribute the recommendations and ask for comments from all the agencies that have a stake in them. Because of this process, "interagency" has become a code word for "established policy" or for "a White House decision."

Okay, so I complain about having no time to prepare. But, in truth, it works in my favor in at least three ways:

1. It means I'm more likely to personally brief the SecDef because none of my bosses will have time to become an expert before Thursday morning.
2. The SecDef's pre-meeting materials are more likely to be what I want them to be because the editors between me and the SecDef will lack the time to review, discuss, and reverse my recommendations.
3. I won't have time to put everything in writing and, when I'm speaking off-the-cuff, I get to say what I want to say in a way that makes sense without it being mangled by all the people between the SecDef and me.

But I haven't yet prepared anything for this brief and I know darn well that you can destroy a year's worth of goodwill on one botched brief to the SecDef. Especially when you've framed yourself as the Department's expert on the subject. If I fumble a briefing like this, the next time I raise this issue, the Secretary and all his minions will look over their half-glasses at me and say, *"But last time you talked about this, you wasted our time."*[24]

The sheer urgency of it kicked me into that weird place where panic splits you in two. A calm, wise Joel floated overhead and chuckled. "Joel," he said, "you should have framed your

---

[24] A screwed-up briefing could tank the issue's credibility and my credibility to the point that no one would press this issue and request a decision for years to come. A botched effort like this can turn an issue into a pariah. And no one who looks for success in her career will choose to work on such an issue. Without some deft work, effective, constitutional reintegration of terrorists could fall into the poison cycle of unfocused effort known in the bureaucracy as "churn." If someone thinks I exaggerate, I invite that person to look at the effort to close the GITMO prison, the effort to conduct effective public diplomacy against extremism, or the effort to convert excess plutonium into fuel for nuclear power plants.

recommendations before now. They thought you had a paper because you drafted a memo to the SecDef saying he should ask you for it. When you raise questions, you should have answers. But you'll be all right. You'll think of the answers now, you'll write them down, you'll print them off, then you'll casually drop by Nick's office and ask him whether he wants to review the paper before you meet with Assistant Secretary Holachek. You have gambled with your career and won before, old boy, and you'll do it this time, too. No problem."

"Of course!" I said to my floater self, and laughed. I sat in the dangerous, no-thinking space of my cubicle and wrote a paper without status—a "non-paper" that listed my answers:

RECOMMENDATIONS

1. Prisoners should be able to choose the faith (or non-faith) of their "reintegration" program, much like servicemen and servicewomen choose their chaplain. This will avoid running afoul of the constitution's "establishment" clause. Given that most of the prisoners were originally Muslim and most of the reintegration programs are operated by Muslims, this will likely have a small practical impact but a large legal bearing.

2. Before transferring a prisoner, the U.S. should visit the site of the reintegration program and review the curriculum or, if there is none, offer to jointly develop one.

3. The curriculum (from step 2) should be presented in outline to the prisoner and the prisoner should be given the option to a) choose the proposed reintegration program, b) request a program based on a different faith or non-faith (this may not be granted if the requested faith is unavailable), or c) remain in his current situation.

4. The U.S. should work with partner countries and with academia to collect recidivism data and, going forward, systematically capture and assess this data to inform future reintegration-program decisions.

I sat there and stared at my computer screen. That was it. Those were my recommendations. In twenty minutes I had answered a significant national problem.

All the rest was maneuvering: I would have to reword it *ad nauseam* to pass legal muster and get the optics[25] right. I would have to contextualize, persuade, reword, communicate, and recommunicate, and, before all that, I would have to defend it against an incoming broadside. While I wrote these recommendations, Harvey sent me a high-priority email saying his DASD was "not comfortable proceeding with a briefing to the SecDef at this time" because "the potential impact on detainee transfers has not been fully assessed."

I ignored the email, printed my paper, made the copies, dropped five of them in five boss's inboxes with notes that said "for your 1530 meeting," and slid the other copies into a folder on my desk. It was 2:45 p.m.

I strolled to the Pentagon courtyard, slouched into an Adirondack chair, laid my head back, and looked at the elm leaves overhead.

---

[25] "Optics" means you have to word it so it doesn't look bad. You have to make sure it doesn't look bad to Congress, the White House, other countries, other faiths, the Washington Post, Fox News, NBC, and a host of chirping commentators who are convinced that, whatever it is, it must be bad.

At 3:10 p.m., I returned to the office and our administrative assistant[26] said, "Nick is looking for you." I walked into his office and sat myself across the desk from him.

"This looks pretty good," he said, holding my non-paper. "Let's see how the 3:30 meeting goes and then we'll need to clean it up a bit."

"Thanks," I said, irritated at the thought of "cleaning it up."

But I regained my good humor before the meeting, because it is important, for policy purposes, to be likeable. I arrived into Ms. Holachek's office before her previous meeting concluded, so I sat back and waited for my turn. Then, when she was ready, I took a seat at the table. But between meetings, the Assistant Secretary, her deputy; the Deputy Assistant Secretary, his deputy, and Nick all started complaining about a thunderstorm that had knocked out their electricity. For the last five days, they'd gone home to no food in the refrigerator and no air-conditioning in the house and had sweated in their sheets for another sleepless night.

Briefing people in that mental state is like teaching calculus to a two-year-old, and my mind grasped quietly for a solution.

I pulled my chair up to the table and passed around copies of "the paper." I waited for them to focus, then I smiled and said, "I could explain the detainee situation but I'm afraid I would be briefing a bunch of powerless leaders."[27] It was one of my best pieces of work—in a cascade of humor, they all laughed, or groaned.

The prim personal assistant said, "Joel, you'd make a great dad," and the two dads in the room scrambled to distance corny jokes from the institution of fatherhood.

---

[26] That's 21st Century for "secretary"

[27] You've got to know your audience before you make a pun like that.

F: The Pre-brief

"The SecDef approved our proposal to draft a recommendation paper for detainee-reintegration programs," I said, "and I've passed around an initial draft to talk from at our[28] briefing tomorrow."

"Who's actually going to the briefing?" Nick asked.

"I'm going," Ms. Holachek said, "and I plan to take Joel[29] and whoever else wants to go. We need to call Detainee Affairs and ask someone from their office to attend." She turned to her personal assistant. "Kala, please call the SecDef's office and see how much room they have for the briefing tomorrow. There's usually enough space in the SecDef's meeting room but we should check. And we should take someone from OGC, too."

"Shall we walk through the recommendations?" I asked.

I presented the problems and explained how the recommendation paper addressed each of them. Ms. Holachek nodded. While I talked, I noted that she read the Non-Paper, and crossed out the word "prisoner" every place it occurred. It was a stupid mistake. Ms. Holachek is a lawyer and she knows that terrorists don't meet the legal definition of "prisoner."

"Have you cleared these recommendations through the General Counsel and Detainee Affairs?" she asked.

"No," I said, and Harvey's email briefly unsettled my stomach. "I was hesitant to send them out for review until we found out whether the SecDef approved our recommendation to draft a paper." Lame excuse, but passable.

---

[28] It's a try anyway—using inclusive language to build the expectation that I will be part of tomorrow's briefing with the SecDef. There is no automatic assumption that a junior staffer like me will be included in such a high level meeting.

[29] Yes!

"Okay, well, we need to get their review before the briefing. Kala, can you call the SecDef's office and the Undersecretary's office and tell them we'll send them a draft copy this afternoon? Tell them we can get a legal review then send them a final version by 1600 tomorrow and see if that's too late."

G: Inter-Office Coordination

So my recommendations remained intact all the way to the Secretary of Defense. But I had made enemies in Detainee Affairs. They were worried about GITMO so they decided to disagree with the whole set of recommendations and argued that the issue wasn't ready for the SecDef's attention. Their Assistant Secretary had apparently been on leave when his deputy, Cynthia Donaldson, offered her lack of comment on the original memo, and I'm glad I wasn't there for the tirade when he returned. But from Harvey's email, I could hear it all in my mind: "You had *one* job," he screeched, "to close GITMO, and now some chump over in CT has decided that, first, you've got to build them a religious menu! We'll just babysit our enemies at GITMO until they choose the ideological amenities for their retirement resort—until they decide we've hired them a suitable life coach—until they're ready to *opt out* of GITMO?"

I politely reminded Harvey that his office had taken a month to review the SecDef memo—which offered a briefing—noting also that, after the SecDef read the memo, we couldn't very well put that toothpaste back in the tube, now, can we? "So, feel free to suggest a better approach to the briefing," I said. Harvey was silent. And his boss was furious.

H: The Constitutional Argument

In reviewing my Non-Paper for the SecDef briefing, the General Counsel repeated his office's position on the original memo: "The constitutional 'establishment' clause has not been generally applied to non-U.S. persons outside the U.S. Therefore, in OGC's opinion, whether the U.S. may support theological re-education programs such as those commonly described as 'de-radicalization programs,' is open to legal interpretation. This is probably an issue for the Department of Justice."

That was annoying. OGC should take a stand on the constitutional issue and they should ask DOJ themselves if they don't want to decide on their own. This kind of hogwash makes OGC irrelevant. But that's okay; it gives me more room to work.

At this point, OGC and Detainee Affairs had maneuvered themselves to the sideline, with Detainee Affairs wanting the issue to simply go away (too late for that). OGC wanted it to just go away, or at least get kicked over to DOJ. Neither of them wanted to get sucked into another constitutional meat-grinder related to detainees.[30]

I switched "prisoner" to "detainee" in the Non-Paper, "cleaned it up" with Nick, and emailed it to Ms. Holachek's office. Kala promptly made copies for everyone in the chain-of-command and provided it directly to the SecDef.

I sat there and asked myself if people like me run this place after all. It would be okay, I suppose—thirty-year-olds running the world. The only problem is, thirty-year-olds were taught by fifty-year-olds who don't believe in anything.
Personally, I've only kept my feet on the ground because I'm a mechanic, and because I talk with people who aren't like me.

---

[30] Remember the questions of what constitutes torture and who is entitled to *habeas corpus*?

Conversation with Someone Different

My roommate is Sam-Bob. He's an ex-Marine, which is, technically, an oxymoron because the Marines say "Once a Marine, always a Marine."

I lived with Sam-Bob for six-and-a-half months before I said his name with a straight face. He's from West Virginia and I had introduced him to a smart-ass named Dave at my church. Dave smelled out the West Virginia thing because of Sam-Bob's name and started telling West Virginia jokes:

Dave: "Did you know the toothbrush was invented in West Virginia?"

Sam-Bob: "No?"

Dave: "Sure. If it was invented anywhere else, they'd have called it a 'teeth brush.'"

I laughed and still regret it.

Dave: "You know you're from West Virginia if you're at a dance, the caller yells 'ho-down,' and your girlfriend hits the floor."

I didn't laugh and I saw Sam-Bob's good nature wear thin.

Dave: "If you marry a girl in West Virginia and then you move to Kentucky, is she still your sister?"

Me: "Sam-Bob, let's go home."

It's not my church's fault that we have an insecure kid from New Jersey in attendance but, unfortunately, that's the last time Sam-Bob set foot inside my church. That's the first time I said "Sam-Bob" like it was a perfectly normal name, too, and I've considered it normal ever since.

That's also the day I quit teasing people about where they're from. I still act arrogant about being from Texas, of course, just so people will believe I'm from there. But I lost my accent long ago for professional reasons.

A year after the "ho-down" incident, I spent some time in New York City and came to understand Dave better. At a party, I met a guy who worked for the U.S. mission to the United Nations. He tried to impress a girl I'd met by loudly dismissing people who work in "parochial, national, backwater" places like Washington, DC.

I've lived in enough places to know that every place is a small place and it will stifle you if you don't get out of it sometimes and exercise a little humility. But New York's self-congratulation and self-admiration surpasses even Texas, and it lacks the humor. They talk about diversity in New York like it's the only virtue in the world and they've got a monopoly on it—like diversity is another New York brand that others only plagiarize—like the rest of the world could fall off into space and they'd still be fine there in New York because they already have everything the world offers.

After experiencing New York City, I felt more kindly toward Dave. He grew up in New Jersey, shat on by people who saw his state as their toilet and they bullied him until, in self-defense, he turned it on everyone else.

But I didn't know how to show grace that day when he mocked Sam-Bob. I only wanted to yell at him and tell him how Sam-Bob is the son of a West Virginia preacher, how Sam-Bob enlisted in the Marines from sheer patriotism during what we once called the War on Terror—a West Virginia kid who cared for New York because New York is also America.

Sam-Bob's a quiet guy and tolerant for a Marine. He mans the security desk of a defense contractor, asking guests to sign a guest sheet on the reddish marble desk where he sits. "Take the elevator to floor seven and you'll sign in again there," he says in a helpful voice. He insists he's not a rent-a-cop and spends his spare time reading war history, trying to understand what the hell happened to him in

Afghanistan, and training himself to think kind thoughts toward the mass of shallow humanity that passes his desk.

When I'm in my senses and I have a tough problem, Sam-Bob is the first one I ask for help. And he's good at helping because he thinks different from me. That's also why he's annoying.

"Hey, Sam-Bob," I said, Sunday after my first tangle with Harvey from the Detainee Affairs office. "What are you reading?" He turned his book to show me the cover. "I thought you already read *Rogue Warrior*," I said.

"Yeah, man. Great book. But this is the other Dick Marcinko book: *Strategy for Success*."

"I thought the other one was *Vengeance*."

"That's the other, other one. It comes after *Violence of Action*. But you can read them in any order." Sam-Bob chuckled. "It's great. Did I ever tell you how this guy swears? It's some really creative stuff."

"Yes, you read me an entire paragraph of it. I had my hands in some kind of goop I was cooking and I could have kept my head cleaner by clapping them, goop and all, over my ears."

"See, now I know you're lying. Since when have *you* cooked?"

"Okay, fair point. But could you put down your Delta Force fantasy for a second? I've got a serious, real-world problem and I need your advice."

"Hey, man, this is real-world stuff. And it's not Delta Force, it's SEAL Team Six. Big difference. Besides, Dick Marcinko is legit. He really stuck it to the Navy. They hated him but, when it came time to take out terrorist number-one, what did they do? They called up Dick Marcinko's old outfit and shot the old bastard, once and for all, through the eye."

"Yes," I couldn't resist, "and they couldn't stop bragging about it. And you know what? No one will work with us now because they're afraid, if they do a good job, we'll tell everyone about it and get them killed."

"Whatever, man."

"No, this is serious, Sam-Bob, and you of all people should know it. You talk about terrorist number-one. Well, the rumor got out that the U.S. had used a vaccination campaign to collect information for that mission. And you know what? Now thousands of children will die from preventable diseases because people think every vaccination is a ploy for the CIA to track them down and shoot them. And none of the local doctors will work with us, because they think all Americans are from the CIA and we'll throw them under the bus, too, like we did the last guy."

"Dick Marcinko wouldn't throw people under the bus," Sam-Bob said.

"Really?" But I'd had enough and swerved hard to change the conversation. "Look, I've got another issue, and I need your advice. It's dead serious."

"What are you working on?"

"Detainees."

"I've worked on a few detainees in my day."

"Sheesh man, talk to your psychiatrist about that. Or a defense attorney. I'm talking about detainee *policy*. We're force-feeding them religion and that's not right."

"I don't think they need more religion—or more force-feeding, for that matter. Those prisoners are already religious enough to throw their own turds at us, and they'll hardly eat unless you put a fucking Koran on the dinner tray, with green beans and this certified kafka, purchased from an Arab-Jew-kosher-meat dude with some pita bread on top. That's dinner. And then they sniff to see if it meets their 'delicate sensibilities' before they scoop it up in their hands and smear it everywhere so when they're done eating, I swear, the only thing left clean is the silverware."

"Maybe you should just say 'Koran' without any adjectives," I said. "It could help with the turd problem. And I think you mean 'shawarma'?"

"What did I say?"

"You said 'Kafka'."

"Whatever, it's how the Arabs cook their goats or sheep, or whatever it is they cook."

"Kafka wrote a book about a guy who turned into a bug, then got neglected by his family."

"I'm just saying they eat weird food. I don't see why you're getting all technical about it. At least I didn't mix up the *force-feeding* and the *religion* like you did."

"But I said 'force-feeding' because I was trying to get your opinion about *indoctrinating* them."

"Like switching their Korans for Bibles, or something?"

"Or hiring someone to tell them they were confused and the Koran really tells them to love Americans."

Sam-Bob frowned. "They'd never suspect *that*, now, would they? If America suddenly turns expert on the Koran and it happens to not say what it used to say and now it says God loves America?"

"But what if it wasn't America saying that? What if it was a Saudi guy?"

"A Saudi guy bought and paid for by America?"

"Exactly. How else are you going to convince them to lay off with the terrorism?"

"We used to shoot them."

I almost laughed, but managed to keep a straight face. "And did that convince them to lay off?"

"It convinced the ones we shot."

"But it left their families and their tribes with nothing *but* terrorism to say they weren't okay with the arrangement, right?"

"Turn them over to Dad."

"Huh?"

"I said 'turn them over to Dad.' Dad could talk a coalminer into starting a pebble collection. He could sell ice to a penguin. And that's who it'd take to change their minds.

"One time, Dad and Mom convinced this pancake-makeup-wearing whore to teach fucking Gerard Manley Hopkins classes. She switched her fishnets for culottes, started a flower garden with petunias and stuff, then held readings there in the evening. And the miners came to listen. Darndest thing I ever saw."

I sat there and looked at Sam-Bob. He'd draped his knee over the arm of our stuffy red chair and stared across the hall into the kitchen. "Well, Sam-Bob, if that's what it takes."

"If you gave Dad a little time, he could convince a terrorist to shout hallelujah and sing God Bless America." He looked at me. "By the way, have you ever, you know, *seen* a detainee?"

"No. Why?"

"No reason. Just thought I'd ask."

"Have you seen one?"

"I guarded a prison, man. How do you think I know about the kafka and the turds?"

The Brief and the Poem (I)

Every morning I drive twenty minutes from my house to the Pentagon's remote North parking lot. I park on an imaginary line that runs due north from the turnstile where I swipe my badge then walk onto the hallowed Pentagon grounds. I nod to the guard and cross a footbridge over highway 110. Ahead, Robert E. Lee's mansion sits atop a hill, flag at half-mast, surrounded by Arlington's scrubbed gravestones—stones that shift and realign their rows as you pass. Abraham Lincoln buried the dead on Lee's plantation to ensure that, by defending the south, Lee had forever forfeited his home to be a memorial to the people who died in his war.

To the right of Lee's house is Rosslyn's business district, sporting the glassy, mid-rise office buildings prohibited by height restrictions in DC. I scan past the Francis Scott Key Bridge to Georgetown University's chapel, and further to the right—on the horizon—the National Cathedral sits heavy on DC's highest ground. From there, you drop your gaze to the Lincoln Memorial and then shift to the right where the White House is lost in the trees. I try not to notice how the Washington monument recalls the white hoods and winking eyes of the Klan, and switch my focus to the Capitol dome, then to the Jefferson memorial and the Potomac, with Roosevelt Island in the foreground below an airline, swishing at low altitude on approach to Reagan National Airport. Then I look at the Pentagon, built to house the Department of War—its bleak, steel-rationed walls defeating even the gardeners' attempts to soften its appearance.

To the right of the Pentagon, a helicopter hovers, sets down, then deposits the Secretary of Defense. I will meet with him in one hour.

But he was late. The DASD for Detainee Affairs, a man I'd never met—named Hodges—sat in the waiting room when we arrived, then he stood to shake hands with Ms. Holachek.

"I'm glad you could come," she said.

"When someone talks to the Secretary of Defense about detainees, it's my job to listen," he said. From his photo, on the Pentagon's "policy wall," I had not guessed DASD Hodges was this young—or this tall. He wore his hair slicked unnaturally back, and dangled marfanoid hands at the end of his arms, their unusual length incongruous with his little door-knocker beard. When Mr. Hodges stood over Ms. Holachek to greet her, she looked portly, pleasant, and grey by contrast.

"I wish we'd had time for a pre-brief with you," Ms. Holachek said with genuine warmth. "But I've asked Joel to keep us fully synced since this is an issue that touches both our offices."

"Yes, it does," he said, then sat back in his chair and picked up a newspaper. "I'm just concerned that your approach will make it harder for us to close GITMO," he said in such a growl that I think he meant for only me to hear it.

I sat across the waiting room from DASD Hodges, with Ms. Holacheck and three of my intermediate bosses, while the clock ticked and Mr. Hodges rustled the sports section of the New York Times. He would be an attractive guy except that his skin had the texture of an eggshell.

I tried to keep our conversation on benign topics because I knew he listened. But then Nick asked Ms. Holachek whether she intended to be the only one who spoke in our meeting. She said she meant to frame the issue, then make the whole group available to answer the SecDef's questions. I saw that Mr. Hodges stared at her over his paper and I asked her in a low voice whether she expected him to talk. She looked across the room.

"Ron," she said, "we were discussing the order of the briefing. I intend to introduce the team, then outline the paper that Joel circulated with your team. But you're welcome to take a portion of it as well, if you like."

"I'll just listen," he said.

We sat in silence. I looked at the relentless clock and felt queasy. We'd already lost fifteen minutes of the thirty-minute meeting and this was my big chance to clear the logjam I'd been chipping at for the last year. A rushed meeting is worse than no meeting and I was hoping we could reschedule. But no.

"He's ready." It was the Secretary's secretary.[31]

We filed through the door and there, in his wide office, stood the Secretary of Defense. "Good morning, and thanks for coming. I apologize that I'm running late."

Famous people throw me off in person.[32] Why is it these guys are always smaller in person than on TV? And gentler, too. Maybe they get used to people being intimidated by their position and they compensate with an understated manner.

He shook hands with each of us. We seated ourselves, and the Secretary asked, "So who's briefing today?"

Ms. Holachek said, "Mr. Secretary, I was planning to introduce the topic and then turn it over to Joel for the specifics."

"You must be Joel?" the SecDef said, looking at me.

"Yes, sir," I answered, relieved that my voice cut in.

"Excellent! It's a little unusual for me to engage so early in such a discussion, but detainee issues are important." He sat at the

---

[31] Even in the 21st Century, a Secretary's secretary is okay with being called a secretary.

[32] I had only ever seen the Secretary once during an awkward incident in the Pentagon locker room where he very nearly towel-snapped me as I happened down the hallway between him and the towel receptacle.

head and leaned forward, elbows on the table, hands clasped in front of him. I wondered whether they'd built the table below standard height just to accommodate this posture.

The SecDef went on: "Your timing is good. As you know, this is a topic of personal interest to the president. He pulled me aside yesterday after a National Security Council meeting on Pakistan and asked me where we stand on GITMO. I told him my staff is doing some creative thinking and that you'd provide me with recommendations this week.[33] I read your paper and it needs a short section on what we've done to date, plus a few more specifics on how your proposals will help us close down GITMO.[34] But I promised the president that, when I get back from Indonesia, I'll take my staff to brief him."

The SecDef focused on Ms. Holacheck. "It looks like we'll be doing more direct briefs to the president. I'm not sure what's going on over at the White House, but the president told me he's tired of having all his information filtered through the National Security Staff and the White House Chief of Staff. I apologize for being so brief here but, good work." He smiled. "Sandy, please work with my staff. Tell the White House I spoke with the president about this and then work with them to schedule a POTUS briefing. Whenever we can get it scheduled, I'll bring you and …"—he turned to me—"what's your name again?"

"Joel."

"I'll bring you along, too. I apologize again, but we're negotiating to keep our supply route open through Pakistan. What's-his-name from CENTCOM is on the line and I can't put him off."

And, with that, the Secretary of Defense stood and walked toward the door. "We'll talk when I get back," he said, winking at me.

Fuck!

---

[33] This is not good.

[34] This is even worse.

Sorry, I don't swear, but this is horrible. I'm toast, in fact. I have sacrificed every working relationship I need for a wink from the Secretary of Defense and a meeting with the president—a meeting I don't want, on a topic that belongs to someone else—a topic that is the opposite of everything I'm trying to do. Here's my list of the ways this is horrible:

1. I'm not trying to close down GITMO. I'm trying to establish legal, ethical, and constitutional guidelines for detainees.

2. Closing down GITMO is someone else's job; I don't want it and they don't want me to have it. They will all be outraged that I've gone behind their backs and talked to the SecDef and the president about their issue.

3. I've got nothing to offer on closing down GITMO. It's an impossible problem, it belongs to someone else, and I'm not even a lawyer!

4. No matter what I say and no matter what's true, everyone will think I promoted myself and sucked up to the president. They will sabotage *everything* I do from now on. "*You want to go it alone,*" they'll say, "*well, then, go it alone and let's see how that works out for you.*" It's beyond a teacher's-pet problem. I'll have undersecretaries and Senate-confirmed officials jealous of the attention I'm getting.

DASD Hodges left the room ahead of everyone, his face visibly contorted. Ms. Holachek said, "I can't say I've been in a meeting quite like that before."

Nick forced a smile as we walked along the Pentagon's outer ring and said flatly, "Congratulations, Joel. Let's sit down when we get back to the office and discuss our approach to the POTUS briefing."

I nodded. Back in the office, two of my co-workers stood in the hall, waiting for Nick.

"So?" they asked. "How did it go?"

"It was terrible," I said, and brushed past them. If I hadn't snapped at them, I'd have cried, so I snapped. Imagining their "someone's PMSing" looks behind my back, I dropped my papers on my chair and escaped into the hall. I went to the restroom but recognized someone who'd walked in before me, so I diverted to the escalators and headed for Starbucks.

"Small decaf Americano?" the barista asked.

"Yes, thanks," I said, relieved that not all my relationships were shattered.

She gave me the drink and I sugared it, creamed it, capped it, and then I knew what I would say to Nick.

"Close the door and sit down," Nick said when I entered his office. I did.

"Nick, I'm not doing the briefing."

"Hold on, hold on," he said. He looked quizzical and I thought he might laugh at me. "Let's think this through a bit."

"I've thought about it," I said, "and I can't do the briefing. Guantanamo Bay belongs to Detainee Affairs or State Department— heck, maybe it belongs to Joint Staff or the Navy—and the SecDef doesn't even care about setting a policy for reintegration programs. He just wants to close GITMO. I'm sorry," I said, "I was only trying to get an IPC so we could put together a reintegration policy and be done with it. That's what our memo said. I wasn't trying to advise anyone on GITMO!"

"Put your coffee down," Nick said. I hadn't known I was shaking. "We'll figure this out but, after what the Secretary said, I think you'll have to attend the POTUS brief. We just need to figure out how to coordinate it ahead of time and make sure everyone's onboard. Let's see if Detainee Affairs wants to put together an information briefing for POTUS and then we can tag on something about reintegration."

My panic subsided a little. It sounded simple. Maybe I could just tag along for a presidential briefing on detainee issues. I felt my face relax.

"What do you think of that?" Nick asked.

"That makes sense."

In fact, it was pure genius. I had tripped myself into a coveted thing: an audience with the president. And what would I do? I'd pull an "aw shucks" and turn it over to the people who really needed it. Then the people who hated me for talking about their issue would love me. They'd been trying for months to get this.

That's the way it is with these things. If you know what you want, you'll never get it. But if you go out for something and then take what comes along … well, then there's always something in it you can use. Nick pushed his tissue box across the desk and smiled while I blew my nose. I gave a single-chuckle at myself so he'd know I was over it.

"I'm seeing Ms. Holachek about something else this afternoon," he said. "I'll run our plan past her and see what she says."

I had an urge to swallow this graying, fifty-year-old, ex-CIA guy in a hug and sob into his shoulder but, being a mechanic from Sampson, TX, I did what you should always do with such an urge: I stifled it and said, "Thank you very much."

Then, I opened his office door and he said, "You should go home early today."

"Thanks."

I left the Pentagon, feeling washed out, like I'd spent my tears dry. Red lights blinked from the Washington monument, as they had this morning—as they had before my life spontaneously disassembled then reassembled itself. I laughed feebly to myself at the silliness of it all and recited a poem:

"The Girl

One day life stands
Gently smiling like a girl
Suddenly on the far side of the stream
And asks
(in her annoying way),

"But how did you end up there?"

How could you do a life like mine if you didn't memorize
poetry?

The Government Website

Why do I fight these battles? Why do I keep trying to set things right when I gave up on the bureaucracy years ago?

Maybe I am hungover from a Joel Alden who lived once and tried to improve people's lives. A Joel Alden who taps earnestly on his keyboard at the State Department. A Joel who looks up at the sound of a knuckle rapping on his cubicle wall.

The office clown, Eric Sproul, stands in his doorway with a new guy. "So this is Joel Alden," Eric says, "our small-town mechanic, turned conservative crusader, turned human-rights staffer. Add rail-splitting to that resume and you could be someone in this town, hey, Joel? Joel, meet Wesley, our new intern."

"Wesley? Good to meet you," Joel says. "We should grab coffee sometime but I'm running to a meeting now." Joel listens while they walk on and Eric continues his narration.

"You've walked into a living, breathing, social experiment, Wesley. The State Department has proven through its human-rights bureau that prisons do not in fact need to be secured. The doors can be left wide open and, with proper conditioning, the prisoners will leave and return to these padded, joy-sapping cubicles of their own volition and pore for inhumane hours over reports on the most depressing subject matter so that, at the end of the day, the reports can be posted for further inaction on the State Department website. It's a sort of sweatshop to end all sweatshops, if you know what I mean. Here's the kitchen and the coffee that makes the whole place go, and let me introduce you to Sandy 'the-keeper-of-the-chocolate' Waller ..."

Walking to his meeting, Joel wonders with irritation who appointed Eric Sproul to show the new guy around. At his meeting, Joel pulls back a chair from the table where a Foreign Service officer from the State Department's China office has centered himself opposite the wife of a Chinese man imprisoned for teaching the Bible to his neighbors.

"Can you please do something for freeing my husband?" she asks.

"First, I can assure you that we take claims like this very seriously. Any violations of human rights or religious freedom are a significant concern to the U.S. Government." Joel knows from the speaker's smile that he has considered whether to say "significant concern" or merely "concern" and that he feels generous for his choice.

"I ask that you please speak to the government of my country on this," the wife says. The colleague's smile fades with generous annoyance; as a non-native speaker of English, the wife has clearly not appreciated the significance of "significant."

"I would like to thank you for bringing this issue to our attention," the colleague says, trying again with patience toward the challenges of cross-cultural communication. "U.S. officials engage regularly with their counterparts in the host government on a range of issues, including human rights."

"The last time, when they have taken my husband, they injure his back with too much beating. This time, is even longer. I ask for your help soon."

"As we meet with relevant Chinese officials, I can assure you that we will continue to engage on these issues."

Joel escorts the stricken wife from the building and he wishes to assure her that he at least has heard her story and shares the pain. But, having sat through the meeting in complicit silence, he cannot say even this.

He returns to his cubicle and searches the internet for enough corroboration to strike the inevitable "allegeds" from his colleague's record of the meeting[35] and to defend this story against embassy Beijing's inevitable deletion attempts in next year's report on the state of human rights in China. Joel thinks darkly to himself that, if this misery cannot be relieved, it must at least be recorded in the State Department's official record of Things That Happened[36]—and, as Eric Sproul would say, "posted for further inaction on the State Department's website."

---

[35] *Alleged* extrajudicial detention, *alleged* physical abuse, *alleged* religious persecution, *alleged* intimidation of family members . . .

[36] If he had been alive to hear of it, Joel Alden's father would have quoted Psalm 56: 8, saying that Joel had recorded the woman's suffering and "placed her tears in a bottle."

PowerPoint

The two weeks after our SecDef brief were unpleasant. It seems that DASD Hodges told his colleagues at the White House, State Department, and the Joint Staff that they owed POTUS a GITMO brief. In response, the Joint Staff issued formal taskers to Joint Task Force Guantanamo (JTF-GTMO) and to the Navy, requiring each to generate a brief for the president. JTF-GTMO produced a PowerPoint presentation on the history of detainees and their conditions at Guantanamo Bay (free access to good food, medical care, exercise, religious literature, etc.), and the Navy laid out a legal description of how Congress and the courts have blocked the president and the Navy in its—the Navy's—noble efforts to purge the Guantanamo Bay *Naval* Base of this blot on America's good name. I printed these briefs, and when I fanned the pages in front of our industrial paper-shredder, it frowned visibly and shook its head.

I'll tell you now that I blame PowerPoint for most of what's wrong in the world today.

In a time before I was born, people sat together to discuss an issue—at least I think they did. They listened to each other's tone-of-voice, read facial expressions, watched body language, and followed the twists that come in a conversation. All parties were alive while they talked. But now we rely on the most flaccid of tools: speaker and audience both staring at a screen—inane words and generic, approved[37] pictures endlessly tweaked to fill the white spaces on a slide.

A poor briefer walks into the room. He wears a blue shirt with an insignia and he's a man who should have walked with a clear gaze and a firm handshake. But, instead, he lugs piled printouts on his hip like a child that has almost slipped free by unshucking himself from his own shirt. The briefer slides the briefs from his hip onto the table, where they slump to the side and he snatches at one that has slipped over the edge. He apologetically shoves copies across the glassy table to the early arrivals, then starts fiddling with the computer terminal in the corner. But, for some reason, the room's projector is stuck in video-teleconference mode. The thermostat-looking controller in the corner appears to be a touchscreen, but it doesn't respond so the briefer thinks it may be remote controlled. He looks around for the controller then changes his mind and asks an administrative-looking person outside the room to call tech support (tech support was *supposed* to have the room set up for this). As the briefer steps out to talk to the administrative-looking person, he meets a general who has arrived for his brief. The briefer nods to the slumped papers and invites the general to "Grab a brief and we'll start shortly."

The general sits at the head of the glassy table and flips through the slides while he waits. He turns the brief endwise to squint at a pie-chart that's too small. He frowns and circles a typo. Then he flips to the back and reads a slide titled "recap." He wonders whether the briefer intends to spring a decision on him today. "How soon do you need a decision?" the general will ask over his half-glasses. The general suspects that they will ask him to endorse a vague recommendation on the spot and then, because it wasn't clear, they'll have room to interpret his approval however they like. It will

---

[37] The Pentagon has a comprehensive database of pictures for use in official Pentagon briefs.

be like a disembodied "yes" that you can keep in your wallet and spend however you like. That's why the general's "how soon" question will make them squirm—because it's a reasonable question and, if they say "today," his question will point out to the staff that they have taken all the thinking time for themselves and then they've asked him conspicuously to *not* think but just say yes to them on the spot.

By now, a technician has arrived and switched on the screen. The briefer hisses that the room should have been already set up and the technician apologizes because he is a contractor and contractors always apologize because they want to keep their contracts. But then the technician reminds the briefer that all briefers are required to take A/V training before using the briefing rooms.

"I've never even heard of this training," the briefer snaps.

"It's listed on the employee-learning website." The briefer nods then. He has never heard of that website but he knows it was probably in one of the new-staff emails he ignored.

But the briefer has no time for this. He looks at his watch. He is four minutes late, so he dims the lights, flips to slide one, and says, "Good afternoon, I'm Colonel Joseph Hampton and I'll be your briefer today." Then he flips to a slide that says "Agenda" and reads it.

The room is dark. The briefer has no idea where he wants his audience to focus. On him? On the screen? Fifteen minutes into the presentation and he has made eye contact with no one but, because the room is dark, no one finds it odd. The general nods. He yawns in the darkness but his briefer pushes blindly through. Damn the yawns; full screen ahead.

Were this briefer's slides written to stand alone? Why then does he read them like a bedtime story to a general who is, we presume, literate?

Are the slides the speaker's notes? Then shouldn't he place them on the podium, turn up the lights, and look his audience in the eye?

Did he design the slides for his general to review them afterward in his office? Then why not hand them out at the end?

Or has the speaker brought some graphics to go along with his speech? If so, this is good. But, in the Department of Defense, this is the least of PowerPoint's uses.

In fairness, PowerPoint doesn't *cause* crappy communication. It just makes it look professional.

Microsoft didn't invent empty content—bad writers learned it long ago. They wrote impossible memos to give the appearance of doing something. The difference is that people are only now taking our beleaguered PowerPoint Colonel to task while they've had centuries to skewer the empty-memo-writing bureaucrat:

> *"Some writers have the unhappiness, or rather Prodigious Vanity to affect an obscurity in their Stiles, indevouring by all meanes not to be understood, but rather like witches to cast a mist before the eies of their Readers."* – Samuel Butler (1612 – 1680)

> *"The best way to be boring is to leave nothing out."* – Voltaire (1694 – 1788)

> *"The first rule for a good style is to have something to say; in fact, this in itself is almost enough."* – Arthur Schopenhauer (1788 – 1860)

> *"Speak English,"* said the Eaglet. *"I don't know the meaning of half these long words, and what's more, I don't believe you do, either."* – Lewis Carroll (1832 – 1898)

> *"Whenever you feel an impulse to perpetrate a piece of exceptionally fine writing, obey it – whole-heartedly – and delete it before sending your*

manuscript to press. Murder your darlings." – Sir Arthur Quiller Couch (1864 – 1944)

"[Jargon] looks precise, but it is not. It is, in these times, safe: *a thousand men have said it before and not one to your knowledge has been prosecuted for it."* – Sir Arthur Quiller Couch (1864 – 1944)

"What is it that brings on this long-winded wordiness? I'm not sure but I have a hunch that a writer, feeling defeat in advance, gets lengthy and vague in self-defense." – Congressman Maury Maverick[38] (1895 – 1954)

"A memorandum is written not to inform the reader but to protect the writer." – Dean Acheson, Secretary of State (1893 – 1971)

"Too many readers are intimidated and humbled by what they can't understand, and in some cases that's precisely the effect the writer is after. But confusion is not complexity; it's just confusion." – Patricia T. O'Connor (1949 -)

Uncommunicating is as old as government. PowerPoint has merely become the most popular way to neuter yourself, bureaucratically. Because it looks more professional than mumbling or writing bad memos.

So I oppose PowerPoint. It is one way I push back at my broken world. I have propped a book over my computer—bold letters stamped onto a yellow cover: "Real Leaders Don't Do PowerPoint." Nick frowned when he saw that. And now, when he sticks his head into my cubicle and asks me to build him a

---

[38] Maury Maverick, is another TX rancher who got into government. He got his name associated with antisocial cattle and then he invented the word "gobbledygook": twin accomplishments that make him my hero.

PowerPoint deck, I take up the book and finger its letters contemplatively until he reframes his request.

You'd understand my passion on this if you were asked to "provide input" on the two GITMO decks that worried our shredder. The Navy couldn't have dropped its ordnance farther from the target if it had staged an interpretive ballet with a voiceover explaining GITMO to the president. It was enough to make a fellow cry for the wasted days and wasted years—the wasted lives spent on this empty work.

So how do you "provide input" on a thing like this? First, you think of the president. What does the *president* need?

The president needs someone to talk with who is authoritative, informed, and honest. A person with no electronic crutch.

I have a brilliant friend, Andrea, who designs "3-D virtual humans" for the Army. Holograms. And what are these holograms designed to do? They're designed to teach social skills.

Isn't it time for the Army to send their socially-deficient soldiers on a camping trip, give them a phrase-book of basic interactive language, then make them write an old-fashioned essay on what they learned out there? And then the Army can put its hologram money toward reducing the federal deficit.

My solution is all very well for the Army, of course, but how do you respond to a useless product in the bureaucracy?

Deftly. I sent a polite email to Joint Staff, JTF-GTMO, and the Navy, thanking them for their comprehensive information and for generating it so quickly. I told them we were instructed to bring no more than ten people to the POTUS briefing, of which five could be from DoD: the SecDef planned to attend personally (1), two OSD individuals had been requested by name[39] (3), Detainee Affairs would provide the primary briefer[40] (4), and the Joint Staff should select one person to attend for the military (5). The Joint Staff designee should plan to use the two informative briefs (Navy's and JTF-GTMO's) as background information to answer the president's questions.[41]

One time a man travelled to a damp village in Norway. It rained the whole time he was there. Some years later this man returned to the village and arrived in a rainstorm. He crossed a street and extended his umbrella companionably to a local boy who walked with him: "Does it always rain here?" the man asked.

The boy shrugged. "How could I know?" he said. "I'm only seven."

See, I know why people use PowerPoint. It has nothing to do with using the best format for your message, it's how nervous bureaucrats micromanage a briefing when they can't be present. They make the briefer submit his slides for review so they can protect their interests. PowerPoint is how dozens of petty kings negotiate what they will say to their emperor. It's how competing bureaucrats compromise among themselves before talking to a foreign government (or a foreign part of their own government, like Congress).

PowerPoint has not only destroyed the art of conversation, it has become the tool of choice for a paralyzed, micromanaging, no-one-in-charge, consensus-based decision style. Take away the tool and you take away the power.

---

[39] I have masked the fact that I was requested by name and my attendance is displacing a 3-star general who, I learned later, had already scheduled a jet to fly him from Florida to DC for the briefing.

[40] I am also masking the fact that no one from Detainee Affairs was requested by name.

[41] There is no reason to be mean. That's why I thanked them for the (misplaced) briefs, gave the briefs an accurate compliment (they *were* informative), and then marginalized them.

So, if not PowerPoint, what is the solution? How should we brief the president?

A trusted person should gather the views of her colleagues and then go talk with him. The SecDef has promised the president a briefing on GITMO. The SecDef has designated Detainee Affairs as his lead for this topic, so Detainee Affairs should choose a briefer. The briefer should take another colleague to keep her honest and she should speak with the president as requested, and then she should communicate back what the president has said. This is a simple, no-bullshit code that requires character, trust, and honesty.

Was there ever such a code? How would I know? I'm only thirty.

The Conversation with an Almost Lover (I)

"Name someone—anyone—who changed the world by working a job that offers a retirement plan," Joel demands in frustration. "The State Department gives their human-rights staff a leash that's just long enough to pretend they're serious, but too short to change anything." As he talks, Joel knows he has given up on his job in the State Department human-rights bureau.

After three proper dates, Joel has invited Janet over to his house for their first not-really-a-date. It's just sort of, *hey, want to cook dinner together at my house—something simple, like salads?* Janet says yes, even though she's not sure they're dating per se, at this point, and it's something that doesn't need cleared-up today, but it does need cleared-up pretty soon or it will be strange for her to be there cooking in Joel's tiny kitchen while Sam-Bob gets himself off the couch and goes in the bedroom to put on something more formal than his sweat shorts, and Sam-Bob wonders whether he's welcome in the main part of the apartment because the other two kind of fill it up since the dining room and the TV room and the living room are really the same room.

"You wouldn't believe the Presbyterians in Africa," Joel says. "You can go to a village in Z______ and they'll all be in church on Sunday, dancing barefoot with this haze of dust, and anywhere a pinhole of light comes through the roof, it makes a shaft where you can see the particles swirling. People stare at you because they've never seen a white person but, you know what? They're standing up front with a choir director. They're wearing red robes and singing four-part harmony. And there'll be a pastor up front, too, telling them that Jesus died for their sins. And do you know why that is?"

Janet is wearing Sam-Bob's apron—it reads "World's Best Dad" over a spatula-wielding cartoon with a cumulonimbus hat—and she's trying to find a space in the conversation to ask whether Joel wants tomatoes on his salad and Joel gives this yeah-sure nod about the tomatoes so he can use his actual words on the amazing Presbyterians. Janet eats a tomato chunk, licks her finger, and dumps the rest over the salads.

"And, do you know why they're wearing those robes and telling each other about Jesus?"

"Why's that?"

"It's because of the Scots. In the 1800s, they had barely enough to eat back in Scotland, but they felt so strongly about God and about Africa that they packed all their earthly belongings and moved there to tell the Africans about God. And do you know how they packed their stuff? Like, since they hadn't made suitcases yet, what they used to carry it all?"

Janet has placed their salads on the table and she's putting another salad on the table, too, because she has clearly made enough for Sam-Bob without even asking, and she has also placed these little bowls of fixings on the table and all Joel has done while he talked is to hand-grate way too much cheese, so Janet leaves most of the cheese on the cutting board where he grated it and she puts a little bowlful on the table, along with the avocados and the beef and the chips and the chives and the salad dressing that she has made with ingredients already in Joel's kitchen, that he had no idea could be combined that way into a surprisingly-tasty salad dressing, seasoned mostly with pepper.

"What did they use to pack their clothes?" Janet asks, and maybe she seems a little tired.

"They packed their clothes in coffins," Joel says, and gives a wait-for-*that*-to-sink-in pause. Then he repeats his mission trip leader's final punch: "Now *that's* commitment to the gospel."

"It's also a little morbid, wouldn't you say?"

"But, Janet, that's the point. Good things aren't safe. So why are we trying to be safe?"

"So what are you thinking you'll do?" Janet is incredibly good at telling when Joel is driving at something. And she probably knows where he's going with it all, but she gives him a chance to say it himself, which is part of the sensitivity that makes Janet amazing.

"I'm just thinking, what would it be like if we had that kind of commitment? You and me, here, today?"

"Well, what do *you* think it would look like?" The whole meal has turned from a "to be" and now it's an "is" sitting there on the table. Janet fills three glasses with water.

"I don't know how to fix Africa," Joel says. "White people have been trying and failing at it for hundreds of years."

"But …?" Janet has set the glasses on the table and cocks an eyebrow. If this is Janet's version of flirting, Joel decides it is very sexy.

"But there are some wonderful Africans who care about Z_____, and I'm thinking, what if there's a way to help them? To support their vision for their own country?"

"Maybe you should come work with me at USAID."

"So we can live in a walled-off neighborhood, eat mangoes, hire servants, contribute to our retirement plans, and give America's left-over stuff to starving Africans?" Joel's hungry voice has pushed its edge through the surface and Janet answers it with a question about the salads. She had noticed this edge when the food was slow coming on their second date and maybe she wonders whether Joel could ever learn to sense a small, human thing like that in her.

"Shall we eat these salads while you tell me your plan?" Janet says. But she is really asking him to release the food for eating; she's inviting him, as is his custom, to pray before their meal. And she is asking him to answer Sam-Bob's unasked question about whether he is welcome in the main area of the house.

"Sam-Bob. Food," Joel calls toward the bedroom door. Then he turns back to Janet. "So I met this guy named Joseph Banda. He goes out and talks with the pastors and the chiefs in the countryside. The people trickle in from their fields and sit under a shade-tree while he talks with them about how Jesus was a leader like the pastors and the chiefs, except that Jesus led by washing people's feet, healing the sick, and teaching the people a better way to live. When Mr. Banda talks to them, it looks like it must have looked when Jesus taught. Outdoors. With fields and birds and dirty feet for inspiration—to use as illustrations for what you're saying.

"What if I just volunteer with him? With Mr. Banda? I could help him set up a website, tell people what he's doing in English—Mr. Banda's English isn't very good, which is fine as long as he's talking to his own people, but it gets garbled every time someone from the outside tries to understand what's going on—like an embassy or a church group, or maybe an aid group that wants to build clean water wells in the tribal areas where he's working. I'm thinking Mr. Banda could build credibility with some projects like the wells and then run for president and lead by example. You need someone like that to make sure foreign aid really works for the people and to make sure government officials serve their people instead of taking all the best bits and leaving the people to fend for themselves, like what's happening now."

Janet is nodding and listening, but she has sat herself at the table, sprinkled the fixings over her salad and she's drizzling the dressing on hers while Joel kind of absently takes each bowl and sprinkles it over his salad after she's done.

"Do you want some salad dressing, too?" she asks.

Joel nods and says, "Janet, this looks amazing."

Sam-Bob comes out of the room, lights a cinnamon candle, and plunks it in the middle of the table between the chives and the cucumbers. He winks at Janet, sort of like, isn't Joel a piece of work because he should have lit the candle first thing but, with a little tending, maybe Joel'd be alright.

"I'm thinking of moving to Africa," Joel tells Sam-Bob.

"I'm thinking of moving to Afghanistan," Sam-Bob says.

"Only you'll have health insurance," Joel says.

And Sam-Bob says, "What I need is life insurance."

"But you've got that, too."

Then Sam-Bob is irritated and asks whether they were inviting him to actually *eat* the salad or just to join their chat about dying.

"When you get back from the war, we should live together again," Joel says.

"When you invite people to your table, you should also invite them to eat the food on the table."

So Joel prays, asking guidance, protection, wisdom, and safety for them all. Finally he thanks God for the salads and, most especially, for the hands that prepared the salads.

When Joel is done, Sam-Bob looks at Janet and says she's got nice hands, because he thinks it's ironic that Janet's hands are the only body part Joel thanked God for. Sam-Bob says she should be careful flashing her hands around in public and attracting attention like she does.

And Joel thinks to himself: even if God has given up on America, maybe He still works in Africa. I should go and see, he thinks.

The POTUS Brief

On the chosen day, I drove over the Memorial Bridge in a black suburban with the Secretary of Defense. Harvey and DASD Hodges still resented me for getting us into this, so they'd manipulated me into drafting the SecDef's prep materials, then, while "reviewing" the materials, Harvey tried to reverse everything I'd said. But I added back one bullet he deleted from the SecDef's talking points: We have certain legal and constitutional concerns with so-called 'de-radicalization' programs for terrorist detainees (turn to Sandy Holachek for explanation).

Ms. Holachek had told me privately that, if this came up with the president, she would refer it to me. In the end, Detainee Affairs built their own short, sensible PowerPoint brief.[42] It laid out the detainee situation and offered the president options for breaking the gridlock:

- Find a champion for this issue on Capitol Hill and ask Congress to lift its ban on transferring Detainees to the U.S.
- Appeal to the public and shame Congress into action
- Press to change GITMO's "non-U.S.-soil" legal status[43]
- Bypass laws restricting the movement of detainees out of the prison at GITMO, arguing that they abridge the

---

[42] Such a thing does exist after all.

[43] This would give the detainees access to U.S. courts and standard U.S. judicial procedure. It would also infuriate Congress and probably Cuba.

president's constitutional authority to act as Commander in Chief of the military[44]

- Publically threaten to pursue either of the last two recommendations as a way of forcing Congress's hand to do the right thing

These recommendations belong to Detainee Affairs and, as CT advisors—as advocates for proper reintegration programs—my office did not express a position on them. This was part of Nick's "aw shucks" approach to the president's GITMO brief.

Equipped with our messages, we drove through the White House gates onto the rarified pavement of West Executive Avenue. To our left loomed the giant wedding cake known as the Eisenhower Executive Office Building, while to our right sat a building that mimicked a classy dentist's office: a lost-in-the-trees annex to the White House, known as the West Wing—perhaps the most understated real-estate in the world. We walked with the Secretary through the just-for-friends basement entrance and the Secretary turned right. But Ms. Holachek pointed left. "Mr. Secretary," she said, "we're meeting in the West Lobby upstairs."

The SecDef apologized, winked at me, and said, "Ah, yes. That's my Sit Room habit, but we're in the Oval today, aren't we?" I nodded and got cotton in my mouth from knowing the place I was in.

We walked up the stairs into a narrow hall. I glanced around for a waiting room and stared when the vice-president came through a door in the hallway, in his shirtsleeves, holding a rolled newspaper. The placard on the door where he'd been read, "Gentlemen."

---

[44] Nearly every year the president, in what is called a "signing statement," declares that his constitutional status as Commander in Chief exempts him from certain new provisions of law.

I'm an adult and I'm aware that biology applies without distinction to all persons. But still, that killed the aura—the VP with the rolled paper—and made the place weird.

The VP nodded as he passed. I nodded back. Ms. Holachek opened a door on our right and we sat ourselves in the waiting room under an icy painting of George Washington Crossing the Delaware. The Secretary sat in a chair, and I sat on a couch between Ms. Holachek and DASD Hodges.[45] Completing the horseshoe, a three-star admiral from Joint Staff sat alone in a chair.

But I had barely sat when the receptionist stood, walked directly to me, asked to speak, and took me to a corner of the room.

"Are you with the Secretary of Defense?"

"Yes."

"The entrance you used isn't for visitors."

"I'm sorry, but the Secretary took that entrance."

"The visitors' entrance is there." He pointed to some French doors with windows to the outside. One of them opened, held by a Marine in a white cap, and in walked the Secretary of State with a wisp of windblown hair, a lawyer-looking man, and an Assistant Secretary of some kind. She nodded to the SecDef.

"Okay," I said.

The receptionist seemed unhappy with my answer so he opened another set of doors and practically pushed me through them into a hall decorated with Norman Rockwell paintings. He walked me to a staircase and said, "If you have to come up from the basement, use these stairs."

"Okay," I said. I was inside the White House with the Secretary of Defense. I'd just seen the vice-president and the Secretary of State, and I stood there trying to think about the paintings.

---

[45] I changed my mind; his skin is not eggshells, it's the texture of icing on a birthday cake.

"Okay?" he said, then followed my gaze. "That's a painting Norman Rockwell did of people waiting in the West Lobby. It was bigger then. The lobby was." He gave me a moment to look. "I have to be at my desk," he said, and I followed him back.

In the lobby, the Secretary of State still stood. "Is Robbie in?" she asked the receptionist. "I wanted to catch him before our meeting with the president." She crossed the room and walked through the not-for-visitors' door where we'd come in. Robert McFadden is the president's national security advisor.

I sat by Ms. Holachek. "Everything all right?" she asked.

"Yes, it's fine. He showed me some Norman Rockwell paintings."

A girl wearing a navy skirt-suit and a matching leather portfolio entered from the Rockwell hall and asked the reception guy whether the Secretary of State had arrived. "She's in Mr. McFadden's office," he said.

The girl carried her portfolio through the same doors we'd come through, then reappeared and said, "The president will meet with you now." She led us past the West Lobby painting, down a short hall on the right, to the President of the United States, who stood, as an ordinary man stands, in the door of his office and shook our hands. I shook too, and sat next to Ms. Holachek on a couch, and DASD Hodges sat there, too, with his giant hands folded across his crotch.[46]

My feet rested on an eagle's talon, somehow woven onto a presidential seal in the oval rug. The Secretary of State, her staff, and "Robbie" McFadden were already there.

The only thing special about the Pentagon is that it is a pentagon. That, and it commands the most powerful military in the history of the world. The only thing special about the Oval is that it is

---

[46] His skin really isn't the texture of a birthday cake. It's more like the pith you find when you pare away the skin of an orange.

an oval. That, and it houses the most powerful man in the world. It's a plastic version of what you see on TV, airbrushed or over-dusted somehow.

The president sat at the end of a nested, oval seating arrangement.

"We haven't all spoken recently so let's introduce ourselves. I'm the president," said the president. Ms. Holachek chuckled. The president got a kick out of it and I think the SecDef and SecState had heard that one before.

"I'm the secretary of defense."

"I'm the secretary of state."

"I know. I appointed you," the president said, "but I'd like to meet your staff."

"This is Sandy Holachek," the SecDef said. "She's my assistant secretary for special operations and low-intensity conflict."

"Can someone explain this clearly to me for once?" the president asked. "What the hell is low-intensity conflict? It sounds to me like the relationship between DoD and the State Department."

The SecDef should have laughed, but didn't. "Team America is one team," he said. "Think of 'low-intensity conflict' as a situation where our enemies die quietly somewhere with a little help."

"And 'high-intensity conflict?'"

"That's an invasion or a bombing campaign."

"And what about a small bombing campaign to help our enemies die quietly?"

"Ah," said the SecDef, his humor returned, "Sandy would be my point person for that." And then he plowed ahead with introductions. "Next to Sandy is Joe.[47] He's the one who reminded me of the detainee issue a few weeks ago. Next to him is … Why don't you introduce yourself—you'll do yourself more justice than I would."

---

[47] My name is Joel, Mr. Secretary. Joel. The president should know that.

"I'm the Deputy Assistant Secretary of Defense for Detainee Affairs," said the Deputy Assistant Secretary of Defense for Detainee Affairs. "Sandy is responsible for counterterrorism, but I run the primary office in OSD for addressing issues related to Detainee Policy."

"Yes," the Secretary said, and then nodded for the Admiral to introduce himself.

"I'm Vice Admiral John Kapuscinski, Joint Staff," he said.

"Robbie, why don't you start us off," the president said, looking at the National Security Advisor. The State Department staff opened, then closed their mouths.

"Mr. President, you asked DoD to provide an update on detainee issues and, I understand, they also wanted to discuss the role of de-radicalization programs in …" Mr. McFadden searched for a word.

"In transitioning terrorists back to peaceful society," Ms. Holachek said.

"Yes," Mr. McFadden said.

"Joel is our expert on that," Ms. Holachek said, "and I've brought him along because he has done some good thinking in that area." Ms. Holachek believes in giving her staff a chance to represent their own ideas—it's part of her "leadership-development model." Usually I like it but, right then, I wished she'd ramp it down a notch.

"Joel? Like the Bible?" the president asked.

"Yes, Mr. President," I said. But I slipped him a business card so he would see I'm from OSD, not the Bible.

"Ah, thanks. 'Joel Alden, counterterrorism advisor to the Secretary of Defense, Office of the Undersecretary of Defense for Policy,'" he read. It was a *faux pas*, of course, to give the president my business card, and I felt a *We can't take him anywhere* vibe radiating from everyone—except the president; he seemed amused. He must get tired of everyone acting stiff around him.

"So what's this issue with de-radicalizing terrorists? Is that part of low-intensity conflict where you help people die quietly? A dead radical is a de-radicalized radical?" He raised his eyebrow at the SecDef, who remained silent.

I couldn't quite tell whether this question was serious, but I could tell the SecDef didn't care to talk about low-intensity conflict anymore, so I said, "No, sir." Everyone looked at me. "A number of Islamic countries also have a domestic problem with terrorism. The so-called de-radicalization camps are places where these countries send young terrorists, and they hire Imams to teach them a more benign form of Islam. They see it as a step toward integrating former terrorists back into society."

"I've heard of this before," the president said. "It's theological boot camp for terrorists."

"Yes, sir."

"And you're going to tell me we don't know whether these camps work."

"Yes, sir. We transfer detainees to certain countries where they will be put through these reintegration or 'de-radicalization' programs. But we lack a clear policy for how and when theology is an acceptable tool for countering terrorism. DoD's lawyers believe this is an uninterpreted area of constitutional law." My calculation worked. The president is a lawyer and he took my bait.

"That could be much larger than simply a counter-terrorism issue," he said. He looked at the Secretary of State. "Don't we work with Islamic moderates on women's rights and economic empowerment—basket weaving, stopping AIDS, and such? Don't we give money to churches and mosques for some of that?"

"Yes, Mr. President," she said. "This is a broader issue. I will ask my staff to review it again, but all State Department programming passes a careful legal review and we have established what I believe are responsible parameters on this issue."

I wanted to challenge the Secretary on what these parameters might be. But I'd already walked myself out on a willow branch over a river full of vipers, while her people sat there, silent, with hatchets, waiting for an excuse to chop off my branch.

"Mr. President," I said, "I would suggest that terrorist reintegration also raises some unique issues beyond what we face with humanitarian funding. For instance, with humanitarian programming, all faiths are, at least theoretically, given the opportunity to apply for the government grant money. Christian organizations, Muslim, Buddhist, or Secularists can submit proposals for U.S. money to educate children or to rescue orphans. And people choose whether to participate in the programs we fund. No one is forced into any of them if he disagrees with the theology. And, regardless of who administers the grant money, the U.S. sets parameters to prevent churches or mosques from using the money to evangelize or proselytize for their faith."

"Is that true?" the president asked, looking at the Secretary of State.

"That sounds like an accurate description," the Secretary of State said. The State lawyer whispered in her ear and I judged that her staff had not prepped her for this conversation.

"I would suggest setting a similar policy for counter-terrorism programs," I said, "particularly when it comes to terrorist de-radicalization and reintegration."[48]

"That sounds reasonable," the president said.

---

[48] This will come back and bite me. I know it. I doubt the State Department has established clear parameters in this area and I don't want to pattern DoD's policies after the State Department. But this is the only way I could find to rescue my issue without contradicting the Secretary of State. And I spoke up to distract the president from her whispered conversation. I do not want State to lose face in front of the president; I want them to get the policy right. They can see this, right?

"Shall I have my staff provide a draft policy for review?" the Secretary of State asked.

I panicked quietly and tried to catch the SecDef's eye. I needed him to go to bat for me on this. But he didn't see it.

"That sounds reasonable," the president said. "Thanks for offering."

Dammit, State Department! This is *my* issue, not yours!

"What else is on the agenda?" the president asked.

"Once State pulls together a draft, my staff will hold a meeting for the interagency[49] to review it," Mr. McFadden said.

I fell into despair. State had swooped in and stolen me blind, right in front of the president, and no one cared. State's idea of cooperation is that everyone works for them. I will give them my papers—they will rewrite them in passive, equivocal lawyers-speak— they will take all the credit until something goes wrong, then they will blame me for starting it all. That's how the State Department works.

Back in the suburban, Ms. Holachek said, "Nice work, Joel. That was really impressive." I parted my lips. "The president was genuinely engaged and you explained the issue well. You even got the conversation back on topic when the Secretary of State tried to head you off. That's not easy and you did it quite nicely."

"Thanks," I said.

---

[49] "The interagency" doesn't exist. It's an irrational concept. "Interagency" is code for an interagency *meeting*. The White House maintains a fantasy that its decisions represent some sort of government-wide consensus; part of how the White House pretends it doesn't lord it over the rest of the government is by calling White House decisions "interagency decisions." The White House thinks it's true because it meets "with the interagency" before it makes its decisions.

The Conversation with an Almost Lover (II)

Joel slips behind the trees with Janet, trespassing in private scandal after the National Arboretum has closed. They gaze over the housetops to where gold glistens on the Basilica of the National Shrine of the Immaculate Conception. Janet leans against a tree and she toys with a stem of grass. Joel wonders why a girl never knows she's gorgeous in a plaid shirt and jeans.

"Did I tell you that Seth decided not to run the shop?" Joel says. "None of us liked mechanicking but, since Seth was the youngest boy, we always thought maybe he'd do it."

"Yes, you told me," she says.

"The shop was hard to stomach after Dad got killed. But I still wish we'd found a way to keep it open."

Janet quietly watches an inchworm that has found the end of her sleeve. It flails over an incomprehensible gap, reaching for the blue veins of her wrist. "If Seth won't run the shop, what will he do when he graduates?" she asks finally.

"He says he wants to be a machinist."

"Isn't that a lot like being a mechanic?"

"Machinists work standing up. Seth says, whether it's the newest or the oldest profession, he won't be paid to lay on his back."

Janet frowns. "Where does he pick up stuff like that?"

"I don't think his new friends have helped much. He's had a tough time since Dad died."

"I'm sorry to hear."

"Seth doesn't have a passion for anything. He's not trying to make the world better like you and me."

"Do you think we're making the world better?"

"No. But I think we could."

"I think we've made the world better just by sitting here and letting this city be seen."

"But I'm talking about our jobs. Like working at USAID or the State Department."

"Joel, do you know what I learned about USAID's budget this week?" Joel stares and Janet goes on. "USAID assumes that Congress will support its budget, not because Congressmen care about development overseas, but because they see how much of USAID's giveaway stuff is made in each Congressman's district."

"Sounds like the Department of Defense to me. Ever hear of buy-America provisions?"

"What's that?"

"Congressmen are forever trying to make the Department of Defense buy all their equipment in the United States. They say it's for national security reasons, but really it's to make the military buy overpriced stuff made in their hometowns."

"But this is different," Janet says. "USAID calls itself the Agency for International Development when, actually, they destroy industries overseas. No one over there can afford to make mosquito nets or malaria pills, or water wells or whatever when USAID buys them in America and then gives them away for free. It's worse than Wal-Mart! Wal-Mart only undercuts local businesses by selling stuff cheap. USAID does it for free." Janet has said something liberal against Wal-Mart and she's angry, but Joel feels the incongruous urge to kiss her. Because caring can be incredibly sexy.

"Think about it," Janet says. "What would have happened to your dad if some foreign agency set up a free mechanic shop in Sampson, Texas?"

"He'd still be alive," Joel says and regrets it.

"And, you know what? Sometimes I think the governments overseas prefer for us to give them American stuff because, when you ship it into their country, it gives them a one-stop place to steal it. Did you know that customs jobs in Azerbaijan are so lucrative that the customs officials' families have to buy their jobs for them? The jobs are expensive, too. But, it's an investment. Once you've got the job, you can steal a little from everyone that moves through the port—businesses, relief workers, whoever. And Azerbaijan isn't unusual." Janet stops. Then she looks in Joel's face. "Joel, you know I didn't mean to bring up your dad, right?"

"I know. I don't know why I say stupid stuff like that."

She takes his hand and massages it with the pad of her thumb. "How are your mom and your baby sister doing without the shop?"

"They're fine. But Naomi will give you an earful if you call her a baby. She'll tell you that she just took the SAT and I recommend against reminding her that it was actually the *pre* SAT."

Janet smiles. "I would like to meet Naomi sometime." Then she looks away at the dome of the blue basilica. "Joel, do you really want to go to Africa?" She turns to him again and squints into the sun.

"You can't make a difference doing bureaucracy jobs in this town. You've got to go where the needy people are."

"I think I'm making a difference at USAID." Janet is looking at the dome again.

"How can you say you're making a difference when your agency is ruining poor people's businesses?"

"Because I'm pushing for them to be better than that," she says. "Joel, do you enjoy what you do?"

"Sometimes."

"But usually?"

"I never thought about it."

"Maybe you should."

"Do you enjoy what you do?" he asks.

"I do," she says. "Most of the time."

Follow-up Notes (I)

After the POTUS brief, I managed to see no one on my return to my cubicle, where I found separate "How did it go?" messages from my counterparts at State, Joint Staff, and also one from Harvey.[50] Because I was the only working-level staff in the room, my peers all had to rely on me for the specifics of what their bosses said: I'd have to tell Joint Staff that their boss said nothing (and, by extension, their PowerPoint work was useless); I'd have to tell Harvey that we only talked about my issues, not his, and I'd have to tell State they were now in charge of my issue and that I was "standing by to help." I couldn't stomach any of it so I wrote, "Interesting meeting. No big changes. I'll send a readout tomorrow." I pasted this into three separate emails and hit send. It was 5:30 p.m. and I only wanted to drink.

I circled my chin in the air to disrupt the knotted muscles in my neck. Then I sighed and stepped into the hall, where I encountered a courier and knocked my knee against a lock drooping from the corner of his bag. I held the door for him and pointed to the reception desk.

When I returned five minutes later, our receptionist slid an envelope across the desk. "This arrived for you," he said.

---

[50] Harvey does not like me and he does not like what I'm doing. But, still, he wants to know what I know. And he knows he'll get the straight story from me. Straighter than he'd get from his boss—whose skin is actually the texture of a fabric flour sack. He has learned that I'm honest—that I put the truth over my own interests. People don't know this, but honesty is an investment—a cost up front that, with a few losses here and there, will pay you back for years to come. Honesty turns into credibility and credibility is tremendous power.

"Oh?"

It was sealed like a wedding invitation—with "Mr. Joel Alden" written carefully on the back and "EYES ONLY" stamped symmetrically at either end of my name.

I took the envelope to my desk, slit the flap with a scissor blade, and unfolded a half-size paper that bore a blue letterhead: *President of the United States*. The text, written in fountain pen, said:

Dear Joel,

I appreciated your detainee briefing today. It is essential for me, from time to time, to seek unofficial advice and I would be honored if you would make yourself available in this capacity. If you are willing, please contact my assistant.

Sincerely,

President of the United States

At the bottom, in a different hand, was written:

Please reply to tamara.l.walz@eop.gov. Let me know if you have questions.

Joyfully, Tammy

I rummaged absently for a picture of Janet I keep in my wallet for the purpose of knowing it is there, and I looked at it because her face was calm like it was the day I took the picture—the day the wind did not lift her hair like it should have done to make this the sexy kind of picture a man keeps in his wallet.

I read the note again, blinked, and said, "This is strange. This is very, very strange." And, because it was so very strange, I started to methodically recall the details of our conversation, trying to isolate something I'd said to elicit such a response from the president. But, before I got past the low-intensity fiasco, my brain warmed to an image of myself advising the president, confidentially, through his presidential challenges, and chiding him where I found narrowness in his thinking, and then, when he needed time alone, I circulated quietly among his advisors and guided them with my barely-perceptible hand to just and righteous conclusions—advisors who were never quite aware that I was at the White House, just that now the place ran more easily, with less conflict, more clarity, more vision.

But then my vision soured from an unbidden suspicion that the president did not, in fact, want my advice but that he had dangled this lure in front of me so we could meet and he could require me, beyond my power, to put DoD into its proper place behind State Department—a view arising from a mistaken idea that some departments fall below others in a hierarchy of government.

I rotated my chin again and stood, then walked out of my cubicle and looked at Nick where he sat hunching at his keyboard. He hunches everywhere, to seem gentle and not scare people. I almost told him to take off his jacket when he sits in his chair like that because it scrunches the tail and then people see the wrinkles when he walks around.

Then I left the Pentagon and did not suspect that the president wrote this note because he had associated me, irrationally, with the strident prophets of the Bible.

The Conversation with a Lover

Joel has returned from his time in Africa and he watches a film with Janet. But the film has ended and he tells Janet his troubles while she rests her ear on his chest.

"Hear anything in there?" he asks.

"Yes."

"A block of ice rattling around?"

"No, Joel, I hear the heart of a good man."

Joel relaxes. Whatever else is good, here or there, in this country or that, above the earth or below it—whatever—this is good.

"Joel," Janet says. "You had a good dad. You know that?"

"Why do you say that?"

"Because God is the only father I've ever had."

"I know."

"I've got a man's genes somewhere in me, but he left before I was born."

"I know."

"I met him twice, in a restaurant, and he told me he was proud of me. That's all. And do you know what I said to him? I told him I was proud of the man he could be."

"What did he say to that?"

"He shook his head. I told him I meant it, but he said it was too late. He said, 'You're a beautiful girl, Janet,' then asked the waiter for our bill."

"Well, he was right about that."

"About what?"

"That you're a beautiful girl."

"I know. But I wanted to hear you say it."

"So what would you say?" Joel asks. "Is God a better father than your dad?"

"Yes, Joel," she answers. "He's a good Father."

"Has He talked to you more than twice then?"

"Of course. He's God."

"Five times? Ten?"

"He talks to me every day, Joel."

"Really? Then, next time, when you two chat, would you send Him my way? He's seemed awfully distracted lately and I have some questions about Africa."

"Joel, you have to hear His voice in other people, in the world, the weather, and in the little feelings you have when you're quiet. Those are God. They're from Him."

"They're all God, I suppose," Joel says. "Janet, I respect your faith. I can see how it has made you the person you are. And I love the person you are. But, if everything good in the world is God, how is that Someone? Isn't 'God' just a name for the good things in the world? And what about the bad things?"

Joel thinks for a bit. "Janet, I lived in Africa," he says. "I looked at their blank eyes, their putrid sores, and their smiling, lying faces. I looked for God but He wasn't there. And if He is not there, He is not anywhere.

"You're a good person, Janet. You've shown me that the world has good things. But how does the world look any different if the good things are God or if they're just good things?"

"I wish you could believe, Joel."

"I did," Joel says, "and it didn't work."

Follow-up Notes (II)

Dear Ms. Walz,

Good morning. I received your note from the president requesting my unofficial advice. Please let me know what I need to do and, if you're able to provide more specifics on what the president wants, that would be very helpful.

v/r,[51]

Joel Alden

P.S. I would normally inform my DoD leadership of such conversations. Is that okay?

And, Tammy responded promptly:

Dear Mr. Alden,

The president will be pleased to hear. He views these meetings as separate from your duties at DoD and prefers that you be discreet about them.

---

[51] v/r stands for "very respectfully." Military people use it as a sign-off, the same way normal people say "sincerely."

The president did not give specifics on what he hopes to talk about. After your meeting yesterday, he handed me the invitation note along with your business card, and he said, "I think this guy has more to say. Let's see if we can get him in here." The president believes that everyone has something he wishes he could tell the president and he will probably sit down and ask what that is for you.

If you prefer to send him your thoughts in advance, please send me a short email and I will provide it to the president. I will work with the scheduling office and be in touch with you shortly.

Joyfully,

Tammy Walz

This was still strange. Very strange. But strangely sensible.

Before I could get my head around any of it, I received another message:

Mr. Alden,

You are scheduled to meet with the president from 6:00 - 6:30pm next Tuesday, August 6. Arrival instructions are attached. My contact information is below. Please call if you have any questions.

Joyfully,

Tammy Walz

The One-man Skit

"Sam-Bob," Joel says in those last months while things were still good with Janet. "I'm going to *The Queen Vic* with Janet and Lauren. You should come."

"Like a double date, or something?" Sam-Bob asks. "I went out with Lauren once and I don't think she cared much for me."

"I told you to shower before dates," Joel says.

"I did shower, like, twice, and even put on cologne."

"Did you demonstrate your swearing prowess on the date?"

"Just a sample—so she'd see what I was talking about with Dick Marcinko. It wasn't really even swearing—just explaining how someone else does it."

"See, that was your mistake," Joel says. "Lauren's a clean girl. After your date, she told me she was looking for a cleaner sort of guy. I figured you'd forgotten to scrub the dead skin off your neck. But it must have been the swearing."

"You know what?" Sam-Bob says.

"Screw me?"

"Yes. How did you know?"

"It's a trade secret. But you really should come. Lauren's moving to Texas and you may never see her again. It's your last chance to demonstrate the fine manners that your mother taught you before the Marines turned you upside down."

"You know what, I think I will," Sam-Bob says.

Lauren serves as the one-person DC staff of HFC—*Help For China*. She combines semi-conscious chic intrigue with downhome Kansas charm—tall, a flawless face, flats, and a long, straight skirt.

She betrays the kind of beauty that would shine through a feed sack if that's what she wore. This is not lost on Sam-Bob. But Lauren has fallen in love with a guy at HFC's Midland, TX headquarters. Or, more accurately, he has fallen in love with her and she has decided to give him a chance.

On *The Queen Vic's* second floor, a bartender surfs soccer channels and Joel asks Lauren to "Remind me, again, why a China group is based in *Midland, Texas?*"

"That's where Sandy Pope lives," Lauren says.

Sandy Pope. Why does Joel think of a man in a dirty white dress when he should be thinking of a philanthropic billionaire?

"Besides," Lauren continues, "there's nowhere for a Chinese man to hide. HFC's director, Don Wang, knows every Chinese person in Midland and, if there's one he doesn't know, then that one is a spy from the Chinese Government. It's very convenient, when you think about it."

"I can see a sort of logic there," Sam-Bob says. "But just wait. The good old People's Republic will soon buy up the Republic of Texas and ship its oil off to pollute the Shanghai sky. It's only a matter of time." Joel sends Sam-Bob a caution glance, but Sam-Bob once served as a puppet actor in his dad's church and he is off and performing for Lauren:

China Voice: *"Hey um, America, you owe me. Time to pay up."*
America Voice: *"I'll pay you later."*
China: *"No. You pay now."*
America: *"I already tell you: I got nothing."*
China: *"You got Texas."*
America: *"But how can I pay for California without Texas?"*
China: *"We take both and call it even."*
America: *"Fuck you!"*
China: *"You're in no condition to fuck anyone, old man. I leave you New York. I throw in Jersey for extra. You should thanks me."*
America: *"It's* thank *you. Not* "thanks" *you."*

China: *"Actually it's 谢谢. This conversation is over. Learn Chinese."*

Sam-Bob can be hilarious. But this is awkward. Janet glances sidewise at Joel and, under the table, Joel squeezes her hand. *Just let him finish.* They order food.

"Have you found a place to live in Midland, Lauren?" Joel asks when the food has arrived.

"I'm staying in Don Wang's basement for the moment," she says. "There's a wait list for every bit of housing in Midland."

"Everyone's itching for a little sandstorm, I guess," Sam-Bob says.

"Actually, it's oil," Lauren says. "There's a horizontal drilling rig every twenty feet. You wouldn't believe it."

And Sam-Bob is at it again. "You know, when you and what's-his-name have kids …"

"Sam-Bob, I'm dating a guy. His name is Samuel Yoder and we're *dating*, not having kids."

"Yes, yes, one thing leads to the next," Sam-Bob says. "Like I was saying, when you're sitting with the other Midland parents, at T-Ball or something, you'll be having all these conversations:

Lauren voice: *"Hi, I'm Lauren, what do you do?"*

T-Ball Mom Stranger (TBMS[52]): *"My husband is a geologist. What does your husband do?"*

Lauren: *"I rescue Chinese Christians from jail."*

TBMS: *"I see. Well, does your husband enjoy it?"*

Lauren: *"I do it. Not my husband. Me."*

TBMS: *"Well, that's a little forward of you, don't you think? How do you even know they want rescued? Besides, don't you think they'll feel a little silly with a woman rescuing them, and all? What's your husband's name, anyway?"*

Lauren: *"Samuel Yoder."*

TBMS: *"Is that some sort of Amish?"*

---

[52] Pronounced "T.B. Moms"

Lauren: *"It's too sunny here. I think I'll go find a place in the shade."*

TBMS: *"Shade? Honey, we've got oil, sand, sun, and money. If you want something else, you're in the wrong place."*

But Sam-Bob's persistence pays off. Lauren laughs and Janet, too. "You know," Joel says, "there's real potential in this—the China-Texas-oil nexus. A TV producer could do something with that."

"How do you say hello in Chinese?" Sam-Bob asks.

"It's 'ni hao,'" Lauren says.

And Sam-Bob is off again, this time in a TV announcer voice: "Welcome to NiHaowdy y'all, where Texas and China meet in the land of billionaires for the biggest fracking party you've never seen. Today's episode: The Collision of Cuisines: egg roll meets burrito with a side of sweet-and-tortilla soup. It's love on first contact in a place where this beany, cabbage goodness shows just what the world can be when we all get along!"

"Ew," Janet says, and Lauren covers her mouth with a napkin to maintain dignity while she laughs.

Sam-Bob sees his audience in hand and continues: "Join us next week for forbidden footage from the Forbidden City—the savage beating of a Chinese congregation at worship—secretly filmed on knock-off Chinese iPhones and beamed through a hijacked Falun Gong satellite directly to TBMom's iPad, while Confucius, he say, 'That's nuts, man.' Will TBMom learn to care for something besides money and environmental destruction? Will China finally invade Texas to shut down our TV show, once and for all? Tune in again next week to find out!"

A man with slacks and suspenders shoots a dark look and the bartender glances at them while they laugh.

"Lauren," Joel says, "you should really talk to someone about this. Does anyone know a TV producer?"

"Oh, boy." Lauren rolls her eyes.

"The Chinese government might reconsider its actions if the things they do in the dark corners of their country are broadcast the next week for an eager American audience. What do you think, Janet?"

"I think you guys are hilarious," Janet says.

"But you have to admit, there's something in it," Joel says. "Can't you see the Bored Moms of America tuning in for another voyeuristic episode of Wild West billionaires, dust storms, illegal immigrants, vigilante justice, police brutality, and Oriental intrigue? America, the defender of the oppressed. America, the crusty—the hostile host of strangers. Catch it all next week on NiHaowdy!"

"And what will the Bored Dads of America watch?" Janet asks.

"They'll watch the kids," Joel says.

"Okay, you win," she says.

"So Lauren will pitch this to a producer?" Joel asks.

"You send me a producer's name and I'll ask Don Wang what he thinks," Lauren says. "How's that for a deal?"

The Lost Art

Dear Ms. Walz,

Thank you for the clarification. I will be discreet about the meeting. As you suggest, I will also plan to write something to help focus our conversation in advance. Can I ask you one more question, though? Do you know why the president wants to speak with me in particular?

v/r,

Joel Alden

This time I did not receive a prompt response and, while I wrote my readout email for the POTUS conversation, I wondered whether I had outstripped my welcome in sending additional questions to Tammy. I pictured her asking the president and, in my mind, the president grew impatient with her for asking and said disparaging things about me. Then, when my readout was almost complete, I received this from Tammy:

Dear Mr. Alden,

The president must have been impressed with how you conducted yourself in your meeting yesterday. He reads widely and, recently, he has been impressed with how some of the Biblical prophets delivered direct, frank assessments to their leaders. I suspect that, based on your briefing yesterday and perhaps even from your name, he hopes you will understand this.

People find the president an engaging man to talk with, so you should not be anxious on that account.

I hope this helps.

Joyfully,

Tammy

It did not help. I felt unmoored. And offended. My name is Joel, but I'm not a prophet and I'm not trying to be one. Is the president expecting me to tell him something from God?

I felt injured, irrationally, and I became disturbed at the thought that, in my offense, I denied what my parents raised me to be—what they *named* me to be. It was a self-negation—a betrayal of the dead.

I sat, arms folded on my desk, forehead resting on them. The day had grown impossibly long and I heard footsteps, a sigh, and the chirp of someone alarming the office.

"Oh, hey," I said, "don't lock me in. I'm still here." I stood, looked over my cubicle wall, and saw my Deputy Assistant Secretary[53] looking surprised.

"Oh, I didn't know you were still here," he said. "I talked to Sandy this evening. She said you were fantastic with the president yesterday."

---

[53] Nick's boss. He's a man named Bruce Horvath and, where detainees are concerned, he understands that there are already enough hands moving the piano. So he sort of stands there, waiting to buff the scratches out of the floor once we've set the monster down and folded enough layers of cardboard under the front leg to stop it from tottering.

"Thanks."

"Really, you should be proud of yourself. Sandy said you did a great job delivering the brief. That's a big deal."

"She pushed me into the pool and waited for me to swim," I said, trying to smile.

"I want to hear about it, but I told my wife I'd be home five minutes ago."

"Okay."

"Tomorrow?"

"Sure. Of course. Just let me know when."

"You should go home."

"Thanks. I will."

He walked out. I felt confused and walked out the door, too, which I locked. But then I leaned on it, realizing I should have set the alarm.

I walked to the outer ring of the Pentagon—the E ring—with my slung backpack, and rode the elevator down. "Have a good night, sir," the night guard said, nodding, his shirt puffed with armor.

"Thanks. You too."

I was distracted and troubled. If I hadn't grown up like my namesake, what was I? If I no longer thought Joel was good, what did I think was good? If I was not who I was raised to be, who was I?

Driving home, I imperiled the responsible drivers with rear-facing child seats, who flowed with me over the 14th Street bridge; over the reeking fish market; through the Third Street Tunnel under the National Mall, and through "the H St. Corridor," still recovering from the last round of race riots in 1968.

Once home, I read the Psalms for hours, with Scotch, comforted vicariously through a boy who had read them and been comforted—a boy who loved the humanity, the grief, the confidence, the joy, the anger and revenge, the relief, the repentance even, and the humility of it all. The Psalms are where you ask a haunting question, you let it fester into despair, then it ruptures and is healed.

Did my parents name me Joel as a mockery? Yesterday morning I intended to prevent the U.S. from forcing "benign Islam" on terrorists. In the afternoon I maneuvered the Secretary of State to a draw. Today the president asked me, simply, to be the man I was raised to be. And I recoiled.

I stood, saw that I was still wearing a tie, and rummaged for a bowl of cereal before bed.

A Childhood Milieu

A: The Mother

How did my mother's son come so completely untrained? The Joel who asks his mother one day why a person would kill a baby before it is born—having determined in advance that this is a thing that is not as it should be.

The Joel whose mother answers that some people, at their point in life, do not want babies.

"But why don't they want babies?" he asks.

"Maybe the mother doesn't like the father," Mom says, "or maybe she doesn't want to be seen with a baby when people think she shouldn't have one."

Joel thinks and then asks how could a person kill a baby inside before it was born? "I guess you're old enough," Mom says and, even though he's only nine, she hands him the 7th grade science book.

B: The Textbook

So Joel reads his Christian textbook. He reads things that burn through the crust of his soul and sear a Hard Place inside, hurting and driving him somehow to stop the pain. To know and not act is to be no prophet at all. A mailing should be sent, he says, alerting his friends to this thing that ought not to be done and asking them, in turn, to alert their friends. By such a scheme all will soon know and they will stop the thing. But his father discourages this without reason so Joel sits and watches baby Seth blow a bubble on his lip, not knowing his brother has failed to protect the children.

C: The Scripture

From his church, his father, and his name, Joel learns Jehovah is the Lord. He must remember all that Joel says in the scriptures and repeat it back without error, and so Joel nods his head in rhythm while he recites strange words to his father before bed.

It shall come to pass in that day, that the mountains shall drop down new wine, and the hills shall flow with milk, and all the rivers of Judah shall flow with waters, and a fountain shall come forth out of the house of the LORD, and shall water the valley of Shittim.

Egypt shall be a desolation, and Edom shall be a desolate wilderness, for the violence against the children of Judah, because they have shed innocent blood in their land.

But Judah shall dwell forever, and Jerusalem from generation to generation.

For I will cleanse their blood that I have not cleansed: for the LORD dwelleth in Zion.

Jeremy is older than Joel and he is named after Jeremiah, who is also in the Bible, but Jeremy does not remember everything because Jeremiah said too much.

D: The Radio

Joel's father owns a shop in Sampson, Texas, where, together with a man named Luis, he repairs the county's fleet of trucks and other stray cars, whose owners tolerate Mr. Alden's wait list for an honest mechanic. In this shop Joel learns to find what is wrong and to set it right, while the blood drains from his arms and, when the wrench has slipped, the blood returns and seeps through the grease on his knuckles. A spattered radio on the shelf tells him he lives in a country where others don't work because the government pays them from the money it confiscates by law from the people who do. And, if this is not enough, the government, through a deficit, will make their children bruise their knuckles again to pay it off in years to come.

So Joel lies through angry summers on a mechanic's creeper and, alone in school, studies with the intensity of someone who intends, through simple truths, to save the unwanted children and to dissuade a country from trying, through its budget, to defy math.

E: Music

Joel Alden is good at math because he teaches himself with invisible labor. He also excels with invisible effort at oboe, patrolling with this tender instrument against further encroachment on the borders of gender propriety and maintaining a meager life of choice beyond the prescribed trigonometry, the slick intake manifolds, and the crusted exhaust.

And that is how Joel comes to play Mahler next to Coleen in all-state orchestra. Coleen asks kindly about the grease in his cuticles, and she relates Joel's determined loneliness to her life with the clingy band boys who lack the guts to say they like her, and the brainless jocks who ignore her for showing too little leg.

"But I don't want to be a mechanic or a musician," Joel says. "Some people think I should be an engineer because I'm good at math. But I'm only good at math because I work harder than the other kids and because I learn it from a book instead of wasting time with bad teachers."

"If you don't do music or engineering, what will you do?" Coleen asks.

"I want to study people so I can change them."

"But why do you want to change them?"

Joel Alden looks into Colleen's face, too angular to seem quite beautiful to uncharmed eyes, and he tells her of the unborn souls.

"Do you go to church?" she asks.

"Yes, why?"

"I thought so. Want to go meet my friend Susan? The last two years, before you messed things up, Susan and I always juggled for first and second chair in Oboe."

F: The Novel

So Joel Alden is born to good, practical folk who require strength of will and who only acknowledge things of the heart in music or in the old language of scripture. But doubt comes creeping. Joel doubts about his soul at night when the mind is open to terror and, seeing no such doubts in others, keeps them deep within.

Then he finds a novel. A novel is a low form—entertainment—which is tolerated only as a weakness among practical folk. And Joel discovers by chance that his human heart is not alone. Jean ValJean is strong—a criminal, a mayor, a man who runs a factory—but he bleeds inside for what is evil and for his hope in something good. He is human as only Joel is human, driven by nobility and torment of the heart.

But few share this kinship. Fewer still in this dry edge of Texas. A soul such as Joel's must leave Texas and find his people elsewhere. A small flame makes Joel human inside and it must not die. The flame must be guarded as the most precious thing, carried with a cupped hand, with wax trickling down and a light that flickers against the dark walls while his family sleeps. It is the only *real* thing perhaps, and must be carried to a friendlier place—this secret credential that lets humans know other humans—to follow them, and perhaps even to lead them. To know and handle the heart is the work of leaders among men. And Joel knows that, though it is fragile, this flame in his heart is stronger than the strength of strong men because it is the thing that guides them. Men respect strength, but they only respect strength under the control of a human heart and a good mind. Everything else, they fear.

Joel sees this, dimly. And he decides with it. And this is all that matters.

The Readout and the Legend

I email-blasted the sterile "outcomes" from our conversation with the president to my colleagues at State, Detainee Affairs, Joint Staff, and the White House:

- DoD briefed the president on the unique constitutional, legal, and policy considerations of theological terrorist-reintegration programs. Attendees agreed that parameters should be established.
- State agreed to provide a draft policy for review (Action: State by August 14).
- The White House National Security Staff agreed to convene an interagency meeting to review the draft policy and provide an interagency recommendation[54] for the president's review (Action: NSC by August 21[55]).

---

[54] With a little tweak of words I have turned the National Security Advisor's nonsensical "the interagency" into the sensible "interagency *recommendation.*" Also, note: six months ago it wasn't okay for me to email the White House directly. But now it is. That's because I have now attained "super staffer" status. This means I can "go direct" to important stakeholders like the White House and then back brief my leadership on what I've done. "Super staffer" is an unwritten, unspoken thing so I made up a name for it. But it's real: it's what happens when your leadership likes what you're doing and they trust the way you work.

[55] I have listed the meeting a week *after* the draft policy is due from State. This is to remind the White House and the State Department that DoD will need a week to review their draft before meeting to make a recommendation to the president. But, despite this reminder, I'm sure State and/or the White House will wait until one or two days before the meeting; then they'll release a problematic draft that will, regardless of its position on

A formal outcomes message for such a meeting must be sent by the White House. But I sent this email under the guise of "offering my informal notes/observations," because everyone wanted to know what happened at the meeting, and because my counterpart at the White House was not present in the meeting. Of course, I cc'd my counterpart at the White House; hopefully, she'll tweak my email just enough to pretend it wasn't mine, and then she'll send it out as an official White House meeting record.

All this—the pinnacle of my career to date—and I didn't care. I was doing reflexive, autopilot work while my mind was obsessed with prophecy.

I ate soup for lunch Friday in the sheer hope it would stay in my stomach and calm my adrenaline.

As a face to the world, I propped up Joel the matter-of-fact bureaucrat: he wrote the "outcomes" email, spoke with his counterpart at State, and provided his old non-paper to State in exchange for State's promise to provide a bootleg version of its draft policy while the draft was still undergoing internal State review.[56]

Bureaucrat Joel did this while the real me quailed at the president's words and didn't care a bit for the Pentagon's policies.

But, while I quailed, a small legend circled back to me from my DASD; Mr. Horvath wanted to know whether the SecDef had really butchered SOLIC's mission description so badly that the president wanted to shut us down: did the president really disagree with the concept of low-intensity conflict? Or did he just not understand it? I guess, if you look at it from the outside, SOLIC does sound a little weird.

Islam, subtly establish the State Department as a co-decider on everything regarding DoD and detainees. I know this. It's how they work. But I have at least suggested a reasonable timeline that would prevent these tactics.
[56] Even if the rider is asleep, this horse still knows how to wear its saddle.

"Remember when the president first heard of the Defense Threat Reduction Agency?" my DASD asked. Ha! The Defense Threat Reduction Agency? Why not just call it the Defense Make Things Better For People Agency? Or why don't we just go with Denis Kucinich and switch from Defense to Peace. "Department of Peace," Mr. Horvath said, swiping an imaginary banner over the Pentagon's front door.

"But really, is there a problem with low-intensity conflict?" my DASD asked, suddenly serious. "Did the president really make fun of the SecDef over it? Sandy Holachek said you bailed him out."

"I didn't bail him out, I just moved the conversation along to detainee reintegration."

"Sounds like a bailout to me. You totally bailed out the Secretary of Defense." My DASD shook his head and frowned. "You know, I can respect that."

Rumors travel. I'm okay with that.

The shell-Joel absorbed this praise and made modest responses while the quailing-prophet Joel looked up from his corner and watched with a wan smile.

Meanwhile, I did what I could: I booked a room at a bed and breakfast in Harpers Ferry, then drove through the mountains while the sun sank behind this quirk of geology where the Shenandoah and Potomac rivers merge and cut through the Shenandoah ridge.

Hopscotch

In the midst of his ideals, Joel Alden must overcome enormous, practical problems. Multiplication, for instance.

"Do public school kids have to learn this?" he asks.

What is the logic of 7x8? The thing is impossible.

Father switches the flash cards patiently in the evening. Then they give it up and tumble on the floor together with Josiah and Jeremy.

"Do a flip, Daddy! Do a hang-by-the-feet!" Joel's head throbs, upside down, and Mr. Alden laughs. A laugh is a treasure in these small parts of life. After work. Before bed. On days when work has not lasted as long. A laughing sliver of "may" between life's musts.

But still Joel does not remember his times tables. And he must. Mom must confront; Joel must learn.

She takes chalk and orders Joel out to their slab of concrete. He *will* learn. Joel stares, scrunch-faced, fingers laced across his middle, and watches her draw. Hopscotch? Hopscotch with strange numbers?

Mom hops on the numbers and is not good at it. These things should be left to children.

"Let me do it," Joel says.

"But you have to say the numbers when you hop. See? Hop with your left foot in this box and say seven, then hop with your right foot in the other box and say eight, then you jump both feet into the box that says fifty-six. See?"

"Mom, I know. I can do it."

And Mom draws new boxes with other numbers while Joel hops them and chants. Joel is a good hopper; he knows and shows it off. The chalk fades underfoot and, when the answers are rubbed out, he says them anyway.

He drinks water in the kitchen afterwards. "Some kids think multiplication is hard," he says. "But I think it's kind of easy."

Out the window looking onto the road, Joel watches a truck hoisting a dead heifer aboard. He has seen it a dozen times. A ramp drops from the back and you loop a chain around the foot and pull a lever to run the winch. Her tongue drags in the dirt and she bobbles aboard, then you snag the ramp with the same winch, pull it shut, and you're off to collect another bit of dog food. The truck has a logo on the door: *Your Local Used-Cow Dealer.*

"I hope I never have a job like *that,*" Joel says and, turning from the window, he sets his glass up on the counter where Mom has started dinner.

A Historical Milieu

A: The Old Town

I followed the road where it squeezed through the Shenandoah ridge along with the train track, the river, and the marshy canal. Then I found my room in a converted mansion standing on a cliff at the back of town—a town deliberately frozen in a time when people would build their town on a hill and held ideas they would die for. So close to DC—but worlds away.

At Harpers Ferry, Thomas Jefferson once stood by an odd rock, gazed down at the river in its gorge, and proclaimed that this view alone was "worth a voyage across the Atlantic." Then, some generations later, at the bottom end of town, John Brown holed himself up in the Federal armory and fought to end slavery (though a prescient Fredrick Douglass had told him he would not come out alive).

John Brown had told his men their defiant act would trigger a slave uprising, but they dropped their spark into a wet powder keg; it seems they neglected to tell the slaves about the rebellion.

So John Brown had a sword driven into his chest. That would have all been neat enough, but the sword, as the report goes, "either not having a point or striking something hard in Brown's accouterments, did not penetrate."

B: The Prophecy

So they made an example of him, as mature governments do, and John Brown lived to prophesy on the day they stretched his neck:

I, John Brown, am now quite *certain* that the crimes of this *guilty land will* never be purged *away* but with blood. I had, *as I now think vainly,* flattered myself that without *very much* bloodshed it might be done.

C: The Lecture

And though John Brown was commonly thought a madman, Henry David Thoreau traveled and spoke to gathered townsmen, comparing Brown well with our nation's founders: "They could bravely face their country's foes," he said, "but he had the courage to face his country herself, when she was in the wrong."

Then Thoreau reminded his countrymen of how Brown had fought well in Kansas and prevented slavery there:

[Brown] said, truly, that the reason why such greatly superior numbers quailed before him was, as one of his prisoners confessed, because they lacked a cause—a kind of armor which he [Brown] and his party never lacked. When the time came, few men were found willing to lay down their lives in defense of what they knew to be wrong; *they did not like that this should be their last act in this world.*

D: The Cowardly Fantasy

With these thoughts in my head, I woke up early Saturday and hiked Maryland heights—a place still littered with the civil war; I passed a polite sign noting the place where Abraham Lincoln turned back on his tour, stymied by the bitter grade.

But I persisted, and then I sat, delirious with endorphins, squinting, as an eagle squints down its beak, on a toy train that toiled through a toy town, past a toy Brown, and toy tourists who entered toy museums to stare at their waxy past. And I asked myself: is there a single line that runs unbroken from then to now?

We are rid of that, aren't we? We live in a time when no one must choose what will be his last act in this world.

I will speak with the president as he has asked. If I have nothing to say, I can still speak. I have told him that I am no prophet and we will chat pleasantly by the fire.

E: The Lecture (Continued)

Before bed, I read the rest of Thoreau's lecture on John Brown. Thoreau railed against the people who could watch John Brown's trial, knowing he would be hanged, and still sleep: *If there is any such who gets his usual allowance of sleep, I will warrant him to fatten easily under any circumstances which do not touch his body or purse.*

And Thoreau said of himself: *I put a piece of paper and pencil under my pillow, and when I could not sleep, I wrote in the dark.*

The thing struck hard, as a hailstone strikes the ear, and something from Sam-Bob turned unfunny in my mind.

The president excoriated lawmakers yesterday on television, telling them, if they did not approve his expansion of our debt, he would hold them to account for breaking our economy. He demanded that Congress spend their children's money now and he stated flatly that all other positions were narrow, cynical, and partisan. It was reckless and extreme, he said, looking into the camera.

I had known of this wrong thing since I was a child—one generation enslaving another through debt. Now the president has asked to speak with me and I knew Thoreau would look dimly on me for my silence.

Is there something that will break us faster than for parents to betray their children? For one generation to sell the next into debt?

How can our leaders face their parents? Parents who each gave a brother, a friend, a cousin to defeat the Nazis, to defeat the brutal Communists—a generation of stolid men, wounded and silent from what they saw—a generation that suffered to give its children the greatest peace—the greatest wealth the world has ever seen. And still it was not enough. The next generation took it all. They taught *their* children that the parents were backward, prejudiced people—powerful men who maintained their power at the expense of the poor. Today's leaders pocketed their parents' gift, disparaged them, and then spent their children's money, too, because, for them, it was never enough.

Is this not what a prophet would tell the president?

Sam-Bob knew this when he made skits about China. My father knew it, measuring his dollars, as he did, in bruises and in a chronic ache to his back. And the antagonists on the radio knew it, too, although they gave the president reason enough to call them extreme. I know it, myself, because I did not invent math.

I lay on my bed at Harpers Ferry convinced that, having escaped DC, the clean breeze of truth blew through my mind and displaced the brown air that had settled there. I determined to do something to prevent myself from retreating when I sat with the president and dissuaded myself of the truth because it required an inconvenient conversation. I pulled out my Blackberry:

Dear Ms. Walz,

In preparation for our meeting, please pass the following to the president:

Dear Mr. President,

I write because your assistant offered to provide you with a note to prepare for our meeting and because, in your invitation, you asked for my unofficial advice. I am prepared to offer it, such as it is.

I laid my blackberry aside, having reclaimed the Joel of my childhood, and then slept short of my usual allowance of sleep.

Sunday morning I awoke to an email from Tammy (does she work all the time?):

Joel,

Wow! I'll make sure the president sees your email before your meeting. Good luck!

Joyfully,

Tammy

I sat there, dazed at what I had done, and ate only soup for the next two days.

The Handwritten Note

When math is done for the day, and dinner, Ronnie Alden reads to his children: Jeremy, Josiah, Joel, and Seth. They curl their toes under the couch cushions for warmth, eyes sober and wide, following the print on their waxen pages.

Daniel 5:

1 Belshazzar the king made a great feast for a thousand of his lords, and drank wine in the presence of the thousand.

2 While he tasted the wine, Belshazzar gave the command to bring the gold and silver vessels which his father Nebuchadnezzar had taken from the temple which had been in Jerusalem, that the king and his lords, his wives, and his concubines might drink from them.

3 Then they brought the gold vessels that had been taken from the temple of the house of God which had been in Jerusalem, and the king and his lords, his wives, and his concubines drank from them.

4 They drank wine, and praised the gods of gold and silver, bronze and iron, wood and stone.

5 In the same hour, the fingers of a man's hand appeared and wrote opposite the lampstand on the plaster of the wall of the king's palace, and the king saw the part of the hand that wrote.

6 Then the king's countenance changed, and his thoughts troubled him, so that the joints of his hips were loosened and his knees knocked against each other.

7 The king cried aloud to bring in the astrologers, the Chaldeans, and the soothsayers. The king spoke, saying to the wise men of Babylon, "Whoever reads this writing, and tells me its interpretation, shall be clothed with purple and have a chain of gold around his neck, and he shall be the third ruler in the kingdom."

8 Now all the king's wise men came, but they could not read the writing, or make known to the king its interpretation.

9 Then King Belshazzar was greatly troubled, his countenance was changed, and his lords were astonished.

10 The queen, because of the words of the king and his lords, came to the banquet hall. The queen spoke, saying, "O king, live forever! Do not let your thoughts trouble you, nor let your countenance change.

11 "There is a man in your kingdom in whom is the Spirit of the Holy God. And in the days of your father, light and understanding and wisdom, like the wisdom of the gods, were found in him, and King Nebuchadnezzar your father—your father the king—made him chief of the magicians, astrologers, Chaldeans, and soothsayers.

12 "Inasmuch as an excellent spirit, knowledge, understanding, interpreting dreams, solving riddles, and explaining enigmas were found in this Daniel, whom the king named Belteshazzar, now let Daniel be called, and he will give the interpretation."

13 Then Daniel was brought in before the king. The king spoke, and said to Daniel, "Are you that Daniel who is one of the captives from Judah, whom my father the king brought from Judah?

14 "I have heard of you, that the Spirit of God is in you, and that light and understanding and excellent wisdom are found in you.

15 "Now the wise men, the astrologers, have been brought in before me, that they should read this writing and make known to me its interpretation, but they could not give the interpretation of the thing.

16 "And I have heard of you, that you can give interpretations and explain enigmas. Now if you can read the writing and make known to me its interpretation, you shall be clothed with purple and have a chain of gold around your neck, and shall be the third ruler in the kingdom."

17 Then Daniel answered, and said before the king, "Let your gifts be for yourself, and give your rewards to another, yet I will read the writing to the king, and make known to him the interpretation.

18 "O king, the Most High God gave Nebuchadnezzar your father a kingdom and majesty, glory and honor.

19 "And because of the majesty that He gave him, all peoples, nations, and languages trembled and feared before him. Whomever he wished, he executed; whomever he wished, he kept alive; whomever he wished, he set up; and whomever he wished, he put down.

20 "But when his heart was lifted up, and his spirit was hardened in pride, he was deposed from his kingly throne, and they took his glory from him.

21 "Then he was driven from the sons of men, his heart was made like the beasts, and his dwelling was with the wild donkeys. They fed him with grass like oxen, and his body was wet with the dew of heaven, until he knew that the Most High God rules in the kingdom of men, and appoints over it whomever He chooses.

22 "But you his son, Belshazzar, have not humbled your heart, although you knew all this.

23 "And you have lifted yourself up against the Lord of heaven. They have brought the vessels of His house before you, and you and your lords, your wives and your concubines, have drunk wine from them. And you have praised the gods of silver and gold, bronze and iron, wood and stone, which do not see or hear or know, and the God who holds your breath in His hand and owns all your ways, you have not glorified.

24 "Then the fingers of the hand were sent from Him, and this writing was written.

25 "And this is the inscription that was written: MENE, MENE, TEKEL, UPHARSIN.

26 "This is the interpretation of each word. MENE: God has numbered your kingdom, and finished it;

27 "TEKEL: You have been weighed in the balances, and found wanting;

28 "PERES: Your kingdom has been divided, and given to the Medes and Persians."

29 Then Belshazzar gave the command, and they clothed Daniel with purple and put a chain of gold around his neck, and made a proclamation concerning him that he should be the third ruler in the kingdom.

The boys follow the words in their Bibles but Seth lies on his side, asleep on the carpet, because he is too young to read.

The Conversation

"Joel, it's good to see you." The president walked into the West Lobby and greeted me with a wide smile—the sort you match and then realize you meant every tooth of it because you feel so much goodwill for a man who's that happy to see you.

"Thank you for the invitation, Mr. President," I said.

"Shall we sit outside?" he asked. "We have great staff here. I just ask and someone brings me a table and some tea or lemonade, or a beer—would you like a beer?"

"I'll drink what you're having, Mr. President."

"Well, I've taken up this summer habit of mixing iced tea with lemonade."

They brought a perfect, wrought-iron table with a glass top, an iced pitcher, and two glasses.

"They'll put us behind the trees by the East Wing so we can chat beyond the reach of staring eyes."

"I see," I said.

The president seated himself across the table from me and looked at me with the eagerness of someone who has anticipated a good conversation. "It's unusual that I invited you in here," he said, "but I'm glad you agreed to come."

"It wasn't the sort of invitation I could refuse, Mr. President."

"But this is not as unusual as you think," he said. "Did you know that, when the Secretary of Defense travels to a war zone, he always has lunch with a group of frontline, enlisted warriors? None of their commanders are allowed and none of the Secretary's staff."

I shook my head. "No, sir, I didn't know that."

"The Secretary of Defense has a great staff," the president said, leaning back in his chair. "But that's not enough. When you're a cabinet secretary or a president, you have a great system to feed you what you need to know. But still the system screens certain messages that a president needs to hear.

"My staff gets nervous when I hear things they haven't reviewed. And who can blame them. But, to understand this country, I need to talk with people like you. Some things need said that can't be said in a meeting room."

"I see, Mr. President."

"I've been reading the Hebrew prophets," he said. "Have you read them?"

"Most of them. Years ago."

"There's an unsettling line in Amos. He talks about a time when prudent men keep silent." The president looked at me as he spoke and then he stopped. But I thought his introduction wasn't complete so I nodded and waited.

"Have you ever seen something and thought, 'The president needs to know this?'"

"Yes, Mr. President, I think most of us have."

"And did you tell?"

"I spoke with you about detainees."

"Yes, you did," he said. "And I was impressed. But the other times? Did you speak then?"

"No."

"No one ever does. You see, everyone thinks like a prophet but no one speaks like it. Not to me, at least. Why is that?"

The question seemed unfair, so I said, "Most of us never have the chance to speak with you, Mr. President." But I knew, when I had said it, this didn't answer the president's complaint about the people who do speak with him.

"Joel, do you know why I invited you here today?"

"Because you're looking for a prophet?"

"Well, maybe. Do you think we have prophets today?"

I pondered that and finally said, "I'm not sure we need them now."

"And why not?"

"We have a constitution, separation of powers, free media, the Government Accountability Office, the Inspector General … Don't you think that's enough without prophets telling us how we're wrong?"

"The lawyers parse everything I do, my opponents make partisan arguments on the internet, and senators grandstand for their constituents. And that's a shame because what if a president needs a prophet?"

I smiled a little.

"A couple of days ago, a guy came into my office, told me I was tampering with religion the wrong way, and handed me a business card. When that happens, a president has to sit up and notice. So I cancelled my last meeting for the day and asked my Chief of Staff for a Bible. The poor guy looked confused and asked whether I wanted him to call Bono or Franklin Graham. But I told him I really just wanted a Bible."

I smiled again.

"Robbie was still in my office and he said he'd get me one. A few minutes later, my national security advisor sent me a link to bible.com/joel. That guy understands me freakishly well."

The president sounded droll and gazed at the edge of his table where a spider braced herself and rappelled unselfconsciously to the ground, like her cousins do in all the barrios and all the palaces of the world. The president smiled and re-poured our glasses of lemonade, but without unfurrowing his brow.

"I sat there and read Joel, and then I read Amos because it comes after Joel. Amos has a verse that has inspired my Administration. It says, 'Let judgment run down as waters, and righteousness as a mighty stream.' I campaigned on good judgment, you probably know that, and we put that verse on the wall in my campaign headquarters."

I sat there and thought vaguely that he'd have done better to call Bono than to read the Bible and discuss it with *me*.

"But Amos is hard to read after that," the president said. "He gets cruel." He pulled a paper from his inside pocket, unfolded it, popped the creases straight, and glanced down the page. "Amos accuses foreign nations of injustice. Then he pronounces God's judgment: 'As a shepherd rescues from the lion's mouth only two leg bones or a piece of an ear, so will the Israelites living in Samaria be rescued.'"

The president raised his eyebrows at me.

"That's quite an image," I said.

But then he jumped back to what he was saying before. "I have critics, Joel. They make partisan arguments on the internet. They warp the truth to hurt me and they're not telling me what I need to know. The IG[57] and the GAO[58] aren't telling me, either. And that's why we need prophets.

"I myself spent years in church and I know of how Joseph prevented famine by advising the Egyptian King. I have read about the prophet who spoke to David after his sin. And then there's Daniel—a man who spent his life advising the Persian kings and then told the chilling: *mene mene tikel upharsin*. Do you know what that means?" he asked.

"You have been weighed in the balance and found lacking," I said quietly.

The president gave an appreciative nod. "Would anyone bring that message to me if I needed it?"

"I don't know, Mr. President."

---

[57] Inspector General
[58] Government Accountability Office

"You told it to me straight about detainees a couple of days ago. That was closer than I usually get. How is it that my administration is full of people named David, Daniel, and Joel—but none of you are prophets?" The president turned from the lawn and looked at me to see what I would say. He was serious but I think he toyed with me also, to see who I was.

"Parents name their kids," I said, "but doesn't God appoint prophets?"

"And how do you think God appoints a prophet?"

By Janet's rules, I should get to know the president before I tell him anything. So I decided to toy back with him.

"God appointed Isaiah by burning his mouth. He got Joseph sold into slavery and falsely accused of having sex with his master's wife and then Joseph took over the jail and started a side business of interpreting his cellmates' dreams. Moses was tending sheep when he saw a …" The president held up his hand and chuckled.

"But what about Daniel? Didn't the king summon him to speak?"

This time I chuckled and started to feel comfortable talking with this man. "I was raised to admire the prophets," I said, "or at least the idea of a prophet. But, you have to understand, it's surreal when a president emails you because your name is Joel and he asks you to be a prophet. And, now that I'm here, you're asking me about finding leftover ears and God writing your doom on the wall?" I stalled a little. My comfort turned pale—maybe it's because I said *doom*—and I felt a brief terror, like this man was baiting me to judge him like Daniel did.

"After your assistant emailed me," I said, "I re-read the book of Joel. And I was troubled. Joel's judgment was deadly. He told Israel, in the name of God, to destroy the Gentiles. How can I speak like that, Mr. President? And would you trust me if I did?" I looked at him to see his response, but he stared at the table, lost in thought.

Finally, he said, "Still, would you tell me something like Daniel did? If you knew it was true? If you knew I needed to hear it and you were sitting here with me, would you tell me?"

The president looked at me then. His manner was still professional, but I heard unease in his voice.

I didn't know what to say so I sat there, and then I thought again of Janet's rules.

"Mr. President," I said finally, "you seem convinced there is something you need to hear. Something that's not being said. Why is that?"

The president's professional manner slipped. He gave a curtailed gesture, dropped his hand on the table, and then deflated slowly, the air sighing from his nose while his body slumped in on his lungs. Then he inhaled, his shoulders bobbed, and he said, "I'm not leading a country anymore, Joel. And it's not because I can't lead. It's because there's no country."

"What do you mean, Mr. President?" I asked, a little shocked.

"I give speeches, and I know America pretty well—campaign stops, polls. I've got advisors from every walk of life. But, more and more, I find myself saying things, not because I believe them, but because we need them to be true."

Now he spoke intently, looking across the table at me. He arched his brow. But I had nothing to say so I nodded. He looked puzzled, like he had served me a tennis ball and I stood there while it skipped off the court and jangled the fence. He frowned, like he still believed there must be a reason why I stood across the net from him, and I wondered again why he thought I was the person to play this game with him. But then he pulled another ball from his pocket and threw it up for a serve.

"You know, FDR said, 'The only thing we have to fear is fear itself.' He said that because fear is self-fulfilling. If people think they'll be afraid, then they're afraid. A lot of what makes an economy bad is simply people who expect the economy to be bad." I wondered whether he was still answering my question or if he'd gone off into his own head. Did he still serve his balls to me? Or did he serve them blindly at me while I watched?

"Hope is self-fulfilling, too," he said. "Even wanting hope is a hopeful thing. If we believe we are a good, united nation, then we will become a good, united nation. That's why I say what I say in my speeches. But, underneath, we don't know who we are to each other anymore. That's why I asked to talk with you today."

I nodded and he seemed to decide I was worth his time after all, like maybe I was the boy who picks up the balls from along the fence and throws them back while you practice your serves. He went on. "Every president says, 'The things that unite us are greater than the things that divide us.'" On this line, he gave an uncanny imitation of himself giving a speech and I must have snickered. "You like that?" he asked. "There's more where that came from."

Then he turned serious again. He shifted his chair to look out where the lawn dimmed and colored in the evening light. I studied him there, legs crossed at the knee, face profiled against rose-light on the East Wing. Then my mind did the hovering-overhead thing and the hovering Joel laughed at me, sitting there stiff in a chair with the president.

I felt a micro-slump in my shoulders—the difference between tension and good posture. I listened again and thought the president needed a confessor more than a prophet. I thought smugly that being a confessor must be an easy job and I remembered that I got hired that way once when I interviewed a man who loved his own voice so much that I only asked a few questions and he talked himself into believing I was, "a very perceptive person." So he hired me, and I laughed.

The president went on: "But no matter how often I say these things—no matter how much I know they can fulfill themselves—I see them slipping away. They're no longer true.

"I try. I really do. But as I write my speeches, the things that unite us are harder and harder to find. And the things that divide us stay. I feel them looking at me. They're like a toad. And you ignore the toad, but it's still there looking up at you and bobbing its throat." I laughed but he glanced at me like I'd said a joke about his dead mother.

He looked away then and seemed to think.

"You know," he said, "you don't win an election anymore by running to be the president of a nation. You win by being president of different groups. You don't speak to them as humans or as Americans, you speak to them as farmers, teachers, or gays. You talk to union members, businessmen, women, blacks, Latinos, Jews, Muslims, Secularists. You convince them you are like them, that you love what they love, hate who they hate, and that you will give them something once you're elected.

"Don't get me wrong. I've tried very hard to articulate our national values—an honest wage for an honest day's work, that we're all created equal, democracy, rule of law, freedom of the press … I believe in these things. But I still sense that we're not a nation—we're a collection of people living in the same place. In fact, we don't even live in the same place. We live in different places in this country—hundreds and thousands of miles from each other—or we're segregated in neighboring neighborhoods." He blinked a couple of times and looked away. "I'm tired of trying to invent an American story that includes us all."[59]

I sat there hearing the president confess, and it sounded like something I had always known. But it was disconcerting, because I thought it was dangerous for the president to see this thing for what it is and to say it in naked words like that. I wondered whether the president was the last person to discover this: every other country is a place, a race, a language, but America is an idea and if the idea dies

---

[59] This made me think of a Latin phrase I heard once: *E Unum Pluribus*

we become a collection of parts that used to be a whole thing—like the parts of a car that has lost its bolts. Somehow, I thought it was the president's job to hold it all together, and still he sat there talking to me like he'd watched it all happen and he'd given it up. So I felt something like despair, like there was no point in throwing balls back across the net again for such a man. I would let them pool along the fence until his bucket was empty.

There was no need to deliver the hard message I had imagined for him over the weekend. I have spent enough time on a farm to know you can whip a stubborn animal into action, but not a dying one. The president was speaking sincerely and I watched to judge whether he had enough life left to put himself back together. I smiled at the sadness of it, then smiled because it is much easier to listen than to speak a hard message. The stress that had consumed me for the past two days drained away.

"What's funny?" the president asked.

"You're easier to talk with than I thought," I said. "It's intimidating to talk with the president of the United States and I was afraid you expected me to be a prophet of God."

He frowned. "Based on your email to Tammy, I thought you had something to say."

Sometimes I blush. I hate that about myself. And I know the president saw it as he switched his tri-folded papers from a printout of Amos to the email I sent from my bed at Harpers Ferry.

He read aloud:

"I write because your assistant offered to provide you with a note to prepare for our meeting and because, in your invitation, you asked for my unofficial advice. I am prepared to offer it, such as it is.

"Perhaps there are issues about which your advisors and your critics alike are afraid to speak frankly. They will tell you the truth as it suits their purposes; I will tell you the truth as I see it. Neither method, I'm sure, will produce the Truth exactly, but I believe mine will come closer. I think it may also be less pleasant. I would apologize for this in advance but I think it cannot be otherwise, and I would be remiss if I apologize to you for the world being as it is."

If I could have disappeared right then, I would have. My words sounded profoundly arrogant as he read them. I had somehow planned to pull a Nathan and tell the president about a man who had the money to pay his debts but, instead, sold his children and spent his money on a nicer car. The president, I thought, would be appalled at this story. Then I would tell him that he is the man—the one who sold his kids—and, for proof, I would point at the deficit.

I had vaguely pictured the deficit as something squishy and void, pooling around the president's feet and filling his shoes, and I thought I would point to it when he blamed the guy for selling his children and I'd say "What about that?" in my stern, explain-yourself voice and the deficit would be so obvious there, soaking through the leather of his shoes, that he could only acknowledge the reasonableness of what I had said.

But, sitting there in front of the East Wing with the president, this plan seemed absurd beyond belief.

"Mr. President," I said, "I'm sorry. I wrote that email late at night."

"That's okay, I've written some of my best speeches at night."

"Really, Mr. President, I wrote that before I had the chance to meet you and hear from you directly."

He stared across the lawn and I think his shoulders sagged. "Are you going to say what you came to say, or are you afraid? Like my advisors and critics." He raised his eyebrows and I think he mocked me when he said this.

When he turned and looked at me, I've never seen someone look so alone. I had a weird feeling that the president needed someone to hug him and tell him everything will be all right. The last thing I wanted was to lob the grenade I had prepared for him in my bed at Harpers Ferry.

"What were you going to tell me?" he asked.

"Mr. President," I said, "I was going to accuse you of abandoning your parents and of robbing your children. I was going to lambast you for ignoring the deficit. I was going to tell you that you're antidemocratic because you spent my generation's money before we could even vote. I was going to say you've campaigned with brutal efficiency against anyone who takes this problem seriously. But, when I say it now, I realize it's lame. It's not even my generation you're robbing—I've had a vote since long before you ever ran for president."

"So, that's it? You're going to walk it all back now?" he asked, like a man betrayed. "You figure you'll come here, have a pleasant chat, and drink my lemonade? Then you'll leave and brag to your friends that you had a private meeting with the president?" He looked hurt. And insulted.

"No, Mr. President," I said. "That's not what I think."

"Then what do you think? Say it."

That made me mad. Mad that the president thought he could take a random counterterrorism employee and summon him like Daniel to be a prophet. It's unprofessional. And it's twenty-five centuries out of date. But, mostly, I despised myself for thinking I was tough, then turning to jelly when the time came to speak.

"Mr. President," I said. "I'm mad because your generation is stealing our country blind." I waited to see if that grenade caused any damage. Nothing. "You don't have the right to take money that belongs to your children and spend it on yourself, on your healthcare, on your retirement, and that's what you're doing with the deficit."

He stared ahead without moving so I tried another line: "Mr. President, I'm young. I'm hoping to live in this country for another forty, fifty, or sixty years. But, at this rate, there will be no country left. There may be a slave country—a slave to its creditors—but there will be no free country. That's what you're doing and it's not right. It ruins the trust that holds our country together from one generation to the next."

Can a liver tremble? I think so. I sat and my core trembled at what I had said to the President of the United States. I waited for him to say something. Finally, he said, "I know the deficit is a problem. But you're wrong about two things. First, the deficit is not a policy problem. It is the result of a problem with our culture, and a president cannot control the culture.

"You're also wrong about the children. I believe firmly that we must invest in the next generation. It's a cornerstone of my presidency. I've advocated for children's healthcare, for education, for school loans. In fact, these are part of the reason we have a deficit." He tapped the tabletop. "I will not balance the budget on the backs of our children."

Something swarmed up in my gut when he said that. Did the president think we have a deficit because he just cares too much about children? Like it's the children's fault that he's destroying their future? Blame the culture and the children for your failures, why don't you, Mr. President!

"But education money isn't for children," I said, more forcefully than I meant. "It's for parents. Maybe selfish parents are part of the culture that's getting you down?"

He stared at me. "Parents?"

"Yes," I said. "My mom taught me math by playing hopscotch on our driveway. My parents gave me a good education without schools, on a laboring man's income, and it didn't cost the government a dime. Schools aren't for children. Schools are a free place for parents to send their kids so the parents can do stuff without them."

The president frowned. "I think we both know schools are a lot more than that, Joel. Schools teach a whole range of developmental skills, life skills, occupational skills, social skills ..."

That was condescending. The president had invited me—a grown man—to play this game with him and now he treated me like a child who scrambles after his bouncing green balls. I found a bucket of my own, where it had blown, empty, to a corner of the court to lie with the shriveled leaves and gum wrappers. Methodically, I filled my bucket from the president's lousy serves, then I stood it beside me on my end of the court. I raised my racket, looked across the net at him, then threw a ball high in the air.

"And what kind of social skills do the schools teach?" I asked. "Isn't school a place where kids learn to beat up on people who are weaker than them, to make fun of others for being fat or gay, to do drugs, to have sex, to make cliques and mock the misfits? Doesn't every adult you ever met have some kind of post-traumatic school complex?"

"You can stop," the president said, his tone dark.

We sat there for a long time. My words surprised me a little and I knew I had crossed a line. I was homeschooled. It's true. And I can only imagine how unhinged my little tirade must have sounded to the president. I wondered if I might be dismissed.

After a brooding silence, without looking at me, the president asked, "Do you drink whisky?"

"Sure, Mr. President."

"Bobby, bring two glasses of that whiskey we just got—the Scotch," he said over his shoulder. Then we waited. Bobby appeared with two glasses and poured them. I paced myself with the president, which was fast—we drained the glasses within five minutes.

"Joel, I don't think you're a prophet," he said. "What I want to know is why you got into government."

That threw me off. I sat there for quite a while without a word. "Because I wanted to make a difference, I think."

"And are you making a difference?"

"It's so slow I can't always tell. But I try, and I think things are changing."

"What sort of difference do you want to make?"

"How so, Mr. President?"

"Are you cutting taxes? Making sure poor people have jobs? Rescuing AIDS orphans? Making America the greatest?"

This felt like a trap. "I have opinions on some of those issues, but I don't work on them."

"What do you work on?"

"Defense. Counterterrorism in particular."

"Why? What difference do you want to make in defense and counterterrorism?"

"I believe the world is a better place when the strongest country and the best country are the same country."

"That's good," the president said. "I like that."

"In the Pentagon we have a formula," I said. "Threat = Capability × Intent. It's a good formula. We use it to rank our enemies. But I've come up with another formula for our own country: Greatness = Strength × Goodness."

"I see. Maybe I'll write that one on my office whiteboard and give it some thought."

"Write it on the oval office wall with a sharpie if you want to be remembered for something," I said. The president squinted at me and I realized that's not the sort of thing you say to a president. So I plowed forward to cover my *faux pas*. "You could tell your biographer that your kid did it and you spanked him for writing on the walls, but then you decided it was so smart that you left it there for everyone to remember."

He saw what I'd done but laughed just the same. Then he asked, "So are you working to make us strong or to make us good?"

"Both, I hope, Mr. President."

"And how's it going? Do people appreciate you for trying to make us good?"

I smiled. "Sometimes."

"But usually?"

I had to think hard on that one. "When you make policy there are so many factors. You have to consider them all. And the result may not be what's right."

"So, if we're not doing the right thing, what is it we do? Balance out the competing pressures and call it policy?" He held his hands up to an imaginary marquee and read: "America, the sum of its influences." The marquee lingered a bit, then he looked at me and asked, "Is that what we have?"

"I guess so."

"And people who want to do the right thing, for the hell of it, because it's the right thing, are they one of the influences?"

I had never heard it put like that and it surprised me that the president thought about these things.

"Maybe the right thing is one factor," I said, "but I don't think it gets weighed very often. I don't think we agree on what is right to start with, and I don't think it usually outweighs the other factors."

"What sort of other factors are you talking about?"

"Doing what's good for the economy. Doing what we think will make us safer. Maintaining influence with our allies."

"What sort of allies are you talking about?"

"Saudi Arabia. When's the last time you called out the Saudi government for systematically oppressing and murdering women—for keeping them all as prisoners under house-arrest and for stoning them if they're falsely accused? Have you ever criticized the way the Saudi royal family uses the country's oilfields as their personal bank account?

"Or what about China? When's the last time you spoke of how they torture Christians and Falun Gong? Or Kazakhstan—or any country with a supply route into Afghanistan—when's the last time you challenged their abuses?"

The president stood there, across the net, and watched my serves skip off the court in front of him. He made no effort to return them and my bucket was nearly empty, but I kept on.

"Didn't you advocate for Russia to join the World Trade Organization at the same time when Putin cracked down on his political opposition and we learned the sordid story of how they tortured Sergei Magnitsky to death in prison because he exposed massive tax fraud? While Putin sold arms to a brutal dictator in Syria and left the Syrian people with no alternative but the most hideous of organized terror groups to protect themselves from their own government?"

The president didn't answer immediately and I thought of his first inaugural speech and of where I had watched it in Z____ with all the small-time dignitaries after riding my motorcycle through the watery potholes. And I quoted:

"'I do not stand here saying that America is perfect, but I ask people of goodwill the world over to join us in the struggle to become a more perfect union. As president, I can say that America is a friend to free people everywhere. And to those who struggle for freedom but have not yet achieved it, I say, don't give it up. We are a friend to you as well.'

"It was a good speech," I said. "Do you know where I was when you said that?"

"These are complex issues, Joel," the president said, finally, with a sad note in his voice. "We have essential economic and security relationships in these places and, if we give them up, we make the world more dangerous. How can I defend women from the Taliban if I offend the countries that give us a supply route into Afghanistan? How can I negotiate a reduction in the world's most dangerous weapons with one hand while, with the other, I'm exposing the Russian Government for corruption? As President of the United States, I can't throw these relationships away just to complain, on principle, about things that are beyond my control."

"I know, Mr. President. But you asked what influences drown out people who want to do the right thing, for the hell of it. Those are the influences."

"My Administration has taken on some pretty powerful influences."

"I'm sure you have, Mr. President."

He looked at me for a long moment. "So what about you? Do you fight to do the right thing in your job at the Pentagon? Do you push back on the factors that 'drown out doing the right thing?'"

"I try to, Mr. President. We talked with you last week about terrorist reintegration. I pushed hard to bring that issue out of the shadows."

"And why did you push for it?"

"Because we don't have a terrorist reintegration policy and I think what we're doing is wrong."

"And what do people say when you tell them what they're doing is wrong?"

"They usually act like I'm being difficult. Sometimes they get offended, as if I'm accusing them of something."

He smiled. "You do come on a little strong."

"You pushed me, Mr. President."

He nodded and asked for two more glasses of whisky.

"Do you know why we have a deficit?" he asked.

"Why?"

"It's because all the good causes take more money than all the good taxes can produce."

"Fair enough," I said. "But, as one of my professors used to say, 'For every good program, there is an equal and opposite tax. That, or a double and opposite debt.'"

The president winced, but didn't respond. "Do you read Lincoln?" he asked.

"I've read some."

"You've read the second inaugural address?"

"Yes."

"I've memorized it," he said. "Lincoln is talking about the Civil War and he says, 'Both parties deprecated war, but one of them would make war rather than let the nation survive, and the other would accept war rather than let it perish. And the war came.'

"That's the situation we're in with the deficit. Both parties deprecated a deficit, but one of them would make a deficit rather than raise taxes on anyone, and the other would accept a deficit rather than let poor people, old people, and children go hungry. And the deficit came."

The president had returned my serve—a serve I didn't think he could reach. His response was cleverly placed, too, and that needled me. For one thing, the president had appropriated Lincoln's words to himself, a particular line I had always disliked. Lincoln used it to pose as an observer, an interpreter—a man acted upon by history and not one who acts—a passive victim of the war, not the president prosecuting the war.

I had always thought this was Lincoln's most pathetic line. A confession that he was out of control. Careening into a car crash, you throw your hands up and holler for Jesus to take the wheel.

Lincoln needed someone to kick him in the butt and say: "You started the war and you're President of the United States, so own it and end it. Don't give me this poetic, interpreter-of-history crap. Don't burden me with your bullshit coping mechanisms for the horror of what you have done."

And the line sounded even more pathetic coming from this president's mouth. But, instead of saying so, I thought of something clever: "When President Lincoln said that, wasn't he trying with everything he had to end the war? Didn't he believe the war was an awful thing and then seek to end it as quickly as possible?"

"No," the president said, "he did not seek only to end the war, but to end it on his terms."

"In a way that preserved the union," I said.

"And in a way that ended slavery."

"But he wavered on that," I said. "He doubted whether even his lifelong goal of ending slavery was worth such a war."

"Yes, he did. Until Frederick Douglas stiffened his spine."

We sat in silence for a bit, then I said, "Do you have the same horror of the deficit? Are you determined to end it as soon as possible?"

"Yes, I think I am determined to end it."

"But only on your terms?"

"Yes."

"And what are your terms?"

"I have laid them out many times: I will not balance the budget at the expense of our most vulnerable people. I will not use the deficit to betray our commitments to old people, sick people, poor people, our children, our students—who face an unprecedented cost for a college education—or the veterans, the police, and firemen who protect us. And we must continue to invest in the next generation. I will not allow my opponents to use the deficit as a pretext for choking off the livelihood of the most vulnerable among us while the rich pay some of the lowest taxes in the industrialized world."

He had reverted to campaign rhetoric. How many times have I sat in front of the TV and argued with this talking head? Now I sat with a listening president. He had landed a shot on my side of the net and I should do something with it. But tennis doesn't have to be about defeating the other person. It can be about having a great volley. Sometimes it's best that way.

"Mr. President," I said, "I think one of the reasons we fight in this country and we don't find much in common is because everyone feels like you do on this. We all think we're defending a vulnerable person who, but for our support, would be steamrolled by a cruel, callous machine on the other side."

The president was listening so I went on: "There's probably a better way to say this but, I've found, in Washington, DC, it is very hard to keep your head the right size—to care for the world without taking its whole weight on your shoulders—to care well for a piece of the world when the whole of it is so off-center. There are things that outrage me, and I think they should outrage me because they're outrageous. I've seen how Christians are treated in China, India, Egypt, Iraq … The way women are treated in Afghanistan, Saudi Arabia, Iran … or villages in Africa. But how do I care for them? How do I do what I can about these outrages without becoming forever enraged? How do I care without presuming to be God?"

I paused, and was about to go on but the president spoke quietly: "Whether there is a god or not, I can tell you, there is work that must be done in this world that should not be done by unaided mortals."

That blew me away. For campaign purposes, the president is, of course, a Christian. Beyond that, only he knows how much God means to him. He went on. "How do you love this game and play it well when, in fact, it's not a game and people live or die by how you play it? How do you love it when it's so serious? And how do you play it well if you don't love it?"

I sat thinking about that and then the president continued: "You know what stresses me?"

"What?"

"Things you can influence."

"How so, Mr. President?"

"You're not stressed by the things you can control, are you? You set them straight and you're done with it. You're not stressed because you're in control.

"And the things you can't control? Well, those aren't your responsibility. So you can give them up. You *should* give them up. If you try to control them, you'll just hurt yourself. And you'll hurt others. That's why I love travelling. When I'm in Air Force One, I'm totally out of control. I've got the best damn pilots in the cockpit and there's not a thing I can do to make the airplane fly more or less safely. No stress.

"What stresses me is not the things I can control or the things I can't control. And you may wonder what else there is. I'll tell you, it's the things in the middle—the things I can only *influence*. And, you know what? When you're president, that's everything. You can't control the economy, terrorism, the climate, the budget, the deficit, our allies, the tone of politics, the American culture. You can't control America's attitude toward the world, or whether our kids have good schools, but you can *influence* all these things. And you must influence them, or at least try. And, when you try, you'll never know whether you did all you could. You'll always wonder whether you could do more—whether you should do more. You'll wonder whether someone else could do it better.

"And you know what else? When you're president, you have the one job in the country that everyone thinks he could do better than you. They look at everything you can influence and, if it's not perfect, they blame you. For everything.

"So here's the president's dilemma: How do you cope with a world where everything can be influenced but nothing controlled?"

The president turned his near-empty glass and I felt the pain in his voice. The frustration. And I wanted to offer sympathy. We had somehow agreed to end the competition and let the balls roll to wherever they stopped on the court. We stood leaning on the poles that anchored our net, tapping the racket strings absently on our palms. Then he went on.

"So I know I'm not God, Joel. I can't control things. I'm aware of that. But I have to look out, the best I can, for vulnerable people because they rely on the Government when there's no one else. They rely on me."

I considered this and we sat silently for a good while. Dusk had settled on us. Our spider had finished her web and she sat waiting for gnats. Bobby refilled the whisky. I thought the president hadn't noticed, because he stared at the trees but, then, without looking, he took a sip.

I waited, then finally ventured, "Mr. President, I've never had a partisan job. But I've worked under both parties and for some advocacy groups. Like you, they all picture a victim they're protecting. Everyone thinks he's a David facing Goliath. They all see themselves as a rag-tag band of people sacrificing to stop the other side's cruel, political machine from crushing someone.

"I have pro-life friends and they picture a defenseless, voiceless child who has been conceived through no choice of its own. They believe this child is a person who deserves the chance to live out his life on this earth. They're fighting to save this child from a cold doctor and a cold world that would kill him for their convenience. And they're fighting to save the mother from a life of guilt—a life of heightened risk for cancer, sterility, depression, suicide, and other documented consequences of an abortion—the consequences people try to hide from her."

"You can stop, Joel. This is not what I wanted to discuss." It was the dark, quiet tone he'd used earlier.

"I understand," I said and cringed. This was a risky road I shouldn't have taken. But, to stop now was to lose, so I played the one card I could play to rescue the situation. "But, Mr. President, that is half of the story. My pro-choice friends are also protecting someone."

He looked intently, then said, "Yes, and I'll tell you who that is." I saw something shifting in his eyes. He was wary. But now he wanted to press the issue. The president prides himself—as all politicians do—on his ability to assess people, and he wanted to know whether he'd misjudged me as someone who would talk honestly with him. He wanted to know whether I would fall into blind opposition. He wanted to know whether I was someone he could trust.

"Your pro-choice friends also have a picture of the person they defend," he said, watching my face. "She is young—maybe fifteen—pregnant through love, loneliness, insecurity, temptation, persuasion, adventure, or too much pressure from her boyfriend. Maybe she has been raped. She's young and her body can only bear a child with great risk to her health—to her life. She lives in a culture where the stigma of unwed motherhood will follow her for life. Her father will be outraged to know she's pregnant, and will look on every hardship in her life as the just consequence of her choices, and this will prevent her from falling back on her family—the one prayer of a chance she had to raise a child in a healthy home.

"And now you're going to say that both sides see themselves as a motley band of good-hearted people defending vulnerable people from devastation—protecting them from the other side's cruel juggernaut, and so they hate each other and swear to destroy each other in the name of righteousness." He looked at me, and I'm sure he almost winked. "Did I get that about right?"

"Yes, Mr. President," I said. I swallowed, and then I went in for it: "Mr. President, the vulnerable person I'm trying to defend is everyone who will live in America thirty, forty, and fifty years from now.

"Last week you argued on TV, once again, that without a drastic increase in our debt, America's economy would collapse. You looked into the camera and suggested that, if I oppose more borrowing, I will be the one making it collapse. But I think it's you. You're trading the whole of tomorrow for little pieces of today. Already, this country owes more money than our whole economy produces in a year."

The president sat, silent, his brow furrowed, so I went on.

"Earlier you said that all the good taxes can never pay for all the good programs. Later you listed people who benefit from your programs and said you would not balance the budget at their expense. But what if it isn't possible to end the deficit on those

134

terms? What if the math doesn't add up? What will you say to tomorrow's vulnerable people who read history and curse your name because you're the person who used their money to pay your own debts? What do you say to the historians who will shake their heads and conclude that we were all dead before our ship even sank? Because, otherwise, we would surely have seen it coming and stopped it."

The president looked at me. "I would tell them they should also curse the people who cut taxes in the face of the worst debt crisis in the history of this country."

"But isn't it a weak defense to remind them that other people were also looting their country?"

The president bristled and sat back in his seat. "You sit there and criticize me, but what do you want me to do? Turn old people out in the streets while the fat cats feather their nests? Is that what you want?"

We sat there in silence. The president drained his glass and set it on the table with some force.

"No," I said finally. "I don't want that. I don't envy your options. I guess I'm asking you to face the debt for what it is: the overwhelming moral problem of our time. You compared the deficit to the Civil War and I like that. President Lincoln had terrible options. But he was a man of formidable virtue and political talent. He looked on the blights of his age—slavery and secession—and called them evil. He looked through these blights and saw that they were not a technical, legal problem. They sprang from human selfishness—from human depravity. Ending slavery posed an economic problem, too, and people felt trapped by that. But Lincoln knew that, no matter how impossible it seemed at the time, rich and poor alike must learn to live together in this country without enslaving a whole race. He asked for profound sacrifices from his fellow Americans, rich and poor, and because of that, he removed those blights from America. He did not pass them on to the next generation as the ones before him had done. Isn't that what made him great?"

The president stared at the dark lawn, legs crossed at the knee, hand absently holding his whisky glass.

I continued. "Don't we have to do the same thing now? No matter how difficult, shouldn't we—rich and poor alike—learn to live now without enslaving the next generation? Surely the debt is an easier problem to solve than slavery—for a rich nation to simply live on its own income."

He sat there and I could tell he was thinking. "You know," he said, "Abraham Lincoln had a nation to call on."

"And half of that nation did not even believe he was their president!"

"I can sympathize," he said and produced a half-smile. "Joel, I'm having a hard time finding any unity to call upon in this country, and I'm having a hard time addressing this problem without it. Tell me honestly, does your generation really believe in something? Do they believe we have a culture worth tending? Do they understand the concept of something worth sacrificing for?"

"Mr. President, I've thought about this before and, if you want to know my honest opinion, I can tell you."

"Nothing has stopped you so far, has it?"

I smiled. "My generation has opinions. Maybe we even believed in ourselves for a while. But I can't say we believe in anything, really. We're thirty-year-olds taught by opinionated fifty-year-olds who believe in nothing. We care about our country, but we don't know how or why so, mostly, we care about ourselves."

"That's what I was afraid of," he said. "That's why I can't solve the deficit."

"How so, Mr. President?"

"The problems with the deficit are delayed problems. They don't cause pain now. So, if people only care about themselves today, how will they care about the deficit?"

"Mr. President," I said, "I wonder whether you have really tried. What would happen if you ask the country to sacrifice? What if you called on us to rise to this occasion? Maybe you'd find a national resolve that wasn't there before. What if you ask Americans to think and sacrifice together as Americans rather than as Jews or Christians, or union workers or businessmen? What about calling on people to be noble? Would that be self-fulfilling, too, like hope?"

The president sat there for a long time, circling his finger on the rim of his glass. Finally, he said, "Joel, to make the kind of change you're talking about requires a change deep in our core as a people. A change in who we are to each other—what our country is to us. It's more than tweaking some government policies." He looked up at the darkening sky, then at me. "Joel, it's very hard to create a change like that partway through a presidency. My current policies won't make it happen. I can see that. But I haven't given up on this country. I would like to know what you think it would take.

"I've come to believe the causes of the deficit are deeper than stubborn political opponents, broader than the demographics of aging baby-boomers, and more than extra spending to stimulate the economy. And the answer is more complex than letting the economists do their math and getting the politicians to follow it. It has something to do with who we've become in this country. I can't put my finger on it, and I can't figure out what to do about it, but I'm president and it troubles me. I'm afraid it has less to do with the government and more with the *people* who elect us."

Those words would poison a campaign. I loved his honesty but it wearied me that he had once again found someone else to blame.

He covered the top of his glass with his palm, maybe pondering the apostasy of what he had said. Then he continued, "Joel, will you study this question, then come back and tell me what you think?"

"Sir, you want me to solve your problem with the American people?"

"Yes, I think so. And I want to know whether I'm alone in this."

"Alone?"

"Is anyone else responsible for our Nation, Joel?" he asked. "Is there anyone else advocating for who we are? For who we are to each other and who we are to the world? Or is it only me? Is a lone president supposed to shape America while all the rest stand there, click their tongues, and point out what I'm doing wrong? Our Founding Fathers envisioned a Nation—a whole society—of which Government was just a part—an unusually *small* part. But who are the other parts? Do they know who they are? Do they still show up for work?"

He sat and brooded, then went on. "Have all of our other leaders given up on the American project? And what can a president do when they've all given it up?"

"But, Mr. President, we have a lively community of leaders outside Government. We have NGOs, businesses, churches, universities, artists, writers—"

"And what do they do, Joel? Do they spend their energy encouraging our people and building our culture? No. They lobby the Government. It's like they, too, believe government is the only way to shape our society."

"But they do a lot more than that, Mr. President. Maybe you don't see it because you've been in government for so long."

"And what else do they do, Joel? I'll tell you: they cater to the consumers. And, if it's a university or an artist we're talking about, can you honestly tell me they believe in America? Do they tend our culture? Are they working to make us better than we already are? Didn't you just tell me these places are full of opinionated fifty-year-olds who don't believe in anything?"

I sat, depressed, looking for a way out of this, and I thought of Elijah, who, in a moment of bitterness, claimed to be the only one who still believed in Israel's god—the only man who had not bowed his knee to a foreign idol. Finally, I said, "Mr. President, you're not the last person who believes in America. But what if you were? Perhaps then you would be the first man of our renaissance." He chuckled. "And, if you're the first one, you can count me as a second."

It was dark now. The Washington monument blinked its red eyes across the south lawn and the Jefferson memorial huddled beyond. The White House lights shone on the president's head but his face was lost in shadow. We sat in silence. Then the president said, "I'm happy to lead the nation, Joel, but there's no nation left to lead." He paused, and finally muttered, as if to himself, "How did this happen?"

"Mr. President," I said, "I grew up with Bible-believing Christians, and they would have an answer for that question."

"What question?"

"The question of how this happened."

"I'm sure they would."

"They would say we lost our nation when our families frayed, when our churches lost their respect—when we quit believing in God."

"Are you a Bible-believing Christian?"

"Not really."

"Me either."

"But I haven't decided they're entirely wrong."

He shrugged. "Me either."

"And I believe you're mistaken to blame the problems of our time on forces beyond your control."

He said nothing to this.

"Do you still want me to look into your question?" I asked.

"Yes, I do. Maybe it's for me. Maybe for my successor. Maybe it's something I can only work on when I've returned to private life. But I have to understand it the best I can."

The human Joel was reeling—paralyzed—at what the president had asked, so Joel-the-bureaucrat took over: "What kind of an answer do you want me to deliver, Mr. President? I'm sure a wiser person than me could write volumes on this topic."

"Maybe you can write something, too. Not too long, though. People who know what they're saying write short books."

I smiled. "People write long books because they lack the time to write short ones."

"Yes, exactly. Didn't someone say that in a letter? Once you've taken the time to write your short book, we should meet and talk about it."

"I'd be happy to," I said. "But it will take a few months. I want to read some and ask my friends for advice so I can get this right. You need to hear more than just my thinking."

"That's too long," he said. "People don't think well when they have that much time. They diddle around, feeling important, and then they do some good thinking in the last week or two. But by then they've generated too much material to put it all down and they get confused."

"Then what do you want?" I asked.

"How's two weeks?"

"Can I have three?" I asked pathetically.

The president reached across the table to shake my hand. "You've got a deal, but I have to ask you to be discreet about this."

"I will," I said.

"I'll ask Tammy to set up a meeting at the end of the month."

* * *

I walked out of the White House, past the squalid, permanent protest in Lafayette square, and rode the bus to my house, fogged from the whisky, and sat at my desk for hours writing up notes from the meeting.

As I wrote, I became more and more troubled. The president seemed to think history asked too much—that it had assigned him a super-human task—and I was troubled because it is not our place to protest history's demands. A father does not complain that the car is heavy. He lifts the car off his child. Whether the task was reasonable or not, I had, so far, failed to convince the president that it is *his*.

The Log Cabin

"Father, can I go to work with you today?" Joel has learned that even a prophet must occupy himself on the dry days when he lacks mystical writing to interpret.

"Not today, Joel," Father says. "I'm overhauling a big truck."

So Joel waits, reminded that he is a child, and he reads: *Little House in the Big Woods; Farmer Boy; Little House on the Prairie; On the Banks of Plum Creek; By the Shores of Silver Lake; The Long Winter; Little Town on the Prairie, and These Happy Golden Years.* He reads too much and his mother chases him from the house, smiling. "Go play with your brothers."

Josiah, Jeremy, and Joel find fence posts, and fence posts + imagination = telephone poles, or logs if needed, and then a cleverly stacked cabin with a flat, jostling roof. One brother inside, domestic on this occasion, and the other two atop their house—a better posture for prompting and then surviving the inevitable collapse.

Then Joel crawls with his brothers through the tall weeds. A father who earns the rent only barely after long labor does not manicure his yard.

Joel's mother irons dark patches on their knees but leaves the worn tips of their boots to breath. She worries, of course, but insists on the boots. What else can a mother do? "We killed a rattlesnake, Mom. Or Jeremy did, but I helped. Here's the rattle," he says, holding it high on a chubby palm. "See? Look, Mom. Eight sections and it's not even broken."

"Okay," she says. "I'm glad you killed it. Why don't you put it in your room and wash your hands. Your father should be home soon and we'll have supper."

Rorschach

When you work under pressure, on real-world issues, you need friends to give advice and keep you grounded, to remind you who you are and why you're doing it. But that presents a problem. I have signed too many non-disclosure agreements.

So what do we do? We go silent and rely on our own depleted resources. Tragic, lonely, and foolish. "I could tell you what's hollowing me out," we say, "but it's secret so I would have to kill you."

"I've got one for you," I said to Sam-Bob Saturday morning when I found him wearing his worlds-best-dad apron and dropping vegetables into the skillet for an elaborate omelet.

"You've got to get the grease really hot," he said, "so the peppers will sizzle and then blacken on contact."

I reached up to preempt the fire alarm and saw that it was still preempted from last time. "Can you put the battery back in the smoke detector when you're done cooking?" I asked.

"If you're here, you'll see the smoke and put out the fire. If you're not here, the house will burn down anyway. So what's the point of a fire alarm?"

"No? Okay, then I'll put it back." I set the egg-timer for thirty minutes to let the smoke clear. He turned away from the stove to grab some sliced veggies and his apron twirled neatly.

"Nice dress," I said.

"What do you want?"

"I need your advice."

"I say screw the fire alarm and cook your food right. That's *my* advice."

"But I've got a real issue," I said. "It's dead serious."

"So you want to talk?" he asked. "That's refreshing." He shuffled his peppers in the grease. Then he said, "Pull up a stool, and talk to Mama." He swayed his hips and twirled his dad dress. "You've been so secretive lately, I thought you'd joined the CIA."

I guphumped in lieu of a laugh. "Close. But I've got another problem that's just as secret."

"I see," he said. "And shall I presume you're going to talk about it here in this room that, for all you know, could be bugged by the Chinese, the Iranians, the Israelis, and the—"

"The Israelis?"

"Oh, nothing. I'm only saying, this living room isn't exactly certified for a classified conversation."

"I'm worried more about the Washington Post. This one's hot and it would travel fast."

"I've heard Rupert Murdoch has wiretapping capabilities to rival the French," he said.

"The French?"

"Oh, nothing. What's on your mind?"

"Really, I need you sworn to secrecy."

"Shit, man, I'm already taking so many secrets to my grave there won't be enough room for them in a king-size coffin." Sam-Bob folded two omelets over his blackened veggies, then he slid them from his two skillets onto two plates. "Do you think you can get custom coffins?" he asked. "Is it like a hotel where you can specify? 'I'd like a grave for three: two coffins—one queen and a twin.' Or maybe a roll-away? That'd be awesome. I should call the morgue and ask."

I laughed. It's how Sam-Bob makes life interesting for himself and it cracks me up.

"Hey," I said, "leave the morgue out of this. You won't need it. And, if you do, it'll be my problem, not yours."

"You make a good point," he said.

"So you'll fit my secret in your coffin with all those ghosts of Afghanistan?"

"I'm afraid your secret would get bullied in a crowd like that," he said. "It's no place for sissy secrets."

I laughed again. "This one has some bite," I said. "It'll be fine."

"Said the bureaucrat to the warrior."

"Remember when this bureaucrat tackled a warrior, in fair and open combat, and ground his back into the beach—with witnesses?"

"I was recovering from a cold."

"You were certainly sniffling. And it *was* terribly insensitive of me—wrestling a warrior who should have been on runny-nose leave."

"Will you tell me your secret, or shall we keep reminiscing of that one time when you won something?"

"So you admit I won!"

"What's your secret, man?"

"Are you going to keep it?"

"Of course. What's going on?"

"The president has asked me to provide him with recommendations on some things, like how to solve the deficit."

"No shit?"

"I could sign it in blood."

"I wouldn't mind seeing some of your blood."

"Oh, drop it." I went on. "I had a lengthy conversation with the president yesterday."

"No shit. Just you two?"

"We drank whisky."

"No shit? Why ...?"

"Let's leave the innovative swearing out of this," I said. "The president asked my advice on nearly everything—like how to convince my generation to care and how to unify our country."

"Good luck with *that*," Sam-Bob said, and wiped his thumb absently on his shirt where he thought the apron still was.

"He was dead serious," I said. "I think I'll take some vacation next week and go home to think it out. We're meeting again in three weeks."

"Well, I'll be damned."

"Watch your language."

"There's nothing creative about being damned. Dad says most of us are."

"Are what?"

"Damned."

"My dad thought that, too."

"So what are you going to tell the president?"

"That's the second question," I said. "The first question is how am I going to figure it all out?"

"That's easy," Sam-Bob said, and I creased my forehead horizontally because that was not a normal thing for Sam-Bob to say.

"Easy?"

"We're going for a bike ride."

"I'm going to answer the president's question by riding a bicycle?"

"Exactly!" Sam-Bob said. "We'll play *Rorschach With the City*."

"What the heck is that?" I asked.

"It's a game I made up. And we can play it together because I'm tired of *Rorschach With the Security Desk*."

"I don't have time for games," I said.

"Two minutes ago you were all – *'You're burning the house down* and *nice-dress-Sam-Bob* and *I'm a hero because I wrestled you sick* and *I've got a problem that only you can help with.'* Now I'm helping and you're all *'games are silly?'*"

"What's this game anyway," I asked. "What are the rules?"

"The first rule is put your pants on," he said, with an x-ray glance through the tabletop at my boxers.

We pedaled up Maryland Avenue toward the Capitol, until Sam-Bob squeezed his brakes in Stanton Park and nodded to the statue of a horseman who points his gull-poo-stained finger over toward the Canadian embassy. "Tell me about that guy," he said.

"I don't know who he is."

"Guess."

"Stanton?"

"No. It's Nathaniel Greene."

"Nathaniel Greene?"

"Exactly. Tell me about him."

"But I don't know who he is."

"Exactly."

I did the horizontal creases again.

"You don't know, so you make it up. Who was Nathaniel Greene?" he asked again, with all the patience of a drill sergeant.

"But I told you—"

"And *I* said, you make it up!"

"Okay, then," I said. To be honest, I'd never even noticed the statue in Stanton Park, because it's on a pedestal and it's too big to see. But I tilted my head back in the universal pose for looking up at a windmill. Mr. Greene wore a goofy hat, folded up in the front and the back, leaving a winged brim on the sides, as if his ears were the only part of him at risk of sunburn. The hat made two perfect bird-nesting spots, one on either side of his head. But no birds nested there, and I used my inner bird brain to determine that it is too hot for hatchlings. Then I used my history brain to assess that a man with a hat like that was a man confused about whether he was still British.

"Time's up, bro. Who's Nathaniel Greene?"

So I jumped in. "His mom told him he was born to be a hero," I said. "But, to be a hero, he needed a cause. So, for irony's

148

sake, he decided to convince thirteen British colonies that, in the long annals of human crime, a small stamp tax stands out above all the rest."

"Nice," Sam-Bob said. "Now, see that girl with the sports bra, the spaghetti straps, and the yoga shorts? The one throwing a ball with that giant blue ice-cream scooper thing?"

I looked and did the universal pose for I'm-ogling-you-but-I'm-wearing-sunglasses-so-it's-okay. I was getting the hang of the game so I jumped in. "She's from University Town Indiana and she always jumps to beat the next fastest person to call it 'the middle of nowhere.' She cohabitates with a guy who jogs and bikes a lot to keep his abs flat, even though he's not that young anymore. They've cohabitated so long that they've bought a house together and adopted nagging as their primary love language, but it still seems edgy to her because she believes her mom thinks in phrases like *living in sin*. She likes looking sexy in this accidental, I-didn't-notice-my-pixie-tattoo-showing-on-my-incredibly-well-muscled-thigh-when-I-threw-on-these-compression-shorts-this-morning-and-walked-my-dog-to-the-park kind of way.

"She likes her mom's disapproval and the I-passively-survive-Christmas-each-year-with-my-small-minded-family self image. But she mainly despises her mom because she believes her mom thinks the greatest techno/cultural innovation of the 20th Century is the home-canning set they bought from the Sears and Roebuck catalogue in the 1980s, so now they can survive the Great Depression, or Armageddon, for instance, just by stowing strawberry jam in mason jars that she stacks in a pyramid at the back of a storage shed that she also bought through the Sears and Roebuck catalogue and assembled in the back yard where the girl used to have a swing set that was held together at the joints with spiky plates hammered into the wood instead of nails or bolts, and the girl resents that the swing set is gone even though her mom says she's obviously too old to use it so why should *she* care unless, of course, she has changed her mind about having some grandkids?"

"Really?" Sam-Bob said. "You think she's old enough to say 'Sears *and* Roebuck?'"

"She looks younger than she is because she's never had kids and because she uses highlights to cover the gray in her hair. Besides, she definitely imagines her *mom* saying 'Sears *and* Roebuck.'"

"Well, then," Sam-Bob said, nodding. "Shall we ride on?"

I thought I'd done a good job on the girl in the park and I wanted to top it for the Capitol. But Sam-Bob rode past the police posted by the corner of the Capitol grounds and made like he'd cruise down Capitol Hill without a glance. I shoved a couple of steps on my pedals, pulled even with him, and asked whether he intended to Rorschach the Capitol.

"You can't Rorschach something you've thought about before," he yelled.

"Why not?" I yelled back.

"It's like introducing yourself to someone you already know."

"But we could still stop and make up stuff about it."

"But then we would never get where we're going."

And that's how we invented the word-association, speed-play version.

Sam-Bob pointed to the Capitol and I yelled, "The Apotheosis of Washington." He frowned like I'd said something obscene, then cranked his pedals to keep up his momentum from the hill. As I worked to keep up, he rode against traffic across the parking lot, then ran a red light crossing First Street, and I sniffed mustard in my nostrils from a hotdog truck. Sam-Bob cranked his way down the bus lane along the National Mall, back erect, calf muscles bobbing white in the sun as he pedaled, fingers laced across his belly in the universal look-mom-no-hands pose. I followed until he nodded toward the little Louvre-esque pyramid between the two buildings of the National Gallery of Art. Then he looked at me and waited for an answer.

"Trying to transcend," I bellowed, and he looked annoyed again.

He nodded to the Archives.

"Dim documents." I thought he smiled.

On our left, he pointed to a suspended concrete donut—the Hirshhorn Museum. I like the Hirshhorn Museum. It displays a book with pins glued to it. Why? What is it? It is nothing. Only a book with pins glued to it. Why should this thing be any more or less than any other thing?

"Cultural defibrillation," I shouted, and I'm pretty sure he grunted.

We rode to the spire of the Washington Monument, covered in scaffolding, with the White House peeping at us through the trees on our right and Jefferson's pantheon to the left. Sam-Bob nodded to Jefferson.

"Narcissist."

We turned a hard left, rode over the Potomac[60] and, from there, off the end of the Reagan runway where planes fly a few feet over your head before landing. We stopped and listened to the air torn and lashing overhead where a plane had flown through.

"Those planes are doing that to the air all over the world all the time," Sam-Bob said. "But you'd never know it if you didn't sit here and listen for once in your life."

We pedaled on, suspended between the Potomac and a thundering power plant, through Alexandria's sleepy waterfront, to silent woods where a man can think. I pedaled and sweated, until I stopped thinking of clever answers and my body had worn itself into

---

[60] There's a legend that George Washington threw a silver dollar across the Potomac. Scientists say it's impossible, of course; the river is too wide. But the scientists forget that, back then, a dollar went farther.

peace, and from there into weariness. And finally we sat on George Washington's lawn.

We looked across the brackish river to Maryland's forested riverbank.[61] Behind us stood a mansion radiating its owner's confidence that he'd set his nation on a good path. A house built around the ideas of grace and hospitality.

"George Washington," Sam-Bob said. "Go."

"Quitter," I said.

"Huh?"

"Are we still on the speed-play version?"

"No."

I looked up the hill at Mount Vernon: whitewashed blocks of wood with sand embedded in the paint to give them the impression of stone. Who is Washington? A man who thought appearance was, itself, reality? A man who believed manners show the real content of a person? A leader who believed that his rules should also apply to him?

"He's a quitter," I said again. "Pretty much the model quitter, in fact. Quitters lead so people can do well after they're gone. That's why the first thing General Washington did after he won the war was quit."

"Ah," Sam-Bob said. "He quit *after* he won the war. I think that's key."

I squinted at Sam-Bob. But he was done talking so I went on.

"In the 1700s, when generals won wars, they didn't quit, they ruled. But General Washington resigned and moved here. To this

---

[61] They made a rule that Maryland has to keep the view just like it was for George Washington. That way Virginians can gaze out from their condos at the forest across the river and think thoughts that are frontiersmanly and therefore noble. The Marylanders must conceal themselves under the forest canopy lest they distract the noble Virginians. But the Marylanders can still gaze between the branches at Virginia's condos and think depleted, suburban thoughts when they're in the mood.

very place, where he lived as a private citizen and encouraged his guests to carry on the work he'd started.

"He quit, and that may very well be why America is free today. In fact, George Washington quit twice. He came back years after retiring from the Army and served as a wildly popular president for eight years."

"Wildly popular?" Sam-Bob asked.

"Okay, I get it. Wooden teeth, wig, stilted smile—he was probably tamely popular, but the point is he was popular, and the other point—which is the main point—is that he quit."

I don't think this counted as Rorschaching, but Sam-Bob had an amused dimple at the corner of his mouth so I went on:

"But before he quit, he set the place up to run without him. That's what people need to learn. If you love someone or someplace, you will not make them depend on only you. Dictators and micro-managers need to learn from George Washington, who is probably the most famous double-quitter in the world. George Washington wanted people to outgrow him. But tyrants, on the other hand, cut everyone off at the knees so they can stand tall.

"Everyone should aspire to grow up and be irrelevant, Sam-Bob. That's my story and I'm sticking to it."

"You've got a man crush on George Washington," he said, with a wait-you-think-Sandra-Bullock-is-hot? inflection.

I ignored Sam-Bob's comment, hugged my knees, and looked across the Potomac. I thought of the president's complaint that he was alone with the American project. "Sam-Bob," I said, "do you think we have people like that anymore?"

"Like what? Irrelevant?"

"People who see politics as a minor role in the life of a statesman. Didn't our Founding Fathers intend to build a Nation—a whole society—with Government as just a small part?" I said, parroting the president. "If you asked George Washington what he did for America, wouldn't he talk first about his life as a surveyor, a soldier, a farmer, or a drafter of the constitution? And wouldn't he say that retiring was the most important thing he did as president?"

Sam-Bob grunted and I thought of Emerson, of John Brown, Frederick Douglas, and Thoreau. And what about George Whitefield, Jonathan Edwards, Harriet Beecher Stowe, Andrew Carnegie, Mark Twain, George Washington Carver, Thomas Edison, John Steinbeck, Albert Einstein, Martin Luther King, and Harper Lee? They were never in Government, were they? But, still, they shaped America—they took responsibility for the *idea* of America—as much as anyone. But where are they now? Have they all given it up and left the president alone to advocate for who we can be? And what of Franklin, Adams, Washington, Madison, Hamilton, and Jefferson? Citizens and statesmen first and political leaders second—people who bravely faced their country's foes, *and* people who had the courage to face their country herself, when she was in the wrong? Where have they all gone?

"Yo. Dude. Hello." Sam-Bob had stood. He offered his hand and pulled me to my feet.

"You didn't answer my question," I said.

"What? About your crush on men in wigs and tights?"

"I don't care what they wore," I said. "But do we have *people* like that now—great men in all walks of life? Do we have people like that anymore? And, without them, how can America stay America?"

"They had them, we have us," he said.

"But that's not good, Sam-Bob."

"Depends."

"On what?"

"Depends on you."

"You're not helping here, dude."

"They had their problems, we have ours. Do you really want to trade?"

We mounted our bikes again and retraced our ride.

"Why'd you call Thomas Jefferson a narcissist?" Sam-Bob asked finally, just before we cycled single-file onto the footbridge across the Potomac and back to DC. I thought about it while I rode, then I clipped the chain link with my handlebar because an oncoming cyclist crowded me. He wore product-endorsed spandex and had elbow rests on his bike so he could ride in the posture of a charging goat.

"Thomas Jefferson built his house as a monument to himself," I said, when we'd cruised down the other side and stopped to stare at his white, Roman-ish monument. "He built a wall in his study that he could twist around backward. His slaves would put food on it and spin it back. That way, Thomas Jefferson could lift his chicken livers or whatever off a little shelf on the wall and eat them without having to actually see the person who served his food.

"He built a silly French mansion on top of a hill and talked about freeing his slaves so he'd seem all noble. But his house—his little self-monument—cost so much they had to sell his slaves to pay it off when he died. One little man's ego-accessory, bought by a hundred men's bondage. He did free a couple of slaves, of course—it was the closest he came to admitting they were his own children."

"So much for the great men of the past," Sam-Bob said. "Glad to know how you feel about the man who wrote our 'dim documents'—the fine bronze man who stands here and gazes out across our national Mall."

"He stands here forlorn," I said, "looking over the heads of the niggling humans who traipse past to stare at him with their hungry kids. He's stuck, forever gazing across at George Washington's even bigger monument. It's like even Thomas Jefferson could never be quite good enough for Thomas Jefferson."

"And what about it?" Sam-Bob asked. "Do you give good old GW a free pass on the slave stuff just because he could quit like a champion?"

"He should have been a better quitter than he was," I said. "But at least he built his house for his guests and his family. Not as a living mausoleum for his own ego."

We stopped one more time on the National Mall, where a bunch of congressional staffers played kickball. One team wore neon green shirts that said *The Indiananators* in white letters, with *Indiananators* in a sort of cursive script. The other team wore black shorts and black shirts, except one that I'm pretty sure was navy blue.

"Tell me about them," Sam-Bob said.

"The Indiananators are self-conscious because the shirt vendor misprinted their shirts. They used white ink even after the whole office huddled around that jock guy who's "pitching"—the one who never heard the news that he doesn't live in a frat house anymore—and they've all assured the jock that they personally saw him select "black" from the drop-down menu when he ordered the shirts off the vendor's website, but now you can hardly read the shirts because they're white-on-neon-green but it was too late to get them reprinted before the first game so the team let it drop, but they still feel kind of pissed because they look silly out there when they were supposed to look all cool. But it's really just as well. *Indiananators* just looks dumb, because it's trying to be goofy, but it's not really, and what does it say about you if you even fail at being goofy?"

"Yikes," Sam-Bob said. "Good to know what you think of the shirts. What about the people? Any thoughts about the people?"

"The people?" I said. "Those people came here to fix the world. But it didn't work so they decided to play kickball. And now, even if they had a chance to save the world, they wouldn't know it because they're not looking for it. They just want to keep the corn growers happy so they can get elected again and keep playing kickball."

"Somebody's a little testy today," Sam-Bob said.

"I'd ask you to understand but, then, you've never sat and chatted with the president."

"Really?"

"You haven't, have you?"

"Many times."

"Huh?"

"I guarded Camp David, dude. That's how I got my start in biking—riding through the woods with the president."

That kind of shut me down. He should have told me that before so I wouldn't make a fool of myself.

We rode home and, while we locked up the bikes, I asked him another question. "Why do you call this Rorschach?"

"Because, when you make up stuff about strangers, you're not learning about them, you're learning about you."

I stared at him and he glanced up at me from where he sat on his heels fitting a U-lock through the spokes of his bicycle.

"Who taught you about all this Rorschach stuff anyway?" I asked.

"It's the G.I. Bill, man. I've been taking classes."

The Poem (II)

"Father, shall I go to work with you today?"

"Yes, Joel, I am overhauling several trucks this summer and I would like your help."

That day the lift falls for the first time and Joel uses a hand jack, with panicked deliberateness, to lift the truck from his groaning father.

"God has done this to make me more like Him," Father says of the crumbled bone in his wrist, now pinned together in a cast. "My selfishness will be crushed like my arm."

Joel hears this from a man in pain. A man who has never learned to be both weary and pleasant. A man who is always weary— to rest would have been the kindest thing he could do for his family—and Joel doubts.

Years later, pressed for creativity in class, Joel will remember this time and he will write:

Men

Men respect men who work.
Father tosses a paper bag over his shoulder.
He strides, boots pressing the irrepressible grass
then he ruptures the bag against the barrow
and powder hangs over it, in the still air.
No effort.

Joel tosses his sacks, too.
Eighty pounds of concrete shouldered against one ear
then eighty pounds against the other.
His collarbone strains and rallies to bolster the bags.
He strides. He ruptures them on the barrow, too.
No effort.

But Joel respects the load
with the respect of one man for another
who bears up under the same strain.
Respect? Yes. But not love, quite.

Do men love? Yes. But only while pretending not.
A persistent conversation that meant nothing, really.

Do men lust? Of course.
And they show it in snide comments among themselves.

Do they respect? Yes.
In a nod toward the guy who carries two bags, modestly
when he could have done three.

Are men infatuated? Yes.
And do they show it? Of course
but mostly while drunk.

But love? Men only love while pretending not.
"Yeah, she's all right," he says, slurping coke
from a newly cracked can, and then he squints at the sun.

But men do love.
They love each other, privately, while working.

And perhaps it shows
with your hand on my shoulder
a calloused finger snagging the fabric
when parting for a long time.
Will I see you again? Huskily. God knows.

Men love, deeply it seems, while pretending not.

Joel admits that Father's chronic anger has ended with his broken wrist. But Joel will say nothing of this during the time of his father's life.

The Span of My Worlds: A Milieu

A: The Vivid Imagination of a Vague Problem (II)

For the next three weeks my muscles held a tension that reminded me of a task that was not forgotten, even when I focused elsewhere.

The president's questions collided with the Rorschach game in my head until my brain foamed and threatened to spill over its edges. Who are we to each other, and who is responsible for our culture? I floated intergalactically again, with these new questions echoing ever louder in the silence. But there was no answer.

No one in my Government thought it was his job to decide our policy for detainees. So everyone appealed to the president. And no one takes responsibility for tending the nation we received from our forbearers. What a fine situation!

The president's questions agitated and scattered soda on a bit of vinegar that had pooled quietly in my brain. Something that may have once been a thought had reduced itself in my head to a vague unease that swirled beyond reach and haunted me.

So I picked up what tools I had and brought them to bear. I had, from time to time, tried to force this menace into a thought so I could fight it, man-to-man, with the clear tools of reason. But it would shimmer beyond reach, dispensing a vague sense of oozing doom, like a delirium that paralyzes you in a suspended land of terror to be smothered by something with no substance—freezing you in a place where a body may suffocate in the purest air.

When awake, I pretended this did not exist, but I fooled myself, creating distractions at the times when such things creep in:

turning on music as I dozed, or playing the radio while I drove. But now, in the pressure of the moment, I forced the wretch to speak. And it did speak, in a strange, iambic rhythm.

It is the nature of such a thing only to be told when you sharpen its edges beyond what they ever were. But maybe that's the purpose, after all, so I offer you the strange scene that follows:

(Begin Scene)

My father has left me his slithering city, built from stolen labor and hollow wood. He made me rich with his filthy funds, exploited his buyers, perpetrating crappy construction, and he abused the men who did his work—used men, abandoned and left to recover if they could.

But I tell his men they are free, and together we will wipe my father's stain from our land. We will wreck what he built, telling the cheated owners to join us, and work for the day when all that remains is pure. We are wrecking, tearing, until, in their frenzy, the men even wreck the cranes, all in their haste to crush our glassy city.

But I stand out above the mayhem. I raise my hand through the drifting grit and, in the ensuing silence, ask them: "Friends, why do you now break the tools? We must use them to destroy the old way, and only then shall we remove the tools and set ourselves free."

Then we work until all is wrecked, smelting the metal and pouring it back into the earth. And now we purify ourselves—each man purifying his brother with death—so only I am left, alone on the earth. I stand heroic and hold a sword, saved for myself. I watch the sun glint on its blade and I think of what is done, of all these sordid wrongs—man's wrongs—and I see that no one else remains. Only Joel stands here recalling them to mind. I brace the sword on the good earth and sigh, leaning upon it to pierce my chest and drain the blood of man from this earth.

But something remains. Must this sword linger and trouble a new race?

162

So I use a stone to grind the sword away—reducing my dagger to a shard. And with this shard I open my veins in peace, having purged myself with this last shred of our evil world. Freeing the globe from our hideous sin. But in my hallucined haze, the matriarch of a new race comes. She picks up the shard, weighs it in her palm, and closes her fingers upon it. Then she shows it to her wondering child and, even as my blood settles in the clay, I see that our plague will stay, everlasting upon the earth.

And, deep within, something sinks, gaunt and hollow with the pointlessness of it all.

(End Scene)

B: The Phone Call

In this scene, I lost myself. But I had to recover it or I couldn't know who talked with the president, and it would become false for me to speak.

So I called my mom and, while the phone rang, I picked at the vines that squeezed themselves through the cracks in my concrete steps. When Mom answered, I told her I was stressed by some things and I wanted to come home to see her and my sister Naomi.

C: The Handoff

There is no vacation from a job like mine. The world does not stop. You work from vacation—doing shoddy work and having a shoddy vacation—or you trust someone else to do the job while you're gone—someone who has another job of her own and who is easily outmaneuvered by the bureaucracy because she does not understand your issues and, naturally, does not care as much as you do because she has other issues that she cares about most.

Jamie is one of the best co-workers I have had. She does good work and everyone likes her. On time. Respectful. Well-spoken.

Confident. She wears a splendid collection of fitted blouses and, when I talked of terrorism with her, once, I thought I'd forgotten Janet and I wanted to ask her out. But I hadn't and I didn't.

The only problem is that Jamie doesn't have a lick of sense about making policy. She's one of the splendid people who makes the world go round. But she only does it once someone else has decided the direction it should turn, how fast, and on what axis.

After deciding I couldn't afford a work-from-home vacation, Nick asked Jamie to cover for me while I was gone. I explained to her how the taxpayers were paying to feed crap Islamic theology to terror suspects, not because we thought the theology was true but because we thought it would make us safer. And I told her how no one really knew how this was done, by what rules, and whether it worked. In fact, no one even knew whether it was legal or constitutional. And I told her how important it was for us to answer these questions—but that it irritated pretty much everyone for me to be asking them. And Jamie got it. Or at least she got that I cared and she cared, too, because she could see that I had gone about it all for the right reasons.

I told her that I wouldn't check my work email on vacation but that I would pick up the phone if she called and that she should not hesitate to call. Also, I would check my personal email and she could send me a check-your-other-email note there if something needed my attention. Then I said she should keep Nick up to speed on everything and that I trusted her judgment.[62] You see, every vacation has communication rules—you've got to set them before you leave and then follow them because, like it or not, your job is still *your* job when you're on leave.

Then I left. I removed my laptop from my bag and placed it directly on the belt. I removed my shoes, wallet, cell phone, and keys

------

[62] This is not strictly true, of course, but saying it is the price of an out-of-touch vacation.

164

to give the screeners a clean view of my shadowy, naked self and then I contemplated how to orally inflate my life vest by blowing into the red tube that would dangle conveniently from my shoulder in the unlikely event of a water landing. I gazed mesmerized at the overlapping plates on the luggage carousel, then I stood, wrist draped over the handle of my roller bag on the curb of the Rick Husband International Airport, named for Amarillo's tragic son: a former chief of astronaut safety, commander of a shuttle that had unfortunately strewn itself across Texas years ago.

D: The Car Ride

"You've lost weight," Mom said as she drove us out past the Amarillo tiltrotor plant, then signaled her merge tentatively onto Interstate 40.

"That was on purpose," I said. "I was collecting pounds in my cubicle. How have you been?"

"It was dry this spring and a freeze killed most of the wheat. So there wasn't much of a harvest."

"I'm sorry to hear."

"We had some good rains in July, though, so the maize looks okay."

"That's good," I said.

"And the disaster package looks like it will come through this year so people are doing fine."

"But how are you?"

"Naomi and I have been repainting the living room and we'll have Grandmother over for dinner this evening. She comes over most evenings. Or sometimes I take something into town and we eat it there with her. How have you been? We weren't expecting you home this summer."

"I'm fine, Mom. I just got tired out and needed a break."

"I know you've been working hard at the Pentagon and all."

I said nothing and I thought about the deficit.

"How's Janet?"

"I don't know, Mom. We broke up."

"I know. But do you stay in touch?"

Mom drove while I stared out the window. A wisp of dark smoke ran alongside the road and disappeared in the distance. I traced it back from the orange horizon to where it pixilated into a million starlings outside my window, flying in line to a place none of them knew.

"There's no point staying in touch, Mom. She didn't really leave the door open."

"She's a great girl, though. You should call her sometime."

I said nothing. Naomi rode in the back seat reading *The Lord of The Rings: The Two Towers*.

"Mom, I had a meeting with the president."

"You did! That's great, Joel. Sometimes things are a little tough here with your dad gone and all, but I want you to know we're proud of what you're doing in Washington."

"Mom, he wants me to give him some advice. He wants to know what I really think he should do. Not just on Defense or Counterterrorism. He wants to know how he can get in touch with what's going on in America—to change some of the things that are dragging us down."

"Joel, that's wonderful! I can't think of a better person for him to ask."

My family has always thought good things happen to me by accident, without trying.

"Please do me a favor, though, and don't mention it to anyone," I said. "I've got to figure out what to do and I'd rather not have everyone congratulating me or trying to give me advice."

"Sure, Joel. Naomi, did you hear that?"

"Yes, Mom, I heard."

"I thought you were reading about Frodo and Sam in Mount Doom," I said.

"I was multitasking," she said. "And they don't get to Mount Doom until the third book."

"Okay, then, Legolas and Gimle counting corpses at Helm's Deep."

"That's in the middle of the book, I'm near the end."

"Okay, I give up. I just didn't know if you heard what I said about the president."

"Which president?"

"President …?"

She laughed. "I know which president, Joel. Take a breath. You're in Texas."

"Okay, maybe just don't mention it to your friends."

I still sounded stressed in principle but, ever since Naomi laughed, I knew I'd be fine; I would meet with the president and tell him what he needed to hear—and this time I would do it without barricading myself at Harper's Ferry and shouting at him in my head.

"So, Naomi, what are you doing?" I asked.

"I'm reading *Lord of the Rings: The Two Towers*," she said. "I'm near the end, after Helm's Deep. Remember?" Then she muttered loud enough for me to hear, "They really do knock your brain a little flat there in DC, don't they?"

"Oh, stop!" I said. "Are you excited about college? Going to succeed where I failed? Going to straighten Wheaton out once and for all? When do you leave?"

"Fifteen days and fourteen hours."

"That's rather precise, isn't it?"

"I have a counter on my phone."

"Ah, yes," I said. "I have a phone."

"Let me see it." I handed her my phone. "When are you meeting with the president?"

"I don't know for sure."

"About when?"

"In two-and-a-half or three weeks."

She muttered, "Okay, let's say August 25." Then she asked, "What time would you say?"

"I don't know. Last time it was six in the evening."

"August 25 at six p.m. Okay, there. You're meeting the president in sixteen days twenty-two hours and … twenty-three seconds." She handed me the phone and I watched the seconds tick off.

"Did you know that *Lord of the Rings: The Two Towers* is the first movie I ever saw in a theater?" I asked.

"Yup. Because it came out two months after Dad died and, with him gone, who's to say you couldn't watch movies anymore?"

"Ouch," I said, and I felt Mom sigh at the wheel. She always thought Dad was too strict about the movies, but she hates for us to imply that our lives got better when he died.

It's not true, of course—that our lives got better. There's a hole in our lives where Dad was and we each live privately with an image of a transmission dropped into his chest. Had he neglected the safety catch? Had Luis neglected it? Why did the hydraulic hose break where the farm store had repaired it last time? Does any of it make any difference now? And, since it's so sucky having your dad killed, shouldn't you enjoy that you've lost the bad things about him, too? Like hating movies? But we should respect Mom, of course. And we should respect Dad, too, even if he is dead.

I decided to talk with Naomi about this in private. There was no need for her to throw these barbs at Mom.

"Also," Naomi said, "it's because you watched the movie that you think the Battle of Helm's Deep comes at the end of the book instead of in the middle."

"Then I defer to greater expertise," I said.

D: Wood Cutouts

Mom turned the car into our driveway and I saw that the gravel had furrowed under a succession of tires until the rainwater ran along the road and gullied the tracks. As Mom drove, she kept her tires on a ridge between the gullies to prevent the car from busting its oil pan. Her headlights swept the farmhouse in the twilight and I saw that my aunt Sandy had applied her wood stencils, her scroll saw, and her router to Mom's house in her recent craze for negative spaces. Blue dummy shutters bordered the windows; one window featured double-heart cutouts and the other showed cutout doves with their meekly rounded heads.

Tell me something: that board had no heart until you cut it out. You only know it was there because now it's gone. Why is this? Was there not a fist in that board, or an eagle to cut out? Or does your saw only find doves and missing hearts?

Mom stepped into the house first. She switched on the front light for Naomi and me to lug my bags onto the porch, and I knew from the damp smell of ragweed that Naomi had mowed the yard today because I was coming home. I smiled at her, carrying my bag, knocking her knees against it while she walked.

"You can roll that bag," I said. She plunked it on the sidewalk, then roller-shoved it over for me to carry the rest of the way. Then she retrieved her own bag from the car. I looked back and waited for her, glowing in the trunk light until she slammed it, dipping the car's shocks with her force. A girl's voice in a woman's body, black-and-white in the gray evening but wearing a purple backpack. "Did you know that this lawn is the first time I knew I could make the world a better place?" I asked for no reason.

The Lawn

"Granddaddy taught me to use his Moz All," Jeremy tells Joel.

"What's a mozall?" Joel asks.

"It's Granddaddy's mower, stupid. Uncle Bobby had to go away to the hospital and I told him I can mow as good as Uncle Bobby. And Granddaddy's Moz All is the same as ours so I can use ours now, too, and mow the place myself."

Joel is impressed and watches while Jeremy drags the ancient mower from the shed, flattening a path through the weeds. Jeremy unscrews a plug, declares it low on oil, finds a bottle, and dumps it full. Then he opens the gas cap and fills it from a rusted tank overhead.

"Now, before you pull the cord, you have to choke it," he says. "Use full choke until it fires, then half choke." He pushes a lever on the engine then steps on the mower deck.

"You put your foot here because, if you put your foot anywhere else, the blade will chop it off," he says. "It's very dangerous."

He pulls and the blade spins in full view. His hair flops forward, blonde in the sun, and sticks to the sweat on his forehead. He'd had an argument with Mom and she didn't tell Father, but she stopped buzzing his hair with the clippers like she did for Joel because she didn't want Father to punish him for arguing about his hair again when Jeremy had more important things to learn than short hair.

"This mower is good for weeds because a safety guard would get in the way," Jeremy says. He tugs the cord again, the twisted belt spins, and the motor gives a poof. Jeremy tweaks the choke, then pulls again. The Moz All shudders, then it rattles, and stands there trembling and fanning specks of dirt.

"Go inside!" Jeremy yells. "This mower could hurt you!" So Joel watches from a window while Jeremy pushes through the weeds. He runs the mower aground in a hidden gully and grinds a half circle in the dirt.

Afterwards, they examine a dent in the shed from a rock thrown by the mower. Jeremy's jeans are spattered with mutilated weeds and, as they walk, grasshoppers spring out, rolling ahead in a wave, forced to flee in fear from their shredded habitat.

Jeremy captures one from a stray stem and picks the legs from its body while they sit on the steps. "We could make Mom a lawn like Granddaddy's," he says.

"But Daddy says he won't be bothered with watering a pretty town lawn."

"We could water it ourselves."

"But it would die if we go on a trip or if we grow up and leave someday."

Jeremy thinks about this and tries to lift the wings from his naked grasshopper.

"We could make a native lawn like Granddaddy's. No one would have to water it because it's the same grass that grows in the pasture."

"But where would we get the seed?"

"I saw some in the Burpee catalog. We could maybe ask Mom to order some."

"But we can't just plant grass in the weeds can we?"

"We'd hoe the weeds, stupid. Or maybe I could use the rototiller."

He holds up his bug-eyed grasshopper, scrunching to look it in the face before wiping a brown drip from its mouth. "Quit drooling, little buddy. Tobacco is a nasty habit." He turns to Joel. "Let's go ask Mom to ask Daddy for some dirt to fill the holes."

"Look what I found in the sink," Mom says when they enter and the screen door has settled from its diminishing crashes. She holds a rock the size of her fist.

"How'd it get there?" Joel asks.

"Probably through that hole," Mom says, pointing to a ripped screen over the sink. "It's a good thing I had opened the window or it would have broken the glass, too."

Jeremy is stricken. "You won't tell Daddy, will you? I'll find a way to fix the screen."

"We'll figure something out," Mom says. "What were you coming to ask me?"

"We want some dirt," Joel says, being better composed than Jeremy.

Mom's lip twitches. "What do you want dirt for?"

"We're going to make you a lawn," Joel says, "but we need dirt to make it flat."

Mom looks out at the mowed weeds. "I would like that," she says. "But the yard is sloped now so you'll need something to hold the dirt up at the bottom if it's going to stay flat."

"Like what?" Joel asks.

"Maybe you could use those old railroad ties stacked by the shed," she says. "Then I can ask your dad for some dirt."

"Yes!" Jeremy says, and they run out, crashing the screen door again, to study the cracked, tarry, old ties. Mom would make things okay with Daddy about the torn screen.

The Pen that Probes a Wound

I ate dinner, chatted with Naomi about her worship band, said goodnight to Mom, and climbed the stairs to the attic, even though Mom told me I could stay across the hall in the other bedroom where I could stand without bumping my head on the ceiling. "No thanks," I said. "I like my old hobbit hole." And I winked at Naomi.

Walking up the stairs, I saw that Aunt Sandy had kept the cutout hearts and the doves. She'd painted them and mounted them over the handrail opposite the senior pictures Mom took for Josiah, Jeremy, and me when we graduated. She'd left a gap for Seth, still believing he would take his GED and qualify for her patient wall of pride. And she'd added a picture of Naomi. I stopped and looked. Naomi wore a touch of lipstick, with her hair un-straightened but glossed somehow, and her eyes held a Mona Lisa smile that spoke faintly of mischief and of judgment for the matte-eyed doves mounted opposite her.

In my room, I slid open the roll-top desk I'd rescued all those shriveled years ago when Grandmother upgraded her furniture. It smelled of dust and I wiped it clean with my palm. Then I sat there and read Louis L'Amore—a brave story of crossing the ocean long ago—until my eyelids drooped. I wondered vaguely what my office did about detainee policy today and I smiled to find something so insignificant in my head.

In the morning I sat on the gray lawn, plucking at the persistent perennials in the native grass, until the sun rose in silence. I sat at peace with the president's problem and it revealed itself a bit to me.

To speak well with another person, you must understand who he is. You must shape every message to its receiver. I had learned this. But I didn't know the president or, more precisely, I knew him only a little. Then, sitting there on the dawn-lit plain, I discovered something else: I knew myself even less—my knowledge of the president was a great silence with a few clear bits of sound, while my knowledge of myself was a great, cacophonous noise.

Once upon a time, I played my role in a neat family that fit into a neat world: definite groups with definite edges between them. Clean Baptists left alcohol alone and so they knew they weren't Methodists.

Even the jokes went stale: Why do Baptists do church twice on Sundays? Well, Baptist preachers have to reprove their people more, or the Baptists will sin fearlessly, knowing that no sin is big enough to unsave a soul in God's eyes. Methodists, on the other hand? A Methodist preacher can trust his people because the Methodist God always cocks an eyebrow at His people, asking whether they've changed their mind about going to heaven after all.

But that's not me anymore. Now I live with people who have drifted in upon a city where we don't belong. Simultaneous citizens of everyplace and no-place, all floating on an unsettled sphere of our own creation where every island drifts and a body cannot say a thing is here or there because the thing has drifted, so they only describe the sorts of things that tend to occur in such places and they trend over a range of patterns with characteristic deviations from their average while observed from a drifting post, and the shifting methodologists argue for a median to displace the mean old average as a center to tie the shifting things to an anchor that ties itself only to the mean thing to which it is attached. And they feel superior because they've overcome the old divisions.

When dad died, I left summer school, then returned to college after the funeral to escape my maddened mind. I worked methodically at the algebra equations—working them slowly in a spare Chicago dorm, then moving through more problems in the for-extra-practice book, even though I had done them all the year before at the roll-top desk in my room.

Jeremy and Josiah were home that summer and they worked with Mom to sort stuff out. What else to do? To sit with my family beyond the requisite week of grief would be more than a body could bear. The grief goes on but, after that week, no one speaks to you of it; they've exhausted their script for the families of the dead and anything more makes them stupid. They pretend to understand, but they cannot understand. And they say gawdawful things when they say anything: It's all part of God's plan. God means it for the best. Your dad is in a better place now, Joel. Sometimes the greatest miracle of all is that God sustains us in our grief.

Keep your saccharine poison and let me grieve. My dad died. So I do math. Okay?

But somehow, sitting there on the solid Texas earth before breakfast, I looked at my problem with the president and saw quite clearly: more than not knowing who the president is, I had nothing to say because I did not know myself. I couldn't brush off a father's death with platitudes and, while I did algebra, my body, without asking permission, quietly gave up on God. Isn't that more rational than to plead with a God who seems bad? How, after all, do you trust a God who lets a father die, then bolts His door against the cries of the orphan? He was not there. When I tried in the pits of grief to hear Him, He spoke not a word.

But, when God was gone, I found no one in his place. So I followed a hollow god. I did the things of life like I was supposed to do them. They were empty, but they were not pain. And the people thought I was okay because I did calibrated Christian trash-talk at the bowling alley and I mouthed the lyrics to pop songs that only seemed edgy at Wheaton. When the other students returned for the fall, they asked how my summer had been and I said, "My dad died. Thanks for bringing it up." They laughed, then discovered later it wasn't a joke.

Why do I look back on painful times that are gone? On the family we used to be? On children who have melted and regrown themselves as someone else? Those times were good. And they were crap. But they are gone. So why?

To see America, you have to look at it from one place and not from another. To look at it from everywhere is to not see it at all. And now I knew I was blind, because I did not, myself, know who I was. I did not know where I stood.

But sitting there with ragweed smeared on my fingertips, I squinted at the newly risen sun, and saw clearly back to a childhood that was mine—to a person that is somehow still me.

I returned to the attic where I'd worked the lonely problems of so many Saxon books. Where I'd written adolescent stories to revive my mind after days of mechanicking. Writing at the expense of sleep—consoling and compounding the miseries of the day. I sat there again and wrote vignettes from my past. And then I saw myself quite clearly—a child in the family we used to be.

I pulled a string that dangled in my memory, then pulled and pulled until the whole thing fell loose as I sat and cried and tried to write the pictures—of my father on the mountain, a log cabin that crashed, hopscotch and dead cattle, the lawn where Jeremy and I made our world better—and I saw the family gathered earnestly each night, Bibles draped over our childish legs. Mom and Naomi wondered if I was unraveling. I could see it in their eyes when I ran two pens dry and then asked for more paper after the first fifty sheets were gone. And I saw fear in the micro-glances Mom used to stop Naomi before she talked.

A computer works in the office but only a pen works on the heart. I numbered my papers and circled the numbers, then I peeled the pages off when they were full and dropped them to the floor. When my brain froze or my hand cramped more than I could take, I stopped and gathered the pages into a stack at the top of my desk where they sat under a broken-antlered deer I had claimed as a memory of my grandma when she died. I wondered whether I was unraveling, too. But I went on. I wrote, straight through for two days.

In my memory, I killed a hoard of rats, harvested a crop of maize, advised my mom against shooting a bathtub, lost our calf to a broken leg, rescued cattle from a bizarre bondage they had invented for themselves, learned supply-and-demand from the Soviets, and I watched my father work Seth to bitterness. I discovered buried treasure, I remembered the time my father apologized, and I saw my mom there, deescalating it all while no one noticed. I remembered the times without bitterness and wrote them down.

Did any of this tell me who we are to each other in America? Did it tell me who is responsible for our culture?

One image from Jesus is still popular: to remove a splinter from my neighbor's eye, I must first remove the beam from my own. Only then will I see my neighbor's eye clearly. Many people have torn offending content from the Bible; they have broken the Bible and left it for dead. But they still pick out this morsel from the corpse—it seems, as a society, hypocrisy is the only sin we still agree on.

Before I blame my countrymen for abandoning their culture—before I presume to measure the president and declare him lacking—I must measure myself. I must find the child I was and perhaps see that he has kept something I have lost—something wise to offer the president.

The Wisdom of a Child

Father has gone, at his own expense, to learn advanced maintenance for the new generation of diesels. It's the way the world is going and, once he gets certified, he will raise his rates. You can't get the old diesels anymore and so, pretty soon, the learn-it-as-you-go mechanics will be gone. You'll need more than wrenches, a parts-washer, and a creeper; more than an air compressor, a sand-blaster, and a truck jack: you'll need a diagnostic computer to tell you which chip to replace—which isn't mechanicking at all.

After two years, the regulations say, only certified people can touch the new trucks, which is terrible because certified mechanics may not even be mechanics; maybe they're just certified. They could work on the trucks and never know which direction the engine turns. No need to listen for the cylinder that misses. No need to pull the injectors and scratch the carbon to see which one is bad (do they teach you *that* in the certification course?). No need to look at an overheating engine and see that the fan clutch has failed (they're electric fans now, anyway, and you replace the fan motor if one goes bad. And there's a diagnostic for that, too, probably.).

"They won't stop until they've taken every *man* in this country and reduced him to a *technician*," Father says. Then he grasps a suitcase with his soap-scrubbed calluses. He kisses Mom on the mouth, then Mom shuts the door to preempt an opportunistic house-fly, and Joel watches the wisp of dust behind Father's tires as he drives away.

So Father is gone. Then Josiah sees something out the window. A coyote, which should know better than to come through in daylight, trotting like his path just happens to fall between the people house and the chicken house. He'll take one. By the neck. For the road, since it happens to be there. He winks, tips his hat, and trots on.

But such a thing cannot be. You bastard! That chicken is human!

Josiah shouts. And Joel runs with him for the door. The coyote turns and stops briefly, a Rhode Island Red dangling from his mouth. *Something wrong?*

"Hey! Get out!" the boys shout.

Mom has a gun. She hates guns—she has only gotten it for backup, but she lowers it because the boys run shouting between her and the coyote. He has dropped the chicken and he will leave. There is nothing to shoot.

"We got the chicken, Mom," they say. And they have. "Where can we put it?"

Jeremy hugs the chicken, its head pulled into itself. It huddles still, then pushes a claw against his ribs.

"Why don't you put it in the bathtub," Mom says.

The bathtub? Of course, in the bathtub. And four anxious heads peer over the edge to see how the chicken has fared.

"Is he okay?" Joel asks. The chicken spasms.

"It might be best to kill it," Mom says. Of course. They should kill it. Because it will die anyway. But how?

"I could wring its neck," Mom says. But she knows she won't. "Or I could shoot it."

Joel looks on with concern. Mom can forget important things and Dad helps with that. Only now Dad is gone.

"You can't shoot it," he says.

Mom looks at him. "Oh?"

"It would make a hole in the bathtub," he says, and Mom stifles a smile.

"We would take it outside first," she says.

Josiah snorts. "Of course."

"No one would shoot a chicken in the *bathtub*," Jeremy says.

And Joel sees that he has said a stupid thing. They will say nothing of it, though, and he has determined that it must not be spoken of again.

Then the chicken solves their problem herself by falling limp from her spasm, and the boys cast her away from the house, beyond wafting distance.

Only the story has not ended, nor even reached its climax. On Sunday, Joel's family eats after-church roast at Grandmother's house and, upon their arrival, Grandmother talks on the telephone, cord stretched around the doorframe to the next room. And Joel hears her tell of a child who thought his mother would shoot a chicken in a bathtub.

Joel is undone. In town, one woman calls another and they tell each other of the stupidest kid in the county. A radio host chuckles when his staff places a note in front of him. "This just in … oh, ho, ho, this is a good one, folks. This kid … oh, boy, we've got a dim bulb here!" he says, and throughout the realm people pull their chairs up to the radio and listen. And their sticky-faced children snicker.

Tears drip from Joel's chin while the perpetrator, his formerly loving grandmother, squeezes him in mock comfort, telling him he has made a wise and intelligent remark to protect his mother, foretelling the unintended consequences of indoor gunfire and all. Even Mom has betrayed him. (How did *Grandmother* hear it?) And Joel sees that the world's two gentlest souls have abandoned him.

So he sits on Grandmother's green couch, moving his mouth over silly words in *The Butter Battle Book* while the family eats. He imagines he has not heard it when the cruel family laughs over a joke at the table and they tell Grandmother her roast is the best roast ever when it is the same stupid roast she makes every Sunday, with the carrots and the nasty onions, so what's so special about that?

The Brother-Sister Conversation

After supper my first day home, Naomi persuaded me to start a movie with her and the next day we finished it. Then, on day three, she caught me alone after breakfast when Mom had stepped out to feed our table scraps to the chickens. She stood herself, fist on hip, at the foot of the stairs and said, "Joel, you've been here two days and you've done nothing with me. You've hardly even gone outside and the weather is perfect."

"Hey, we watched a movie," I said. "A two-night movie—*The Return of the King*."

"More like *The Return of the President* is what I'd say you were thinking about," she said. "Here, I've got a riddle for you: He sees his family without seeing his family. Who is he?"

"Ouch," I said. "Naomi, I've spent a lot of time in my room thinking about our family."

"Then I've got another riddle," she said: "He rolls his eyes around backward to see what's in front of him. Who is he?"

"Hey, you can stop now!" I said, genuinely hurt. "Let's do something together."

"Well, now, it's kind of you to offer," she said, and paused reflectively. "Doing something together? That's a good idea. I'm glad you thought of it. First of all, I'm going to show you the tornado that nearly tore our place down—the one I told you about on the phone but you haven't asked about since you came home."

So I walked out of the house behind my little sister. She was pretty. I'd noticed it before. But her sarcasm gave her an edge I hadn't seen. She ran across our small pasture, toward a gap in the middle of the barn, her ponytail bobbing in the wind. Then I caught up and we stood between the two ends of the building, where the tornado had sliced it like you'd cut out the middle of a log fallen across the trail.

"You know, I started milking a cow right here when I was seven years old," I told her.

"Yup. I know," she said. "And you walked barefoot through the snow, uphill both directions, leaving blood in your tracks." She said it, but the fire had gone out of her voice.

"How close were you when the tornado hit?"

"I was in the house with Mom."

"Were you scared?"

"Kind of."

"Precise tornado, huh?" I said. "Taking out the middle of the barn like that and being so tidy about it."

"It couldn't have done a better job if we'd stood out here and given directions to the tornado driver," she said.

That gave me the absurd image of an old man sitting atop the cloud, driving it cautiously with two levers, squinting through half-glasses at his work.

"Ha!" I said. "We could use a tornado like that to clean up a few things around here, couldn't we?"

"Yup," she said.

"What would you do if you could drive a tornado?" I asked.

"Besides go into the demolition business, make a ton of money, and build a house somewhere so my brothers would come home and live there with Mom and me?"

"Yes," I said. "Besides that."

"I'd probably hover outside your house, give you a list of demands, and twist your car around in little circles until you met them."

"And if I didn't meet them?"

"Then I'd drop it kind of hard."

"And what are your demands?"

She sat down in the grass. "First, I demand that you sit here," she said, and I sat.

We sat a long time, until the flush of wit was gone.

"Joel," she said. "Why don't you believe in God anymore? Is it because Dad died?"

"Maybe," I said. "Or maybe it's because I went to Africa. I don't always know."

"Will you come to church with Mom and me tomorrow? We're going to the Baptist Church now. I'm playing a piano special for the offering."

"Sure," I said. "I would love to hear you play."

"Jeremy and Josiah didn't go to church with us when they came in June."

"I'm sorry. I'd love to go." I paused and we both saw the last tint of morning orange drain from the clouds. I looked at Naomi. Finally, I winked and asked, "Will you set my car down now?"

"Sure. I think I'll go pick on someone else," she said. "Seth's junker isn't worth my time so maybe I'll play with Jeremy's car. He's got himself a new Lexus that should twist nicely."

"Remind me not to get crossways with you."

"Remind yourself," she said. We got up and she draped my arm around her shoulder, took my phone, stood facing away from the barn with me, and snapped our picture. Then she swiped and tapped. "Thirteen days until you meet the president," she said, handing the phone back. My phone's screen was now a shot of Naomi and me standing in the middle third of our old milking barn.

The Joke at Someone's Expense

As a boy on the farm, in the barn, my childhood-self learned many things—things no one would say aloud. He learned from watching the patterns.

For instance, if you grow extra beans in the garden, you can give them away. You say, "Would you like a mess of beans?" and people know it's a gift. But if you offer "a pound of beans," then you're selling them. But selling is just for outsiders who think farmers are quaint and they buy stuff like they'd tip an odd performer at the circus.

Also, there's chores versus work. They seem the same but they're not: chores are around the house; you have to do them but you don't get paid. But work is away from the house and you get paid for it. Also, chores take a little time every day—maybe thirty minutes or maybe an hour—but, with work, it goes on and never ends; you just get tired and stop so you can sleep and work more tomorrow. Work is repairing trucks at Father's shop or helping the neighbors with their harvest. Work is not for children.

But Joel has had chores since he can remember. Locking the cow in her pen at night so she'll make good milk without the taste of pasture weeds and then, in the morning she will trot joyfully, udder swaying, to be milked. She tilts her neck, fitting her stubbed horns between the bars, and falls in upon the feed, ignoring the annoyance when Joel clicks the stanchion shut to prevent an ill-timed retreat. Joel leans against her hind quarter, shifting her weight and moving the near leg clear of her teats. He dusts the night's dirt from her udder then, sitting on his stool, squeezes his forearms numb, pressing a gallon of milk through nature's pin-holes. Today will be no problem; Joel is on time.

But Buttercup keeps an unforgiving schedule. Once the feed is gone, she will abruptly withdraw what milk is left, set her feet against the stanchion, wait briefly for Joel to notice, then urinate prodigiously. At this, Joel will respond in haste, seizing the manure scoop, and directing Buttercup's yellow cascade away from the milk. Then he will look at the milk and search his memory to see whether he'd gotten the bucket out of range before the urine struck. And he will decide whether to cast his morning's work among the weeds.

When, after many months, the milk has dried up, father will send Buttercup to live with the neighbor's herd and, some months later, she will sequester herself far in the pasture and be found licking a wide-eared calf, staggering under her caresses. A calf who nurses from the same udder, bracing his forefeet to slam it impatiently with his head. A calf who grows to four-hundred pounds, then lies broken in the corral.

Father, Joel, and Seth look to see what is wrong. The calf stands and one leg buckles under him. He stumbles, then stands again on three legs, ventilating through flared nostrils. "Don't bother him," Father says. "His leg is broken." But, as Seth walks away, the calf charges madly.

"Watch out!" Joel yells. Seth looks in shock as his pet runs and tears its leg. He watches in horror and climbs the fence to escape, off the top into un-supporting air. Behind him, the calf crashes its head into the steel rods and Seth drops hard on his knees. He stands and dusts his jeans while their weary father laughs. He laughs and laughs until he weeps with mirth. Seth glances up weakly and Joel looks at them both. With Dad, few things are funny, but those few contain all the pent-up hilarity of the universe.

In the morning, father seats himself with the family for breakfast. He has awoken himself laughing at three a.m. and he retells the story over breakfast, mimicking Seth's late looks of horror: one when he sees the calf bearing down on him, and the other, a half second later, when Seth feels himself climbing and falling through the un-supporting air.

Mom, eyes tearing from the contagion of their father's mirth, looks at Seth and eye-smiles to him, assuring him that there is no mockery. And Seth reserves for himself a dark chuckle at their father's amusement.

The calf could never comprehend that to heal is to suffer and, having lived shy of the usual time on earth, Joel finds him dead at the end of the lane to await the dealer in used creatures. This is their father's doing.

Buttercup bawls for two days, like a cow in heat, then she trots joyfully, again, to be milked. With no calf to share Buttercup's bounty, Mom picks up the phone. "Would you like a bit of milk?" she asks. "We have some extra."

The Frisbee

Jonah was going to Tarshish. But who cares that he was going there? The point is that he got thrown overboard on his way and then got swallowed by a fish, right? Jonah never cared about Tarshish. But then he did care. He cared because Tarshish was *not* Nineveh, and Jonah hated Nineveh. Ergo, *he found a ship going to Tarshish; he paid the fare, and went down into it, to go with them to Tarshish from the presence of the Lord.* Jonah took all his Nineveh crap and threw it at Tarshish.

That's what I did with my roommate Nathan the December after Dad died. We had a grueling week of tests and it was my last chance to rescue a rough semester of grades. So did I focus on my tests? No.

I discovered my Frisbee. And I threw it with Nathan for hours, mesmerized at how it bobbed in the air, at how it flew straight for so far then slumped off to the side. A whistling cold front hit Tuesday of finals' week and I threw the Frisbee hard into the wind. I threw it like I meant to destroy Nathan's face and he urged me on. "Bring it! Throw it! Don't let this silly-ass bastard of a storm beat you." And his words garbled in the twisting air. My eyes watered from the cold—from the glittering snow-light—and I remembered one winter when our neighbors, the Hodsons, got a shipment of cattle, who had pink-eye, and their eyeballs froze from watering in the cold.

I threw like I intended to behead Nathan with a discus. Then, with the form of a French waiter balancing his tray, Nathan would lift the Frisbee from where it hovered and bobbed in the air. I would squint at him like an enemy while he snapped it back hard at me to out-speed the wind. Frost grew on his whiskers, icing and thawing with each breath, and finally freezing into crystals that grew and dangled under his nose. I held out my numb palm, heard the flat impact, and smiled at the damage his disk did to my hand. Then I flung it back at him.

We did this for hours that week. Then I wrote my tests while biting my lip under the conviction that x *must* equal y—with x being the constant Frisbee pain in my hand and y the variable pain where I bit my lip to balance it out. That was the year of my first literary feat: for two hours in class I wrote a comprehensive survey of Western history and literature since A.D. 1500—twelve pages of verse that garnered an A-plus from a teacher who hated me in particular, for my attitude.

Why did I cower in these memories now, in Texas? Jonah had an urgency for Tarshish because it was *not* Nineveh. I threw the Frisbee because it was *not* the test. I wrote about my childhood because it was *not* the president's problem. But, however hard he made it for himself, Jonah *would* go to Nineveh. He knew it the whole time. I am certain.

My memories swirled and churned across time until my problem snapped into focus and the answer sat before me. Janet. Because Janet had always been at peace with the griefs that, for me, were too much. Because she could hear me and sort the best of me from the worst better than I could ever do it for myself.

I thought of Naomi, too, and of her books. I needed a fellowship of the ring—someone to throw a Frisbee with me until I could face the test.

Janet was wise. She could tell me about myself so I would understand it. Who else can do a thing like that?

But Janet broke up with me. In February. At sunset. Just past the golf course on Hains Point, where I sat dry-eyed on a retaining wall that stood crumbling against the everlasting Potomac. She loved me, she said, and she broke it off because she loved God more than me and because I didn't believe in God. And then she switched churches so she could go on believing without me.

Why did I still go to church when I saw that there was no God? Hope, I guess. Hope that I was wrong and that I might still discover something true. Besides, the best people I knew were Christians. Hypocrites, of course, because they fell short of their ideals. But they fell short respectably and they were good to me. They can tell you what they believe and they didn't make it up; it's something they received—from tradition and from scriptures— they'll tell you what it is and they'll accept you without making you believe it.[63] How could I leave a place like that?

____

[63] Something the Baptists and the Methodists never quite learned.

The Call for Help

On Thanksgiving, after an excessive lunch, Father leaves to finish an overhaul he has committed to the county for its winter fleet. In the rest of the world, people laze when it snows, but, in Sampson, Texas, the crews plow through the night, then the farmers rise at dawn and tow enormous rolls of hay over the ice because cattle cannot graze through the snow. And the county relies on its contracted mechanic to ensure the fleet is fit.

On this tryptophan afternoon, Mom answers the phone.

"Sure," she says. "I'll send Joel." She turns to me. "That was the Hodsons. Can you take your dad's welding trailer to the West Pasture? They've got cattle in trouble."

"And they need a welder?" Joel asks.

He finds Mr. Hodson the Elder and Mr. Hodson the Younger wrestling two mud-crusted cattle in their corral. The Younger's hat lies flat in the mud with a nasty hoof-print in it, and the two men stand, soaked to the knees and spattered.

You've got to protect your water pipes from the rubbing of itchy steers, and so the Hodsons had welded themselves a nine-square tic-tac-toe grid and they'd wired it to their water pipes to stop the rubbing. But today, two cattle have yoked themselves through squares three and four of the grid, then stalled to wait for rescue. When rescuers arrive, however, the steers break the pipes in fright and flood the corral. One runs, not warning the other. But he trips with his foot through square nine of the grid and splashes heavily, nostrils bubbling in the muck. This throws his yoke-mate sideways and presses a rod into his throat.

The Younger props the bubbling nostrils free on his boot, then both men heave the other calf until its spine presses on the rods in lieu of its throat and they feel for the dampness with their hands as the breath flows again. But, with air, the two beasts revive, heave themselves afoot in terror, then stumble and choke again in their unequal yoke.

Again, the Misters Hodson fall to the heavy work of unstifling their beasts. The Younger waves Joel's trailer alongside and directs him to strike the torch. Joel twists the oxygen valve. He sharpens the billowing flame to six pricks of blue. The cattle flinch at the torch but the men kneel hard on them. The calf's hairs darken and curl while Joel squeezes the oxygen valve and blows the dripping steel away until the first beast is free. With more ease, Joel cuts the second steer loose until it, too, staggers free and stares in confusion.

"I'll be damned," the Younger mutters then and Joel follows his gaze to where the first beast stands still, having inserted its head between the rods of the corral for comfort.

The Call for Help (II)

To: Janet Lestersen
From: Joel Alden
Subject: I really need your help

Dear Janet,

I have been asked to accomplish a task that is beyond my ability. Otherwise, I would leave well enough alone and would not write to you.

I had a strange meeting, and I was asked, from the highest level of our government, to explain who we are to each other in this country and who is responsible for tending our culture. Does this task belong to the government alone? Or does someone else also take responsibility for our country?

I promised to think about it and provide them with recommendations. We will meet again in two weeks.

Janet, I don't know how you did it but, when I was with you I thought more clearly than at any other time. I need that now and I wonder if you would help me with this task?

I am writing a fuller account of what prompted the meeting and of why I offered the advice I did, initially. If you are willing to work with me on this, I will send you my detailed notes from the meeting.

I am home in Texas now to do a bit of thinking. Your rules have helped me with this. After all, how could I describe what has happened in this country without describing what has happened with my family?

Joel Alden

When I had written this, I walked downstairs, past the hearts and the matte-eyed doves. I sat in Dad's old recliner and gently rocked myself. The chair squeaked and my eyes watered at the memory of a man who, after a day in his shop, would prop a miniature pillow and a heating pad against the small of his back to ease the pain. I rocked, at peace with my sadness, until Mom entered from the kitchen and sat in the carved rocker where she had nursed her five children and lulled us to sleep.

But Mom could never sit with idle hands. "Would you like some tea?" she asked, and I said yes, although it was August and shimmering outside.

With a cup of tea in her hands, Mom sat and, at length, asked whether I had found what I needed at home.

"Yes," I said. "I've been remembering Dad."

"He would be proud of you," she said.

We rocked for a long time.

"Mom, I'm not a prophet," I said.

"Why do you say that?"

"Because the president wants me to be a prophet. That's why he asked for my advice."

"You don't have to be a prophet, Joel."

"But didn't you and Dad raised me for that? Naming me Joel, and all?"

"You were always someone who saw what needed to be done and you did it."

"Why do you say that?"

Naomi stood in the doorway and looked quizzically at us. Then she poured herself a cup of tea and sat on the end of the couch where it was her habit to read.

"Because that's all you're supposed to do," Mom said. "Let someone else decide whether that makes you a prophet."

"But why do you say I always did what needed done?"

"You did your Dad's work when he had his arm in a cast. Remember that? We had decided not to expect it of you. But you expected it of yourself and that kept the family afloat."

Naomi blew the steam from her tea and looked across it at me.

"Even when you were a boy, you would see a job and just do it. Do you know how rare that is?"

"But it's how I was taught," I said.

Mom smiled and rocked gently so as not to disturb the tea in her cup. "Remember the time you stopped me from shooting the bathtub?"

"You never would have shot the bathtub."

"Not with you to look after me." She smiled again and I attributed a wink to her, although, in my entire memory, she has never winked.

I sipped my tea, the recliner squeaked and, outside, up the rutted lane and across the road, I saw a stranger greasing his combine on the old Hodson farm.

"Mom, I emailed Janet and asked for help with the president's project." She smiled again. Her hands lay idle around her empty cup so she stood and went to the kitchen, where I heard her strike a match to light the burner on her old gas stovetop.

The Story of What Was

To collect a bit of extra income in the fall, a Joel Alden half my age rises before dawn, completes his Algebra by ten, when the maize is dry enough to harvest, and drives himself through the crisp air to the Hodson farm. The law does not permit a proper driver's license at his age so he compensates with experience; at fifteen he has been driving almost half his life.

At eight, Joel first hooks his left arm around the wheel of an F-150 and holds it firm to counter the clutch's pressure. With his right arm he shoves the lever into gear. "Easy on the clutch," Father says. "There it is. Now, a little power, and you're off. See? Nothing to it." But Joel would not back a trailer for three more years—you can't back a trailer until you're tall enough to see over the seatback. But that's okay. Some people are adults and they can't even do it. Some people are drivers-ed instructors and *they* can't back trailers! They can *tell* you how, but can they *show* you? It's not their fault, really, but kids who don't grow up on farms have a hard time making up for the things they missed.

Joel drives the Hodsons' tractor during harvest, pulling it precisely alongside while the combine trembles, scissoring the stalks in front while, behind, it shifts the grain to a cart lumbering dumbly after him, attached by the tongue to Joel's tractor. He drives in peace, observing each day which way the wind blows along the ground, then choosing to empty the combine on a segment of the irrigated circle where his view is unobstructed and the tractor's radiator will remain unclogged by the dust.

And Joel knows which way the wind blows aloft by the movement of the clouds. He notes which storms are building, which have anviled, and which are dissipating—but, more importantly, which are passing by and which are bearing down upon him. Driving slowly on the flat earth, Joel sees what few people ever see: nature's beauty in Sampson, Texas is always there, ignored in full view, above the horizon—an art show each day, never repeating, with an evolution of light, shade, and color—all in this place where "nothing ever happens."

Mr. Hodson The Elder drives the combine, smiling, tapping his foot on the coupled brakes, and looking benevolently down on the mayhem from his fishbowl. He empties the combine and Joel drops back to await the next dump. Mr. Hodson has retracted the combine's spout but the dribs of grain continue apace, scattering among the stalks. Joel surges his engine, shooting black smoke from the tractor's nose, and he flails across the breadth of his window. Mr. Hodson looks up and waves back with a smile. Then he sees Joel's gaze and his finger pointing behind. Mr. Hodson's face lights up, he face-palms the unloader switch, points his thumb unwittingly at a hawk overhead, and resumes tapping the combine's brakes to a rhythm in his head, known but to him.

Harvest is a time when farmers are wound tight. They work themselves to exhaustion, recovering their year's profit from where it hangs ripe and vulnerable to wind, rain, lightening, and—above all—hail. They work the hours of the sun and more, and so do the mechanics, truckers, and the grain handlers at the elevator.

The farmers' children operate heavy machines costing hundreds of dollars per hour. They feel the machines' rhythms in their seatbacks and listen for a belt that begins to slip, a bearing grinding itself dry, a glug of weeds standing unexpected in the grain to clog the threshing cylinder. They watch the gauges to know when the radiator has collected too much chaff and they open the engine box, adding a suffocating wave of diesel heat to the hot sun. Wiping chaff from the radiator fins with the fingers of a crumpled glove, the maize dust—nature's fiberglass—trickles under their collars and promises that the children will itch the long hours until their next shower. But the engine runs cool now and this is what matters. Their fathers would offer a withering critique had they missed a sign and broken something they needn't have.

Joel likes Mr. Hodson The Younger. He spits tobacco juice and winks while he rubs it into the ground with his boot. Texas is ridiculous and it is his, so he laughs. He leaves his semi-truck for Joel to fill from the cart, hands his dad a packed lunch from the wife, and runs the combine while The Elder sits with Joel and eats. But, while The Younger drives, the combine stops. So Joel drives The Elder with stalk-shattering urgency to see what has happened. The Younger has extended a ladder behind the combine and they climb after him to where the red engine sits silent in its oil. A hole gapes in the engine and, at their feet, askew, sits a piston—one of the engine's giant plungers—attached to the remnants of a rod that had thrashed its bearing and ground itself until the engine shattered.

Joel waits for the farmers' rage. The engine was overhauled last year; this is a catastrophic failure of the manufacturer, the mechanic, and of the operator—his son, who failed to detect what *must have been* ominous warning signs.

The Younger looks at The Elder and Joel averts his eyes. Then The Elder stirs. He winks, looks at the bloody piston, and says, "Well, what do you think is wrong with it?" At this, The Younger turns his head back and laughs until his tears blur the last of the summer's puffy clouds. The Elder uses a nifty bag phone in his pickup to call the shop and ask them to lease him a combine for the rest of the season.

At home that evening, Ronnie Alden hears the story. "That's what they get for running a cheap red combine," he says.

The Violent Email

To: Joel Alden
From: Janet Lestersen
Subject: RE: I really need your help

Dear Joel,

Thanks for your email and for your kind words. I can see you've had a lively time of it lately. Congratulations on that. You're a deep thinker, Joel, and a good person for them to ask.

I'm dating someone. You may have heard. He's a thoughtful guy, too, and he may be helpful to you. I talked with him about it and we'd be glad to help with your project if that's what you want.

Please send along the materials and then give me a call when you're back in DC. My number is the same.

Warmly,

Janet

I read her email, then closed my computer and did great violence to some innocent creatures in my mind.

The Violence of Action

After a summer of sweat in the truck shop, Joel drives again to the Hodson farm in the hope of a new season—hope for the first day of the fall harvest. With The Younger, he shoots grease for hours into the combine's hundreds of Zerks. They air the tires on Joel's cart, slide its drive shaft over the tractor's splines, then grease the flex joints.

In the afternoon, the combine trembles to life and slides into the white strip of male maize they will sell for feed. They will harvest the broad, red strips next and sell the hybrid female at a premium for seed. But the grain registers wet at 15% so The Younger proposes they spend the balance of the day cleaning the Hodson barn.

They laugh, sweat, and inhale dust as they throw rotted bales of hay from the barn. Joel seizes the rusted wires and feels them crumble. He grasps the tumbled pile at his feet, so the straw ends scratch at his wrists, and he learns the sweetness of a drab task done in a new place.

Below the hay, rats live in their labyrinth. Joel and The Younger expose them as they clear the last layer of hay, starting at the door and moving toward the back. The rats move, too, pressing together as their civilization shrinks and grows crowded. The Younger stands—with a hayfork, a shovel, an axe handle—while Joel lifts hay and the rats scramble. The Younger clubs at a rat. Another bolts for the door but he switches targets and collapses its skull. The remaining rats plead and press their mates for a bit of the remaining space.

"I think the shovel is best," says The Younger. "Whack them with the flat part. Want to try?"

So Joel whacks, crushing the little bastards until the hay dust has settled itself to mud on the sweat of his forehead. The Younger jiggles the remaining bit of hay to disturb its occupants. They climb over each other in hiding and the hay seethes. In the corner nearby, a bucket accumulates a gallon, two gallons, three gallons of crushed corpses.

The Younger calls Joel at home that evening. "Want to know how many rats it was?" he asks. "I counted them."

"How many?"

"Seventy-one."

"Wow!" Joel says. "Well, give me a call when the maize is ripe, or if you want to go rat clubbing again. Until then, I'll be stuck here doing schoolwork."

The Sermon

I had never seen Mom wear makeup. At sixty, with five grown children, smile lines and grief lines collide kindly on her face. A gentle soul suffering with the utmost grace, she now wore a touch of powder and subtle lipstick. She glowed with the sort of beauty you could see five hundred times and not notice, and then it would strike you so you would fall irretrievably in love and either marry her or die alone years later, coddling a jug of whisky. I felt a sudden conviction that some unworthy man would notice; he would try to replace my dad, and the outrage of it consumed me.

"Shall we go now?" Naomi asked after breakfast. "Joel's coming to church with us, Mom. I promised him a dazzling solo for the offertory."

"Besides, I would hate for you to go to church unchaperoned," I said. I meant it jovially but I forgot to smile. My skirt-dressed Mom and my sister are among the most modest of women. Still, I imagined the world's male population swarming upon them. How did they protect themselves when I was away?

We drove into the Baptist lot, past a loathsome sign: *If God's your co-pilot, better switch seats*. I survived greetings from a congregation where I had never belonged, filled with faces I could almost remember—people who seemed to know me perfectly. "How are things in Washington? Have you got them all straightened out? It's good they've got you there to bring a little sanity."

I did the politician smile, thanked them, and maintained a covert watch against the creeps ogling my mom. They were a squirrely lot, though, and did it behind my back.

Then I sat on a blonde pew in a blond-wood church and looked up at a blonde cross over the bizarre bathtub they used for baptisms. I sat with Mom while Naomi stood at a crappy keyboard far below her and played the music of peasants. She smiled at a wind-burnt, scrubbed-up guitarist and coaxed him through a not-quite-failed rendition of I'm-Coming-Back-to-the-Heart-of-Worship-and-it's-all-About-You-Lord. I imagined the guitar kid sitting knobby-kneed in the tub while his mom gripped his hair and scrubbed dead skin from his face, and I dared him in my head to look at my sister, even once. *Just do it, kid. Remember my face? Well, I'm her brother. Do it again, kid, and this face'll be the last thing you remember.*

Naomi was trying to retard the tempo on a final loop of all-about-you-Lords. She looked at beet-face and nodded to a slower rhythm, but he plowed ahead with his guitar and, in my head, I screamed *look at the leader, you idiot,* and finally he did. Naomi smiled with relief, drew the forgettable song to a close, then sat next to me in the pew. "Nice work," I said.

She smiled. "Thanks." I looked around at blister-face so he'd see Naomi grinning at me—me, not him—but he feigned focus on the pastor.

The pastor stood with his perpetual preacher smile and an appalling gut that drooped over his belt and pointed at the floor. He stepped up the two industrially carpeted steps with a gait that spoke vaguely of knee pain, then stood behind the blonde pulpit—narrow at the bottom and wider at the part where a man pounds his fist. It stood there, shaped like a kite or an old horror-film coffin stood on end, holding a post with a crossbar on the front, designed to crucify Jesus all over again Sunday-after-Sunday.

"It's good to see you all in the house of the Lord," the preacher said, "and a special welcome to our guests. Please stand and be recognized." Naomi stuck her elbow in my ribs, so I stood with polite anger at being singled out. All their necks twisted toward me and I glared through my syrup-smile at one spot: *look here, radish-head, she's sitting next to me and smiling because I'm her brother—her tough, very well-connected brother.*

"We have Joel Alden here, all the way from Washington, DC. Please give him a warm welcome when you have a chance. We're glad to have you here, Joel." I sat and the preacher started in:

"Today, I want to ask you all a question: What's so amazing about grace? Our text is Luke 15:11-32."

Cellophane pages rustled through the congregation—forefinger and thumb licked and used to twist translucent leaves free from the paint that bound them together at the edge.

"We all know this one—the story of the Gracious Father—the story of the Bitter Brother—the story of the Prodigal Son.

"Some of you knew my brother, Red. And you know he died this past June.

"Red was always smarter than me. He knew it, my family knew it, and you knew it. I have only ever beat Red at one thing: football. You see, once I got myself moving, even in high school, no one dared to stand quite square in front of me. The coach over in Hansford taught his boys two ways to tackle. To tackle anyone else, he taught them to grab above the knees and ride the victim to the ground. But he taught them another technique for me and he told them never to attempt it alone. He told them to intercept, redirect, then defer to gravity and, as the story goes, the whole team used to chant this together before they ran out on the field to play Sampson. I'm told the coach elaborated this tactic to his team entirely with bull-fighting metaphors. He explained with fantastic imagination how an agile fighter would drive a sword between the bull's ribs and deliver the snorting beast—snot stringing from the nostrils of its nose—from its torment. *Its* torment, my friends, as if the bull was on a sort of self-destructive rampage and it must be rescued by this generous and pitying Spaniard.

"They called it a *coup de grace*. Grace, my friends. And Red used to remind me of this. I would sit on him for being an imp and it just killed him to be sat on. He was older, smarter, and faster than me and we both knew it. But, instead of crying uncle to get me off like he should have done, he would lie there and, through clenched teeth, he would tell all the ways he was better than me. We both knew his list was true, we both knew his list ended with – *so that's why Dad loves me more than you* – and we both knew it hurt me more to hear this than it hurt him to have me twist his shoulder out of its socket—which I did once, by the way."

Here the preacher winked. The congregation chuckled in good humor and the preacher smiled a sunny smile that still confuses me. He went on.

"Grace. People used that word a lot when I was in high school. The Hansford kids would yell it from the stands—egging their football players on to crush me under my own weight. And it was Red's word for killing me—for putting me out of my misery. *My* misery, friends, as if my misery was something I did to myself.

"Why do I tell you all this? So you will hate my brother? So you will pity me? So you will hate my father, who sat in his chair and read the paper while Red told my failures to me on our living-room floor? No. That's what would happen if the story stopped here.

"In those days, Red said *grace* when he meant death. And Red was half right. You can never quite separate grace from death. But here's where Red was wrong: grace begins with death—it always does—but it never ends there."

The preacher said this in a low voice that hissed almost. He leaned his elbows heavily on the pulpit and pushed his glasses up his cauliflower nose before he went on.

"Grace is not the death we see in our world, grace is what God does with that death."

He used a sticky tab to open his Bible to the right page.

"And Jesus said, A certain man had two sons: And the younger of them said to his father, Father, give me the portion of goods that falleth to me. And he divided unto them his living. And not many days after the younger son gathered

"You all know that I have farmed all my life. Tomorrow, I will go out behind my house, I will hook Dad's old tractor to the drills and I will pull them out of the weeds. Before I fill them with seed wheat, I will give those rusted hose clamps a squirt of WD-40 and loosen them with a straight screwdriver. I will hold the feeder hoses up to the sky and then use a hooked piece of bailin' wire to clear the spider webs out of them. I'll replace the hoses that have been eaten through by mice and I'll grumble because they don't make the tubes of wound steel like they did forty years ago when my dad got me into this business."

An older guy said, "They don't make 'em like that now."

"I'm telling you: with all the rubber and plastic these days, it's a mouse's world. But in the seventies there was nothing for a mouse to chew without breaking his teeth. It was also in the seventies that Red left for college. In the seventies, Red spent the money my dad could never quite find for my own schooling. Red convinced Dad to put up the money for his business ventures. To this day, *Red's* is the biggest honky-tonk in Austin. And somehow, no one ever noticed but it was me, the old Dempster drills, and a little extra money from the gas well that started it up.

"In the Bible Jesus tells us that our Prodigal friend spent all he had. *And then there arose a mighty famine in that land; and he began to be in want. And he went and joined himself to a citizen of that country; and he sent him into his fields to feed swine. And he would fain have filled his belly with the husks that the swine did eat: and no man gave unto him.*

"How does a swine's husk taste? Well, we lost touch with Red. I don't know what he ate, how he made money, or what he lived on. A stranger answered the phone in his house when Dad called and the stranger said he had bought the place on a foreclosure. Dad never talked about Red after that. He never thanked me for the money I had earned or apologized to me for wasting it on a drinking joint in Austin.

"Some of you remember me in those years. Sitting unshowered on that pew at the end, where Sister Beth sits now. To your credit, you told your children to leave me alone. But you loved my wife, Janine, I know, and that's probably what gave her the strength to go on loving me through the hardest years of her life.

"Scripture tells us that, when the prodigal *came to himself, he said, 'How many hired servants of my father have bread enough and to spare, and I perish with hunger! I will arise and go to my father, and will say unto him, Father, I have sinned against heaven, and before thee, and am no more worthy to be called thy son: make me as one of thy hired servants.'*

"I don't know how the swine's husk tasted for Red. But, as for myself, some of you know that I bought a shotgun—a twenty-gauge because, for some reason, I thought a twelve-gauge would be too much to clean up after. I was never quite clear on who I meant to shoot, but somehow I had decided that my family had one man too many. I only had to decide whether it was me or someone else that was extra.

"Something about the weight of a gun feels manly in your hand. Like you're in control. Like you've got power again and you can do something.

"The stock of that gun had a deer carved into it, all perked up, with its head turned toward you. I used alcohol and a Kleenex to dust around the ridges in that carving. Then I hefted the gun and pointed it up at a corner of the room. I started to think about the parts of a person's anatomy and I considered the proper kind of shot for each of them. But still I had not decided whether it was my own body I thought of or someone else's and I wondered whether I would shoot myself the same way I would shoot my brother or my dad. Or did I have a double-standard?

"I thought hard about this and it disturbed me that I had no answer. I would have killed any of us but it made me question my character that I felt different about how to do it—between me, my dad, and Red. I had left my gun downstairs and, while I sat on my sofa, experimenting in my head with how to shoot myself, Janine walked in. She stood in the doorway to our basement holding my gun. But the weight didn't look manly on her. It made her shoulders sag, and her holding that gun was the saddest thing I ever saw. Her—finding that gun on the workbench downstairs and lugging it up to ask me where I had gotten it.

"I told her I had bought it off old Donald Sproul. And, do you know what she said? I know you know because you heard her tell it a few years back. She told me to take it downstairs and hang it up properly—out of reach in case some kids went down there. She sat on our couch and waited for me hang it up. Then she told me, 'Ken, your dad is senile, and your brother is gone. But you're still here and I won't let you go because I still love you. I believe in God and I believe in you. I don't know how much life I have left but I want to live it with God and with you and I want to live it with you both on good terms.' And then she told me she had an appointment to check on a lump in her breast—one she had known about for way too long.

"So that's what happened to me. It was the *coup de grace* that puts a wounded man out of his misery—by giving him back a life he never had. Hearing what she said hurt more than shooting myself would have hurt. I'm sure of that. But it hurt good. And that's how I switched from the guy in Sister Beth's pew, over there by the window, to the one who stands up here every Sunday to tell you what God has done.

"Like I told you before, grace starts with death, but it does not end there.

"You may figure I sold the gun or threw it poetically in a lake. But I didn't. It's still hanging in my basement, and sometimes I go down there with a bottle of alcohol and a Kleenex to clean around the antlers of that deer. I keep it unloaded, hung up out of reach, so your kids will have a safe place to play when you come to visit me. And I've got no shells for it because I never knew what kind to buy.

"Jesus tells us that the starving prodigal *arose, and came to his father. But when he was yet a great way off, his father saw him, and had compassion, and ran, and fell on his neck, and kissed him. And the son said unto him, Father, I have sinned against heaven, and in thy sight, and am no more worthy to be called thy son.*

"About two years ago, Red called me and told me we needed to talk. I told him Janine had died and he said he was sorry to hear. I told him Dad's mind had gone and he said he was very sorry to hear. Then I asked him what he wanted to talk about and he said he wanted to talk in person. I asked him where he was and he said he would be here at my house in two days.

"And then Red showed up and knocked on the door, here at the home where I used to sit on him. And I would have sat on him again, but then I saw this waxy skin stretched across his forehead and I saw that he had withered until it would have taken three of him to tip the scale against me. He said he wanted to live here and he offered to cook or help with bookkeeping for the farm.

"*But the father said to his servants, Bring forth the best robe, and put it on him; and put a ring on his hand, and shoes on his feet: And bring hither the fatted calf, and kill it; and let us eat, and be merry: For this my son was dead, and is alive again; he was lost, and is found.*

"Most of you know that Red died of AIDS. In his last couple of years—some of you will remember—he told us how he had spent time in jail for running a gambling business out of *Red's Honky-Tonk*.

"*Now his elder son was in the field: and as he came and drew nigh to the house, he heard musick and dancing. And he called one of the servants, and asked what these things meant. And he said unto him, Thy brother is come; and thy father hath killed the fatted calf, because he hath received him safe and sound. And he was angry, and would not go in: therefore came his father out, and intreated him.*

"*And he answering said to his father, Lo, these many years do I serve thee, neither transgressed I at any time thy commandment: and yet thou never gavest me a kid, that I might make merry with my friends: but as soon as this thy son was come, which hath devoured thy living with harlots, thou hast killed for him the fatted calf. And he said unto him, Son, thou art ever with me, and all that I have is thine. It was meet that we should make merry, and be glad: for this thy brother was dead, and is alive again; and was lost, and is found.*

"Red had no right to come home and live off my labor. But we farmed together in the last two years of his life and, true to form, Red did all the thinking while I did all the work. And it hurt. Because I'm overweight. My knees are shot. My back is shot. I should have retired years ago and I would have done it, too, but Dad had cashed out the farm and given the money to Red.

"It hurt but, for the second time in my life, the hurt was good. Our farm did better because of Red and, in those years, the two of us paid off almost half our debt.

"It was only because of where Janine left me—because of what God did to me—that Red and I lived together as brothers for the first time in our lives.

"Was that justice? Or was it grace? Justice and grace. So often we pit them against each other. But here is the truth: without justice there is no grace. With no offense, there is no forgiveness. Where no one has fallen, there is no lifting up again. Where nothing is lost, there is nothing to restore.

"Grace does not ignore justice. It takes justice in its stride. It honors justice, then supersedes it. Grace does not diminish sin in order to be bigger than sin. It does not say, *'What you've done isn't really so bad.'* It says, *'What you've done is all that and worse, but I am bigger still.'*

"That's what's so amazing about grace.

"We think grace is kind and sweet. But it is not. It is bitter. It is so bitter I thought for a while that I would rather kill someone. And my blood boiled when Red showed up on my doorstep with his suitcase—ignoring me throughout our lives while I cared for my dying wife and our bitter, dying dad—and then he showed up for me to care for him while he himself died from his pathetic, self-inflicted wounds.

"We're like the Bitter Brother—you and me. Maybe we can accept grace for our own "little" sins, but we're disgusted when grace sweeps up a spectacular sinner like the prodigal son—like Red—and we're left, frowning on the sidelines of this thing called grace. We take it personally.

"We're happy for God to overcome sin, of course—pride, gluttony, or maybe a divorce at the outside limit. But we sit here in these pews with the abortionist, the unwed mother, the lapsing alcoholic, the homosexual, and—god forbid—the politician ... Or maybe we're even okay with that. But surely, we think, we should have some recognition that, if we ourselves have not been quite faithful, we have at least been *more* faithful than *them!* And we object when God kills the fatted calf in an unseemly celebration for *those people*. It is we, the faithful, who should be celebrated as the true children of God.

"Our world is dying for a lack of grace, my friends. We argue with each other in this country about what is just, and some people resent justice because it's a way for some guilty people to accuse other guilty people—because we're all guilty.

"So the world does away with justice. We're afraid to say what is right and what is wrong, because all of us will find ourselves somewhere in the wrong.

"So what is it we Christians have done? We have divided the world into us—the small sinners, who are basically okay—and them—the evil ones, who deserve judgment. And we object, like the older brother did—like I did when I stood in my doorway and looked at my sorry, pathetic, disease-ridden brother. I objected against extending God's obscene grace to *him*.

"In the old days, people bowed before their king and called him *Your Majesty* or *Your Grace*. Kings were thought to be a stand-in for God. And people were beholden to their king. But why? Was it because of the king's power? Was it because of his justice? No. It was his majesty. It was his grace.

"And why is that? Shouldn't a king be just? Yes. Because without justice there can be no wrong. Without wrong there can be no grace. So I tell you this: without justice, grace is not amazing. It is not amazing, because it is not grace.

"What's so amazing about grace is that, with grace, we can still call good and evil by their names. And we can do it without damning us all to Hell. We call good and evil by their names." He leaned forward. "That's justice. And we must welcome the prodigal when he comes home. That's grace.

"I stood there and looked at the ancient Pontiac Red had parked in my driveway, its vinyl top flaked away, its upholstery faded and crumbling about the shoulders. And I looked at Red, standing there with the exhaustion of a man driven by hope and despair, looking for a place to die."

The preacher stepped back, a hand on each side of the podium, his arms straight.

"I have one more parable for you—a parable about the ominous side of grace: Jesus tells us of a servant who owed his master a huge debt. But the servant could not pay and pleaded for mercy. So the master forgave the debt. But that servant went out and found a man who owed him a small debt.

"And then Jesus says he *took him by the throat, saying, 'Pay me that thou owest.'*

"The man pleaded with his fellow servant to have patience but he *refused and cast him into prison, 'til he should pay the debt.*

"Then, *when his fellow servants saw what was done, they were very sorry, and came and told unto their lord all that was done. Then his lord, after that he had called him, said unto him, 'O thou wicked servant, I forgave thee all that debt, because thou desiredst me: shouldest not thou also have had compassion on thy fellow servant, even as I had pity on thee?' And his lord was wroth, and delivered him to the tormentors, 'til he should pay all that was due unto him. So likewise shall my heavenly Father do also unto you, if ye from your hearts forgive not everyone his brother their trespasses.*

"Why did the master unforgive the first servant? I will tell you: the servant was no longer forgiven because the hand that extends grace is the same hand that receives it. If we have sinned and received grace, we must also offer this grace to all who have sinned against us.

"When I put my gun away on that rack, I placed it on the rack for myself but, what I did not know at the time is that I had also placed it there for my brother. And for it to stay there for one of us, it had to stay there for both. If I intended to keep the grace extended by Janine and by God, I had to offer it also to Red. This is a bitter law of the universe. It is a law of God.

"What's so amazing about grace is that I stand here still spilling over at the gut and telling you this story without bitterness. What's so amazing about grace is that Red and I passed so many delightful hours together in my house—in our house—these past two years and that the two of us together forgave dad in the nursing home, even though he had no idea who we were.

"What's amazing about grace is that Red and I sat with so many of you—at ten o'clock in the morning each day at the Dairy Queen—and we drank coffee while Red ate vanilla soft-serve, and a sore slowly took over his mouth then crept out on his lip so your eyes would water to look at it because his body could no longer fight the canker virus and you all told Aggie jokes and laughed with him until he could barely even drink his food through a straw.

"What's so amazing about grace is that Red helped me write this sermon and he only asked me not to give it during his life or at his funeral. So you're getting it here today. And there's no recording. That's because it is just one small story. A story for us here today.

"What's so amazing is that by grace, the people of God are living out their own botched versions of this parable all over our country and all over the world today. And it is right for us to treasure

212

these things to ourselves.

"What's so amazing about grace is that I wrote a sermon at all when I can barely write. I usually just stand up here and say what the Lord lays on my heart and I talk until Brother Don over there starts checking his watch. I know what you're thinking there, Brother James Ferguson, but it doesn't work for you. You start checking your watch five minutes into my sermon and that's not fair. But Brother Don here, he's got a good ear for when I have said enough."

Surprised by the sudden attention, Mr. Ferguson leaned forward in his pew and pushed his slipping glasses up his nose while the congregation chuckled their sympathy and rebuke to him for his impatience.

"There's so much pain," the preacher continued. "Red suffered a lot in the last few months. And his pain died with him. This too is grace. But the grace he gave and received in those months—it lives on. Because, as I said before, grace starts with death but it does not end there. Grace outlives death.

"That is the parable of the Lost Son. The parable of the Gracious Father. The parable of the Bitter Brother.

"If you have never received God's grace in your life, I invite you to come forward now. Don't wait another day. Don't go on living in a soulless world. Everyone in this room is a sinner, like me, and like Red—on the wrong side of justice, deserving punishment, deserving the tormentors. The only difference is that some of us are saved by grace. And none of us who are saved by grace could object to a God who offers the same grace freely to you whoever you are. Whatever you have done.

"If you feel the quiet voice of God speaking to you now, don't wait. Come down to the front of the church and do business with God this morning.

"If you are like the older brother, like I was, and you have clenched your fist against God's grace to someone else, open that fist. Open your hand and offer God's grace freely to your brother, to your fellow sinner, and, for God's sake, open your hand to once again receive God's amazing grace into your own life."

Naomi had slipped out of the pew and over to the crappy keyboard, where she now played *Amazing Grace*. Some people sang along, and some people wiped their eyes, but no one went to the front of the church, so they sang the song a few more times and then gave it up.

I felt dazed, and on the way out of the church sweet people greeted me again. "How long are you here before you go back to DC? Where's that nice girl who came with you last time? We liked her. Are you still dating?"

Behind me, Mom tugged my sleeve. "You remember your cousin Will?" she asked.

I am over six feet tall but, even then, the goofy-grinning guitarist gangled over me, shifting a cracked guitar case to his left hand and extending his right one to shake. "Ah, yes, Will," I said. "It has been a long time, though. You've grown up."

I shook hands with the pastor and said, sincerely, "That was quite a sermon, sir."

"Just call me Brother Kenny," he said. "You caught us on a strange Sunday, but I'm glad you could be here."

In the Buick, Naomi drove and Mom insisted on sitting in the back. Naomi powered the Buick over seventy out of the chalky creek breaks from Samson, past the giant S painted on the hillside and, while she drove, I asked her whether she had known Brother Kenny would give that particular sermon—as in, did she know it yesterday when she asked me to come to church under threat of crushing my car? And, for that matter, did Brother Kenny know I would be there?

Naomi gave me a dim look and kept the throttle pressed low, even though we had got up the hill, and she drove fast on the disconcerting plains. "You people in Washington always think you should know everything about everything," she said.

Actions that Speak Louder than Words

"How stupid can you be? I mean, where's your head? Do you even think before you do stupid stuff, dummy?"

Joel has driven the family suburban by accident into the mud.

Father yanks the suburban door and screams the engine forward, then in reverse, until the wheels catch and he rolls easily again on firm ground. He throws the door open and brushes past Joel, eyes flashing his anger while his mustache droops in disappointment over the sheer ineptitude of the human being he has brought into this world.

Joel takes the suburban, then, to be parked in the white garage and he sees the speedometer dangle at no speed, broken from what has happened. More than a hundred. Less than zero. Nothing.

The Draft Policy

Sitting on the plane Sunday afternoon, I stared out while our wingtip streamed its line across the deep sky, then I dropped my gaze down where some strange boy must have looked up, sweaty from digging for worms with his friend, and I saw this boy point his dimpled finger up, squinting at my trail in the sky. Then I looked in the window of a plane we met, where a man called Joel Alden flew home to visit his mom. The man was a shell. Cut off. Flailing to understand his country without thinking of his past. Trying to know himself but not knowing his family. What a hopeless man, staring blindly out of a porthole in his aluminum tube.

While the plane disgorged its passengers in preparation for my flight, I had emailed Janet a summary of my discussion, "at the highest level of our government," and I agreed to meet with her and her boyfriend Thursday evening at a place called Big Bear Café.

Then, Monday morning, I nodded to the Pentagon guard, walked over the bridge, and entered that massive hive of men holding fat folders while they briefed their bosses en route to meetings at the White House. But I only saw workmen, glistening in orange light, while they shoveled coal into the boiler of a drifting ship. Sacrificing, sweating, and putting in an honest day's work. To go where? Who knows? And who cares? They put in an honest day's work and they go home with honor, with a paycheck, with respect, to their families. Or they go up for shore leave, where they will carouse, fight, and bolster the eternal reputation of sailors. What does it matter where this ship goes? If it is no longer needed, it can still patrol where it was needed ten years ago, or twenty. And no one is the wiser, right? The

Russians are still a threat. The Chinese. The Somalis. The Muslims. Whoever. The ship must sail because there are threats. Then the men can earn their honor and go in to their families—or to the girls they impressed, sloppy and drunk at the bar.

Jamie had energetically "worked the detainee issue" for me in my absence and, when I returned, she sat across a table from me and asked, genuinely, about my trip home. She'd noticed I was working hard, she said, and hoped I had enjoyed the time off.

"It was great to get out of DC for a bit," I said. "Were you okay while I was gone?"

"Fine, I think," she said. "I tried to contact you." Something stirred in my belly when she said this.

"How did you try?" I asked, and then I covered my frustration with a laugh when we discovered she had misread a smudged letter where I wrote my email address on a green sticky note for her before I left.

"Nick had a family emergency," she said. "So, while he was out, I circulated State's draft policy for DoD review."

Jamie had received a general "no objection" response across the department. Then Ms. Holachek's deputy had tentatively approved it to meet a short State Department suspense,[64] while Ms. Holachek was away speaking at a conference on "asymmetric threats."

So I read the draft—in the psychic posture of a bomb tech unwrapping an anonymous Christmas gift.

The State Department had produced an impeccable eight-page discussion of the terms "de-radicalization" and "reintegration." It articulated the national security mandate for people to stop thinking bad thoughts about the U.S. so we can go on living in the world without them killing us. But, more than that, State implied that people overseas should have access to good counselors so they can

---

[64] "Suspense" is passive-aggressive for "deadline"

handle the inevitable bad thoughts people will think toward the U.S. if they perceive themselves to be subjugated by repressive governments that are, in turn, supported from afar by a self-interested superpower. So, more than stopping bad thoughts—which are inevitable and, perhaps, natural in such circumstances—State suggested that the U.S. should seek to "manage" these sentiments into "channels other than violence."[65]

Buried on page six of this draft was one operative sentence—the sentence you would paste into PowerPoint to brief your boss on the new "policy:"

The Department of State, in consultation with other elements of the USG,[66] and relevant international partners, should consider the appropriateness of a program's theological or other ideological presuppositions when determining whether to support a given program.

The main question, Jamie said, was whether to push back on State's listing of itself as the primary evaluator of a program's theology "in consultation with other elements of the USG." Would

––––––––––––––––––––

[65] Wow, State Department. Brilliant idea. What sort of channels? Painting, for instance? Shall we teach terrorists worldwide that Allah mostly wants them to paint their violence toward the West in watercolor (in non-representational depictions, of course)? Or shall we recommend canine therapy? (Call it a kitschy "K-9" if you want Congressional funding.) Then terrorists can learn to care for a dog and, when they learn to love the dogs, it will create a tender place in their angry hearts where they can also love the people who lecture them against repressing women while, themselves, producing pornography at a prodigious rate.

If terrorists can learn to love dogs then they must also see that other people are not bad just because they are different from you and they support regimes that deny you basic human decency in exchange for cheap oil and for giving Israel a free pass whenever it wants to kill itself some Muslims. Good plan State Department. Maybe a little therapy is all the terrorists need.

[66] That's us—the Department of Defense

this perhaps sideline DoD?[67] Did I care? Jamie wondered. Should we try to get State to list DoD as a co-evaluator since DoD is responsible for handling detainees?

I saw that, in my absence, the bureaucracy had chewed on and no one had noticed that, while chewing, it had spilled all the food from between its flabby lips and it now chewed on nothing. And while I was gone, DoD only quibbled about whether the draft policy gave too much authority to State. And somewhere, I knew, a bureaucrat sat and prepared to highlight this process to Congress as an example of collaborative, whole-of-government decision-making on an issue of national importance.[68]

I told Jamie that I did not feel strongly about co-listing DoD as a decision-maker, and then I just slumped there at our meeting table and I thought of giving it up. Where does a person find the sheer energy to press on against so much strategic apathy?[69] The policy should not merely assign responsibility for deciding these questions, it should say what is acceptable and what is not—what is legal and what is not.

I wondered vaguely how many things in government took their shape because the person who cared got reassigned or woke up tired from a crying baby and, for a day, lacked the fortitude to fight.

"I hope this is okay, Joel," Jamie said tentatively. I heard sympathy in her voice and then I felt guilt over sitting in a posture that would perhaps have been appropriate, with my feet on an ottoman and a glass of whisky in my hand after a very hard day.

---

[67] Yes, of course

[68] Yes, Congress, our various departments get along quite well when they discuss nothing—when their strategic objective is to have a polite conversation with starched napkins and ironed tablecloths.

[69] Is it strategic? Yes. I think so. Or maybe apathy is just a tactic to squash a question that leads to an inconvenient answer. Do you answer the question? No. You guide it quietly off the stage.

I sat straight then and laced my fingers on the table. "Yes, thanks," I said and paged through the draft again, trying to comprehend its length. "This is a start. We just need to state what is legal and what is ethical and we need to require our people to collect data on the programs."

Jamie nodded sympathetically. She listed my points—1, 2, 3—in her spiral notebook and I almost fell in love with her all over again when she asked, "Shall I call State Department, then, and tell them that DoD will make more inputs to the paper? We have a new POC at State by the way. Her name is Caitlin. She's really helpful."

"Yes, thanks. Please do give Caitlin a call and I will try to meet with her later this week," I said. Then I looked through my files for the non-paper I had written an eternal month ago before slouching, relieved, into an Adirondack chair.[70] Somehow the page

------

[70] RECOMMENDATIONS
1. ~~Prisoners~~ <u>Detainees</u> should be able to choose the faith (or non-faith) of their "reintegration" program much like servicemen and servicewomen choose their chaplain; this will avoid running afoul of the constitution's "establishment" clause. Given that most of the ~~prisoners~~ <u>detainees</u> were originally Muslim and most of the reintegration programs are operated by Muslims, this will likely have a small practical impact but a large legal impact.
2. Before transferring a ~~prisoner~~ <u>detainee</u>, the U.S. should visit the site of the reintegration program and review the curriculum or, if there is no curriculum, offer to jointly-develop a curriculum.
3. The curriculum (from step 2) should be presented in outline to the ~~prisoner~~ <u>detainee</u> and the ~~prisoner~~ <u>detainee</u> should be given the option to a) choose the proposed reintegration program, b) request a program based on a different faith or non-faith (this may not be granted if the requested faith is unavailable), or c) remain in his current situation.
4. The U.S. should work with partner countries and with academia to collect all existing recidivism data and, going forward, should systematically collect and assess this data to inform future reintegration program decisions.

seemed ancient now, like it should be yellowed and curling at the edges.

Sitting at my roll-top desk in Texas, I had wondered whether I still cared about detainees. It had seemed like a very small issue tucked off in a dusty corner of my government. But I had my answer now. Was I overwhelmed with a bigger question? Yes. But still I cared.

I walked into the office, where Nick sat crinkling his coattail against the back of his chair, and I asked him how his family was.

He shook his head with a dry chuckle. "When you were a kid, did you ever get into a water fight?" he asked.

"Once or twice when my dad was away," I said. "He wasn't much for the boys-will-be-boys philosophy."

"Well, my two boys share your when-Dad's-not-around philosophy. But their fight took place in the bathroom and it was Clorox vs. ammonia. Unfortunately, my wife didn't catch onto it until Joseph ran out of ammonia and went for the Drain-O.

"They're fine now, though. We've installed a locking cabinet in the bathroom. How was Texas?"

"You make my vacation sound placid," I said. "There was no chemical warfare and it was great to see my mom and my sister.

"Unfortunately, though, it looks like State waited for us to leave, then slid an empty paper through the system. Their policy only does one thing: it says State will consider what theology is appropriate—in consultation with other elements of the USG, of course."

I had circled the operative sentence for Nick. He read it. He chuckled dryly again and then I asked whether he would back me up if I told State that, for the draft policy to be implementable, DoD would need more specifics.[71]

---

[71] See how I have proposed a little reverse-psychology—implying that DoD needs *more* direction from State Department?

I laid my non-paper on his desk and said I recommended proposing to State Department that, beyond its current content, the draft policy should answer three additional questions:

1. What are the constitutional/legal parameters for reintegration programs?
2. What is the minimum insight the U.S. must have into a program before supporting it?
3. How do we gather information on a program's effectiveness, and how will we apply this information to future decisions?[72]

"I like your style," Nick said. "But do you think it will work?"

"Honestly, yes," I said. "At least, I think it's worth a try."

I think Nick heard weariness in my voice. "Let's do it, then," he said.

Then he continued. "If we don't get this right, we have no purpose except to come in at nine in the morning, shuffle our paperwork, and leave at four." He leaned forward, laid his palm on my non-paper, and looked kindly at me. "You know that, right?" Then he told me that the office recognized my skill, they wanted to

---

[72] I have answers to these questions. But, if we cut-and-paste my answers into State's paper they will have an allergic response, rejecting our stylistically-alien* material from "their" paper. If we cut-and-paste our answers, they'll give us a "State Department is not prepared to accept ..." response like they do with recalcitrant foreign governments. But, if we pose the questions and ask for *their* answers, they can hardly deny that the questions are valid and, of course, we will be two steps ahead of them in providing some answers.

* State doesn't do bullets; it doesn't do terse; it doesn't format its papers to show the outline: DoD does. DoD thinks its way of writing is clear, actionable, and direct. State Department thinks it is how DoD dumbs down its ideas so Jarheads can understand them, and, more importantly, so Jarheads will not recognize them as "ideas" *per se* and then the Jarheads will read the bulleted papers, maybe, instead of burning them in their primal fires for warmth.

222

keep me, and he hoped they had not overworked me in recent months.

When it came to it, I cared a lot about detainees. I smiled and then teared a little at Nick's words because I could see that my work remained intact.

If we accepted State's draft, the best of my professional work would scatter in the wind. The bearded Stalin would unroll his kit and snap his gloves with new confidence, and, in its little way, this would further damage the U.S. in its effort to be a careful presence in our world. If I failed, it would sit heavy in my gut.

I stepped out, huffed snot into a tissue, and stared blankly at the "Real Leaders" book in my cubicle. Then I walked in again and told Nick that I faced some pressure "on the home front" but that I would work hand-in-glove with Jamie to see this one through, if that was okay.

Words that Speak Louder Than Actions

Joel Alden works with Father, reassembling the front-end brakes of a semi in an empty lot across from the shop, mind yet untouched by the thought of an Islamic terrorist. Weary with the work of a waning day, he sits on a stool, fingering the final lug-nuts.

Reaching forward, shirts stretching across their backs, providing a neat place for a mosquito to pierce the fabric. By weary agreement, Joel rests and defends his father from the whining cloud. "You kill one," he mutters, "and a thousand come to its funeral."

Then they switch. Joel fumbles with the nuts, then screams the air wrench to a grinding halt on each of them. They release the jack, settling the truck once again upon its wheels. Joel coils the air hose from where it lies across the alley.

"Joel," Father says. "You know what I did with the suburban yesterday? That wasn't right."

Joel looks at him.

"Will you forgive me?" Father asks.

"Sure. Sure, of course," Joel says. "I didn't mean to get the suburban stuck."

Joel stifles an impulse to laugh and hug his dad and thank him wildly for this apology. Joy presses up into his neck and forces a vestige through to show in his face. He wraps the hose, hangs the loops on their rack, then cuts the grease from his hands in the solvent of the parts washer.

It is the one offense for which his father apologized and Joel never forgets.

"Let's go home and see if your mother saved us some supper," Father says.

The Painting

I left my house for the Big Bear on a stagnant summer evening. Two weeks were gone and I still had no idea who we are to each other in America—no idea who is responsible for our culture.

I slid a key into the U-lock of Sam-Bob's bicycle and, in the doorway of the apartment building next to my house, a woman yelled to her girlfriend, pink pants stretched over what would have, if inhabited by a different soul, been an attractive body.

"I told my Jaylene to keep her snotty face out of the room, and give me some peace for once. But here she comes all 'Mommy, I'm scared' and sticking her nose into my business. And, George, what does he do? He loses his shit? Like he'd just dropped in from Krypton and he'd never seen a mother before. And so I say, 'I'm a mom, okay!' I've got a kid and, if your little pea-brain can't handle that, you can just go fuck yourself because you, sure as hell, won't be fucking this no more!"

She did an ostrich-neck gesture that highlighted the assets of her shrink-wrapped body, her breasts bobbing heavily in their tube-top. Her friend nodded sympathetically from the sidewalk and the woman went on. "And, Jaylene, she's standing there too scared to cry and I'm like, 'It's okay, hunny. This motherfucker won't be fucking no mothers no more. He don't got the dick for it.'"

I walked my bicycle to the end of the block, too depressed to ride, and the woman's voice echoed after me while she gesticulated with her pink, drug-store fingernails. Darkness smothered me. I knew this was also my country—the president's country.

I felt depressed, as I did once after surgery, walking, addicted to pain killers, hungover from Percocet. Lonely, mind collapsing in failure when asked to comprehend something good, with other bodies on the street looking at me and seeing a healthy young man walking along. And that disgusted me, because they only saw a shell over my decaying core. I looked back at them, too, and they looked like people going happily about their lives. But I saw through it and attributed to every shell a core as rotten as mine.

I walked and thought of the statistics: the women who've miscarried silently or aborted; the half of marriages ending in divorce; the shocking percentage of my fellow people who have been abused sexually or beaten by their partner; the people medicated to resist a looming depression; the eating disorders; the schoolyard bullying; the preponderance of STDs—often terminal; the people dulled permanently by chronic pain and medication; the men addicted to pornography—to seeing women abused for their personal pleasure; the preponderance of people who coexist in relationships that have fallen flat—reminders of failed love, of failed dreams.

I thought of the morbid obesity, of shattered men who joined up believing pain is weakness leaving the body, and the massive addictions to pills, alcohol, tobacco, and other attempts to cope with the misery. I thought of the child who lies through the night in black terror over his eternal fate. And I saw in every face the mask of a devastated soul.

I saw art—the music of anger and despair where millions find an expression of themselves. I thought and I knew that despair engulfed my fellow-men. And what of those un-engulfed? I will tell you: these are the saddest of all, because they have not yet fallen.

I thought of this pain in my country, even where people can seek a cure. A place where people can give their grief a name and talk with a professional whose job is to find a life for them after the pain—through the pain. I thought of this and I projected our despair to people overseas who carry the same pain but deeper and without solace. Who are such people to each other? Who is responsible for them? And God? Who is he? I was disgusted that there could ever be a God.

I thought again of Thoreau:

The mass of men lead lives of quiet desperation …

From the desperate city you go into the desperate country, and have to console yourself with the bravery of minks and muskrats …

Unconscious despair is concealed even under what are called the games and amusements of mankind.

There is no play in them …

My mind sank deeper until I saw, for every desperate creature on the street, another, farther gone, staying home in a broken chair because his mask has slipped—he is miserable and too ashamed to be seen.

In every bright action of my fellow man, I saw a diversion from the misery at his core. A nation of smiling corpses, working, buying, and selling as we imagine a living person should. Each afraid someone will drag away his mask and expose the sham. Stepford wives. Everyone.

These thoughts spiraled in upon themselves and a horror fell over me as a child who discovers his mom bald, asleep, with a wig on the bed-stand and, in his gut, the child knows that all the goodness in his life has been false—inhabited by a hag, chuckling that he was duped—and now he sees that his world was always a sham, staged at his expense for their amusement. He is the fool for believing, for offering up his innocence, and he promises never to believe again.

Beauty is a myth to distract us from what is real. Baal's cheery music diverting us from the fire where an infant blackens in his arms.

A cat purring and arching her back against your leg while she dreams of ripping away the hamster's belly. The greatest romances are but a prelude to the greatest grief, and the greatest warrior still dies in terror over his shattered guts. Innocence for a moment is spoiled forever; this cannot be undone. The whole world: a ghastly Wall where Dead Troops Talk and the Taliban walks among men who do not yet know they are dead—chatting pleasantly over their foaming brains.

What should I tell the president of a place like this?

The Language of a Child

But, if the world is so sad, then what of a man who is at peace with his family? A man who slaps on his cap in the boot room and whistles. "I'm going to run some errands," he says. "I'll be back in a couple of hours."

"Oh, can I go with you?" Jeremy asks. "I've finished my math."

"And me, too?" Joel says.

"Darling, I'm taking Jeremy and Joel," Father calls back into the house.

Driving past the towering Sampson elevators, Father shakes his head. "The wheat price is down another ten cents today," he says. "I'll have to tell Granddaddy."

"Daddy, who decides the wheat price?" Joel asks.

Jeremy snickers and whispers in Joel's ear: "No one decides the wheat price, stupid."

"No one really sets the price," Father says, and Jeremy sticks out his tongue. Joel pretends not to see.

"Then how does the elevator know what price to put on their sign?" he asks.

"Well," Father says, "all over the country people buy and sell wheat—farmers, traders, elevators. Flour mills grind the wheat into flour so your mom can make bread and things like that. Every day the elevator here in Sampson checks to see what price the other elevators get for selling their wheat to the mills, then they post a lower price on their sign and that's the price they pay the farmers. And the difference in price between the small-farmer batches and the big flour-mill batches is the extra money the elevator uses to pay its men and keep the electricity on and buy food for their families."

Joel thinks about this. It makes sense, but it doesn't make all the sense. Finally, he asks, "But, if no one decides the price, what makes it change?"

"That, my friend, is what we call supply and demand." Father smiles. "Jeremy, do you want to tell Joel about supply and demand?"

"What?" Jeremy asks.

"I've told you before," Father says, "remember? About piles of wheat sitting on the road corner?"

"Oh, yes!" Jeremy says. He puts on his know-it-all voice: "If there's a pile of wheat on the corner for anyone to take, no one could charge much for wheat because people would just get it from the free pile."

"That's it," Father says. "The price depends on two things: how much wheat there is and how much wheat people need. Supply and demand. If there are a lot of people and not much wheat, people will pay a lot of money for it because everyone needs to eat. The price goes up because people see that there's not enough wheat so they hang onto what they've got, unless someone is willing to pay them a lot of money for it.

"But what if it's the other way around and there's so much wheat that people can't eat it all? What if there's so much that people put a great big pile on every street corner because there's not enough room in the elevators? Then no one would pay much for it, would they? Maybe they'll just pay a few cents for someone to go out there with a sack and bring it back for them."

This makes sense. But it hurts Joel's head to think of something like a price that's out of people's control.

Father continues: "Every year, people are watching to see if there's a terrible freeze or if it rains enough in wheat country, and they're guessing whether there will be a big harvest. The freezes, the rains, and the guesses change today's prices because people use them to decide whether to sell their wheat today or wait for later, hoping the price will go up."

He pulls up to the curb at the Sampson Farm Supply store. "Does that make sense?" he asks. Joel nods. "Here's a little story," Father says. "Back in the Depression, when your grandmother was a girl, there was so much wheat and the price went down so low that the farmers were going broke. It cost them more to grow a bushel of wheat than they could sell it for. No matter how good the crop was, they still lost money. So the government bought a bunch of perfectly good wheat and dumped it in pits to rot. They wanted to get rid of it so the price would go back up and keep the farmers in business.

"But other people were going hungry because they had no jobs and no money—not even enough money to buy the cheap wheat," Father said, "but the government still kept destroying food to keep the farmers in business. That's what happens when the economy gets out of whack.

"You see, a market is made out of people. It's something people can influence, but it's not something they can control. It's like America. America is made out of people, but no one individual controls America. No one can. America is controlled by all of us and that's what makes us great. If you wanted to get America small enough for a single person to control, you would have to make us tiny and pathetic. And the whole point of America is that we're free men.

"Of course, now the government doesn't dump wheat in pits. It has found another way to influence the market. Now the government watches the rains and the freezes and the crop while it's growing in the field. Then, if it's too much, the government tells the farmers to plow up the extra—that way the price stays up and people don't harvest the useless wheat.

"When I was a kid," Father went on, "the Russians lost their wheat crop because they were Communists. Communists aren't free like Americans and they have no reason to work because someone gives them their stuff for free whether they work or not, so no one went out and harvested their wheat. The Russians were going hungry because they had no wheat, so America sent ship after ship of wheat over to keep them from starving. But what do you think it did to the wheat price here in America when they took all that wheat away and sold it to the Russians?"

"Did it go up?" Joel asks.

"That's right! The supply went down here in America and the price went up. It went up from three dollars per bushel to over ten dollars! The farmers made a lot of money that year and that's when your granddaddy bought that orange tractor he still uses to mow his weeds. When he bought it, it was the nicest tractor we'd ever seen. He bought it new and he bought a new pickup, too, all because the Russians were Communists and they were too lazy to harvest their own wheat. And what happens to the price when supply goes down?"

"The price goes up," Joel says.

"That's right." Father smiles. "That's supply and demand." Then Father says, "I've got to run into the farm-supply store and see if they've got my air-compressor running again."

Once Father is inside, Joel looks at Jeremy. "Looks like I'm pretty smart after all, huh, Jeremy?" Jeremy looks out the window at a beetle climbing the curb.

The Socratic Dialogue

I locked my bike outside The Big Bear Cafe, depressed by the state of humanity. If you'd pressed me just then, I could have thought of nothing better than to set off the apocalyptic blasts our race prepared for itself in the second half of the last century. I could have thought of nothing saner than to turn the Cold War hot and exterminate the whole sorry lot of us.

And there Janet stood, leaning on a stool, dark glasses holding back her hair, looking out from under a peaceful forehead. You cut a dove out of a board and it still looks gentle. And what do birds know of virtue? But doves act their part and Janet's face, too, was shaped like peace and, unless hard-pressed, she lived it. With great fortitude.

Without the person of Janet Lestersen behind her face, you would never remark on it. A lusty eye would pause on her in its scan, then look away for something shinier—a layer of too much fat, eyes set too deep, face too angular. But once you see the person there, Janet's features glow; you're enchanted—drawn in to bask there. You must lean on her and find rest with her in a world that has no rest. With her, it is the plainest thing that a person should grieve what is sad in the world, love what is good, and be at peace with them both.

"Hi, Joel," she said, looking up.

"Janet, how are you?" I reached for a hug and she slid her arm around my waist from the side. I had forgotten how she fit there under my arm.

"I'm fine," she said. "Soc should be here in a bit. He's running a few minutes late."

"Soc?"

"It's a long story," she said. "I'm sure he'll tell you. How are you feeling about your project?"

"I'm terrified," I said. "How are you?"

"I'm fine."

"That's good to hear." Did she catch the bitterness in my voice? Janet broke up with me because I'm not a Christian. But sometimes I think she really broke up because I'm negative.

"So you're terrified," she said. "And why are you terrified?"

"I got three weeks to sort this out," I said, "when the smartest minds have lived and died in despair over the same questions."

"Maybe that's why they asked *you* this time," she said, with this sly, almost-wink thing she does. "And maybe that's why they only gave you three weeks."

"So they're asking me because I'm not smart?"

"You told me once that the smart people can be found doodling at the back of the class, leading street gangs, or dangling from their own rope in the garage." She raised her eyebrow and I winced. But then she softened her face and scratched my shoulder. "You haven't changed a bit, Joel. But you'll be fine. You've got a good head and I'd take that over being smart any day." Then she waved and said, "Soc, we're over here."

He wore green jeans and red canvas shoes, and a faded-from-red-to-pink shirt.[73] Janet stood flat-footed and kissed him in poor taste on the mouth.

"Soc, this is Joel," Janet said. "Joel, Socrates."

"Good to meet you," he said, and waited for me to tell him the same lie.

____

[73] A fake fade. Honest fades are deep around the shoulders from working in the sun but, from the look of his shirt, he must have laid it out on a lounge chair and flipped it carefully from front to back to keep it even.

"Socrates?" I asked. "Do people actually name their kids that?"

"Not that I've heard of," he said. I looked at Janet because I thought the joke wasn't funny, whatever it was. But she stood there and watched us like we were some sort of travelling improv act.

"This is the part where you ask me why I'm called Socrates," Socrates said.

"Why are you called Socrates?" I asked.

"Ah, well, I thought you'd never ask," he said. "Really, I actually did think you would never ask. That's why I prompted you.

"Soc is short for Socrates. But you've already deduced that, I see. Socrates, in turn, is a reference to an ancient Greek philosopher who is most famous for his most famous student—"

"I know who Socrates is."

"Soc, just tell him and then let's order some drinks," Janet said. "There's no need to be mean."

"Indeed there is not," Socrates said. "Which is why I am patiently explaining my name to this newcomer who has asked. Socrates is a nickname, which is—"

"I know what a nickname is."

"No doubt. But my particular nickname is short for 'Upside Down Socrates.'"

"Upside Down Socrates?"

"People found 'Upside Down Socrates' too long, though, and, having declared 'UDS' an unsatisfactory moniker, my friends settled on the name of 'Socrates'—the venerable founder of our discipline. Those closest to me have further shortened it to a name that could be mistaken for an item of unsalacious underwear."

I'd just met him, but I was already as tired of Socrates as Europe is of war. But I wanted to be done with it so I asked, "Why Upside Down Socrates?"

236

"Ah, you're getting the hang of this," he said. "I prompt a question, you ask it, I compliment it, then I answer it. It's a useful pattern.

"They call me Upside Down Socrates because I'm like Socrates, only backward. Socrates was old and wise and asked questions, while I'm young and stupid and give answers."

"What's your real name?" I asked.

"Socrates is real. Besides, my dad is famous. So you can just call me Socrates."

We ordered drinks and I wanted to tell Janet that I needed to meet with her alone so we could talk, unmocked, about issues of national concern. I caught her eye behind his back and gave the palms-up shrug of desperation. In reply, Janet gave an air-swat that said: *that's just Soc, don't let him get to you.*

When I first walked into Big Bear last year, I thought it was cool: the patio, the ivy, the retro music. But I watched while Socrates chatted up the stupid barista and I saw through the sham.

"Can you make me a dirty chai?" he asked.

"Sure thing," the barista said and dumped two shots of espresso into a perfectly good chai latte. I cringed at the contamination of it and looked away. And then I noticed a vinyl record on Big Bear's turntable. I mean, who are they fooling? "Big Bear Café," with a turntable—like they're some sort of lumberjack café from the sixties?

We sat with our drinks. I'd given up at gaining anything from this miserable experience. I had only two goals: avoid felonious conduct and manage this improv act so, at the end of the day, the audience would break in my favor. Surely I could draw a favorable contrast with this creature. Surely I could convince Janet she'd made a bad trade when she went for him.

Seated on the patio, bureaucrat Joel addressed himself to Janet. "As you read in my emails, I was asked to provide some sweeping recommendations to our national leadership. Recommendations on how to unify the country."

"I think 'they' made a bizarre appeal to the prophet Joel?" Socrates said. I glanced at him. "For the sake of simplicity and the furtherance of our constructive dialog, shall we call *them*, 'the president?'" he asked, looking at Janet.[74]

"Oh, for goodness sakes!" I said.

"Having made the motion and hearing no objection, shall we continue to consider the president's questions?" Socrates asked, again looking at Janet as if it was just the two of them having coffee, while I sat like a stranger who reads his paper awkwardly at your table because the other tables were full and you lacked the presence to say no when he pulled out the third chair and asked unexpectedly, "Do you mind?"

"I have considered this a good deal," Socrates said. "The president would have done better to seek advice from a philosopher—in the Platonic sense, mind you—rather than a bureaucrat, but it is nonetheless commendable that he has recognized a deficit among his advisors and sought a remedy. It would seem that your qualifications for this project are thin, consisting primarily of the fact that your parents opened their Bibles to a particular book on the date of your birth. That said, you have done well to recognize the wisdom of Janet Lestersen. I commend you for outsourcing your advice to her. She, in due course, has outsourced her advice to a true philosopher so that the president may still receive the wisdom he ought to have sought from the beginning. I presume, in this, that you are capable of conveying to him, reasonably intact, what you are about to hear and will, no doubt, take notes on as this conversation progresses?"

----

[74] This is a problem.

I chose to ignore this little episode of speech, as it was the kindest response I could imagine. "Janet," I said, "do you have any ideas on how I should address this request?"

"I think you could learn a lot by discussing it with Socrates," she said.

"And why do you think that?"

"You're both smart, analytical guys and you've both thought a lot about the questions the president is asking." Socrates winked at me when she said "the president."

"What you must do," Socrates said, "is understand what's behind the president's questions and then address his questions on that level."

"I know."

"But that's the easy part—the first step. It's what every bureaucrat knows to do. The next part is where you need a philosopher." He glugged his disgusting drink and crunched an ice cube—all without breaking his snide stare. "To make real progress, you must also tell him the questions he doesn't know to ask." He stopped, like he assumed such an idea would need time to penetrate my skull. "Most questions are dishonest," he continued. "Most questions are designed to avoid the truth. But you must design your questions to find it. Most people ask the questions they want to answer, not the questions they need to answer."

"Tell Joel what you mean by a dishonest question," Janet said. She meant to be kind but it only made this feel like a little she-and-him club with me on the outside.

"A dishonest question?" Socrates said. "Ah, yes, in an educational setting, it is useful to provide examples. Let's take the iPad salesman: he walks into a school and asks the administrators, 'How can technology solve your educational challenges?' The salesman likes the question because it helps him sell stuff. The administrators like the question because it helps them avoid their real problems—the ones they would see if they looked in a mirror. It only asks the questions that lead to an easy answer. It only discusses the problems you can throw money at. And everybody wins, right? But the question is dishonest. It avoids the school's real problems—it avoids the honest question." I nodded briefly then remembered I hated him.

Socrates went on: "So here's my question for you: What's the honest question? What is the real question they're avoiding?"

"The honest question about what?" I asked.

"Education, of course? What did you think we were talking about?"

"I thought we were talking about the problem I have to address: Who are we to each other? Who is responsible for our culture?"

"Yes, and I'm telling you how to look behind those questions and ask an honest question that really needs an answer."

"Okay," I said. "So what's the honest question? Maybe they should ask what their educational problem is before they look for the solution."

"Okay, good," Socrates said. "You're making progress. But there's another question behind that one: How do you know there's a problem to start with? And here are some more questions: What are your expectations? What is reality? What is the gap between them? Are your expectations reasonable? What would it take to meet your expectations? Is this something you're willing to do? Is it something you're able to do? Would there be unanticipated consequences to 'doing what it takes?' What are those consequences? Are they worth the cost? And what are the consequences of doing nothing?

"People don't ask those questions, though, because the answers hurt. They ask questions, like the president did—questions that assume their problems are someone else's fault.

"When people ask honest questions, they usually find answers that require them to change, and they don't want to change so they go on asking dishonest questions and complaining when nothing

240

improves. We're like the people who stay away from the doctor because they're afraid they've got cancer. And, you know what? They are the ones who die of cancer.

"'The unexamined life is not worth living.' Who said that?"

"Plato," I said.

"Actually, it was Socrates."

"Actually, Plato put it in Socrates' mouth after Socrates got himself killed."

"Ah, yes, the sad day of the philosopher's death."

"The happy day!" I said. "Socrates asked to be killed—he practically dared them to do it to him, for goodness sakes!"

"That's not strictly accurate."

"Socrates gave a speech in his defense and what did he do?" I asked. "He talked about how much he'd like to die! I'd have given Socrates the hemlock myself! He abandoned his family, then walked around tearing everyone down and mocking them for being wrong. Then he bragged about how much wiser he was than them all because he claimed a goddess had declared him the wisest man alive! And this is the foundation of philosophy?"

"I'm sorry you feel[75] that way," Socrates said. "But Socrates was right, the unexamined life really is not worth living. If you don't think about who you are and where you're going, how do you expect to get there? And tell the president this: the unexamined country is not worth governing. You tell him. Then, if he hasn't kicked you out for that, I'll tell you some examination questions to ask."

He must have seen the look on my face, because he went on. "And why do *I* ask the questions? Well, because the only way *you* are likely to ask the right questions is if *I* tell you what they are. Unfortunately, to ask questions, I have to turn my upside-down self

____

[75] Feelings are okay but every time someone says *feel* he's being condescending. Like *I'm sorry your* feelings *have got you unhinged.*

upside down.[76] Why, you may ask, do I have to turn myself upside down? Well, that's a good question."

"I didn't ask that question!" I said. "If you want to talk to yourself, for heaven's sake do it in a soundproof room!"

"Ah, ha! You want a conversation now? Well, then, why don't you ask some questions instead of bragging about how you want to kill Socrates?"

"Because I'm trying to have an honest conversation, not sit on some mountain receiving wisdom from Yoda."

"Yoda didn't live on a mountain."

"Whatever."

"Do you want to know why people hated Socrates?" He paused. "I asked you a question: *Do you really want to know why people hated Socrates?*"

"Please inform me," I said.

"You know how people hate a know-it-all?"

"Yes," I said, "I have experience with that." Janet got it and frowned.

"Well," Socrates said, "there's something they hate even more: it's an ask-it-all. Socrates was an ask-it-all and they killed him for it. And, you know what else? If you want to get the president out of his funk, you'll have to become an ask-it-all yourself. And, if I have my guess, he'll hate you for it.

"Besides, the president is the wrong person. He isn't destroying this country, the people who elected him are destroying it. And, to change that, you'll have to tell *them* they're wrong and convince them to change. Good luck with *that*. And, if you don't want my help, I can get up, take my girlfriend, walk out, and wait for people to improve. I can do that, if you want. But you said you wanted help."

---

[76] In DoD we have a term for a person who thinks he can carry on all sides of a conversation himself. We say he is a self-licking ice-cream cone.

Janet gripped Socrates' arm in gentle tugs, like she would rein back a horse. She used to hold my arm like that, too—it was like having a conscience attached. She'd sense you thinking a mean thought and squeeze before it came out. And, if she was too late, she'd tell you afterwards. "Joel," she'd say, "I know you didn't mean it, but what you said to Emily at the party was hurtful." And she was right, obviously. I would never have noticed on my own. But she would tell me later and I would know she was right.

We all sat there in silence and Socrates pulled a pack of cigarettes from his pocket. He lit one and I waited for Janet to react. Nothing. Then she spoke. "Joel, I don't think I'll be much help to you on my own." She paused while Socrates dragged on his cigarette, blew smoke, and stared at me. "But Soc and I can meet with you again, if that's what you want, and we can help you sort through this project."

I felt betrayed. Janet had sided with him. But Socrates seemed to assume we were back on good terms and struck into a new conversation.

"I see you looking critically at this cigarette," he said. "But, really, you're looking uncritically. You're thinking it's nasty and unhealthy. And you're wondering why Janet doesn't object."

"You're putting words in my mouth," I said, more in weariness than in anger.

"Come on, man, if you bottle up your thoughts, you just force me to say them. That's what you were thinking. Admit it."

"That's what I was thinking."

"But you've got an uncritical opinion," he said. "Smoking is actually quite healthy."

I let myself be dragged back into his game. "That's just perverse."

"Nope." He smiled. "I mean it. Quitting smoking is part of how we've destroyed ourselves in this country. Quitting so we can live long, pointless lives."

"Are you going to explain yourself or just keep being perverse?"

Socrates snubbed his cigarette, sealed the butt in an old-school camera film case, and lit another. "See this thing?" he said. "These are what make people sane. Little things you can touch and feel with your fingers. Little things that stop the frenzy and measure life out so you can live it. Quitting smoking, switching from tea to coffee—these are all steps down the slippery slope to insanity."

"Keep talking," I said. He had given this lecture before and I knew he would give it again.

"I will," he said. He took a drag from his cigarette, sucked it into his lungs, held, then released the smoke through his nostrils. "You work. And why do you work? I'll tell you why. You work so you have the material to actually live life in the in-between spaces— before, during, after your job. But in America, we work by squeezing out the in-between spaces and working all the time. We call it efficiency." He wrinkled his nose at this word and spat.

"What you need is something natural—something you can touch—to create spaces in life where you can live. People drink coffee alone at their desks so they can work faster. But they brew a pot of tea so they can rest for a bit while the kettle boils, ponder a bit as it steeps, then chat together while it cools. That's the space where you learn who you are and what the whole thing means. And the tea gives you a gentle boost of caffeine—not a frenzied coffee jolt."

"I'm not opposed to tea," I said.

"But this cigarette does the same thing. It's not as good as a pipe, granted, but still, it's not bad. It builds into your body a little reminder that, hey, it's time for a break. You need a cigarette. So you go out, take deep breaths with your friends, let your body relax, and then you go back to your work, balanced, de-stressed, and knowing who you are. You know what the weather is outside and why you're doing what you're doing. You've lived for a bit. It's laziness, maybe, you think? Naw. The tea cools, the cigarette burns down, you know the break has ended, and you go back to work. And what's the downside? Nothing. Only it's bad for your lungs."

Socrates paused and looked at me. But I said nothing. "This concept should make sense to you, Joel," he said. "I'm trying to state it simply. If it would help, I can explain how it works with a good glass of beer?"

"No," I said. "I think you've made your point."

"And you've said nothing to the contrary. Shall I presume that you have taken this to heart? Or do I still expect you to go back, work yourself straight through on hyper-doses of caffeine—or those disgusting energy drinks—then come home exhausted and delete the rest of your life alone with frozen dinners and inane TV shows?"

"You can stop," I said.

"And he evades the question." Socrates threw up his hands to an imaginary audience. "Mature response there, buddy. Well done."

I looked at Janet, hoping to see the misplaced faith in Socrates drain from her face. "I think Socrates is trying to say he'll question your assumptions and help you understand what you're doing," she said. "Soc is just trying to illustrate the irrationality of people who know they want to live long lives when they don't even know why they want to live lives."

Janet. I've seen her take a bruised, decaying peach—an oozing fruit turning to syrup in the sun. She touches its skin kindly while you watch, and then you see in this, the best of peaches a man could eat upon his grassy earth.

She used to make me feel twice as smart as I did with anyone else. And that's what she did now for this kid in green jeans. She took his insults and touched them until they were good—helpful insights presented for my benefit.

"Joel," she said, "I think it will help you to talk through some of your questions like we're doing here. There are a lot of things troubling our country. And, like Socrates said, unless someone points them out, we'll never be able to improve them."

Socrates took this as his queue to start in again. "Ugly people don't like it when you hold a mirror up to them," he said. "But it's your job. If you want to be a philosopher, that is. You have to hold a mirror up to America. She's ugly, I can assure you, and she won't like it. But, for Christ's sake, if a country can't look in the mirror and acknowledge what it sees, it should apply for hospice care."

"This isn't the first time I've tried to cure a country that should be in hospice care," I said obliquely.

An African Milieu

A: Broken Protocol

Socrates said we should live on purpose and I knew Janet once fell in love with a Joel Alden who also believed this. A Joel Alden who, in the twilight of his faith, looked for meaning through helping his fellow man—in Africa, which is known to be noble. Africa is not a place; it is a continent with many places, but Africa credit accrues for them all. So he chose Z______.

Africa credit is not like other credit. Africa's problems are too big: success is known to lie beyond reach so you get trying credit, which is great because trying is sustainable while succeeding is not— you can spend your life trying to build a castle but, once you succeed, you have to get on with the devilish business of living there, which sucks if you're better at trying than succeeding. Success kills the fun. There's a lot of money in poverty but, if the poverty goes away, where's the money? So it's best to help in a place that will stay poor.

Joel doesn't know this yet when he leaves for Z______, but he will learn. The way to make a difference, he thinks, is to get out of government and meet people where they are, to help them one person at a time. He's alone. A volunteer in the big wide jungle—in the Serengeti with antelope: alert, quick, endangered—alive and incredibly beautiful.

A determined American abroad, Joel Alden straps grocery bags over his shoes—bags that might have drifted, scratching, across a parking lot and snagged on a streetlight—and he drives his motorcycle through the knuckle-cutting rain to the ambassador's presidential inauguration party. He putts, in splattered gear, through a line of limos, coat-checks the grocery bags, and watches while the baby-faced Chinese ambassador, through confidential conversations, charms a chamber of dignitaries while tuxedoed servants disperse pastries from a tray.

Joel sees the Embassy's deputy—the DCM[77]—notice him, and frown. "I have made it clear to Mr. Alden that the U.S. does not sponsor his activities in Z_______," the DCM says to a dignitary in his head.

Joel takes a glass of wine from the servant's tray and breaks protocol for fun: "How are you?" he asks. The slight servant smiles with Africa's white teeth. Earlier, he'd served Joel his lunch at the café: roast chicken, rape greens, maize paste, and the delightful ndiwo gravy for flavor. The servant is human, much like the dignitaries. But this is a secret between Joel and him and they won't let it out.

B: The Useless Conversation

"I'm Cynthia Dawson," a motherly blonde says at Joel's elbow.

"Joel Alden," he says, and extends his hand.

"What do you do here?"

"I volunteer with a local leadership-development organization." It's a clumsy explanation. But what can you say: *I'm helping David Banda because he's planning to run for president?* "What do you do here?" he asks.

"Have you heard of Ngwezi Farm?"

"No."

"Well, my husband and I met its founder a couple of years ago. It's marvelous. You have to go there and see it!"

Joel does the combined eyebrow-raise/thoughtful-frown/wineglass-bob that says, *Why don't you tell me about it.*

---

[77] Deputy Chief of Mission

248

So Cynthia Dawson continues. "The founder of Ngwezi Farm left his commercial tobacco farm and built Ngwezi with a system of pipes that bring water from the mountains. He has created a fully-sustainable irrigated farm with no reliance on fossil fuels, chemical fertilizers, or GMOs[78] or hybrid seeds. It's all based on crop-rotation and anti-erosion farming methods."

"Are you trying to make everyone farm like that?" Joel asks.

"Our plan is to educate Z______'s farmers using Ngwezi's best practices."

"How do they farm at Ngwezi?" Joel asks.

"What do you mean?"

"Tractor? Spade? Hoe? Ox-and-plow?"

"Oh! It's all done without the use of fossil fuels or industrialized farming methods that deplete the soil."

"So it's done by hand?"

"And you should see the gardens—tomatoes, vegetables, mangoes, bananas, papayas, high-protein ground nuts, high-protein soy. You really have to see the place to believe it."

"Do they grow enough to sell it and pay their workers?"

"They've just been going for a couple of years but, I'm telling you, it's a sight to see."

Joel feels sudden slack in Cynthia Dawson. "Have you ever farmed?" he asks.

"I've studied crop-ration and other methods to diversify the diet and improve soil conditions," she says.

"And what is your vision for farming in Z______? Will women always bend over at the waist, hoeing their fields in the African heat, trying to grow enough food to live through another year?"

"We have to make things better where we can, don't we? And we know corporate, factory farming isn't the answer. Just look at

---

[78] genetically modified organisms

America with all the hybrid seeds and DNA-splicing and chemicals and global warming. I mean, surely you wouldn't want to hand Africa's economy to corporations like Monsanto!"

"I grew up on a farm in America and it's the most beautiful thing I've ever seen," Joel says, and he turns to where the ambassador has stood to speak.

C: The Useless Speech

"What you're about to witness," the ambassador says, "is one of America's finest traditions. You're about to witness a peaceful transition of power from one government to another—a transition reflecting not the will of one political party or another but the collective will of the American people."

Joel looks out the window at some frayed banana fronds in the twilight, then back to the projected snow on Washington's projected mall where the new president gives his speech.

"Today," the president says, "we stand for the future, for a more perfect union, for what America can be. We stand here in the firm belief that, despite today's challenges, America's best days still lie ahead."

Inside, Joel rages. Africa needs tractors, combines, train-loads of diesel, and truckloads of high-yield, disease-resistant, hybrid seeds. Until then its people will labor—heavy, swooning, tropical labor on a diet of starch, mangoes, and parasites—and, in the end, they will starve. It does *not* need suburban do-gooders like Cynthia Dawson who watch a couple of documentaries and move to Africa where they're mistaken for experts because their skin is white, and they teach the people how to starve all over again. *They know how to starve, Cynthia! You idiot! But you're teaching them something different, right? Yes, you're teaching them a new way to starve!*

Write a song, Cynthia, he rages on: Starvations: Variations on an
    African Theme

Write a book: Fifty Shades of Hunger

Start a cultural exchange: Send Us Your Smartest and We'll Send You Our Dumbest

Set up a business: Exporting Ideas That Never Worked in our own Country

Do you know how many people have set up idyllic "sustainable farming communities" in the U.S., Cynthia? And every last one of them either worked its fingers to the bone or gave it up—usually both?

The president speaks on: "I do not stand here saying that America is perfect, but I ask people of goodwill the world over to join us in the struggle to become more perfect—to build, in the words of our Constitution, a more perfect union. As president, I say that America is a friend to free people everywhere. And to those who struggle for freedom but have not yet achieved it, I say, don't give it up. We are a friend to you as well."

D: The Useless Conversation (II)

When the speech is finished, Joel positions himself where the DCM will see and he chats pleasantly with the ambassador. He has read the ambassador's bio and identified a mutual friend.

"Do you know Sara Hornberg?" Joel asks.

"Yes!" The ambassador lights up. "How do you know her?"

"We worked together in DRL."

"Really! That's great. Sara Hornberg and I were posted together in Namibia a few years back. Great person! And what's your name?"

"I'm Joel Alden."

"Good to meet you, Joel."

Joel sees that the DCM has turned away to chat with a person he doesn't like.

The Rules of Conversation

"So, shall I presume we will meet again, or would you like to rely entirely on your own resources?" Socrates asked.

Despite myself, I wanted to know what Socrates would say about America's problems. And I wanted to see Janet again. I wanted to shake her and show her what a jerk she was dating.

"Yes," I said, "let's meet again."

"Then I will establish some ground rules."

"But this is my project," I said. "I will establish the ground rules."

"Do what you will but *I* will establish the terms of my assistance."

"And I will establish my terms for receiving it."

"So I will lay the ground rules, then you can propose some 'first-floor' rules."

"Or maybe *I'll* lay the ground rules and then, you can propose a basement," I said.

"Boys, stop it! Joel, please explain your rules."

That shushed Socrates, and I basked in his silence long enough for him to notice.

"To start with," I said, "you're smart. You said we have to hold a mirror up to America but, when we do, I think you'll see that America is smart, too." Socrates snickered like I was even stupider than he thought. I continued, "But America will never understand if we talk in philosopher words. Words that, by the way, I doubt half of the philosophers understand. With that kind of talk, the people will never see themselves in your mirror.

"Ever heard of the French Poet, Charles Peguy?"

"Please enlighten us," he said.

"He was a brilliant philosopher, and do you know what he said?" I waited. No Socratic engagement. So I went on: "Peguy said, 'If you can't say it in the words of a farmer, it's not true.' So there. That's rule number one: 'If you can't say it in the words of a farmer, it's not true.'"

"I don't do redneck philosophy," Socrates said.

"Me either, but, if you can't state it simply, I won't believe you understand it yourself."

Then Socrates tried to switch on me. "Have you heard of Wittgenstein?" And he pronounced it all _VIT-gin-shTEIN_.

"Yes," I said. "The German philosopher."

"No. He was Austrian."

"Whatever."

"He said, 'What can be said, can be said clearly, and where we cannot speak, we must remain silent.'"

"You don't need Wittgenstein to tell you that," I said. "'If you can't say it in the words of a farmer, it's not true.' Remember?"

"Socrates, did you have any rules to add?" Janet asked.

"Okay, sure," he said. "If you want to talk to America, I'll go one better than your little Piggy quote. The only truths that change the world are the truths that change children. So, if you can't explain it to your children, it will die with you. How's that?"

Honestly, I liked that one. But I didn't like Socrates pretending he'd just come up this line of argument on his own. So told him, "I believe it was Frederick Douglass who said, 'It is easier to build strong children than to repair broken men?'"

"Ah, my friend, but why quote Frederick Douglass when you could just listen to me?"

I squinted at him, but Janet jumped in. "I'm glad to see we've established our ground rules," she said. "Shall we meet again on Saturday?"

"I came here to provide your ex with an analysis of the president's conversation," Socrates said, "and I have yet to do that."

"Let's save that for next time," Janet said.

"But how can I expect the august Mr. Alden to think clearly in the meanwhile and come prepared?" Socrates asked.

"I can forward your questions for Joel in an email. How's that?"

An African Milieu (II)

E: Conversations with Old Men

In Z_____, Joel begins to see that, in throwing himself against the system, he is the one that will break. But he deflects the looming forces of cynicism with the joys of small generosity.

He explains this all to himself in his journal:

When I was a child, small things thrilled me: the times I stood with Jeremy, Josiah, and Father, holding hands for balance on a tractor-tire inner-tube in Granddaddy's pond—then a gust would topple us, laughing; the times Granddaddy took us to "El Viejo"—the height of fine-dining in my small life, or the times when my friend Chad came to play for the afternoon.

I still remember the birthday when Granddaddy first gave me $50. This was wealth beyond my imagination. The sense of power and possibility was even better than the spending. I bought a stopwatch for $20 and had more than half of the money left.

As an adult, I seldom get a thrill like that. Perhaps from receiving a scholarship to Wheaton or when I first walked in to work at the State Department. But it's not the same. I only get that birthday-money thrill when I have set money aside as a gift. It's that same feeling: I don't yet know who I will give it to, but it burns a hole in my pocket; whoever it is—whatever it is—it will be wonderful!

But there is still a greater thrill when I think that each person is allotted certain time and abilities. I have a unique mind—a unique personality—and I have 24 hours each day to refine them and to give them for something good.

Joel maintains a website, stating Mr. Banda's vision to, "Develop servant leadership among the tribes." And, in this vision, regardless of the rest, there is joy.

But Joel talks to men who have lived long in Africa and he sees that what hope is left in them has been forced deep to survive the decades. It has gone dormant and absorbed itself into the enormous African patience—a pebble of hope sinking through oceans of despair, releasing tiny bubbles and tumbling to a place where it will rest in the silt—a place where it can survive forever and still reach up to animate the brown things that crawl upon the earth.

Joel writes about this in his journal, too:

Delayed hope is a strange thing. I admire those who have fought for freedom and won. I know what to make of them. They support my faith that good men can protect the vulnerable and the oppressed. But what should I think of the preceding centuries—centuries in which the oppressed were not freed? Centuries of despair made more bitter because they were the dregs of a crushed hope? Where in those times was Martin Luther King Jr.'s belief that "right defeated is stronger than evil triumphant?"

Righteousness may not win in my lifetime. This has been the case for many better men. But what am I to make of that?

I share MLK's frustration with those who are "more devoted to 'order' than to justice; who prefer a negative peace which is the absence of tension to a positive peace which is the presence of justice … who paternalistically believe they can set the timetable for another man's freedom."

Our own government sides with the corrupt government in Z______, even if it means leaving the poor with no advocate. Even if it sets a very long timeline for other men's freedom. We forget that, when we are patient with the plight of the poor, it is the poor who suffer.

F: Entertaining Stories

At a party that evening, Joel plays poker. He smokes cigars and drinks whisky while his British friend tells his story of the day.

"So I rolled down my window and the police said, without looking, that my registration had expired. I told him it wasn't expired and showed him. But the writing was smudged. 'We cannot know,' the policeman said. So he proposed that I pay him 2000 v and I told him no. 'One thousand?' he asked. I still said no and he said 'Perhaps you can give me a Fanta to drink?' I told him no and he waved me off in disgust!"

Everyone laughs. And they tell their stories—"An officer pulled me over but he had lost his ticket book. I just waited him out and didn't pay."—"An officer asked for an iPod. I laughed. Like Americans carry extra iPods!"—"An inspector threatened to decertify our orphanage unless we built a footbridge across the street, *for the children's safety*. That posed a real problem."—"The government held up a shipment of water filters, pending a thirty-percent tax on the assessed value of the cargo. We pushed back and waited them out. The government finally waived the tax and sent us a storage bill for the water filters that happened to equal thirty percent of their assessed value, so we paid. What else could we do?" The expats laugh and top each other's stories into the evening.

G: Therapeutic Emails

Deep in the night, Joel calls a friend in DRL to talk about the injustice of it all and to ask what can be done. "Email me a proposal and I'll send it around," she says.

To: southerlandaj@state.gov
From: Joel Alden
Subject: A Proposal for Countering Corruption

Dear Arnold,

Per our conversation earlier today, this is based on my frustration that corruption has a surprisingly good brand considering what it is. It has the image of flamboyant, "colorful" African leaders and of the entertaining stories we tell about our trips abroad where we had to bribe a policeman or a customs official to let us out of some bogus charge—stories we tell with thinly-veiled glee at having had such exotic experiences. We say "corruption" as a euphemism, the same way we hide in the comfort of "human rights abuses" when, in fact, we speak of fingernails torn out and people raped with sharp objects.

In our minds we've divorced corruption from its effects, much like we marvel at the wonders of the Thunderbirds and of precision-guided bombs without thinking of burning children on the ground and the husband who commits suicide because his hands are blown off and he can no longer provide for his family.

In Z_____ I see these soft anti-corruption posters. They say "Report Corruption!" But I think we should be direct about how corruption causes people to suffer. The U.S. Government—or perhaps an NGO[79]—could sponsor anti-corruption campaigns around this message: "You can't be corrupt and love your country."

We should ask presidents and dictators to put their faces on the billboards and voice the commercials like they do for everything else.

---

[79] Non-Governmental Organization

It's useless, of course. You can't change a system through a shoot-and-forget email, but it does feel good to write.

And then Joel writes an email to Janet. "I love America," he says, "but I came to Africa looking for God and I have never felt more like I live in a place where God is not."

This email will hurt Janet, Joel knows, but it also feels good to write.

The Language of a Child (II)

I rode my bicycle home, down Florida Ave, under the train tracks, and I considered how to win against Socrates. Socrates had some good ideas—considering what we will tell our children, for instance—and Janet knew it. I only needed to tie him in the Good Ideas category, then I could just let him win in the Despicable Human Being category, with Janet acting as judge.

Democracy relies on good conversations with citizens. That's why I said, if you can't say it in the words of a farmer, it's not true. But maybe it relies even more on the children than the farmers. Sometimes I think we only know what we think when we tell it to our children, and maybe my generation doesn't know what it thinks because it doesn't have children.

I don't have kids. But I had to try it. If I presented my world for the ears of a child, could I, perhaps, understand it myself? In my head I explained corruption to my son while we drove:

Jonny: "Mrs. King says we should respect what other kinds of people do in the world even if they are different from us."

Me: "Yes, she's right. But, still, certain things are true wherever you go in the world and whatever kind of people you find."

Jonny: "Like what?"

Me: "Well, for example, a British guy was making rules in India. Maybe he shouldn't have been there to start with. But, still, the man listened to the Indian people when he made the rules.

"Whenever a person died, the Indians would turn the body into ash to keep it from rotting. Do you know how you turn something into ash?"

Jonny: "You burn it?"

Me: "Yes. They would burn the body. That's not how the British did it—the British buried people after they died, like we do. The British guy respected the Indian way when he made the rules, but some of the Indian people thought it was good for a woman to die, too, whenever her husband died. So they would ask the man's wife to fall into the fire and turn herself into ash with her dead husband."

Jonny recoils.

Me: "But the British man knew this was wrong. First of all, the woman should make her own decisions, and, second, the people should help her live after her husband dies and not try to kill her. So the British man said it was against the rules to burn a widow. But the people complained. 'This is one of our ancient traditions,' they said. 'You should respect it even if you don't agree.'

"But he answered them: 'This burning of widows is your custom. Prepare the funeral fire. But my nation also has a custom. When men burn women alive we hang them.' Then he stood there and waited to hang anyone who killed a widow. Do you know why he did that?"

Jonny: "Why?"

Me: "Because killing a widow is wrong wherever you go. And there's another thing: wherever you go, it's wrong to take money that belongs to others, especially if you're taking it from someone who is poor. It's called corruption."

Jonny: "What's a corruption?"

Me: "Corruption? It's an old word for rot. We don't use it much anymore."

Jonny: "What's rot?"

Me: "It's when something falls apart and goes back to what it was before. Rot is when the wheat stubble sits around in the field until it turns back into dirt. Or that raccoon that started to stink a few days after I shot it in the chicken house. Remember? That's what corruption really means. It's a body that stinks and rots and finally stops being a body because it has fallen apart and been eaten by maggots and vultures."

Silence, while Jonny thinks.

Jonny: "Dad?"

Me: "Yes?"

Jonny: "What's maggots?"

Me: "Remember when we had that caterpillar in the jar and it turned into a butterfly?"

Jonny: "Yes."

Me: "Well, a maggot is a worm, too, but instead of turning into a butterfly, a maggot turns into a fly. And remember how we fed the caterpillar peach leaves? Well, maggots don't eat peach leaves. They eat dead, rotting meat."

Jonny: "Yuck!"

Me: "Flies lay their eggs in dead animals, the eggs hatch into little white maggots in the dead meat, then they eat the rotting animal and grow up to be flies."

Jonny: "Ew!"

Me: "Then the flies go out looking for an animal so they can suck its blood. Or maybe one buzzes around and bites a little boy named Jonny!"

Jonny: "I would swat that fly if it tried to bite me."

Me: "I'll bet you would. Corruption is rotten and maggoty, and people who say nothing about it are cowards. Corrupt people are killing others all over the world, but most of the people who could do something about it don't care much because it's killing other people, not them."

Jonny, imagining a zombie: "Have you ever seen a corrupt person? With the maggots and stuff?"

Me: "I sure have. Only, with a corrupt person, you don't see the maggots because they're not eating his face or his body, they're eating the man's soul."

Jonny: "Then how can you see that a guy is corrupt, if the maggots are only eating his soul?"

Me: "You can see a person's soul by watching how he acts. With the guy I'm thinking of, you could tell his soul was corrupt because he took money out of my wallet. What would you do if someone took money out of your wallet?"

Jonny, thinking of his birthday money: "I'd tell him to give it back!"

Me: "And what if he wouldn't give it back?"

Jonny: "Then, I'd call the police!"

Me: "But what if it was the police that took the money from your wallet?"

Jonny, looking like he might cry: "Why would the police do that?"

Me: "Well, it's because they're corrupt. In some places police take other people's money just because they're the police and no one can stop them."

Jonny: "Do they have maggots in their souls?"

Me: "Yes."

Jonny: "But how did you get your money back?"

Me: "Well, that time, I told the policeman I knew how much money had been in my wallet so I knew how much was missing. And I asked him to give it back. He pretended not to know what I was talking about. 'Maybe you counted it wrong,' he said.

"You see, corrupt people usually try to pretend they're not corrupt because they know it's wrong. So this guy pretended not to know about the money. There were even posters in the police station telling people that corruption is a crime—saying we should report it to the authorities."

Jonny: "So what did you do?"

Me: "I looked that policeman in the eye and I looked all shocked—like I couldn't believe what I'd seen—and I asked, 'Are you—corrupt?' And do you know what he did?"

Jonny: "What?"

Me: "He looked up at the cracked, yellow ceiling in the African jail where we were and he laughed. Then he reached in his pocket and handed my money back. And, do you know how much money it was?"

Jonny: "How much?"

Me: "Guess."

Jonny: "One hundred dollars."

Me: "Nope. It was three dollars and fifty cents. Actually, in the local language, they would have called it five hundred victories."

Jonny: "Victories?"

Me: "Yes. The same way Americans named our money 'dollars,' they named theirs 'victories.'"

Jonny: "That's a weird name for money."

Me: "They called it that because, when they created their money, they'd just run the British out from trying to rule their country. So they called their money a 'victory' to remind them of how they'd beat the British."

Jonny: "Were the British trying to rule Africa, too?"

Me: "Yes. They even tried to rule America for a while, until we kicked them out because we wanted to run our own country. The British are good folks. America mostly learned how to run a country from them. The British just had a bad habit of staying on and trying to rule places that weren't theirs. So we had to fight a war and run them out. But, when they stay in their place and America stays in our place, we mostly get along fine."

Jonny: "I'm glad the British don't rule us."

Me: "Me too. But the difference between America and Africa is that America mostly learned good habits from the British, like letting people vote for their leaders, letting people say what they think, teaching people to read and write so they can think for themselves, and only letting the Government take our money through taxes after we've all had a chance to vote on it—not straight out of our wallets."

Jonny: "Dad?"

Me: "Yes?"

Jonny: "Were you in jail?"

Me: "For a little bit."

Jonny: "But why did they put you in jail?"

Me: "Well, I was friends with someone the government of Z_____ didn't like and, when a government is corrupt, being friends with someone they don't like is enough for them to put you in jail."

Jonny: "Did they hurt you?"

Me: "Not really. They just left me locked in a filthy cell for a while and made me sleep on a concrete floor. That didn't hurt me much. The people it really hurts are the ones who are stuck in that country. They're poor and, if they ever get much money, the government takes it and the police are no help. If they complain about it like I did, *they* don't get sent back to a nice place like America. They get stuck on a concrete floor in jail for a long, long time. It's terrible."

Jonny: "I wish we could help them."

Me: "Maybe someday you will. The African governments are right about one thing: they should be able to run their own countries without Britain or someone else doing it for them. But, unfortunately, they seem to have learned mostly bad habits from the British—like using the police to dominate people, ruling people without giving them a vote, and running a country for your own benefit, not for the people who live there."

✳ ✳ ✳

I thought about telling my child all this. Was it true? Was it oversimplified? Maybe. But, somehow, I suspected that the oversimplified version, for a child, was truer than the over-equivocated version for adults.

* * *

When I had written this conversation with my son, I checked my email and found an under-equivocated note from Janet.

To: Joel Alden
From: Janet Lestersen
Subject: Re: I really need your help

Dear Joel,

It was good to see you again today. Socrates asked me to send this to you. I'm forwarding it without comment:

Tell your ex I've read his notes from "the highest level of government" and I have summarized the issues:

1. *(Highest level of government—more commonly called "The President") The prophet Amos is pretty messed up but, still, kings had prophets and they needed prophets and presidents need prophets too so, please, won't you be my prophet?*
2. *(Ex) If the prophets were messed up, I don't think you want me to be a prophet.*
3. *(President) But what if I do?*
4. *(Ex) How do you know there's something a prophet should say?*
5. *(President) Because we have no country. I just pretend we do and I say stuff because I want it to be true.*
6. *(Ex) Every other country is a place, a race, or a language but America is only an idea and if the idea dies we become a collection of parts that used to be a whole thing—like a car that has lost its bolts.*

7. *(President) You came here to tell me something. What is it?*

8. *(Ex) But now I don't want to tell you.*

9. *(President) But what is it?*

10. *(Ex) You're running a deficit and that means you're stealing from children.*

11. *(President) But the deficit is a culture problem and a president can't control the culture. And I do invest in children, like with education and stuff. That's why we have a deficit.*

12. *(Ex) Education is for parents, not for children, so it doesn't count.*

13. *(President) You're no good as a prophet. Why are you in government anyway?*

14. *(Ex) I'm in government because the world is better when the best nation and the strongest nation are the same nation.*

15. *(President and ex) But government does what works not what is good.*

16. *(President) We have a deficit because all the good causes cost more than all the good taxes can produce.*

17. *(President (Lincoln?)) Both parties deprecated a deficit; but one of them would make a deficit rather than raise taxes on anyone; and the other would accept a deficit rather than let poor people, old people, and children go hungry. And the deficit came.*

18. *(Ex) We fight about stuff like this because we all think we're defending an innocent victim from the other side.*

19. *(Ex) These things are so big, it's hard to keep the right size head. (Tell him he could at least try—Soc)*

20. *(President) Some things are too big to be done by unaided mortals.*

21. *(President) President's dilemma: What do you do when everything can be influenced but nothing can be controlled?*

22. *(President) Does your generation understand the concept of sacrificing for something?*

23. *(Ex) No one understands delayed-gratification.*

24. *(President) Then no one will solve the deficit.*

25. *(Ex) But we must learn to live together without robbing each other.*

26. *(President) The deficit is cultural. Does anyone else in this country take responsibility for tending our culture?*

27. *(Ex) Agrees to make recommendations. Then looks for someone smarter whose ideas he can plagiarize.*

Your ex is fixated on the deficit; the president clearly did not invite him in to talk about it but he keeps bringing it up and blaming the president for it. The president keeps giving explanations that blame someone else. I count five different explanations:

Explanation #1: The deficit is a cultural problem and presidents don't control the culture.

Explanation #2: All the good causes cost more money than all the good taxes can produce.

Explanation #3: Both parties deprecated a deficit; but one of them would make a deficit rather than raise taxes on anyone; and the other would accept a deficit rather than let poor people, old people, and children go hungry. And the deficit came.

Explanation #4: No one understands delayed gratification. That's why no one will solve the deficit.

Explanation #5: No one takes responsibility for our culture and that's why no one will solve the deficit.

I have given this summary of the surface issues in the conversation so we can proceed to discuss the underlying problems your ex would never see if someone didn't point them out: if the deficit is a symptom of a cultural problem, then what is the cultural problem:

Problem 1: We educate our children rather than inspiring them. In school we prepare children for jobs when we should prepare them for lives. We're teaching them skills not wisdom. They grow up and they have no idea what it means to be human and, if they don't understand this, how will they know who they are to each other? How will they build a culture worth keeping? How will they build a good government of/by/for the people? (Cultural critique is alive and well, of course—we have developed a spectacular capacity for complaining—but cultural leadership is an abandoned, dying art.)

Problem 2: We develop tools and neglect the craftsmen. (I mean, of course, that science and technology are tools but we're not teaching anyone what they're for or how to use them well.) Tools are valuable because you can use them for a purpose but, if you have no purpose, how can you use them?

Problem 3: We're toast when everyone thinks he's subject to the forces in society, not responsible for them. (The president has fallen into this trap and he has dragged most of the government in with him. We're probably toast.)

Tell your ex the government is like the medical profession: as it sprawls, micro-targets, specializes, and breaks into ever smaller pieces. As these things happen, each person takes care of a tiny piece and no one believes he's responsible for the whole thing. The dentist tells you to avoid sugar and the oncologist tells you to avoid the substitutes. So people are sick. Each piece works but all the pieces don't work together.

The deficit is a "whole" problem. On the whole, how much money does the Government collect from its people and how much does it spend? But, based on your ex's report, the president only cares about "pieces" problems—whether this program or that program is needed. Things like education and healthcare. But, if anyone is in a position to think about the whole, it would be the president, right?

Also, unfortunately, our democracy is government by the masses of our people. But it should be government by the best. Actually our government is a hybrid of the masses and money, and such a government will never convince people to be the type of people who will keep a good government. That would be circular, like a game of telephone where you give advice to the person on your right, you wait for it to be whispered around the circle, then you take your own garbled advice from the person on your left. We elect politicians to tell us what we want to hear and, if they try to tell us what is good for us, they will fail; we will elect a new government to tell us what we want to hear.[80]

A government like ours can never teach people how to live. Living well is something people must do for themselves for its own sake and, as a happy accident, they will create a good government-of-the-people, because good politics is the overflow from a vibrant culture—from vibrant people living vibrant lives.

Tell your ex, if he can solve these three problems, he will solve the deficit and preserve American democracy. Otherwise, we're toast. We're probably toast.[81]

---

[80] But what if it's like a conversation, Socrates? What if it's like a conversation with Janet where you say something and, because Janet is a generous, thinking, feeling person, your idea comes back from her enriched in ways you would never have thought of yourself? What if the conversation between our people and our leaders is like that?

[81] What about cynical hipsters, Socrates? People who sit there and never lift a finger—the ones who give condescending lectures on things they've never even attempted and then pronounce doom on the whole sorry lot of us? Are they part of the problem? What about the artists who think their only job is to point out what's wrong with their world—not to show a better way—not to lead by example—not to build a better world—not to discover something good in the mix and show it off—just to expose what's wrong with everyone else—like your blessed namesake, Socrates. Are people like

Joel, let's talk again on Saturday. Also, Joel, it may not always feel like it, but we're really trying to be helpful. Hang in there.

Warmly,

Janet

that part of the "lost dying art" of leadership? Are they one of the problems I've got to solve too?

The Conversation with an Almost Lover (III)

I chafed at Janet's email, not because it was wrong but because it was despairing, and because it came from Socrates. I read it again and wondered how it had come to this: Africa. Detainees. My country. My family. My love life, too. Somehow I asked the same question about all of them: How did it come to this? And all of them took me back to a conversation three years ago in the National Arboretum.

"To be honest, Seth had a hard time with the shop even before Dad died," Joel says, while an inchworm flails desperately. He grasps the denim cuff of Janet's jacket and faces a devastating void beyond the end. He is a simple worm; he has only ever asked one thing of the world: another quarter inch. But the world has denied him even this and he waves in wide arcs over the meaninglessness of it all.

Janet looks at Joel and squints against the sun.

"I think Seth has a problem partly because he had a blow-up with Dad over his math," Joel says. "I taught him his math when I was in high school because I'd already learned it all myself and because people said I was good in math and I should be an engineer. But, when I went to college, Seth was starting algebra and had a hard time. Apparently, Seth and Dad argued until he told Dad he was done with algebra. He said he'd talked to everyone he knew and none of them used Algebra-Two for anything in their lives. Ever.

"Mom told me about it on the phone and she said, if she'd known Seth was having such a problem with math, she would have helped him with it while Dad was at work. Seth told me he had decided to get his GED so he could take EMT classes and work on the ambulance.

"But Dad came in the next day, after their big argument, and announced that, since Seth had given up on school, Dad had signed an expanded contract to maintain all the Sampson city vehicles and that Seth would be going to work with him at six o'clock the next morning to cover the extra work. Dad didn't even start work until seven-thirty before that, but I think he was punishing himself and Seth both for the algebra thing.

"Seth said he wouldn't do it and Dad said, he *would* do it as long as he lived under Dad's roof. Seth said there were other roofs to live under and Dad said you had to pay money to live under *those* roofs and you needed a job to get money and you needed a diploma to get a job and you had to do algebra to get a diploma, and Seth said, well, then maybe he'd do the algebra after all and Dad told him that train—the Algebra train—left the station yesterday and left Seth standing on the platform smoking his smirky cigarette and watching while the Algebra train pulled out and the only other train coming through for the next year was the train to the mechanic shop.

"The extra work was mostly just grease-monkey stuff— changing the oil and filters, recharging the a/c in the spring, changing a starter or an alternator here and there—the sort of thing Seth could do with no problem.

"After Dad died, we learned that the Sampson City contract had been a good deal for Dad and that he'd used some of the money to buy life insurance. But what I think killed Seth the worst was when he found out Dad had put the extra money in a trust fund to become Seth's when he turned twenty-one."

The Offline Conversation

Janet's email—the forwarded email—sat undigested in my gut while I worked on Friday. I'd got a coffee meeting with my counterpart at State and we sat across from each other in the State Department basement, hands toying with our coffee cups on the table. In Caitlin I sensed a competent staffer trying to solve all the small things at the lowest level and leave only the big choices for her bosses.

She wore stark black glasses and held her hair back with a black headband carved with African symbols. "Is this really the approach you want to take?" she asked.[82]

"Yes," I said.

"You know, if we adopt your position, it will be harder to find reintegration programs that meet our standards? It will mean longer waits, fewer detainees leaving the system, and a significant burden on DoD to monitor the effectiveness of the reintegration programs."

---

[82] Since DoD had nearly rolled over on this issue during the week I spent in TX, Caitlin now considers this to be fundamentally "my" approach. This strengthens me because she can see that I have managed to—almost single-handedly—define my department's position. But it weakens me because she suspects that only my bosses' loyalty to me stops them from conceding my position. She suspects that, if she can defeat one simple staffer, she can defeat the DoD. She suspects that I am what's called a "single point of failure." But this strengthens me, too, because now she sits with me and knows that, in negotiating with me, she is negotiating with the whole of DoD. She knows that, if I agree to something with her, I can probably line up everyone in the DoD to support our deal.

"I think you're describing what it takes to do this right," I said. "Until now, we have borne a heavy cost for doing this sort of thing quick and dirty. But if we get this one right, maybe we'll learn something we need to know to prevent future wars. It will require us to talk directly with the governments that run reintegration programs. We will talk with them about how we can shape our world so that our people—all our people—have languages other than violence to resolve the injustices in their lives. For it to work, State Department has to be on board for these conversations, but I think they're the conversations we will have—the conversations we need to have—as we discuss reintegration curriculums—as we discuss how to rehabilitate the people who have done violence to us. It won't pay off in closing Guantanamo next year. But maybe, twenty years from now, we can stop roving the world with robots to kill the people who hate us."

I looked at Caitlin. I might have been better off without that last sentence, but I could see her teetering—teetering between a Caitlin whose professional goal was to be smart and work an interesting job in an interesting world, and a Caitlin who still wanted to choose a hard thing, reach for it, and make the world better.

I leaned back in my chair and let my shoulders drop. Caitlin glanced over to where a food-court staffer hefted the coffee dispensers, feeling them for liquid weight, then setting the empty ones aside for washing—like something I said had made her need an urgent refill before the place closed.[83]

---

[83] Caitlin didn't want to rally State Department for this cause. It would come at a cost for her because they dislike idealism over at State. At least, they dislike the kind of idealism that believes in something definite and moral and says so in meetings. But, still, Caitlin didn't want to rally her department to crush me, either, because she had a conscience and she believed I was a good person doing a good thing. I had put her in a hard place. That's why she glanced away at the dwindling coffee dispensers.

But she looked back at the table in front of me, crumpled her napkin, and stuffed it in her cup, then recapped the cup, pushed it to the side, and brushed her flawless Barbie hair back over her ear, even though it was already held there by an African headband.

"I'll see what I can do," she said finally. "We should have had this conversation sooner, but I'm glad we've had it now."

"Shall we talk again Monday or Tuesday?" I asked. "I know we owe a response to the White House."

"Yes, let's talk Monday."

"Much appreciated," I said. The food-court staffer had started to wipe the tables closer to us in a sort of communication that, if this is business, maybe we should use a meeting room and, if it's personal, somebody's house could be appropriate.

* * *

When I got home Friday evening, my brain was clotted up from it all so, when I saw Sam-Bob sitting there on the couch, I assumed he'd waited there to un-clot me.

"Sam-Bob, you've got coffin-company," I said. "You know how they say, one is company but two is a crowd? Well, I've got a nasty crowd for you on the POTUS project."

"Can't this wait until my crime is solved?" he said, pausing the TV.

"How long will that take?"

He looked at the TV's progress bar. "About twelve minutes."

"But you always guess who did it by eighteen minutes in and you have seventy-nine percent accuracy, so you pretty much know who did it already. Right?"

"It would be eighty percent if you didn't count that unrealistic, silly-ass plot twist in May, with the little brother who was waaayyyy too timid to do a murder with such a blunt knife. That's just bad screenwriting. No comprehension of human nature."

"And who is it this time?"

"It's the girlfriend," he said. "She has that look. And, besides, she thought her boyfriend was cheating. And the ex-boyfriend just wants to make them suspect him so he can get a piece of the revenge. But he's like the bleachy kid who has never left his basement. He saw the sun once—Bleachboy did—and thought it was some sort of laser attack, but he plays Modern Warfare so he thinks he can totally relate to my time guarding opium fields in freakin' Helmand. You know what I'm talking about?"

"Yes."

"See, now *you're* that kid—the bleachy kid in the basement— because you weren't in Helmand, either, so how could you know what I'm talking about?" Sam-Bob shook his head. "You walked straight into that one, Joel-boy. It's like I set this trap for you and I put a giant sign by the trap saying, 'This is a Trap,' and you still walked into the trap because you were dreaming about ice cream or something."

"Ice cream? Really?"

"You want some?"

"Sure."

Sam-Bob got himself off the couch and walked into our tiny kitchen. "So who's my coffin company? And please tell me this will not mess up my epitaph. I hate sharing an epitaph."

"That depends. What's your epitaph?"

"He fought and he died. But he lived in between."

"Really? So when do you plan to start living?"

"You know what? Fuck you. Um, hey, you want chocolate or … uh … looks like it's just chocolate."

Sam-Bob came back with two plastic bowls of ice cream. I pulled my tie away from my neck and dropped my suit jacket over the back of a chair. The jacket lodged and waited for me to sit, then it slumped sullenly to the floor. So I got up again, thinking I'd drape it so it would balance itself over the back of the chair and not slump sullenly to the floor. But then I jounced the spoon from my ice cream bowl so it laid chocolate on my shirt and then on my pants and then on the floor.

"Long day?" Sam-Bob asked.

"Ugh," I said. "Yes. Long day. Long week. Long life, unfortunately, it seems."

"So who's sharing my epitaph?" Sam-Bob asked, while I dabbed the chocolate from my shirt with a dry paper towel. Then I concluded that I was only dabbing the chocolate deeper into the fibers so I unbuttoned the shirt and threw it in our washer. I twisted the dial to Regular, poured in the powder, slammed the lid, and stifled vague guilt about the environmental impact of washing items of clothing individually.

"Want another bowl of ice cream?" Sam-Bob asked. And then he said, "Oh, wait, you haven't eaten the first bowl I gave you."

"You know what? Fuck you."

"I thought we were watching our language."

"I thought we were, too."

Sam-Bob sat with his second bowl of ice cream. I sat, too, and saw that the scooper-domes in my first bowl had melted themselves shiny. I started to eat the ice cream but then I saw my jacket still there on the floor, with dust detectable where it had rolled in the final stage of its slump. I stood to correct this and my overbalanced spoon tumbled again and made a sort of statistically distributed spatter on the floor, centering by my shoe and then decreasing by square roots at greater distances from the initial impact.

"Oh, for goodness sakes," I said. "Did anyone ever think of making a spoon with a head that's heavier than the handle? Or maybe designing a crappy Tupperware bowl big enough for freaking gravity to hold the spoon *inside*?"

"See, you're thinking: design flaw," Sam-Bob said, "while I'm thinking: operator error. Funny how perspective works." But this time he took a paper towel, dampened it, and used it to wipe up my statistical spatters. While he did that, I took my jacket and delicately licked an outlying spatter from the sleeve. Then I slap-dusted it and draped it symmetrically over the chair.

"Want another bowl of ice cream?" Sam-Bob asked. "I may go for a third."

"Oh, for goodness sakes!" I looked at my melting bowl. "Sit down and listen or your grave will be haunted forever!"

"Well now," Sam-Bob said. "I would need more information to assess this threat. Like who's haunting it? As in, on a scale of one to ten, how pretty would you say—"

"Oh, for crying out loud! Will you stop?"

Sam-Bob had scooped his third bowl and he sat looking impishly at me.

"You remember Janet?" I asked.

"Janet I'm-so-sweet-I-could-smile-and-melt-the-polar-ice-cap Lestersen?"

"Sam-Bob, we've talked about mixed metaphors."

"Yes. I like them. You don't. Go on?"

"I've been talking to Janet about the president's project."

"You asked your ex for help?" He raised his eyebrows and I said nothing. Then he said, "Oh, my goodness, you're still in love with her, you sneaky bastard! And did she go for it?"

"Well, sort of. She agreed to meet with me but, when we met, she brought her boyfriend."

Sam-Bob is a nice guy, but he laughed immoderately at this point and I was a little hurt. So he walked into the kitchen, poured us two glasses of sweet tea, and settled himself like he expected a juicy story.

"I don't even like sweet tea," I said, "and we've just eaten ice cream."

"Everybody likes sweet tea."

I wasn't in the mood for that argument, just now, so I sipped once and set the tea aside.

"So you asked your ex and her boyfriend for help. Who else?"

"You."

"Wow, talk about coffin company! I'm honored. I should call the morgue and see if they can make a custom quadruple. But, first, are you inviting anyone else to our funeral?"

"I'm not planning to," I said.

"Well, okay, then. So you want me to do a hit on this new BF? And then you can console Janet at his funeral?" He stared into his tea, then nodded. "There's a certain elegance to it," he said. "My killing skills have rusted, though. I have to tell you that in full disclosure. But I could be up for it."

"I'm not killing anyone," I said. "Janet is dating an asshole, but he's weirdly smart, which he knows and he's using it against me. He has quirky ideas, and keeps sort of lobbing them at me for spite and, frankly, I wish they were bad ideas so I could just throw them away. But Janet keeps asking me to listen because it might help me with the president. And, besides, if I keep talking to him, maybe I can show Janet how much better she could do with me. But if I stop listening to him, he'll just take Janet and leave. By the way, if that happens, I may take you up on the assassination thing. But not yet."

"What do you want then? Want me to sweet-talk him into being nice to his girlfriend's ex? I could probably do that: '*Hey, man, you don't have to be a dick about it just because you're threatened by a romantic rival who can't speak for himself. Be a decent chap and give Janet's old flame a chance to woo her back. She's only a girl who's way out of your league and irrationally thinks you're awesome. What's to lose?*'"

"Wow, thanks," I said. "You're too kind. But I'll pass on your sweet-talking skills, too."

"Good. Because I couldn't sweet-talk my own sister into liking you. And, believe me, I tried."

"Wow, Sam-Bob, just for the sake of argument, let's say we leave your sister out of this? How's that?"

"In this case, the bureaucrat speaks wisdom. So how may I be of assistance in this convoluted episode of *Presidential Advice and Lost Love*? And, by the way, how did you lose such a great girl to such an awful guy? Can you remind me of that again?"

"Oh, drop it. I'm going to get her back and you're going to help me, because that's what friends do."

"So, you've rejected my assassination services, and you've rejected my sweet-talking services. What do you want? Advice?"

"Feel free. Have you got any ideas for the deficit?"

"Spend less."

I laughed. "And what would you spend less on? The retirement we've promised our old people? Their healthcare? Healthcare for people who don't make enough to live on? The military?"

"Yes."

"All of it?"

"Yes."

"Even the military?"

"Especially the military."

"Well, I'll keep that advice in mind when I talk to the president."

"Any other problems you need solved this evening?"

"No."

"That's all you wanted? Someone to state the obvious?"

I thought about it. Why did I bring Sam-Bob into this? Then I realized: "It's just good to know that, when I die, my secret will have a coffin to share. I need someone who knows what's going on."

"Have you thought of, um … getting a wife?"

"Yes," I said. "I've spent several evenings this week in the forest beating my chest, throat-grunting, and scouting for a gettable wife."

"Have you considered putting out chocolate and waiting in a blind? With your looks, that might be a better bet."

"No," I said. "I haven't got the time for that. Besides, who needs a wife when he's got a roommate named Sam-Bob?"

"No problem," he said. "I'll add 'interim wife' to the formidable list of skills on my resume. I've been looking for something to showcase my sensitive side."

"Your sensitive side is easy to see, Sam-Bob. You just have to hallucinate and squint and you'll see it right there next to the flaming ice, the towering midgets, and the stampeding turtles, and you'll say to yourself, 'Damn, that's Sam-Bob's sensitive side!'"

"Really, dude, you shouldn't say that stuff. It will get out and ruin my reputation."

The Conversation with an Almost Lover (IV)

The inchworm still flails over Janet's wrist and she watches it while
Joel talks. Finally Joel says, "Enough already," and reaches to flick the
worm deftly from this world. But Janet holds his wrist.

"I'm just putting it out of its misery," he says.

"It's not your job to end misery," she says.

The Scripted Interview

I met Janet and Socrates again at Big Bear Café for our next chat. Despite myself, I looked forward to asking Socrates some questions. He gave shrewd answers, which is weird for a scruffy kid disgusted with the world. His sort usually tears down everything and offers nothing in its place.

This time the place was nearly full so we sat with the hipsters at Big Bear's communal table.

"Janet sent me your email," I said. "But you ran off topic. I asked about the deficit, but you spoke about teaching children. How is that supposed to be advice for the president?"

Socrates sighed. "You know, this whole, fix-society-with-new-technology thing is crap. The president is right. The deficit isn't a math problem. It's a people problem. For some bizarre reason, people always appeal to the latest research and the latest technology to fix our problems. But the only way to improve a society is to improve people. And you can only improve people by inspiring them. And you can only inspire children. It's like people's inspiration-receptors die when they grow up and, for the rest of their lives, they've got to live on whatever they got when they were kids.

"There's only one way to inspire an adult—you convince him to inspire a child and, somehow, the inspiration rebounds. That's why a great society writes its best literature for children. And the most inspired adults are the ones that love children and the ones who love children's books."

284

Socrates was on fire and I was down for the count with Janet. A guy who sat in the corner shot Socrates a dirty look and put in his earbuds. But Socrates went on.

"A great society devotes its best minds to teaching children. And it knows teaching and inspiring are the same thing. Literature, art—these are letters one generation writes to the next, then it hands these letters to the kids. It's our way of saying, 'Here's who your parents were, take it, use it, improve it, and, most of all, be wiser for it. We did our part. Now you will decide whether we lived, loved, and wrote for nothing.'"

Socrates leaned across the table toward me while he spoke. He'd gulped half his dirty chai and even sloshed some on the table and I was mesmerized by the flecks of liquid that issued from his mouth. Janet sat next to him, held his hand, and watched my face.

"People will tell you knowledge is power," Socrates went on. "That's crap. People tell kids to take math and science, and that's crap. People don't do great things because they know a lot. Have you ever met a know-it-all who changed the world?

"People do great things because they're inspired. Then, because they're inspired, they find the math, the science, or whatever, to do it."

Socrates was vehement about this and Janet nodded. I glanced to the side and thought I could recover the situation by nodding to the onlookers with a deprecating apology for my guest. But then a couple of people behind me clapped and I saw everyone listening to Socrates and nodding—except for two businessmen huddled over their laptops with headphones. That threw me off. I'd never seen it before—this disillusionment with disillusionment—and I wondered what the heck was going on. Had the next generation got themselves onto something and left me out?

Before I could speak, Socrates recovered himself and said, "That's not what I wanted to talk about. You distracted me, Joel."

"That's okay," I said. "It was interesting."

"We decided that, today, Janet would ask the questions."

"Janet is welcome to ask questions anytime, or answer them," I said. "She's probably wiser than you and me put together."[84]

"I mean, Janet will ask the questions instead of you," Socrates said. "Then I will answer them."

That killed me. Even arrogant assholes seldom do something so shameless. I sat there and waited vaguely for Janet to intervene.

Janet read my face. Maybe she even appreciated that I had trapped my rage inside.

"Shall we start then?" Socrates asked.

"Joel," Janet said, "we thought this might be a good way to bring up some of the key issues and keep the conversation on track. Soc and I have been thinking about several of the questions you've raised and we wanted to provide you with some thoughts."

"You want to stage a rehearsed interview?"

"Exaaaactly," Socrates said, and his voice sounded like a teacher patting a child on the head for a tired classroom epiphany.

"If you have more questions to propose," Janet added, "we'd be happy to add those to the list and address them as well."

"And what if I have some answers of my own?" I asked.

"Then write them down for the president," Socrates said. "Unless you'd like me to review your work first."

"Or Janet," I said. "What if I'd like Janet to review them?"

"We'll both review them," he said.

"Why don't you go ahead with your little interview," I said. Stung by the unfairness of it all, I needed time to plot my next move.[85]

---

[84] A clever move, I think.

[85] Socrates is in bed with the referee. He has fixed the score with her ahead of time. How am I supposed to win a game like that?

Janet looked down at a cue-card on the table. But she paused, looked back up, and said, "We're trying to help, Joel. I hope you know that."

Dammit, Janet! I wasn't going to cry. In no case was I going to cry! And now you do this?

"I know," I said. "Thanks."

She looked back at her card and I glanced at Socrates. He had on this what-just-happened-dude look.

Then Janet started in on their weird interview:

Janet: "Socrates, what about the deficit?"

Socrates: "That sounds like a question, but it's not. Do you have a question?"

Janet: "Do you think the deficit is a problem?"

Socrates: "Yes."

Janet: "Why?"

Socrates: "I *think* the deficit is a problem because the deficit *is* a problem. Now if you want to know why *that* is, we can have an intelligent conversation."[86]

Janet: "Yes, please, or perhaps we could talk about how to stimulate the economy and resolve the deficit?"[87]

Socrates, joining his fingertips with the air of an economist on television: "Well, Janet, first of all, that's a very good question. Contrary to the wishful thinking of our current leadership, the way to stimulate the economy is not by running a deficit. You stimulate the economy by showing people there's still going to be an economy twenty or thirty years from now. Business people will make those critical long-term investments if they see that this country is being managed for the long-haul, not being cashed in like it's going out of business. Those long-term investments will build our infrastructure

---

[86] Does Socrates actually *script* insults into his conversations?

[87] Ah, ha! So Socrates was using the insults to stall until Janet reminded him of his talking points!

and start capital flowing again in the near and mid-term. And the way you show investors that there will be an economy in twenty or thirty years is by managing a national budget that, as a starting point, will not bankrupt the country."[88]

Janet, pausing to make sure he is done: "Besides the deficit, what is killing our country?"

Socrates: "Technology."

Janet: "Why are you against technology?"

Socrates: "I'm not. Do you have any friends who are alcoholics?"

Janet: "Yes."

Socrates: "What's killing them?"

Janet: "Alcohol."

Socrates, shaking his head: "Ah, but surely you aren't against alcohol?"

Janet: "No."

Socrates: "Maybe you even drink?"

Janet: "Yes."

Socrates: "And you enjoy it?"

Janet: "Yes."

Socrates: "Do you drink all the time?"

Janet: "No."

Socrates: "That's why you enjoy it. You drink sometimes. A good drink helps you relax after a stressful day. Or maybe you enjoy a quiet drink while you talk about life with your friends. Then you put the bottles away, go to sleep, and go to work again the next day.

"Alcohol is quite a nice thing if you enjoy your drink then put it away, sleep it off, and go about your life. But if you're a drunk, alcohol doesn't work for you—you work for it. Alcohol is good, but it's not good for *you* because you're its slave.

---

[88] This is probably a good point. But what happened to explaining it so a child could understand, or a farmer?

288

"You don't know who you are when you stare into your girlfriend's eyes. You know who you are when you've stared into her eyes and then you're left to sit by yourself and ponder it. That's when you know who you are, and when you know how much she means to you."[89]

Janet: "So … I asked you what's killing our country and you told me about alcohol?"

Socrates: "No. I told you about technology. You don't know who you are when you're staring at a screen. Emails, social updates, videos, the news, the little podcasts you listen to, or whatever, they're only good if you leave them, smoke a cigarette, watch the sun set, and consider what it all meant. That's where life is quiet enough for you to hear what's troubling you. It's where you see the small things that are beautiful and that make your life good. It's where your brain digests what you've been feeding it.

"The problem with technology is that everyone is trying to work at the speed of information, which is faster than the speed of understanding, and it's waayyyy faster than the speed of wisdom."

Janet: "The speed of wisdom?"

Socrates: "You can think of a thing fast, but you can only live it slowly. And living it is the only way to make truth matter."

* * *

I watched Janet's lips while Socrates went through his maxims for life. The kind of things that seem so profound when you say them, but that other people never hear because they're all in love with their own maxims for life.

"Our decisions are well-informed but badly considered," Socrates said. "Too much information, too little humanity. The genius is a man …"

---

[89] I thought, from the look on Janet's face, he had gone off script.

Janet: "Or woman?"

Socrates: "... who can look into the vast morass of information, pull out the few pieces that matter, and live by them. But most people hoard facts and think this makes them smart."

Finally I jumped back in:

Joel: "Am I allowed to talk?"

Socrates: "Cut! We're in the middle of an interview here. What do you need?"

Joel: "Maybe I agree with you on some of this, or maybe I don't, but who made *you* the purveyor of all wisdom?"

Socrates: "I'm telling you how things are. It's up to you whether to believe it or not."

Joel: "But how did you pick up all this stuff? What makes you so confident you're right?"

Socrates, curling his lip: "Life. Besides, I'm Socrates. A daemon hovers in the corner and tells me if I'm ever wrong."

Me: "Huh? I should believe you because you've got a demon?"

Socrates: "A *daemon*, not a *demon*!"

Janet: "Soc, maybe you should tell Joel about your school."

Socrates: "Huh?"

Janet: "St. John's?"

Socrates: "Yeah, I went to St. John's College. I spent four years reading history's great books. That's how I know so much."[90]

Joel: "So that makes you better than everyone else?"

Socrates: "Pretty much."

Joel: "And that's where you got your nickname?"

Socrates: "Bingo! Socrates, the gadfly of Athenian democracy."

---

[90] I wanted to ask who the heck St. John was. The patron saint of assholes—or a peculiar sort of diarrhea that flows the wrong direction? I made a mental note to present this image for Sam-Bob's inspection.

290

Joel: "Don't gadflies torment people and make them miserable."[91]

Socrates: "Exactly. Hey, can we get on with this interview? Why doesn't someone hold up that 'silence' sign for our distinguished studio audience?"

Janet: "Okay, here's your next question: What will it take to save us from these problems?"

Socrates: "People must change."

Janet: "And what will it take for people to change?"

Socrates: "God."

Janet: "How can you believe in a god who would let the world go to … uh …?"

Socrates: "Shit. The word you're looking for is *shit*."

Janet: "Uh, yes. Do you believe in a god who would wait until …?"

Socrates: "Here, let me read the question: 'How can you believe in a god who would let the world go to shit, then swoop in and bail us out?' And, I'll read the follow-up question: 'If there really was a god, wouldn't he rain down fire or wipe us all out in a flood and have Pat Robertson put the national zoo on a cruise ship to breed a new world population? How can you believe in a god like that?'"[92]

Janet, frowning and glancing for a read of my face: "Soc, will you please hand me back the card."

Socrates, touching fingertips again: "Sure. That's an excellent question, Janet. Really, an excellent question. No, I do not believe in God."

Janet, glancing at the card: "Then why did you say that?"

___

[91] I thought of the horseflies that used to torment our cattle. They looked like houseflies the size of your thumb. Two seconds of a horsefly's bite and Buttercup would kick you off the milking stool in a craze of pain. Charming mascot.
[92] So this really was *The Socrates Show* all along, with Janet for a prop.

Socrates: "Say what?"

Janet: "Why did you say we need God to save us?"

Socrates: "Because you didn't ask what I believed. You asked what it would take to save us."

Janet: "But how can God save us if you don't believe He exists?"

Socrates: "First of all, God doesn't need me. He can exist without my help if He wants. Second of all, whether God exists or not, He can save this country again the same way He inspired the Pilgrims to leave England, establish freedom of conscience, freedom of speech, and eventually convinced our founders that He'd endowed all men with certain inalienable rights—the same way He convinced people to work hard, get married, teach their kids to read, and deal honestly with each other. He convinced our people to free their slaves, educate the poor, start hospitals for the sick, give women the vote, set up honest courts ... (pause, while he nods for Janet to read the next card)."

Janet: "Oh, yes: Come on, Socrates, do you really think God did all that?"

Socrates: "I sure as hell think *people* did it because they *believed* in God."

Janet: "And how sure do you think hell is?"[93]

Socrates, blinking: "What?"

Janet: "Oh, I'm sorry, I think I made a mistake with your script. Where were we? Oh, yes: But the people who did these noble things—didn't they also trade slaves, beat them, keep mistresses, lie about each other to win elections ...? I can't believe you're making them out to be saints and prophets, Socrates."

Socrates: "I said nothing about them being saints. I said they did certain good things because they believed in God."

---

[93] She almost winked when she said that—a great streak of the old Janet!

Janet: "But how can you say that when *you* don't believe in God?"

Socrates: "Because I read history. I read the freakin' Declaration of Independence, the Jefferson memorial, the Lincoln memorial, the MLK[94] memorial. The people who made this country good did it because they believed in God. This isn't theology, it's history."

Janet, winking at Joel: "More recently, Malcolm Muggeridge said: 'There is no wisdom except in the fear of God, but no one fears God, therefore there is no wisdom.' Socrates, do you agree with Mr. Muggeridge?"

Socrates, grabbing the queue card: "WTF,[95] Janet?"

Janet, looking sideways at Socrates: "Soc, speaking as your media coach, I have counseled you to start your answers with some sort of compliment. For instance, you could say, 'That's a great question, Janet,' or 'Thank you for that question.' Even if it's a lousy question, you should still pretend it was a good one and then answer it with something you wanted to talk about."

Socrates: "What?"

Janet, speaking slower, with mirth in her eyes: "I was saying you should start by comp—"

Socrates: "I know! But that Muggeridge thing isn't one of the questions!"

Joel: "Speaking as the note-taker here, I'm pretty sure the interviewer asked the question, so I'm trying to understand how it is, as you say, 'not one of the questions?'"

---

94 Martin Luther King Jr.
95 What the fuck

Socrates: "Oh, shuttup!"[96]

Janet, with a meaningful glance at Socrates: "Well, I think this interview is to-be-continued. Joel, did you want to add some questions for next time?"

Joel, assuming his meeting wrap-up persona: "If I think of any questions, I'll email them to you. Meanwhile, your comments today have given me a good deal to think about. The interview format has proven more useful than I anticipated. In the spirit of dialog, I propose, at the next meeting, to submit myself to a similar interview. This would help me enormously as I refine my answers for the president. Does that sound fair?"

Janet: "I think that sounds fair."

Socrates: [Rage face]

Joel, to Janet: "Shall we meet up in advance to work out the questions and do a bit of media coaching?"

Janet: "That could be arranged."

Socrates: [Fury face]

Joel: "Great! How's tomorrow afternoon for a one-on-one pre-brief? Then the larger group can meet for the interview on Tuesday or Wednesday after work? That will give me time to package some ideas for the president by the end of the week."

Janet: "That should work."

Socrates: [Purple fury face]

Joel: "Well, see you next week then."

EXIT JOEL

---

[96] I was tempted to add a few more comments here: Is this part of your St. John's wisdom, Socrates? Is this one of the things that is true, no matter whether I agree? But I held off, not out of mercy, but because I knew Janet only judges one thing harshly, and that's when you kick a guy who is down. She had taken him down spectacularly and the best I could do was to admire her work.

The Bible

Joel Alden reads after dinner, safe in a childhood with a mother, a father, and a Bible for them all. He reads a biography of Dr. Benjamin Carson, whose mother turned off the TV and required him to read and report to her what he found in the books. Then Dr. Carson became a brain surgeon and put balloons between some twins' heads that were stuck together. The balloons stretched out enough skin to cover both their heads when he had cut them apart. Dr. Carson knew he could chill the babies to slow them down for their surgery, because they were babies and babies can chill without dying.

"Joel, your Father wants us to read the Bible and then get ready for bed," Mom says. Joel looks up peevishly.

"But I'm almost finished."

"How much do you lack?"

Joel flips some look-ahead pages and Mom says they are too many.

Father, having showered after dinner, sits with Seth straight-legged and narrow beside him in the chair. The family joins him, each with a Bible, like every evening. Father notes that it is January 29. "So let's read Proverbs twenty-nine," he says. "We have twenty-seven verses and four readers, so that's six verses each. Josiah, please start us off. You can read verses one to six. Jeremy will read seven to twelve. Joel will read thirteen to eighteen. Mom will read nineteen to twenty-four. Then Seth and I will finish. When we're done, each person can pick a favorite verse and tell us what it means."

Josiah starts to read. Joel looks ahead at his cue verse—the one before he will read aloud:

12 *If a ruler hearken to lies, all his servants are wicked.*

Then, when Jeremy says "wicked," Joel falls in to read, brow furrowed over the Bible on his knees:

13 *The poor and the deceitful man meet together: the Lord lighteneth both their eyes.*

14 *The king that faithfully judgeth the poor, his throne shall be established for ever.*

15 *The rod and reproof give wisdom: but a child left to himself bringeth his mother to shame.*

16 *When the wicked are multiplied, transgression increaseth: but the righteous shall see their fall.*

17 *Correct thy son, and he shall give thee rest; yea, he shall give delight unto thy soul.*

18 *Where there is no vision, the people perish: but he that keepeth the law, happy is he.*

Then Joel stops in relief that he had known all the words, even the big ones, and he listens as Mom reads on in her easy, adult voice:

19 *A servant will not be corrected by words: for though he understand he will not answer.*

20 *Seest thou a man that is hasty in his words? There is more hope of a fool than of him.*

21 *He that delicately bringeth up his servant from a child shall have him become his son at the length.*

22 *An angry man stirreth up strife, and a furious man aboundeth in transgression.*

23 *A man's pride shall bring him low: but honour shall uphold the humble in spirit.*

Joel remembers to pick a verse and he knows that you've got to go first or someone will beat you to the best verse. So, when the reading is done, he says, "I've got a favorite."

"Okay, Joel," Father says. "Please tell us."

Joel reads: "*Seest thou a man that is hasty in his words? There is more hope of a fool than of him.*"

"Please explain what that means," Father says.

"It means, if you talk before you think, you'll be a fool."

"Yes, or even worse," Father says.

Father picks verse eighteen: "*Where there is no vision, the people perish: but he that keepeth the law, happy is he.*" He explains that, if no one gives people a vision of how they ought to live, then they perish—they literally waste away and die—because they don't know what they're living for.

"As the head of this family," Father says, "I try to show you a vision like that. That's why we sit and read the Bible together. And it's why your mom and I make rules for you children. We're not perfect parents—I know I'm not a perfect dad. I still make mistakes and that's why I think it's important that a father can apologize to his kids."

The children stare at him.

Mom chooses verse twenty-one: "*He that delicately bringeth up his servant from a child shall have him become his son at the length.*"

Mom says the verse means that the most important thing—even more important than who gave you birth—is who loves you and cares for you. She says it's a good reminder for her of what it really means to be a parent.

When they have all spoken of their verses, Father prays, then says, "Hugs from my kids, then off to bed!"

"Good night, I love you, and I'll see you in the morning," the kids say with a hug and a kiss for Mom and one for Father. Then, between their bunks, the boys change into sweats against the chill of their winter beds.

Jeremy perches on the cedar-chest to pull on his sweats.

"Jeremy, you're sitting funny," Joel says.

"No I'm not."

"But you've got something on your leg."

"Daddy spanked him," Seth says. "He called Mom stupid."

"I didn't call Mom stupid," Jeremy snaps. "Mom asked me to take the breakfast scraps out for the chickens. But the scrap bucket still had enough room for the lunch scraps so I said it was stupid to take the scraps out before lunch. I didn't know Daddy was listening. He told me if I ever called Mom stupid again he'd whip me until I was black and blue."

But Joel sees around the edge of Jeremy's briefs that Daddy already did. "Well, don't call Mom stupid, I guess."

"I know that now, dummy."

The Conversation with Someone Who was Once a Lover

"So how did the butt-kicking go?" Sam-Bob asked when I'd returned from the Big Bear.

"Awesome! Of course!" I said.

"Wait, *you* kicked *his* butt?"

"Yup!"

"Way to go, bro! I stayed in this evening because I figured you'd need someone to hold your hand while you cried yourself to sleep."

"That means a lot, Sam-Bob," I said. "As much as I would love to hold your hand, it won't be necessary."

"How'd you do it?"

"Strategic restraint. Using the other guy's momentum against him. Fighting via proxy. Good-cop, bad cop, to name a few of my tactics. I don't want to reveal all my trade secrets."

"Sorry bro, but those secrets are out."

I went upstairs and laughed. Then I looked at the counter on my phone. It ticked down: Six days, zero hours, fifty-two minutes, and thirty-eight seconds. The victory faded. I had spent two weeks thinking of the president's question and what did I have to show for it?

With only six days, I was running out of time. I was exhausted from work and from working after work and from thinking in my bed when I was supposed to sleep. Even then, I should have been more bothered than I was about my dwindling time on the president's project. I have pulled off complex recommendations in less time, and, besides, for the first time in six months, I had arranged to sit down alone with Janet Lestersen. Not a bad place to be.

I imagined myself telling Janet some policy ideas for our "interview." But, the whole time, in my mind, I was cutting her off mid-sentence, tickling her lips with my breath, then kissing. A nightmare freezes you in that moment of horror before the unthinkable happens. But my mind had frozen Janet in a moment of relief when I knew she'd really loved me all along. Relief that Socrates was just a grotesque anomaly in her undying love for me.

I told Sam-Bob on my way out the next day that I was going to get Janet back. He paused his TV show and said, "Good luck, bro. But I thought she wouldn't date you because you're not Christian."

"I am Christian," I said, "in everything but theology."

"Ah, pardon me then," he said. "Being angry with a god who doesn't exist and all that. It's a very sensible Christian attitude."

"Oh, shuttup," I said. "Besides, I've found a chink in her armor. She's already dating a guy who doesn't believe in God. And he's an asshole. So why not upgrade to a *non*-asshole who doesn't believe in God? Answer me that?"

"So now you're a non-asshole?" Sam-Bob sat up. "That's great news, man. You should put that on your business card."

"Oh, shuttup!" I said, but laughed. I thought of the president's business card and imagined him putting *non-asshole* in italics after *President of the United States*. The funny thing is that, with this president, it would probably be true. But in DC, no one would believe it.

I called Janet and proposed to meet her at the Arboretum.

"I don't think that's the best place," she said. "Besides, the Arboretum is closed. They're furloughed."[97]

---

[97] Budget cuts. Ugh. This is how our national budget problems get real personal real fast.

So I proposed that we meet at a little coffee shop called Peregrine, next to DC's Eastern Market, "Because they have the best coffee in town."[98]

I rode Sam-Bob's bike to Eastern Market, locked it up, and waited. That's the worst, by the way, sitting there fiddling with your Blackberry, while your life's hopes hang out there waiting for someone to walk up and gently shatter them. And, finally, Janet walked up.

"Hi, Joel," she said.

"Hug?"

"Sure." She hugged me, from the front this time, and longer than necessary.

"You okay?" I asked.

"Sure." Janet has spectacular fortitude. She can mask her own grief with a smile and ask, *But how are you?* Her face radiates peace— always. But, today, it showed weariness, too.

"How are you?" she asked.

"I'm okay."

"Shall we do an interview?"

"Sure. But with caffeine, right?"

"Yes."

I held the Peregrine door for her. She ordered a coffee and, in this day, there is something comforting about that. Just coffee in a mug, without a string of modifiers in front of it.

Janet hugged her cup like she meant to give it comfort and we watched a wisp of steam curl off its top.

"Joel, what do you think of Socrates?" she asked.

"He's an interesting guy."

"Did it help? Talking to him?"

---

[98] How do I know this? *Everybody* knows it. What more authority do you need? But if I wasn't subject to *everybody's* opinion, I would tell you my dirty secret: the best coffee in DC is *Swings*.

"I wish he would quit trying to hurt me," I said.

"Do you say that because he makes you mad or because he's not helping you think about things?"

"Probably because he makes me mad. When you ask him a question, he insults you, then tells you the truth like it's a joke."

"It's his shtick," she said. "He does it to make people think. But he has a good heart."

"A good head, maybe," I said. Janet frowned.

"It was clever, by the way, how you asked for an 'interview' last time we talked. I got an earful from him after that."

"It was clever the way *you* asked him about God." She gave a wan smile. "I don't get what you see in him."

"It took me a while to find out he didn't believe in God. He seemed like someone who would. I told him, if he put all his beliefs together like a puzzle and looked at them, they would make a picture of Jesus."

"And what did he say to that?"

"He laughed."

"That's all?"

"No. I told him a guy as reasonable as him should have a better answer than to laugh. So he said a collection of beliefs doesn't make a person."

"What did you say to that?"

"I told him he had a fair point. And then he said he doesn't want a build-your-own-Jesus anyway and that's pretty much the only Jesus people have."

"But you're still dating him?"

"We'll see about that," she said. She pulled a spiral notebook from her purse and fished for a pen. "Do you have some topics for our interview?"

"Yes. I have some."

"Why don't you read them to me."

So I read them:

- Q: What is government? (A: The right to use force.)
- Q: What is culture? (A: Shared beliefs and customs.)
- Q: What makes a government healthy? (A: A healthy culture and healthy leaders. Leaders who use persuasion and restraint more than force.)
  - Q: (Follow up) Why don't we have a healthy government in the U.S.? (A: We don't have a healthy government because people try to use Government to solve all our human problems.)
- Q: How has technology shaped us as a people? (A: ???)
  - Q: (Follow up) How should technology shape us? (A: ???)
- Q: How would your ideas look in a good culture and a good government? (A: ???)

"So that's all you've got?" Janet asked.

"I've got some longer answers."

"So you've already asked and answered all your questions?" She furrowed her eyebrows and looked down at the table. "Is that just the kind of guys I'm attracted to, Joel?" she asked. "Ones who have all the answers?" And she could just as well have said, *'I want to love you guys. I really do. But sometimes you make it so hard.'*

"I thought of some answers," I said. "But I want to know what you think of them. I'm not sure they're good."

"Then shall we start?"

I set my notes in front of me.

"So, Joel Alden," she started, "tell me: what is government?"

"Well, Janet, I'm glad you asked," I said. And then I told her that government's distinguishing tool is force. Government alone can tell people what they must do and then to exact a penalty when they do not comply. "The only good government programs are ones that are important enough to justify taking money by force from someone who earned it.

"But force should never be our first resort to influence the world and we should remember that, in a government's relationship with its people, as with its relationship to foreign countries, restraint is often the greatest virtue."

"I didn't know you were such a Conservative," Janet said.

"Not, really," I said. "But the world has changed until it is Conservative to state even some basic facts. Don't we have other tools besides Government to negotiate who we are to each other? And if I say so, does that make me Conservative?"

"Okay, then," she said, and looked down at her notes.

It irritated me that she wanted to gloss this over so I pressed my point. "It's like the Army," I said. "People want the Army to hand out candy bars, build houses, run power plants, and train border guards around the world. But that's not what the Army is for. It's for killing people and breaking things—you let them do it or you restrain them, but still it's what they're for. You don't ask them to cut your grass.

"If we make the Army our answer to everything, we'll mess up the Army and we'll mess up the world. And then, when we really need an Army to kill people and break things, they won't know how because they've been too busy teaching kindergarten!"

Janet sighed but let me talk.

"It's the same way with governments," I said. "There's a time when a decent society has to force people into line. You've got to force them to respect each other's property, to protect the weak from being abused by the strong, and to protect people's right to worship or speak their opinions.

"But the Government is like the Army: when we make it warm and fuzzy, we forget its awful power and then we're ripe for repression."

"Thank you for that clarification, Mr. Alden," Janet said, snapping halfway into her interviewer persona. "Mr. Alden, besides restraining its coercive power, what makes for a healthy government?"

"Well, Miss Lestersen, that's a good question," I said. "I'd say the requirement for a healthy government is to be the product of a healthy culture and to have healthy people running it."

"You'd kick people out of government for being sick?" She briefly lost her interviewer aura.

"No, Miss Lestersen," I said. "As Americans, we think people are good and devoted to the extent that they make themselves miserable for a cause. We call it hard work. Really, though, it's exhaustion. We're tired. And exhausted people aren't healthy, they're just exhausted. We demand that our leaders make themselves sick to prove they're worth the job. And then, half the time, we still accuse them of being lazy. Have you ever seen a Congressman's schedule? It's a cruel puzzle designed to see how much you can get a single person to do. And people still believe Congressmen are these red-faced drunks who work three days a week.

"We're the richest country in the history of the world, for goodness sakes, and do we have to work this hard just to survive? We look out on our countrymen and we see two things: work and laziness. But there's no rest." I paused and looked at Janet's weary face.

"Maybe people don't rest because they're starving for something they can't find," Janet said. She looked at me with her sad eye-smile wrinkles and I looked away. Then I looked back at her, because I preferred to show my tears to her than to the stranger who worked behind the bar.

I looked at my notes and plowed ahead, "Miss Lestersen," I said, "healthy leaders lead well. And it takes a healthy, wise population to select healthy leaders. America's strength was that we were a government of, by, and for the people. It made us strong while our people were strong. Now it makes us weak."

"Do you really think that?" Janet asked.

I nodded. And I saw that her eyes had misted. It must have stressed her, sorting this whole thing out with Socrates and me. I felt stupid now, for not seeing it before. "Janet," I said. "I'm sorry. I shouldn't have asked you to do this."

"It's okay," she said. "Let's finish the interview."

"Okay."

"Mr. Alden," she said, with a perceptible sniffle, "How would these ideas look in government?"

I looked back at my notes and started back in. "Campaigning, war, and destruction are quick, loud, heroic things, but that's not where life is lived. Living well is slow, quiet, and subtle. It doesn't cost much but it's devilishly hard to do and most of our problems come from failing at it.

"If we don't learn to love these quiet things, we won't love life. We sprint or we sit. But there is only life in the long race."

Janet looked steadily at me and I'm sure I saw a streak of admiration in her face. I waited, then asked, "How was that?"

"That's great," she said, then looked at her notes. "You mentioned television. How does technology play into this?"

"Well," I said, "technology should be a tool to enrich our lives and develop a shared culture. But, if technology was the answer, we would be living better now than ever before. And are we? We have the best education technology in the world, but do we learn better? We have the best communication technology, but do we connect better? We have the best food science, but do we eat better? We've plumbed the human psyche, but do we have healthier minds?"

"No," Janet said.

"Why?"

"This is your interview."

"It's because our problems aren't technological, they're cultural. They're human. We've learned to change everything but ourselves. We want our leaders to find technical, financial, structural solutions for our problems. But we don't want them to inspire us to change ourselves and be better people.

"We think our leaders are as selfish as we are and, we think, if we follow them, they'll use us for their own advantage. We think all the world's structures were built to favor the strong over the weak. We cut down our leaders, because we no longer believe in virtue. We have no heroes. We're a nation of critics with no artists—critics whose business is to whine about the lack of art. We refine our tactics, but we have no strategy. We have vast means, but no ends. We sail the best ships, but we have no captains. We have master politicians, but no statesmen.

"If we look somewhere—in history maybe—and find a person who seems noble, we recite his failings to ourselves, like children writing backward Bible verses on the blackboard, until we have destroyed him in our minds."

Janet waited to see if I was done. "That was quite a speech," she said. She paused, then added, "You sound as passionate as ever."

"I am," I said, and winked. Janet lowered her eyelashes, then she laughed despite herself.

"So what is the answer?" she asked.

"Well," I said, "are you still dating Socrates?"

"The answer to the technology/human/culture problem, you goof! What's the answer to *that*?"

"Oh, *that*," I said. "I'm working on it. But, if I knew the answer, I wouldn't be asking for your help, would I?"

"Really? Are we here drinking coffee together just so I can help you with a few policy questions?" Now I saw a streak of mischief in her face.

"Even the best student needs someone to check his work, right?"

"The best students do. And the struggling students need it even more," she said. "They usually trade their work with a smarter student they've got a crush on."

"Aw, come on!" I said. But I smiled and ached. I'd forgotten how she teased so carefully. *I see your scheming,* she said. *Nicely done.*

"How are things at USAID?" I asked.

"A lot like they were, I guess."

"Want a refill on that coffee?"

"Sure." When I returned, she gave comfort to this fresh cup, and looked across the table at me. "I meant to ask you a question about USAID," she said, reassuming a mock formality. "Mr. Alden, what do you think about foreign aid? What about giving some of those coerced tax dollars to relieve suffering overseas?"

"Well, Miss Lestersen, I've watched some of the folks doing aid overseas and I don't think people who couldn't run a coffee shop in their own neighborhood should tamper with foreign economies."

"Ouch!" she said.

"Don't worry," I said. "You'd run a great coffee shop. But the rest of the people at your agency?"

"I have another question for you," she said. "I find it funny that neither you nor Socrates believes in God, but you're more confident of your answers than the staunchest crusader at my church."

"Do you think our answers are wrong?" I asked.

"Not necessarily," she said. "I think you're both right about some things. But you may be better at preaching than living."

I blinked. "That could be true," I said. "But do you really think I'm like Socrates?"

"I think you're too similar to like each other." She looked steadily at me, then glanced down at her notes, unaware that she'd done the eyelash thing again. "This is some good stuff, Joel. I don't think you're right about everything, but you've got a good head. You're even big enough—as a person I mean—to learn from Soc's little tirades. I admire that." A glow started in my heart and spread upwards, but I contained it short to prevent tears.

Janet continued: "The problem is that I admired your inspiration and insight when you worked for Heritage and DRL, when you went to Z______, and when you worked in OSD. I admired all those Joel Aldens. They were all sure of themselves. And they showed good judgment. But they disagree with each other. Some of them believed in God and others don't. Some of them believed in limited government and others thought Government could make the world better. Some of them tried to make a difference and others seem to have given it up. And there will be more Joel Aldens. Good ones. The Joel who holds his baby for the first time. The Joel who buries his mother. The Joel who lies on his deathbed. They will think different things, too. But which one is right?"

That undid me—Janet, calm, patient, reciting fears I had never told her. Finally, I opened my mouth. "I wonder the same thing. I wonder when I see most clearly, and where. Is it when I've slept? When I'm caffeinated and thinking analytically (that's when I do my best work at the Pentagon)? Or is it when I've had a drink and I'm reflecting on my past—when I was closest to you? Or maybe I will see most clearly on my deathbed, looking back on my memories when it's too late. Or maybe then I'll be fooled by pain, drugs, and wishful thinking about an afterlife that doesn't exist. Maybe I see best now, when I'm healthy, when death is a distant exercise of the imagination.

"All I know is that, in each of these times, the plain truth seems different. Of course, I shouldn't let circumstances cloud my judgment, right? But I always live in circumstances. So where shall I go for unclouded judgment?"

"That's what I was asking *you*," Janet said.

"But I don't know."

"I know you don't."

"Then why do you ask?"

"Because you should think about it."

"I do think about it," I said. "It has driven me to the edge of madness. But there's no way out."

"But there *is* a way out."

"God, I suppose?"

"You can't keep measuring everything by yourself, Joel. It will drive you mad. Do you know why? It will drive you mad because you're not a constant measuring stick."

"I know," I said. "But it's the only measure I've got."

"Maybe measuring is not your job, Joel. What if it has already been measured and you can spend your life simply understanding bits and pieces of it as you come to them?"

I felt like someone who runs on a treadmill speeding at an alarming pace. It ramps and grinds me to exhaustion. Then a girl taps me kindly on the shoulder and says, *'You should step off and walk with me in the garden.'*

'Ah,' I say, *'but I can get much farther by running straight and hard than by walking with you in a garden.'*

'Not on that machine,' she says. *'Step off, and come with me.'*

I remember walking home across Lincoln Park and staring at Sam-Bob when he asked whether someone stole his bike, and then I said I'd find it for him.

"Did you leave it somewhere on your Janet conquest?" he asked. "It must have gone better than you let on if you forgot the bike?"

"Ah, yes," I said. "I mean, no. I'll get your bike."

The Negotiation

Joel Alden walks across the pasture on a mat of new grass that rises back in the sunshine where his feet have pressed. He is bored, so Mom said he should go out to play. When he came back he could have fresh bread, she said. A loaf that steams when you cut into it.

"But I don't want to play by myself," Joel says.

"Why don't you take Seth?"

"He might hurt himself," Joel says. "I think I'll go by myself."

He finds a stick to throw. "At least I made him dodge," he says of a missed sparrow, then he kicks a mound of earth. The resistance feels good in his shoe and he kicks again while dirt trickles between the laces. A stone dislodges from the mound. It skitters under the paddies of a prickly pear. Joel grasps a spine, lifts the cactus carefully, and pulls the rock from where it has fallen.

"I found a piece of flint," he says, and runs the edge against his finger. "Looks like some gopher dug up an Indian knife." He drops the flint in his pocket, then stops while a thought presents itself. "I wonder what else that gopher dug." He squats to destroy the rest of the mound and, sure enough, two other pieces.

Sometimes you find flint in the pasture. Sure. And it's a treasure. But most of the treasure is buried. So you wait for the rain to turn it up. You could dig, of course, but you would never know where to start.

But never isn't right. You need a clue. Like the old Indian grave. Everyone knew the grave was there, no doubt, and you could find old beads there. But they would never say where *there* was. You would go and there would be no *there* there and they would tell you

you could tell you weren't there because there are beads there and if there are no beads you aren't there.

"Hey, Joel," Granddaddy says of a cliff over the creek, "that's the cave of old Chief Nasawana."

"Really?"

"Yes. If you stand in the mouth and yell, 'Hey, Chief Nasawana, what are you doing in there?' he'll say nothing, nothing at all."

"I tried it," Joel says, later.

"And what happened?"

"It didn't work. Nobody's in there."

"Did you ask old Chief Nasawana what he's doing?"

"Yes."

"Did you listen?"

"Yes."

"And what did he say?"

"Nothing."

"Nothing at all?" And Granddaddy laughs.

Those Indian stories sure were silly. But Joel wishes he had a better clue to where they left their flint. Like an x on a map or a story from a dead pirate. But it's hard for the x's and pirate stories to stay unfound until you come along. And, if you find one, there's always someone trying to beat you to it. (Those are just some for-examples of the trouble with buried treasure.)

But this time, Joel scratches his head. "I need a shovel," he says. He twists last year's stalk from a yucca, prickling his shins, and gouges it upright in the mound for a mark. Then he returns to the house and takes a shovel from the shed. He walks away from the flint for stealth so, if the house was a sun, he'd be walking in the sun's shed shadow.

"Where are you going?" Seth asks from nowhere.

"Where did you come from?"

"Come from? I'm just here," Seth says, standing silly in his laceless hi-tops.

"I see that," Joel says.

"Where are you going?"

"Nowhere."

"Why do you have a shovel?"

"No reason."

"I want to come with you."

"No."

"But I can dig. I'll get another shovel."

"You can only come if everything you dig up is mine."

"Okay."

The Best of Conversations, The Worst of Conversations, and the Poem (III)

We met on Tuesday, the three of us, at Big Bear Café, for the last time. It was a vibrant early fall day and I felt more relaxed.

Ms. Holachek had endorsed my handshake agreement with State Department. State would agree to my proposals: requiring transparency in the content of reintegration programs, allowing detainees to opt out of religious indoctrination, and documenting whether the programs work. In exchange, we had allowed State to delete "effective immediately," and replace it with, "within 365 days after the approval of this document."[99] Even my powder-skinned antagonist in Detainee Affairs had started talking like he had supported this policy all along and just wanted to "protect the time our implementers will need to get this thing right."

The win felt good. But, even more, today I felt relaxed because it was my day for an interview and I knew where I stood with Janet. Socrates could no longer claim her for his team against me and, for this reason, I felt exceptionally gracious.

---

[99] When State pressed for this, I almost quoted St. Augustine: "Lord, give me chastity and continence – but not yet." Or, if Augustine was too obscure, I thought I remembered a song about a girl who says she wants to do right but not right now. But I knew I had won. I should leave well enough alone. I should let them save face after fighting me on this and, in practice, I knew it would take State Department and the military a year to get into compliance with the new policy anyway—whether it said "effective immediately" or "within 365 days after the approval of this document."

As it happened, Socrates was cordial, friendly even, and we chatted like friends.

I thanked Janet and Socrates for their help and told them I had gathered almost enough material to digest into a recommendation.[100]

"Tomorrow will be my data cutoff date," I announced. "I'll take the rest of the week off and write up my findings." I thought of the idealized days at DRL when, at the end of the year, I would close the file, draw a line under everything, and start writing the report. Things keep happening while you write, of course, but you drop those things into next year's file and they wait while you report on the year that has passed. It's a comfortable time—phone set to silent, email shut off, wistful music in your earbuds. You surface from time to time and break your colleagues' concentration in search of human contact. You make an office coffee run. This is the calm time where you write alone and quietly build your defenses against the frenzied politics that will come before the report goes final.

In jobs like mine, you make no final decisions. You only advocate with the people who slice your baby in the end. But you set the baseline—the default. You write the first draft and build your credibility as high as possible for the final argument. And that's half the power.

"We can do the interview, now, if you like," I said to Socrates.

"You don't need to do it for me," Socrates said, sipping his dirty chai. "Janet gave me a preview anyway."

"Do you really like that?" I asked. "Tea with coffee in it?"

"Of course. Try it."

"It's funky," I said after taking a sip. "Not bad, just funky."

"What do you want to talk about?" he asked.

---

[100] Optimistic. I know. Naomi's counter on my phone showed only three days!

"My problem," I said, "is that I've got to write a recommendation. We've discussed our problems. But explaining how things are wrong will always be far easier than putting them right. I've got to tell our leaders something they can do. More than that, I've got to make a recommendation to the people of America. The president can't fix America, because America belongs to the people. We're the ones who waste our country."

"I thought the 'president'"—Socrates made air quotes—"asked you to be confidential about this. I've read the notes you gave Janet. He's putting himself out there just by asking and you can't go broadcasting that in a recommendation 'to the people of America.'"

Socrates had a point. "Maybe I'll send him my recommendations and ask for permission to publish a version for the public."

"But that'll look pretty weird without the context," Socrates said.

"I'll give it some thought," I said. "But, whether I'm only talking to the Government or to everyone, we still have the same problem. I can describe America's problems all day. Everyone is doing it. But most people just complain or offer a laundry list of policy proposals to fix it all. But their lists are mismatched with the problem. Or their 'problem'"—I made air quotes—"is built to support their policy list to start with. It's the how-can-technology-solve-your-problem problem."

"I warned you about this from the start," Socrates said.

"What the heck, though." I said. "It's a hard problem but it's *our* problem. Did we only sign up for easy problems? Or did we only sign up to solve other people's problems?"

"I'm not sure *we* signed up for anyone's problems," he said, with a glance at Janet.

"But we did," Janet said. "Or at least I did."

My eyes must have misted because I knew then that, all along, I had been terribly afraid I was alone in this. I stayed on topic, though.

"My problem," I said, "is that the real solutions aren't policies. They have more to do with people caring for themselves, caring for each other as humans, loving their world, and loving their country. People making good decisions and being healthy. The point isn't to solve our problems with healthcare, retirement, education, or the deficit. The point is to live well. And, by living well for the sake of sheer life, we will solve our policy problems by accident. People will be healthier, they will work, they will care for each other when they're in need, and they will learn. But how can you put *that* into a policy proposal?"

Socrates and Janet both nodded. So I went on. "When you talk about dark, grim things, people think you're serious, unflinching, portraying the world as it is and telling it straight. But, when you talk about a good thing like this, you're an escapist, utopian Pollyanna.[101]"

"Yes," Socrates said. "Ever notice how all the cheap preachers, self-help gurus, and late-night pill salesmen sell their products? They say '*This* will change your life.' They simply assume that everyone hates his life. They don't even say 'This will *improve* your life!' They assume your life is lousy, of course, but, more than that, they assume it's *so* lousy you'll take a chance on change—*any* change! What's the standard for a good sermon? Was it *life changing?* How do you dismiss an okay sermon? 'It was okay,' you say, 'but it didn't *change my life.*' Each week the pastor stands in the pulpit and assumes every person in his congregation needs to repent—needs to make a U-turn. But he assumes they'll never do it so he stands up

---

[101] For what it's worth, does anyone remember that the *actual* Pollyanna broke her back and fell into a depression? If there's a message in Pollyanna, it's not that everything in the world is happy. It's that, despite the whole lousy, load of crap, there is still something good to be found. But even this message is taken as frivolous, fluffy optimism. WTF.

again the next week and tells the same people the same thing. Now *that's* pessimism."

"Well, I've got to recommend something to this country," I said. "But then I'll sound like the latest in a line of tired preachers telling America to change. 'America,' I'll say, 'What you're doing is wrong. Cliff ahead, make a U-turn now.' How's that different from all the diet-pill salesmen peddling a fix to 'change your life' without you having to, you know, *change your life?*"

"Joel," Janet said, "You're better than that. You won't be a street preacher."

"But what's the alternative?" I asked.

"Joel," Janet said, "before you can point to a new culture or talk with America about who we are—before you talk about all that—you have to show them who you are. Then you have to show that you've listened and understood their joys and hurts—their hopes and fears. Only then can you talk in a way that means something. That's a good pastor's secret—he knows what is good and he knows his people, and he loves them anyway." She leaned back and Socrates twirled his empty chai. Then she went on. "Holier-than thou, quick-fixers have yelled their slogans day-after-day until America is tired from the noise. It's accusation and anger with no love.

"Talking with America is like talking with anyone else. You have to be humble. You have to earn a person's trust and show that you love him regardless, over time, and then he will hear anything you say."

I blinked. Such a simple answer. Even Socrates knew better than to talk.

Janet looked patiently at me. Watching, perhaps, to see whether her words had soaked in.

"I think there's another piece of this, too," she said. "You have to see the whole thing. The things that are good, the things that are okay, and the bad things. You have to love them all for what they are. You can obsess over the bad things. You might even be right

318

about them. But people will shut down when you talk to them about it because, if the problems are all you see, you're not really seeing them."

Of course Janet was right, but, still, something bothered me. "But I'll be like a ridiculous doctor, then," I said. "I'll walk up to someone whose heart is failing and I'll say, 'You're generally quite healthy. You've got a good mind, you've got solid lungs, and your musculoskeletal system is in exceptional shape. Your heart is giving out, yes, but you've got to appreciate the good things about your health—you can't just focus on the negative.'"

Janet smiled. "Can I get you another cup of coffee?" I asked.

"I'll get it," Socrates said and stood.

"Joel," Janet said, "you've got to discuss it all honestly, together. The only way you'll ever pull a whole person out of sickness is if you know and love and nurture the good parts, too. For your heart patient to get well, you've got to inspire his good mind so he'll exercise his muscles and discipline his diet. It's the only way you'll ever get a bad heart back to health. And you have to see him as a whole person if you're going to inspire him to do any of it.

"Do you see what's good in this country? Or do you only see the things dragging it down?"

I thought about that. And I thought of my family, of Ms. Holachek, Nick, Janet, Brother Kenny. And what about my church? Yes, probably that, too. "Yes, Janet," I said, "I think I see some good in this country, but all the good things are small."

"Tell the president about them anyway."

"But,"—I couldn't help myself—"sometimes I think the good things are all false, like the silly flowers we have in Texas that wilt in a few days and then live out their lives as these hideous gourds. And there's young love that's the brief bait for so many bad marriages. An innocent child is bullied and then becomes a bully, and what was that innocence worth? When you look at it, the good things all fall apart while the bad things last. That's not what I want. But that's how it is, isn't it?"

Socrates had returned and set a coffee in front of Janet. She eye-smiled at him and returned to the conversation, looking sad. "You've told me this before," she said. "What you've said is true, Joel. And maybe without God you're right. But it's also true that, however ugly it is, the gourd holds seeds that will make more flowers. And even a bleak marriage will give birth to a beautiful child. Do you only care that beautiful things break? Or do you also see that an ugly world keeps making these fragile, beautiful things? Do you only care that America is crumbling? Or do you care that, for all its heartbreaking faults, America is beautiful?"

I felt choky when she said that and it hit me how tired I was from all the work—from all the worry and all the thinking of the past month.

"I can tell you care, Joel," she said, "and I don't think you would care like this if you didn't see so much beauty in it.

"I think the only way you can truly love something is to constantly love what is good, constantly grieve for what it could have been, and constantly hope for what it can be. You can never separate love, hope, and grief. They flow out of each other, and the only way to escape them is to stir them all together—love, grief, and hope—and harden them into bitterness. You will choke them all and you will grow bitter with life itself."

Again, I sat there while my eyes stung and her words sank into a hard place that had, for a long time, made its home in my chest. Finally, I said, "That's probably true, Janet, but, if it's true, it's hard. I've hated a lot of things. I don't think of them as griefs, though, they just make me angry. Growing up, I bruised my knuckles in my dad's workshop—over and over again. It hurt and I hated it. I wanted to get away."

"Listen, Joel," she said, "I'll tell you something about yourself. The mechanic shop was hard on you but it was a gift.

You're like one of those wild turkeys that used to strut through your pasture in Sampson. You grew strong and you can fly because you weren't hatched in a hatchery."

"But now I work in the Pentagon," I said. "I get three weeks of vacation a year. I wait in traffic, format my memos right, pay my rent—I get told when I'm furloughed for budget cuts—and my hands have gone so soft I could put lotion on them. But I hate it. I'm exhausted. If the system works, it will go on until I retire, but where's life for all the people who work in a system like that? What's to love? What's to grieve? What's to hope? How can I tell them America is beautiful?" Janet had spoken wisdom. I knew it. But I had to fight it. I'd done this before. And, somehow, my antagonism always met with more wisdom from her. Socrates sat and watched. She tried again.

"Joel, you're a tree that was planted in the woods. You're gnarled from the storms and you've survived. But now you're trying to stay strong in a greenhouse. It will never work. You bruised your knuckles on steel. You weren't built to be happy working in an office for someone."

"Maybe I wasn't built to be happy," I said, with more bitterness than I meant.

"Maybe not, Joel, but there's more to life than happiness."

"Like what?" I asked.

"Loving the sadness that comes when you see something beautiful. Loving the joy and the grief that come from hoping for something good that may never happen, or from loving someone flawed. Those aren't happy things, Joel, but they're good."

She looked up to the ceiling for a moment, then went on. "Joel, maybe you grew strong because you didn't have a gentle, loving father. Instead you had a man who could be mean, a man who made you angry, a man who made you work."

"I did have a gentle, loving father," I said defensively. "I also had a dad who was mean. I had two fathers and they both died on the same day with the same transmission in the same chest." I stopped. Silence hung there and I saw pity in Janet's face.

Then Socrates spoke: "And what did you think? Good riddance from the old bastard?"

"I walked away and I didn't think," I said. "It was what it was."

"And what was that?" he asked.

"Who cares?"

"What did your mom make of it Joel?" Janet asked.

"She cried. She loved him."

"What about your brothers and Naomi?"

"We all cried. And we told good stories about him. You don't speak ill of the dead. You don't even whisper about it among yourselves. Seth didn't speak at all. To this day, I've never heard him talk about Father."

"So is that what you wrote on your break?" Janet asked. "The bad stories about your dad?"

"No."

"Then what did you write?"

"The truth."

"And what's the truth?" Socrates asked.

"My father was good and bad and other things all together. I tried to show them. Isn't that the best we can do?"

We sat in silence and I thought of my father, of the Pentagon, and of the shop. "I grew up on a farm, working in a mechanic's shop," I said. "Now I work in an office." I stopped to remember why I'd said this. "Sometimes I think the problem is that we are losing touch with our world. Literally losing touch. The people who touch the world—with their hands on wrenches and in the dirt—the people who touch the world and the people who run the world are two different sets of people.

"People become leaders by being smart and reading books. Not by living, doing, and being. In government, business, movies, news—we're all smart, depleted people, deciding what other people should do. Because we have the power. Because it's our job."

"If the world was right," Socrates said, "people would get into government because they're in tune with ideas like justice, honor, and love. The public will resonate with that. Even if they don't know why, people still recognize these things because they are bigger than us."

I saw him trying to impress Janet and I saw him trying to make an excuse for the fact that he'd never touched his world. But, more than that, I saw him trying to be moral because Janet likes that. So I replied, "If you believe in justice, but you don't believe in God, what does that make you, Socrates? A Platonist?"

"How would I know?" he said. "Plato came after me. And I don't talk with people who use words ending with 'ist'—or with 'ism' for that matter. People use those words to package ideas up and dismiss them—to avoid talking about what they're talking about."

"Okay," I said. "I get the gist." And I winked at my wit.

"You want to know what makes America different now than it was before?" Socrates asked, trying to change the subject to something he could get out of a history book.

"What?" I said.

"For generations, people have objected to the world they found when they were born and they've tried to make it better. Upon getting popped into this world, every baby used to think, 'Gosh, this place is a mess, I'll have to fix it.' That has changed, though. We still see that the world is a mess. But now we see how many people have tried to fix it. We see what they've tried and how miserably they've failed and we've given it up. We don't even know what we mean by 'better' anymore."

"So what's the answer?" I asked.

"I thought of something when you two were talking about the shop and the hatchery," Socrates said, and I noticed that he'd got himself another dirty chai. "All along we thought we were trying to make the world better. But really, we weren't trying to make it better, we were trying to make it easier. We said we were trying to improve education, but really, we were trying to make school easier. That's like trying to build a better football team by making your training camp more fun. Maybe Joel got smart because he bruised his knuckles in the shop. And kids used to get smart because teachers bruised their knuckles with a ruler. But now no one bruises his knuckles. So no one grows strong. We're trying to make life easy. But it's not. It never was."

Socrates had used me as a positive example. And I liked it. "Determination," I said. "Knuckle pain teaches you determination." But then I thought and added, "My kids will have to learn that life is hard, of course, but I hope they can learn it without an angry dad. And there's another piece of it, too," I said. "They have to see what is good. They can't just be told—they've got to see what it looks like.

"In the Pentagon, we have a formula—I told the president this and I will put it in my report: Threat = Capability × Intent. If you think about it, it's profound. No one is a threat unless he's both willing and able to hurt you. It's the same thing with our leaders—government, business, art, education, media. Greatness = Strength × Goodness. You can't be a great leader unless you're both willing and able to do something good. And you can't do that until you've lived—lived with other people and lived with your hands in the dirt. America can only be a better place when our strongest people and our best people are the same people. We're all busy telling people how to do stuff without *showing* them. And we're all busy despising power. No one thinks power is a good thing anymore, so no one who's good aspires to it. It's a tragedy. We should teach our kids that it's the noblest thing to become wise, obtain power, and use it for good."

"By teach, I'm sure you meant to say 'inspire,'" Socrates said, with a touch of his old antagonism. "You'll never teach anyone to be good. You teach skills, but you inspire people to be good."

"Yes, of course," I said. "That's why I said you teach by *showing* them." I glanced at Janet.

"But you have to say what you mean," Socrates said. "And this takes me to another point: I've been thinking of how these ideas will be presented to the White House."

"You and me both," I said with a chuckle. "But, luckily for you, I'm the one who has to do it. You get to do the fun part—the brainstorming—the talking. And then there's me."

"Only, I've been realizing," he said, "that most of the ideas we've discussed are my ideas, and I should be the one representing them to the White House."

"Well," I said, with an uncomfortable chuckle, "for whatever reason, the president asked me. Your thoughts have certainly helped, though, and I would be happy for you to look at the final version once I've written it up."

"That won't be necessary," he said.

"Okay. But I wanted to offer. Let me know if you change your mind."

"It won't be necessary for you write up recommendations," he said.

"But it's what the president asked for and it's what I promised."

Janet watched Socrates with a strange intensity.

"But the president has changed his mind," Socrates said.

"What do you mean? Are you the president's spokesman or something?" I asked with a dry laugh.

"No. I wanted to make sure my ideas are represented accurately so I gave them a preview. I gave the White House a heads-up on what you're planning and they decided that it's no longer necessary."

"Soc, what did you do?" Janet asked, still staring at him.

"You have to understand," he said, "that documents like the ones you're preparing are guaranteed to be leaked and they could be quite embarrassing to the White House."

"Did you tell your dad?" Janet asked.

"I gave him a little preview," he said, "and he saw that something like this could only embarrass the White House. It was unwise of the president to go behind Dad's back like he did to start with. When Dad confronted the president about it, the president said he had just wanted to hear what Joel would say. Dad supports getting outside advice, but he told the president that the staff should benefit from the advice, too. The president agreed, of course, so Dad told the president that, since I'm friends with Joel, it would be more comfortable if Joel submits his recommendations through me. So everyone wins."

"But I have not agreed to that," I said, feeling strangely baffled. "I promised to submit my recommendations directly to the president. I offered you a copy but you said you didn't want it. And who's your dad?"

"That's not important," Socrates said. "I've summarized our conversations and provided them to Dad. He realized that we have to be careful how my participation is presented since I was involved."

"Socrates' dad is the president's Chief of Staff," Janet said, still looking at Socrates.

"Be quiet!" Socrates ordered. "Dad said he won't have *a DoD employee* going directly to the president and leaking stories that could embarrass the Chief of Staff."

"I never did anything to embarrass your dad!" I said, furious now.

"Oh, yes, I'm sure you'd never mention that all the good ideas were *my* ideas," Socrates said. "But you'd figure out how to mention me anyway. You'd figure out how to skew something I said and make me look like some sort of asshole."

"*I* would never make you look like an asshole," I said. "But *you* … It's not the dress that makes you look fat, Socrates, it's the fat that makes you look fat."

"Joel, stop," Janet said. I looked at her and, for the first time, I saw disgust for Socrates in her face.

So I took a breath. I felt betrayed and then sad. "So you're part of the system," I said. "Socrates, it's *your* power games that strangle the truth. You're what beats people down and makes them cynical. You've been sitting here all along, blindly supporting the whole corrupt system. Do you care whether it's true? Whether it's just? Whether it's corrupt? Racist, Socrates? Would you care if it was racist? Why would you? 'My dad runs it—I benefit, and, if I can't control someone, I cut his throat.'"

"Race!" Socrates said. "What does this have to do with race? People talk about race when they have no excuses, Joel, so they can blame someone else for their failures."

"Sorry," I said. "I meant that you talk about truth but, when push comes to shove, you support power, regardless. That's what has facilitated half of history's crimes. It's what has maintained every system of hate. It's what stifles people who are injured by the system and keeps them down. You say all the right stuff but, when push comes to shove, you side with the oppressors. And that's despicable."

"I didn't take you for one of the whiners, Joel. Blaming 'the man' for who you are. 'The system made me fail,' they say. They lose the game and blame the rules. And you're one of them, Joel. I saw it from the start and that's why I didn't trust you."

At some point I learned to let angry men play themselves out so I didn't respond. I watched to see how this one would play out.

"'Forces of racism,' they say. 'Structures of hate.' Vague phrases to hide what's real. What's real is that black people kill each other more than white people do. So their neighborhoods are more dangerous! That's what's real, Joel.

"What's real is that black kids don't try hard in school. Black people pass up the opportunities they have and then they whine that they don't have opportunities. And, if a black kid does a good job, they attack him because he's acting all better than them and 'working for the system.'

"They're like you. They don't want the problem to go away. They like the problem. They want to keep it. Complain about it. Market it. Write papers about it. Once you've decided you're a victim, you have to stay a victim or you lose your precious little identity. Is it the structure that keeps them down? Who the hell cares? They see the problems. We see the problems. And they're nasty problems: attitude problems, motivation problems, anger problems. But no one admits it. No one says the truth that's standing there, naked and flabby in front of their faces. No. There's a nice little industry of destroying anyone who walks outside their little lines about what you can say, and most of the truth is outside their lines. And the industry moves the lines, without telling you. So you'd best not talk at all.

"Let me ask you this." He leaned across the table at me and I thought I saw flecks of spit coming. "If you're walking in a city and all you know is that one neighborhood is mostly white and another is mostly black, which one will you feel safer walking in?"

"Most people would walk through the white one," I said.

"I didn't ask about 'most people', Joel," he yelled. "I asked you about *you*. For the Devil's sake, why does everyone want to talk about someone else? We've got all these screwed-up people here in this city trying to un-screw-up all the *other* people! For Christ's sake, which neighborhood would *you* walk through?"

"I see your point," I said.

"It's not a point, you idiot. It's a question!"

"I see your question and I decline to answer," I said. "And maybe we should have this conversation somewhere else. Or maybe we should not have it at all." But Socrates was off on another spectacular rampage. Janet looked calmly at him with the confidence

328

of someone who knows she can vault the bar to safety the instant her partner signals the fuse has been lit.

"Education is practically free anyway," Socrates stormed. "You, of all people, should know that. You can learn everything you need from a book and from walking around with your brain in the on position. 'Oh, but what about engineering and calculus?'" he mocked. "Yeah, you can learn those, too. Buy a good book, stupid, and learn it. If you can't figure something out, ask a friend. It's not genius. It's hard work!

"People don't use what they've got. So why do you think they'd do a good job if you gave them more? It's not that they don't have enough opportunity. They throw away their opportunities, for Christ's sake. They pull each other down and then pass their hate from father to son. So it has always been and so it will be to the end of the world, Amen! But that's a *choice*. And don't blame *me* for your choices."

Socrates glanced rabidly around the room, then hunched across the table and hissed, "Show me you can do something with what you've got. Then you can come to me and ask for more. But for Christ's sake, stop whining! The poorest people in this country have more opportunities than anyone else in the history of the world. Do something with it. And stop writing papers for the president!" He stopped and seemed to wait for an answer.

"That's pretty racist," I said, finally.

"Don't tell me what's racist!" he yelled. "The truth isn't racist, it's just the truth. Don't reason yourself out of it just because you don't want it be true. Face the world, folks. It's what grownups do!

"Structural racism? Structural racism will die when black people make their neighborhoods safer than white ones. People have evolved instincts, Joel. Instincts! Our bodies see patterns and they use this information to keep us safe. As long as black neighborhoods have higher crime—as long as a woman gets harassed more there, walking down the sidewalk, she'll have the sensible instincts they call 'structural racism.'"

I caught some dirty looks from the tables nearby and wanted to shift the conversation. "Socrates," I said, keeping my voice quiet, "what are you doing to change all this?"

"People have to take responsibility for themselves, for Christ's sakes."

"Don't talk to me about *people*," I said, retaining the same quiet tone. "Talk to me about *you!*"

Socrates stopped. He knew I had him caught. He looked like I'd hit him in the face. Then he sniffed and said the strangest thing I've ever heard. "I keep a poem on my wall."

"You keep a poem on your wall?"

"Yes."

"What's the poem?"

"It's called 'Give A Dollar.'" And then he folded his hands and recited:

> *"Give a dollar to every beggar; their lives are hard*
> *Their lives are hard even if they have money*
> *Their lives are hard even if everything's their fault*
> *If I must sleep tonight on the street*
> *a cigarette and a beer are the best I could buy*
> *It's good for you to give a dollar and not ask me why."*

He opened his eyes and looked at Janet, then me, with this look that said, *'If you didn't like my poem, I might cry,'* and, in that moment it seemed proper to give him a cookie, a glass of milk, and a tissue.

"Who's that by?" I asked. "Socrates?"

"Socrates is a fictional character," he said.

And, strangely, it was only there, the day they broke up, that I first saw why Janet liked him. I sat charmed and I imagined Socrates as Tolkien's sniveling Gollum, or a creature from Crane:

Who, squatting upon the ground,
Held his heart in his hands,
And ate of it.

I said, "Is it good, friend?"
"It is bitter — bitter," he answered;
"But I like it
Because it is bitter,
And because it is my heart."

Was it revulsion? Absolutely.
Pity? I suppose.
Justice? Yes, I think so.

* * *

I emailed Tammy afterwards, telling her I was making progress on the president's project and inquiring about the timing of our next meeting. That evening, I received the following reply:

Dear Joel,

Thanks for your email! Your timing was perfect and I asked the Chief of Staff about your meeting before he left this evening. The president will be travelling in the first part of September but he looks forward to reviewing your recommendations once they have been submitted through the office of the Chief of Staff.

Joyfully,

Tammy Walz

I studied the bubbled veneer on my desk and considered that my plan had miscarried. I felt relief from the heavy thing that had weighed on me for these weeks. Then my relief shifted to bitterness at seeing the thing I had cared for crushed—not by the inevitable forces in our world but by the malice and fear of one or two people.

To see a job that must be done left undone. To see truth stifled once again in a country that suffers from so much stifled truth. To see my government, designed for the truth to be spoken, subverting it still. To see a president isolated by his staff and denied what he sought—controlled and fed only what his advisors wanted for him. This is bitter.

I looked down at my phone. Naomi's counter said two days, nineteen hours, sixteen minutes, and thirty-two seconds. And the seconds quietly ticked themselves away.

God's Mark

Joel slices his shovel into the dirt, cutting the wiry roots. He stomps then hauls back, prying the sod loose, ripping out the roof of the gopher's tunnel. Joel and Seth start at the mound, then dig apart along the winding gopher path until Joel's shovel strikes a stone. He lifts the blade a fraction, turns the sod aside, then finger-scratches until he has pulled another knife from the earth. Then he digs again, with more care, until he has unearthed an ancient hunter's entire kit.

Sitting cross-legged on the grass, Joel and Seth pass the pieces between them until they have agreed on the grooves where each would fit on a spear or against the thumb of a squaw who scraped flesh from her hunter's buffalo hide.

"Do you know what Moses did with a piece of flint like this?" Joel asks.

"What?"

"He took his boys and cut off a piece of their penis so they could be Christians."

"Really?"

"Yes."

"I'm glad we don't do that now."

"But their mom didn't like that he'd done it," Joel says.

The Open Letter

"So who kicked whose butt this time?" Sam-Bob asked when I came down the stairs Wednesday. He stood, aproned, turning sizzling veggies in his skillet.

"Aren't you working today?" I asked.

"Nope. I worked all weekend so I'm taking today off. Aren't you working, though? Is the Pentagon taking the day off or something?" He eyed my cargo shorts. I told him I'd taken the rest of the week off to work on the president's project. But he must have heard the problem in my voice because he said, "What? That bad?"

"Depends on your perspective," I said.

"You okay?"

"I'm not sure."

"What happened?"

"On the positive side, I think Janet and Socrates are done."

"That's great! Congrats! We could use a little more Janet around here. When's the wedding?"

"Ha! I wish. But, if there's a wedding, you'll be moving out."

"Aw, c'mon, man, I can cook. I can clean."

"I'll believe the cleaning when I see it," I said. "Sam-Bob, Socrates' dad is the White House Chief of Staff and he ruined my project."

"Yikes!"

"Socrates convinced the president not to meet with me and I think he threatened my job. He said his dad won't have *a DoD employee* talking directly to the president without going through him."

"Dude, that sucks."

"I know."

"What are you going to do?"

"Defense policy, I guess. What else?"

"You could expose the Chief of Staff, or something."

"Sure. But who would believe a thirty-year-old bureaucrat who stands up and says the White House is blocking his access to the president."

"When you put it like that … So what are you going to do? Solve detainee policy?"

"I've already done that. Besides, I'm not sure I'll be working detainee policy anymore. There's another office that's supposed to do that. My real job is counter terrorism."

"Like drones?"

"Like drones. Maybe I'll push for a review of our drone policy. We need a language besides bombs to talk with the people who hate us."

"Speaking of which, have you ever, you know, seen a drone?"

"No. Why?"

"No reason. Just thought I'd ask."

"You know, standing by a giant, mechanical insect won't help me set parameters for killing people with robots. But I can have a look at one if it would make you feel better."

"It would. And one more thing: you can learn Arabic or whatever if you want to, but I'll tell you, they get drones. It's a language they understand. Besides, robots are a way to keep them over there and me over here, so I'm all for it."

"That's part of the problem, Sam-Bob. Besides, whatever happened to pancake makeup and Gerard Manley Hopkins?"

"They're not big on Catholic poets in Afghanistan."

"But the drones are a problem. They hate the drones. And they hate the people who fly the drones."

"Here's a problem: Uncle Sam sent me to war, then he gave my job to robots that mostly just use their cameras to watch the world fall apart, and now I can't find a job."

"But you've got a job."

"A lousy job."

"If you would, you know, apply for another job, I'd wish you luck."

"You know what?"

"Screw me?"

"Bingo."

"I think I'll go call my mom."

"And tell her your roommate's being mean?"

"You're small fry, dude. I'll tell her the White House is being mean."

I told Mom about the whole thing. She listened and said she was sorry to hear it. Then she said, "Joel, I know you've got a lot on your plate right now and I hate to bother you, but Seth called yesterday."

"Yes?" I said. "What did he say?"

"He doesn't call me much anymore."

"He doesn't call anyone."

"I know. I think he's in trouble, but he wouldn't say what kind of trouble and I wondered if you would call him. I think he'd talk to you."

"Sure," I said.

I called Seth and asked him how things were. He mumbled like a teenager. Then he said, "Joel, have you talked to Mom lately?"

"Yes," I said. "I just talked to her."

"You know that church she's been going to?"

"The Baptist Church?"

"Yes, I think that's the one. The pastor's name is Ken, or Kenny, or something. I think Mom is dating him."

"What makes you think that?"

"Naomi thinks so, too. And, when I asked Mom about church, she didn't say much."

"Well, okay, then. And how about you Seth? What have you been up to? Mom said you weren't doing so good."

"Joel, I was there when dad died." The line lay silent while I thought.

Finally, I said, "I'm sorry, Seth. I always wondered." Then, I asked, "Did he say anything?"

"What do you mean?"

"Like, after the truck fell. Did Dad say anything after the truck fell?"

"No. He looked at me. But he didn't say anything. I don't think he could talk." I waited a long time again and Seth waited too.

"Is that what's been eating you all this time?" I asked.

"Yes."

"We should all go home sometime and just catch up," I said. "It'd be good for us all to see each other again."

"Yes."

For the first time in weeks, the White House seemed distant, minor, unproblematic. I said goodbye to Seth and called Mom back.

"I talked to Seth," I said.

"Thanks for doing it."

"Of course," I said.

"Is he okay?"

"He's having a tough time, Mom. But I think he may be coming through it."

"Well, I hope so. He took it so hard when your dad died."

"I know. Mom, are you dating Brother Kenny?"

"No, Joel," she said. "Why do you ask?"

"He didn't ask you out or anything?"

"He asked me to go to a restaurant with him and I went."

"Mom, that's called dating!"

"Joel, it has been quiet here since Naomi left for school. Kenny was pretty broken up when Janine died a couple of years back, and we had a good talk."

I felt a sort of metaphysical vertigo. Wires touched and sparked in my brain. The circuits overloaded and began to melt. So I doubled up the only two cures I could think of: I sent a note to Janet—*Can we talk?* And I went for a run.

For a reason I do not understand, my brain can never implode upon itself while I run. So, when I'm stressed, I run, a lot, with the urgency of someone who must fix his head. And I monitor the pain in my bad knee, nervously hoping it will hold long enough to preserve my mind.

When I returned, Janet had texted me back and I arranged to meet her at the Arboretum that afternoon. She apologized for it all, of course, and told me she had broken up with Socrates (whose name was actually Vincent III).

I thanked her and told her she'd provided invaluable help, and we stared dazed over the roofs of Washington, DC at the golden, Catholic dome in the distance. I told her that I still wanted to give some ideas to the president, or maybe just to the American people. She listened with a troubled look in her eyes—a troubled look that, even then, only disturbed the surface of her peaceful face.

"You know," I said, "the problem with America is that, when your national myth unravels, you no longer have a nation. You no longer know who you are and who you're supposed to be, and that's what makes us a nation and not just a bunch of people living in the same place." I laid back and folded my jacket under my head in the grass. Then I said, "You know, Janet, Socrates was wrong."

"I never should have trusted him."

"No, I mean the old right-side-up Socrates."

"What do you mean?"

"Plato's Socrates from *The Republic*. He was wrong. He said justice is too small to see in a person so you have to supersize it and see what it is in a city. He was wrong about that. Our country is too big to see. All I can see is what has happened to my family since we lost our dad—what has happened since you and I broke up.”

She nodded. Then she said, “I knew Soc’s dad was the chief-of-staff and I thought it would help you to talk with him. I never thought it would come to this and I feel terrible.”

“It’s not over,” I said.

“What do you plan to do?” she asked.

“I have learned a lot and I want the president to understand what I’ve learned. But even if I had a way to send it to him, how could I write it? I could write some conclusions, of course, but they could never show the president what he needs to know about our country. They wouldn’t show how to lead us well—to pull our budget out of its death spiral, to give our people the will to suffer with a diminished nation for now—to hope and work for a better day in twenty, thirty, or forty years.”

“You’ve written the story of how this all came about?”

“Yes.”

“Why not give him that?”

“The whole thing? I thought I’d use it as the basis for a report. You know: background, conclusions, recommendations.”

“If you try to write up conclusions from this, you’ll be like the people who treat the Bible like it’s just some rules buried in a bunch of filler, story stuff—the ones who try to reduce it to a list of basic life principles. The problem is that the Bible is a story—poetry, prophecy, and only a tiny bit of law. And it’s a great story, too, if you’d just look at it.”

“Janet, I’ve looked at the Bible many times and it seems more fake every time.”

She sighed. Sometimes I wished she would lash back at me for saying stuff like that. But instead, she is forever patient, weary, and wise. “Joel, maybe the things in the Bible happened. Maybe they didn’t. But, for you to call it fake is to wave aside one of the most profound explanations of the world. You can do that if you want, but it's not honest. You may not find the Bible satisfying, but ask yourself: why is there a universe at all? How do you know there is something wrong in your country, and why do you want to put it right? Find a better explanation if you can. Then come back and call this one fake and we'll have an honest conversation about your beliefs and mine. Get angry and say irrational stuff if you have to, because I get it—my dad left me, my boyfriend just betrayed us, but come back when you're done and let's be honest. That's all I ask."

* * *

At home I took Janet's idea. I wrote a memo, then emailed it to her, asking what she thought.

* * *

FROM: JOEL ALDEN

TO: THE PRESIDENT OF THE UNITED STATES

CC: THE CONGRESS OF THE UNITED STATES
        THE PEOPLE OF THE UNITED STATES

SUBJECT: Recommendations For America

BLUF: Only Small Things Are Good

PROBLEM: The president is trying to lead a culture that lacks a common foundation.

- For an explanation of how this project came about and reached its conclusion, see the story at TAB A.

RECOMMENDATION: We must get back to a time when a doctor cared for a whole patient, a teacher taught a whole student, fathers modeled right lives for their sons, and people considered wisdom to be a politician's or a businessman's greatest asset. If there never was such a time, or if we cannot get back to it, then we must get ourselves forward to such a time.

Agree__________   Disagree__________   Other__________

RECOMMENDATION: Read the Biblical book of Proverbs and do what it says.

Agree__________   Disagree__________   Other__________

RECOMMENDATION: The answer to evil is first to be good and love what is beautiful, and then, where you must, defend it from evil.

Agree__________   Disagree__________   Other__________

Attachment

TAB A: Joel Alden: Who I am and Why I Have Made These
        Recommendations

Prepared by Joel Alden, Citizen, United States of America

* * *

A couple of days later, Janet looked across the table where we sat in the back of Bourbon Coffee, a few blocks from the Capitol. "Joel," she said, "that is the weirdest memo I have ever read. What will you put at TAB A?"

"I'll put the whole story there."

"I like it."

"I hoped you would."

"When you tell the story, will you change Socrates' name to keep him from getting in trouble?"

"No."

"You don't like him, obviously, and I doubt your story will make him look very good."

"I'll write what he said and what he did and I'll let him look how he looks."

"No matter what he's done, he's another hurting person trying to find his way in this world, Joel. I hate to see you using this project to humiliate him. Will you at least change his name?"

"He already changed his name. I'll use the name he chose: Socrates."

"But, from your story, people will connect him with his dad."

"That is the cost of what he has done. He forced me to address it in public. Because of what he did, the only way for me to reach the president is to publish this as an open letter. Either that, or I leave Vincent and his dad to distort what happened and lie about us to the president. I can either let Vincent's lie win or I can tell the truth in public. They've arranged the world so that I have to hurt them to do the right thing. I don't see any other way, Janet. Somehow, I wonder if you knew it would be this way all along."

"I know, Joel, but resorting to the press with internal conversations like this will make you come off as nasty, won't it?"

"I will tell the story as truly as I can so no one looks better or worse than he is—you and me included."

"I can respect that.[102] I have another question, though, Joel. Do you think it will help? Maybe this is one of those times, like the president said, when prudent men keep silent."

---

[102] I could have kissed her. No one knows how hard it is to do something like this. You are just one small person. If you're effective, you set yourself up to get accused, skewed, and hurt by powerful, moneyed, men. It's hard

"I don't know. But, if I won't tell the truth, how can I complain when other people won't tell it?"

"I can respect that." She sipped her water, then asked, "Do you think the president or the Americans will act on any of this?"

"I don't know. Sometimes I think we've just grown tired of governing ourselves. It is hard work—it was always hard work—but we used to be up for it. Now we're just tired. So we elect people who won't do anything hard—people who play with our silly fears. And, if they tell us a hard truth, we elect someone else." I inhaled and held it for a moment, then I asked, "Janet, can I tell you something?"

"Sure."

"Janet, I think Seth killed Dad."

"That's awful. Why would he do that?"

"Maybe he didn't kill him. Maybe he just let him die."

"But why?"

"Dad could be difficult. He worked Seth awfully hard. I don't know why he would do it."

"Does anyone else know?"

"Maybe. Probably, we all suspect it. But why would we let ourselves say it?"

"What do you plan to do about it?"

"Nothing. I just want him to find forgiveness and some peace, and be part of the family again. There's enough pain already."

---

in the best of times. But it is only crushing when you do it alone. With Janet standing there, I could do this even if all the world abandoned me and made me out to be a bitter loser. I will speak a truth—one that people usually avoid because it causes pain. And they will hold the pain against me even if it is a healing pain. Which of us has not reserved our blackest hatred for the dentist whose face leers over us while we're alone, speechless, and tormented at his hand? The best I can hope is that my country will treat me as its dentist. And I can bear this hatred if Janet knows what I have done and that I have done it with a pure heart.

Janet looked kindly at me until I teared and looked at my napkin. Finally, she said, "Joel, I'm sorry about Seth. But I have another question for you."

"Yes?"

"What will you tell the president about why, instead of writing a book about the country and the deficit—instead of making policy recommendations—you've only written him a book about your family—about your trip home, some vignettes from your past, and some weird talks with your ex?"

"I'll tell him it's the best I've got. If he wants to understand this country, he can look at my family. If he wants recommendations, I'll tell him I'm moving back to Sampson. I'll marry someone and we'll teach our kids who they are. Their grandmother will hug them and I will tell them who their grandfather was. I'll tell the president, if he wants a recommendation for America, he can bring America to see my fumbling little family. I'll tell him only this small thing in America is good."

"Make sure you put that in the book," Janet said.

* * *

That evening, I found another note from Janet.

Dear Joel,

I've looked through some of my favorite books. I even read a book by your French poet and I have some recommendations for your memo:

RECOMMENDATION: In the words of Ecclesiastes: "It is good for a man to … rejoice with the wife of his youth, to eat the fruit of his labors … etc." (Look it up.)

Agree__________   Disagree__________   Other__________

RECOMMENDATION: In the words of C.S. Lewis: "A husband and wife chatting over a fire, a couple of friends having a game of darts in a pub, a man reading a book in his own room or digging in his own garden—that is what the State is there for. And unless they are helping to increase and prolong and protect such moments, all the laws, parliaments, armies, courts, police, economics, etc., are simply a waste of time."

Agree__________   Disagree__________   Other__________

RECOMMENDATION: Charles Peguy spoke of what is good and he said it is a father who kisses his son on the crown of the head: "Something taken for granted, something very good, without importance."

Agree__________   Disagree__________   Other__________

* * *

Janet,

These are very good. I will put them in the memo.

Yours,

Joel

THE END

Epilogue

I added Janet's recommendations and, at the memo's bottom, I wrote in my own hand:

Mr. President,

I'm sorry I was forced to do this in public.

As you suspected, I have written a long book because I lacked the time to write a short one.

I think what you need, Mr. President, are advisors who live well, think well, and who aren't tired all the time. I don't know how we can do that in Washington, DC, but we've got to.

Joel

P.S. Did you ever think of moving the Capitol to Colorado? – JAA

End Note

If you enjoyed this book, please leave a review on Amazon and visit my website where you can join my mailing list for future books and stories: www.micahharris.com

And send a note telling me what you thought of the book.

Acknowledgements

"Writing a novel is a terrible experience, during which the hair often falls out and the teeth decay. I am always highly irritated by people who imply that writing fiction is an escape from reality. It is a plunge into reality and it's very shocking to the system." – Flannery O'Connor

Writing is filled with a heartbreaking array of contradictions. The temperament to write well and the temperament to sell books are seldom found in the same person. Writing is intensely lonely while it must also be intensely relational. Good books cleanse and strengthen the reader's mind while writers are notorious for being ill: sick men and women teaching others to be healthy.

For me, the answers to these contradictions are the many people who have cared for me.

I have seldom felt more loved than I did the weekend Bill and Annie Mahr opened their mountain home for a group of my friends to spend a weekend telling me what they saw in this book. These friends told me of their dread that Joel would do something horribly cynical with Pastor Kenny's sermon. The bureaucrats among them told me where I had gotten the furniture wrong in the State Department coffee shop and they debated to the point of tears whether Joel had participated in the cheap business of throwing them, as a lot, under the bus (where the good people of our nation habitually throw their bureaucrats). My friends pointed me to the places where Socrates, or Joel, or Sam-Bob did things that made them want to burn the book and forget it ever existed.

These people spared me a terrible amount of loneliness and they offered a taste of the relationship an author seeks in writing such a book. The faults that remain in this book are likely due to my stubbornness in absorbing their critiques.

So I say thank you to Bill and Annie Mahr and to my early readers: Paul Borchers, Leanne Cannon, Rakel Cleveland, Katie Doherty, Kara Jones, Patrick Moore, Jessica Rodgers, Melissa Swearengen, Matthew Taylor, and Cristina Taylor.

I must repeat one of these names in particular because, on a day when we had both fallen on hard times, Jessica Rodgers met me at a pie shop. I told her I had decided not to attempt this project as a full-length novel. She told me, in her forthright way, that I would regret this choice and, since the moment she said it, I have known she was right.

I am thankful to Jed Royal who modeled how to be a man of relentless goodwill in the Pentagon and then, later, while working an overwhelming job at the White House, he read the manuscript of this book and showed such delight in it that I knew I had to see it through to the end.

Thank you to Madelyn Creedon for the generous introduction and for showing a combination of raw competence and good cheer in two formative places for me: the U.S. Senate and the Office of the Secretary of Defense.

I could not have produced this book as it is without the help of two staggeringly talented editors: Catherine Adams and Eamon O'Cleirigh

In the Summer of 2016, I sat digesting in the sun after a Sunday lunch at St. John's College, Santa Fe. A man looked up at me from the next bench and, in the hours that followed, we tripped from one topic to the next until we discovered that he was a novelist and a publisher, and I was a novelist without a publisher. That afternoon, we followed the shade from bench to bench, until the cafeteria opened for dinner and, by Tuesday evening, he had read this book in its entirety and offered to publish it. In the subsequent months Dr. Robert Richardson insisted, on bringing this book into print. The words "thank you" feel flat but I use them nonetheless because they are the words supplied by our language for moments such as this.

I also use these words for Kenneth and Jean Harris who gave me a hard, abundant childhood on the plains of Texas, along with my six brothers and sisters. And I use them for my grandmother, Dorothy Hudson, who, to my knowledge, is the only person to have read this entire book within 12 hours of receiving it. We miss you.

This book includes the poem, *The Girl*, by Lars Gustafsson and translated from the Swedish by John Irons. It also includes a quote taken from *The Portal of the Mystery of Hope*, by Charles Peguy, translated from the French by David Louis Schindler Jr. You should read Peguy's whole book because it is a sustained meditation on the small gestures that must, so often, bear the full weight of the thing we call life.